SWEET LIKE CHRISTMAS

LIZA JONATHAN

First edition, October 2021. Library of Congress ID pending

Amazon ASIN B09FZ26J4S

Paperback ISBN- 978-1-951209-07-0

Attention Bookstores and Libraries:

Returnable paperback versions of this title can be ordered on Ingram Spark at wholesale rate. Library versions of the paperback can also be ordered on the Ingram site at www.ingramcontent.com

 Created with Vellum

CHAPTER 1

CORN+FLOUR BAKERY, DOWNTOWN
LEWISBURG, WV

LITA NOE DIDN'T SHOCK EASILY. She prided herself on that point.

But one look at the text her uncle had just sent, and she nearly coughed up her morning order of Mountain Mud coffee.

Her buddy Ross used his position behind her in line to rub her shoulders in sympathy. "Christ, Lee." He snickered. "What's on that phone? 'Cause seriously, you're gonna cough up a lung here."

Groaning, she sipped her coffee again to correct that swallowed-it-down-the-wrong-way sensation and debated whether she should show it to him. Lord knew, once he saw it, Ross would never let her hear the end of it.

But she flipped the phone around anyway, masochist that she was. "*This* is what Uncle J wants me to wear to his costume ball on New Year's Eve," she told him, pointing to the picture of the barely there proposed outfit—Leeloo, from the movie *The Fifth Element*.

Gah. The "costume" could pass for five strips of Ace bandages, strategically placed. Any one of which, were it to slip by more than a half inch, would leave her functionally naked.

Ross widened his eyes for a second but, predictably, soon launched into a round of way-too-loud whooping and clapping. "Awwww, yeah. Now *that's* what I'm talkin' about. I'd spend good money to see you in that!"

Heat leapt to her cheeks, and she gave him a shove. "Would you *stop* it?"

His bright blue eyes flashed with amusement under his choppy mess of goth black hair. "What?" he smirked.

Lita elbowed him in the ribs. "You know half the town will be wondering what we were talkin' about."

They both scanned the establishment to find that yes, in fact, *all* the people waiting in line for their breakfast had looked up from their phones. Lita cringed. The ambient pop music playing in this quaint downtown bakery bounced loudly off the exposed brick walls, and the chatter hushed. But no one said anything or asked them any questions, though. Just a couple of fond smiles and head nods from the friends and neighbors she knew. And the kitchen staff were way too busy to care.

She blew out a breath.

"See?" Ross nudged her. "This is West Virginia, honey. People care. But they're not gonna get *that* far up in your business."

She supposed that was true. Besides, she and Ross had grown up in this cozy, historic town of about three thousand people, nestled in the shadow of the Allegheny mountains.

Everyone here knew them, if not directly, then by reputation. She was the tough punk chick who did tattoo art on the side and had mermaid-colored braids down to her waist. Ross was the highly talented metalworker and mechanic who liked to party. Of course, everyone had heard of their employer, Holliday Hot Rods—an antique car restoration and collision repair shop that was getting a national reputation for museum-quality work. Most people understood that she and Ross had been tight since high school, too.

They'd been BFFs since sophomore year, and they were twenty-eight now. So that was what—thirteen years now? Messing around with each other like this was simply what they did.

Still. She'd rather it not get around that her uncle was encouraging her to streak her way through Hairball in the Holler this New Year's Eve, thank you very much. No matter how fabulous the man was trying to make the event. She shook her head at her screen. What was that queen thinkin'?

She and Ross leaned a bit more discreetly against the pastry case, and he hung his head over her shoulder to get a better view of the outfit. "Think he'll want you to wear the red wig?" he asked her.

Lita snorted. "And miss the chance to show off his handiwork? Not likely. My head is the best billboard for the salon he could ever have."

Ross broke out another one of his lopsided, sly grins. "You do turn heads, Lee. Thought you'd be used to that by now."

Was she? It wasn't something she even thought about anymore. She'd been the girl with the crazy colored hair and the nose stud since middle school, thanks to having a family in the beauty business. Her mom and Jesús, Mom's brother, had always been hairdressers. But when they'd gotten a tip on a salon that was selling for cheap here in Lewisburg, they'd moved the family up here from Florida. The move had been the right one, allowing Mom and J to truly launch themselves as beauty influencers.

Divalicious was regionally known, mainly because of Uncle J. His before-and-after makeovers had become a legit

Instagram and TikTok sensation. And their reputation had been well earned, not only from their work, but from the deep relationships Mom and J had formed in the community. The Hairball in the Holler regularly earned into the six figures for the Greenbrier Valley foodbank system. And they did it by making the event into a spectacle—a parade of hair artistry, costumes, and J's posse from his days on the drag queen competition circuit. Around here, it was *the* place to party on New Year's Eve.

Ross placed his hand over his heart and sighed dreamily. "All I can say is, if I saw you wearing that, I'd be up all night. And when I say *up,* I mean up—"

Lita laughed, cutting him off. "Stop slobbering, dog." That boy never missed an opportunity. But *she* knew *he* knew that act wasn't playin' with her. Eager to get the topic off the prospect of her soon-to-be exposed skin, she wagged her finger at him. "Hey, don't pretend that you didn't get a message too. I heard the alert. So what cosplay is he putting you in?"

Ross smirked and showed her his phone.

Shirtless Neo—from *The Matrix*, complete with black patent leather pants and a matching patent leather trench. Lita had to grin at the perfection of it. Ross may be a little rough around the edges sometimes. He was rangy, and mouthy, and dressed in baggy urban streetwear that didn't suit him. But she'd seen enough snatches of his skin over the years to know he was chiseled under all that, with the palest of complexions and a collection of some seriously cool, black-and-white surrealist tats.

Ross Mason had a certain something about him. A presence, maybe. He could *totally* pull off Keanu. But she wouldn't be telling him that anytime soon. The boy's ego was big enough.

Lita was about to lob a joke about patent leather and

rashes when the door whooshed open, and she lost her train of thought. A blast of cold wind and glittery snowflakes skittered over the threshold as two new customers stepped over the threshold. The middle-aged man and old woman caught Lita's attention, mainly because she'd never seen them here before. The woman was a tiny little thing, bent with age, but with long, wild, curly white hair and flashing blue eyes. Despite the fire in her eyes and the determination in her expression, she hobbled, leaning heavily on the man she was with.

Her son, maybe? Grandson? It was hard to tell. When you considered the man in one light, he seemed like a guy in his twenties. In another, he seemed ageless and weathered, his hair radiating a faint, silvery hue. The man was tall, well-muscled and dressed in expensive camo pants and military-grade boots, a black long-sleeved tee, and a black pea coat. Like he was three different military branches at once, and yet none of them at all. She studied the way he patted the old lady's hand. He clearly was catering to her, and helpful, but she didn't see the warmth of a family bond there. A bodyguard? Or a caregiver, maybe?

"Here, get in front of us." Lita waved to them. "We're in the front of the line. You won't have to stand so long."

The old woman sized them up, and for a second, Lita almost stepped back a step at her penetrating gaze. Then a smile broke across her well-lined face, sweet and surprised. She hobbled over in their direction. "Oh! Aren't you kind? You see so little of that these days."

"It's no trouble ma'am," she murmured, letting the old lady pat her arm.

Suzie, the bakery's owner was working the rush today, and she waved to get her attention. "Hey Carmellllliiita!" she sang out, as she rushed around behind the counter. "Your breakfast bowls are all done, and I put those two extra

5

coffees in the carrier for the rest of the crew. But the tray of cinnamon rolls for the shop just came out of the oven. It's cooling on the counter. Give me a minute for the icing, okay?"

Suzie hustled up, all smiles and warm welcomes, and handed the bags to Ross. Lita grinned gratefully at her. Suzie was a sharp businesswoman, and smart enough to know to have the same Holliday Hot Rods order ready every Monday. She and Ross were a bit early today, so they settled in to wait, checking their phones.

Lita listened with half an ear while Suzie took the order for the old lady and her companion, only glancing up briefly when the man excused himself to the back of the restaurant to take a call.

Resigned to her romantic fate, Lita grumbled under her breath as she opened her Tinder app. If she wanted to find a *date*-date to a complicated costume bash like the Hair Ball, she was cutting it a bit too close.

Honestly, she felt a little weird about opening the app up outside the confines of her apartment. The last thing she needed was for someone to spot her standing there, scrolling through Tinder, looking desperate. Yet, considering her last boyfriend in a long line of crappy boyfriends had ghosted himself away six months ago, "desperate" was pretty much exactly what she was.

Okay, maybe not desperate.

Option deprived.

She thumbed through her latest string of choices and stifled a curse. *Really?* All these matches were guys she either knew or in many cases, had dated at least once already. *That's small town life, isn't it?* She hovered over the button to increase the search radius when she heard Ross snort overhead.

"What's the matter, Leeeee, have you kicked the local dating pool already?"

"You're one to talk," she huffed. "*P-snap.*"

Ross's face reddened at his old nickname, and he shuffled on his feet. "Man. You get a tongue piercing for *one year* in high school, and all of a sudden you've got a rep with the ladies."

Lita rolled her eyes. "Not that I'd know."

Ross leaned an arm on the pastry case and gave her another long, lingering perusal, like he was about to make another one of his standard flirty jokes. But it was a feint. The man snatched the phone from her hands instead.

"Hey!" she yelped.

"Well now," he crooned as he tapped the screen. "Let's see who's up in queue here. There's Bo-hunk Gaither." He shook his head. "You don't want him. He's an even bigger dog than me, and that's saying something. And gawd. Here's Marcel French. Seriously, the guy who assists at the podiatrist's office? What a nerd!"

"He's an intern!" she protested.

"Even worse. He's *interning* to learn how to saw people's bunions." He shuddered theatrically, still smirking. "Ugh, he's a total mama's boy. And haven't you heard? Marcel has a secret stockpile of size-five high heels that he likes to lick in his spare time. Not that I'm proud to know that 'lil tidbit. Next!"

Lita crossed her arms over her chest and glowered at the man. But Ross kept thumbing.

It didn't take long before he stopped and raised a pierced eyebrow at her. "Uh-oh. Lee? What's Cam Longstreet doing in here? Didn't you catch him cheating on you last fall?"

"Last summer, actually, not that it's any business of

yours. He keeps showing up in my matches. What can I say?"

Ross wiggled the phone between his fingers. "*Why* are you putting yourself through this?"

"I need a date for the Hairball, *okay*? You happy? Now can I please have my phone back?"

His eyebrows slammed down into a flat line, and he scowled. "Well, *duh*. You don't need a date. *I'll* be there."

Now it was her turn to snort. "You can't be serious."

"Why not?"

"Because. I need a *date*-date." She swiped at her phone, but he jerked it away.

"Why, Lita?"

"Because!" She lunched for it again, this time jumping up a little against his surprisingly hard chest, but still missing.

He grinned and held it up higher. Which was totally not fair. He was only five foot ten, but that was still ten inches taller than her. "Nut-uh." He cackled. "Not until you tell me why you'd rather go with..." He scrolled to the next choice. "Oh, now here's Mr. Gassaway. Our old high school guidance counselor! He *definitely* wants to know if you'd like to match with him. I could just see it. 'Oh, Lita, I think we should schedule a session to talk about your future with my pants...'"

She jumped for it again. And again. "Oh my freakin' God! Would you *stop*?"

But Ross kept right on giggling every time she jumped for her cell, and if she didn't know better, she'd swear he was enjoying all their squirming and bumping. Finally, she popped a foot on his knee and levered herself over his shoulder. She got her hands on her prize, but he stumbled backward, *hard*.

And right into that sweet old lady in front of them.

The woman didn't fall—*thank little baby Jesus*—but the sudden nudge made the poor dear lose her balance enough to drop her tray. Her breakfast sandwiches and drinks went flying.

Their *"Oh no!"* was so similar and simultaneous, it came out sounding like stereo. They leaped forward to help the woman.

"Ma'am, we are so, so sorry. Are you hurt? Is everything okay?" Lita patted the woman down, checking for injuries, while Ross gathered up her tray and snatched paper towels to soak up their spilled hot chocolates. Ugh! Now the whole place was seeing what goobers they'd been. Oh man, little marshmallows were floating across the floor.

"I'm fine," the old woman chirped, though to Lita's ears, her voice sounded thready and frail. "Can't say the same for my breakfast."

Well. Hadn't they made royal asses out of themselves. And now this poor woman... Lita just about died of embarrassment as everyone stepped out of their way. She helped the old sweetheart toddle over to the window side bar, and hike herself up rather rather painfully onto the high stool. By now one of the employees had stepped up with a bucket and mop—yet more trouble they'd caused.

Ross ran off, got a clean tray, and set it down on the table. "Ma'am, this is awful. We can't let you pay for new food." He motioned over to Suzie. "Hey, can you remake her order? I'll pay for it."

"Okay." Suzie shrugged. "But all these people will be ahead of you. And we have more phone orders. It could be a few minutes."

The old woman grimaced. "Oh no! I guess we'll have to keep going without anything to eat then. My traveling companion said we're on a tight schedule. We can't afford to wait. And I was *so* hungry too."

9

The poor sweetie had the most hangdog expression Lita had ever seen. She and Ross exchanged a helpless glance, until Lita spotted the bags of food they'd ordered, all warm and ready to go on the counter.

She pointed it out to the lady. "You know what? You can have ours."

Ross nodded in agreement and jumped up to fetch the bag. He unloaded it into another fresh bag for her to take, while the old woman murmured protests like "Now-now, I couldn't" and "But you'll miss your breakfast." But Lita could tell from the way the lady's eyes sparkled that she was secretly pleased. Finally she agreed to the idea, and thanked them over and over.

Ross held up a hand. "Don't thank us. This never should've happened in the first place. I was the one messin' around like a moron, and that's on me. I'm *so* sorry ma'am."

The woman glanced over her shoulder to confirm that the man who'd brought her was still on the phone, and then turned back to give them both a good, hard look.

And that struck Lita as odd. Because the strangest expression passed over the woman's face. An odd twist on a knowing grin, like all that bumbling sweetness had been a mask, and it'd slipped for a hot second. But then the lady was back to smiling at them with such a helpless, elderly guilelessness, Lita felt terrible for even having the thought. Come on. The woman really was a lil' old darling.

As if to illustrate that thought, the woman smiled down at the slim bag of cookies she'd managed to hang onto, even after all the mayhem. It appeared to be all that remained of her original order, and she held it out to them, motioning to them to take the two seats on either side of her.

"Here," she insisted, pushing the cookies into Lita's hands. "You're going to have to wait a long time for your order now. No sense you bein' hungry too."

Lita couldn't help protesting at that. She and Ross bickered back and forth with the woman, not wanting to take anything from her after they'd ruined her meal.

Finally the old lady put her hands on her hips. "Hasn't anyone ever told you it's rude to refuse an old biddy's hospitality? Now, you go on and eat those while you wait for your food."

That earned a sheepish chuckle from both her and Ross. Chastened, he took the bag from Lita, pulled out a cookie, and handed it to her. She took the remaining one.

Lita hadn't realized how hungry she was until the cookie hit her lips. And it was delicious—an oversized sugar cookie shaped like a round Christmas tree ornament, with a little heart stamped out of the middle. Oh, it was a sandwich cookie—Linzer style with red jelly peeking through on the heart part. Whoever decorated it had mad skills. The icing was brilliant green—glass smooth and covered and tiny edible silver-and-gold balls in elaborate scrolling designs. Honestly, this cookie was really too glittery and gorgeous to eat. When it caught the sun coming in the window, it glowed in her hand.

"Mmm." Ross licked his lips as he chewed. "This does hit the spot. I can't remember when I've had a better cookie."

Lita couldn't help giving Ross a little side eye at that. It wasn't like him to get so excited over a frilly cookie. But then again, she couldn't deny what he was saying, because she felt it too. The cookie was addictive—perfectly golden crisp and tasting like vanilla and almonds. Yet, it wasn't like anything else in the Corn+Flour case today, or any other day that she'd seen. Which was odd, now that she thought about it. But she kept chewing anyway.

The old lady grinned with satisfaction as they ate, and she reached up to touch Lita's face. The woman did it in such a warm, wonderful, grandmotherly way, Lita didn't think to stop her. "Now look at you," she crooned, patting Lita's hair now. "Aren't you sweet? The sweetest girl I ever did see."

That earned a bark of laughter from Ross. "Trust me. Lita's a lot of good things, but *sweet* ain't one of them."

Haha muy gracioso, idiota, Lita wanted to say, and probably give him a pinch too while she was at it. But she couldn't. No, she was too busy locking eyes with this odd old bird. As if she was pinned somehow—captured by strange blue eyes that, like the cookie, almost seemed to glow.

The old lady cackled a little, still cupping Lita's cheek. "Oh, but you *are* sweet, darlin.' You're sweet like Christmas, and between now and the New Year, you'll see exactly what I mean. There won't be a single, lady-lovin' man in this whole town who'll be able to resist you."

Ross's eyes rounded in shock, and he stopped chewing. "Wait—*what?*"

"And you!" the woman clucked, rubbing her hand on Ross's arm now. "You're sweet too. Sweeter than you'll ever let anyone know. But just for the holiday season, you won't be able to hide it anymore."

And then came the freaky part. The *oh-my-God-am-I-really-seeing-this?* part. Ross stared at the woman like he was mesmerized, too. And right where the old woman was touching him, his arm glowed with that same strange pixie-dust sparkle from earlier. It hadn't been the snow. It was that woman. She was *doing* something.

Her intuition was screaming for her to smack woman's hand off him, or something. But this whole thing was so fucking bizarre, she was stunned, frozen, like her brain couldn't get the signal through.

And it was getting worse. Now his eyes were glowing

silver, then gold! Lita suppressed the urge to scream. Frantic, she scanned the rest of the restaurant to see if anyone else was seeing this, but everybody was acting completely normal.

When she checked again, Ross seemed totally fine. He polished off the last of the cookie. And now, Lita was shocked to find herself sitting there, holding up an empty hand where her cookie used to be. *Dios mio. Have I really eaten it all?*

She must've. But why couldn't she remember eating it?

Was she losing her mind? Had she really seen all this glittery glowing business? And what would all this *mean*, anyway? That a nice old lady gave them a present and said nice things to them?

Lita rubbed at the back of her neck, wondering how her day managed to take this weird turn. She really needed to get a grip. She must be seeing things.

The old lady smiled again with an expression so sweet and innocent, Lita was beginning to question her own senses. This old biddy was harmless, wasn't she?

Lita wanted to ask the woman some questions. But just then, the old lady's companion came back. She and Ross explained what had happened with their breakfast and apologized all over the place. His gaze darted between two of them, then he narrowed his eyes at the old lady, looking suspicious.

"What?" The old biddy grinned. "We were having a nice talk!"

The stranger didn't bother to introduce himself or the old lady, he simply apologized for being such a bother. She and Ross insisted they had been the problem, not her. Still, Lita watched the way the man's eyes darted around the room, and he clenched his jaw. There was something he wasn't saying.

The stranger shook their hands and thanked them for breakfast. But he seemed to be in a big hurry. He quickly propped the old woman back on her feet again, and as he walked her out, Lita could swear she heard him say something like "You need to stop meddling" and "It's their business" and "You can't make them lo-"

Ugh! The door closed behind them, effectively cutting off any chance of hearing what the man was saying. So, Lita simply watched the two of them and every mincing step they took as he helped her over the snowy sidewalk. They disappeared around the corner.

She and Ross exchanged wide-eyed expressions.

"Did you feel that?" she asked him.

Ross shrugged. "What?"

"That tingling, when she touched you!" Lita insisted. "I did! It didn't hurt, exactly. But I swear, when she touched my cheek, it felt like she was pushing glitter through my bloodstream."

He snorted. "She made you *feel like glitter*."

"Hey, you weren't able to see my face because she was blocking your view. But I could see you. When she touched your arm, your face got all..." Her words drifted off. The way he reared back and furrowed his brow, she could see he had no idea what she was talking about. Concern was written all over his face, and she'd been friends with him long enough to know what he was gonna say next. Probably some dumbass thing like she needed to get more sleep, or stop watching *Twilight* reruns or something.

"Got all *what?*" Ross asked her.

She shook her head and waved a hand at him. "Yeah, you know what? Never mind. Must've been a trick of the light or something."

Ross cracked a smile, like he was gonna say something, but Suzie flagged him down again. She pointed to the bag of cinnamon rolls she'd just put up on the counter. "Cinnamon rolls are up and your new orders too. You're good to go, guys."

Ross pushed himself to his feet to go grab the food.

Lita stood up too, brooding as she gathered up their mess. Dammit, she just couldn't shake the creeping suspicion that *something* had happened.

She gave herself a little shake. *C'mon. Don't be ridiculous.*

This was just another ordinary Monday. Just their standard Monday-morning breakfast run for Holliday Hot Rods.

But somehow, there didn't seem to be anything ordinary about it at all.

CHAPTER 2

THEY WERE LATE, of course, bringing breakfast in for the crew. Ross knew they were going to get an earful about it as soon as they rolled in. He loved his boss, Hunter Holliday, who was generally pretty chill. But the man could get awful hangry if he wasn't fed.

And Hunter's number two, Hopper Vance? *That* man nearly tackled them at the door.

Hopper snatched the bag right out of his hands. "God you two—what took so long? I'm about ready to eat my arm!"

Ross couldn't help grinning at how this big, bad biker in front of him could be undone by cinnamon rolls. He nodded to the man's enormous guns. "And that arm of yours could've fed you for a week."

"Very funny, squirt." Hopper grinned back and ruffled Ross' hair just to piss him off. It was the sort of thing the man was always doing, mainly because Hop stood head-and-shoulder taller than him, and the two of them were pretty tight. An ex-con with no family of his own, it had taken Hopper longer than most to become a part of the Holliday Hot Rods family. But when Hopper had married his wife Delilah a couple of years ago, he'd opened himself up to everyone and everything. Now, the man had decided their role in the Holliday Hot Rods family was big brother-little brother. It'd become the running joke between the two of them, and it never failed to make them both smile.

Ross slapped the man's hand away, laughing.

They walked everything back to their breakroom, and Ross took a careful inventory of the cars waiting to be worked on as they did. He shook his head at the sight. The place was packed. Seemed like half the town had brought in their cars to get the dings and rust fixed before they traveled for the holidays.

The shop was full up on orders for custom classic car design, too. They had four stripped-down vintage car bodies laying in pieces right now, one of which had to be finished so it could be given as a Christmas present. He had a stack of Hunter's Auto CAD drawings to put up on the laser metal cutter this morning, and a whole afternoon of welding work that would realistically take him well into the night.

But it was all good. He loved this place, his job, his coworkers, his home. He grinned at the Chipmunks Christmas album thumping through the speakers, and the Polar-Express-themed mural Lita had painted for the Christmas party they were sponsoring for families in the local foster care system. From the smell of the paint, it was still drying.

And that's what Ross loved about the place—that spirit of creation, of possibility, that seemed to hang in the air. Holliday Hot Rods was more like a big, mechanical makers space than your typical grimy garage. It was a huge, rehabbed shirt factory that Hunter had inherited from his dad when he'd retired. Ross loved the mayhem of it—the sparks, the classic car parts stacked up in every corner, the noise, and especially Lita's funky artwork, painted large and in charge on every wall like a tangle of refined graffiti. Hell, he even lived here, in the studio apartment Hunter had built in the old supervisor's mezzanine. Seemed like everyone at the shop but Lita had taken a run in it, for one reason or another over the years. And at only two hundred dollars a month rent, Ross had been taking his turn for three years now, so he could save up to buy property of his own one day.

He'd worried it might be weird living above the place where he worked, but it hadn't been. It was simply home to him. And he was making real progress on his dreams here. Buying a house and paying it off. Having acreage and some space to call his own. It was so close now...

Hunter ambled up, attracted no doubt by the big tray of cinnamon rolls Lita was setting out. He snatched one out of the box and jammed it in his mouth before he could even get a plate. "Ummmm," he closed his eyes. "Ah, man, they're still warm."

Lita pinned him with one of her no-nonsense looks that was one part den mother and one part smartass, and handed the man a proper plate. Then a napkin. Hunter gave her a sugary, unrepentant smirk, and wiped the icing from his close-trimmed beard. Now two big flannel-wearing gear-heads were officially undone by baked goods.

"*Jaysus*," Hunter groused, as he stuffed the last of the roll in his mouth. "I thought you guys would never get here."

Lita snorted. "You know what? You can thank Ross for that."

"*Me?* I think we both created that accident."

"Yeah, right," Lita rolled her eyes. She reached in the bag and passed Hunter his breakfast bowl. And a fork. And another napkin. "It would've never gotten so out of hand if you hadn't been actin' up. You should've seen him, guys.

First, Ross is reading my phone over my shoulder. Then he steals it! *And* makes fun of my love life."

What love life?

The words jumbled and crowded in his mouth, ready to rush out. But his lips slammed shut. Like some unseen hand had shut his mouth for him. He tried to open it again, ready to follow up with some epic burn that they could joke about. Maybe stick a pin in the tension that always seemed to simmer between them. Well, the simmering, *I-wish-I-could-tell-you-how-bad-I-want-you* tension that was on *his* side, at least.

But his mouth wouldn't open. He took a deep breath. And another one.

The total silence got his coworkers looking up from their biscuits, waiting for him to give it right back to her.

And he wanted to. But when he finally was able to pry his lips apart, "You're right" came out.

Huh? Wait a minute, wait a minute...

He opened his mouth again, and "It was totally my fault," came out. "I never should've butted in like that. I think maybe I picked on your dating life because mine isn't any better. Can you find it in your heart to forgive me?"

Ross had the sudden, overwhelming urge to clap his hand over his mouth, or even holler, maybe.

He hadn't meant to say that. He hadn't meant to say that! Those words—those thoughts—they weren't even his!

He'd actually intended to say the exact opposite, but what could he do now? Admit he didn't have any control over the verbal diarrhea that came out of his face?

Lita, for her part, simply sat back in her seat and narrowed her eyes at him.

"What?" he managed to say, trying his best cool, *I meant to say that* pose.

A disbelieving smile spread across her pretty face. "Yeah, Ross, I can forgive you. And thank you."

"For what?"

She shrugged. "For admitting when you're wrong. It's...nice."

"Mark your calendar," Hopper called. "It'll never happen again."

Ha-ha. You're fuckin' hilarious, dickhead. He thought about saying it. But somehow the moment felt wrong now, so he kept his mouth shut. And that was *his* decision this time.

"I still don't get how Ross horsing around held you up so long," Hunter mused.

Lita jumped in and answered him, giving the guys a pretty accurate description of how they'd messed around until she'd basically ended up pushing Ross right into that odd old lady. When she went into the bit about the old woman patting her hair and saying she'd be irresistible, he expected the guys to crack up laughing.

But they...*didn't.*

Ross and Hunter both stopped chewing and slid each other a glance. Like a *did-you-hear-that?* kind of glance. For crying out loud, they weren't taking this whole thing seriously, were they? The men actually seemed concerned. To his shock, Hunter and Hopper both started digging for details and peppering them with questions.

What did she look like? And the guy she was with?
Did she say she'd be back?
Did she say where they lived, or where they were going?
Did anyone else see what was happening?
You're sure they were strangers, and nobody knew them?

Ross went slack-jawed with amazement. From the way they were carrying on, you'd think their brush with a strange old biddy was the mystery of the decade. He was so blown away, he must've been a little dazed, because Lita put her hand on his arm and shook him a little.

She turned those big, green doe eyes in his direction. "I don't know about the old woman's touch. I think I definitely felt tingles, like sparkly kind of tingles, when she touched me. What about you, Ross?"

Ross sighed. She was at this whole thing again, and he wasn't sure where she was going with it. And now this weirdness with the blurting. He couldn't even say what that had been. He sure as shit wasn't admitting to that. What, that he didn't have control over his own mouth? That was *nuts*.

Honestly, he couldn't quite remember much about what the old woman had said to him. He'd been too worried about what she'd said to Lita, about all the guys she was going to attract. That's some next-level freaky right there. "*Something, something, sweeter than anybody knows*," was all he could remember the woman saying to him. And he couldn't remember whether he'd "tingled." But he could say one thing for sure. His arm was tingling now because Lita was touching him.

That, unfortunately, was nothing new. He'd always felt that way, jittery and warm, even when the girl gave him a friendly pat.

Ross let out a long sigh. "What's this about tingling? I don't even understand what you're getting at, Lee. Are you tryin' to tell me we were visited by a witch who put some kind of spell on us?"

Lita's exasperated expression seemed to say *you got any better ideas, dumbass?* She sighed resignedly. "You have to admit, the whole thing was strange."

He sighed too. "Yeah, on that point, we're agreed."

Hunter chucked his wrappers in the trash can and stood up. "We may never know what that old lady was going on about. That said, I'd suggest the two of you be extra careful and keep a close eye on each other. There's no telling what could happen."

Hopper frowned. "What, you don't think that—"

Hunter held up a staying hand and shot the man another one of those weird speaking glances of his, like he was willing Hop to stop talking. What were these two not saying? "I'm *saying*," Hunter continued, "the mountains around here are full of legends and ghost stories and magic of all kinds. And it wouldn't be the first unexplained thing to happen in these parts at Christmastime. You know, strange pulls of the moon and the lay lines and all that. So... watch yourself. Okay?"

Lita gave Hunter a wise little nod, like she'd bought into this whole line of bullshit lock, stock, and barrel.

What the actual hell?

Ross laughed. He couldn't help it. Whether he was nervous, or incredulous, or what, he couldn't tell. But the fact that everyone was so serious about this was plain ridiculous, and that's all there was to it.

No one laughed with him. "Wait up." He waved a hand at them. "You mean to tell me that every last one of you believe what that old woman said? That Lita is somehow gonna become the siren of Greenbrier Valley? Like a bunch of men are going to follow her around like the friggin' Pied Piper or something?"

Hunter and Hopper didn't answer him because Lita beat them to it. Her eyebrows slammed down, and she waved her finger at him. "Oh no, you did not say that. Whassa matter, ese, you don't think I could?"

Shit. How was he supposed to answer *that*?

He'd been crazy about her for so long, he could totally see how any guy would want her. Lita Noe could be any man's wet dream—with those big green eyes, and hair he wanted to dig his hands in, and a body so dope it put him in a sweat just thinking about it. But it was more than that. It had *always* been so much more than that. He was crazy about her spirit, and intelligence, and that fiery, take-no-shit 'tude of hers. He loved being with her, and working side by side, and laughing at the same inside jokes .

No matter how many times she'd friend-zoned him, he'd loved her since the day she'd sashayed into his homeroom like some badass unicorn. He was just trying not to be too pathetic about it.

If there was any magic affecting him right now, all these mushy thoughts he was having must be triggering it. His mouth was tingling like a beyotch right now. And that scared him. What inconvenient truth was he going to say this time? He clamped his mouth shut, desperate not to embarrass himself again. Unfortunately, Lita took his silence for an insult.

She stiffened and reared her head back. "Oh, really? Why not? I'm not pretty enough?"

"No! *God*, no. It's not that—"

"What then? I'm not smart enough? Don't have a college degree? Too bossy? Too loud? Come on, what is it, then?"

Hunter and Hopper watched him with bated breath, cringing. Both of them had enough experience with women to know how badly he'd stepped in it here.

Ross knew it too. And he had that sensation again, like words were backing up like train cars in his head. All the things he would probably say:

Because you always pick the wrong ones.

Because you'd don't suffer fools lightly. And there's a shit-ton of fools around here.

Because you're not every man's cup of tea.

And they were all true, every one. But instead, when he

opened his mouth, "'Cause you're too amazing for all of them!" blurted out.

That was true too. But he'd surely never meant to say it.

Far from being disgusted at that way-too-gushy remark he'd made, Lita smiled, her whole face softening into a wry, surprised, lopsided grin that made his heart ping helplessly. "Huh. There it is. Proof there's magic in the world, after all."

Ross couldn't do anything but grin back stupidly at her. Damn, her smiles. They were like a ray of sunshine on a cloudy day, weren't they? He was addicted to them, and always playin' the fool for them too. If he couldn't have her love, he could have *those* anyway, like a little gift that was just for him.

Hunter must have taken note of how awkward this whole situation was getting, because he was grinning from ear to ear at the two of them.

Hopper snorted. "Something was definitely in those cookies, man. I doubt Ross has ever called anything *amazing* in his life. The boy's getting' so basic he'll be giving out meme wisdom on YouTube pretty soon."

Ross laughed, happy for the out Hopper had given him. "Don't tempt me, man."

And just like that, that was the end of it. They could all get back to reality and put all this weirdness behind them. Ross breathed a huge sigh of relief as everybody shuffled off to their workstations.

Ross was busy picking off the last bites of his breakfast when the front door clattered open. When he poked his head back around the corner to see who it was, he swore under his breath.

It was Pervis Langdon, II. Or Pervy Junior, they used to call him in school, coming in with another friggin' repair on his POS vintage Jaguar. Perv was every bit as much of an uppity asshole now as he'd been in high school. He'd been two years ahead of them but had always acted like his shit didn't stink. *He* was on some special kind of upscale track the rest of them couldn't possibly understand, let alone aspire to. His dad was the president of the local bank system, and he'd made good and sure Junior here was Vice President at the Lewisburg branch, straight out of college.

Lita was the closest to the intake desk, so she trotted up to talk to the man. But Ross didn't trust this prick. He decided to watch Pervis from the relative safety of the breakroom, which was on the other side of reception. He'd step out there if the boy got into any of his typical entitled bullshit with her. Ross swore under his breath, waiting for the moment Perv would treat Lita like a servant, or worse, some separate life form—the crazy lil' woman with the rainbow hair who couldn't possibly have a brain in her head. Ross could set his watch by it.

But the minute the man's eyes landed on Lita, that wasn't the reaction she got at all. Oh no, Perv's eyes got wide, and he stood up to attention in his expensive loafers. His gaze raked over her from her head to her toes, and that little sumbitch actually wiped his hand over his mouth, as if he'd spied the most delicious morsel on the buffet.

"Well, well," Pervis crooned, grinning like a fool. "If it isn't Lita Noe, all grown up. Why don't you come on over here and talk to me, darlin'?"

Darlin'?

Ross growled. Maybe that old biddy at the coffeeshop was up to something, after all...

CHAPTER 3

Ross COULD TELL Lita was suppressing an eye roll and trying to put the customer first. Given how much she loathed this poser, it was almost funny to watch.

Almost.

They'd moved around to the driveway now, where Perv's car sat in a glowing green puddle of power steering fluid. Ross propped a shoulder against a shadowy corner and watched in case she needed help with this guy. And that boy was *definitely* acting strange today.

Perv was the kind of guy who was all about appearances. Starched shirts with cufflinks. Real silk ties. Designer horn rims and short blond hair slicked back from his forehead. He had a modern, mountainside house bought with Daddy's money, and a lemon of a vintage Jag that unfortunately, made him a frequent flyer at Holliday Hot Rods.

Every time he'd come here, Perv had barely spared a glance at Lita. When he did, the man had always regarded her like she was some kind of zoo exhibit—the crazy Hispanic with the rainbow hair, devoutly to be ignored.

But today? Perv must be smokin' something. The man was acting like some kind of switch had been flipped, and now Lita was the most appetizing woman on the planet. He leaned up against the car, all loose limbed and smiley, and dangled his keys out of front of him. When Lita curled her hand around them, he yanked them backward, making her almost fall against him.

Scowling, Lita planted her feet, pried the keys from his grip, and gave that asshole a dirty look. Perv snickered but opened the door theatrically for her so she could pop the hood. She did, only taking a minute to find the release.

Hop ambled up behind him, sipping his coffee. "This is what we're doing?" he murmured. "We're letting Lita handle Mr. Personality today?"

Ross crossed his arms over his chest and narrowed his eyes, never taking his focus off the scene. "She hates it when we butt in. All that business about the customers needing to take her word for it. She may not be a mechanic, but she can estimate as well as us, you know."

"Yeah, well..." Hopper snorted. "Not too hard to see something's wrong."

True that. When she came around front and popped up the hood, they both grumbled. Somehow that dipstick had let one of the fuel hoses crack too. Wisps of smoke rose from the engine block.

But that wasn't what Ross was watching. Lita leaned over the engine to get a closer look. And Perv, true to his name, stepped back, leering at Lita's fine ass in those low-slung jeans.

Oh-ho-ho *no*, buddy. His whole body stiffened with anger, and his hands itched to punch this oily motherfucker.

Lita popped up, pulled a rag out of her pocket, and wiped her hands. Ross could see her pointing to the engine and trying to explain something but Perv didn't seem too interested in her words. The guy stepped right up in her space, smiled dreamily down at her, and twirled one of her long pink braids around his finger.

Lita was so surprised, she seemed to freeze for a second. But Ross didn't.

Blood fuckin' boiling, he shot out of the garage and pushed that creep back in two seconds flat. "Hey, man." He stepped between them. "We have a no-touching policy around here. No harassment, either."

Ross glowered at Perv. Eye to eye. Man to man. And it was the strangest thing. Any other man would've been all puffed up and defiant, spoiling for a fight. But Perv? Confusion flashed over his face, and he blanched, seeming disoriented.

He leaned over Ross' shoulder to keep ogling Lita, though, and started smiling stupidly again. "Awww now. Harassment? I was only trying to be a gentleman. Can't a man ask a lady out on a first-class date? I've got tickets to the Charleston Symphony, Lita. The Christmas Pops concert. I'm going with Mom and Dad, and we've got an extra front-row ticket for a pretty lady like you."

"No, Perv!" Lita barked. "What's gotten into you today? I'm not going to the symphony with you today, or any other day. We're here to talk about this completely undriveable car, and it's gonna to cost five thousand bucks to fix it."

Relief rolled over Ross in a sweet wave, and he smiled at the way Lita'd shut that asshole down. He wondered if Perv would pivot to his default setting—negging and haggling over the price.

But the argument never came. No, Perv kept grinning at Lita. "Sure." He sighed. "Whatever you need to make it right, Miss Noe. You've got a blank check, as far as I'm concerned."

Hop, who'd been standing there too, let out a concerned-sounding harumph. "I want to make sure we manage your expectations here. What you're bringing us is a major repair. These parts are going to be tricky to source. And the repairs themselves will require us to take the engine apart to check for leaks and clean it. The shop is jammed with work already. Realistically, I don't think we can get your car done until the middle of February, maybe."

The man didn't even blink. "No problem." He kept grinning, never taking his eyes off Lita.

"Pervis!" Hopper snapped his fingers. "Hey! You heard me, right? Mid-February! And I'll need to be paid twenty-five hundred upfront so we can order the parts."

Pervis nodded blankly and handed his whole wallet to Hopper so the man could run his card. Frowning at the weirdness of it all, Hopper shook his head and trotted off to get the man his receipt.

Pervis stood there, silently checking out Lita's ass as she closed up the hood and rolled the car over to their secured lot. And Ross stood there, grinding his teeth, watching *him*. Like a hawk.

Hopper came back and handed the man his wallet. Pervis took out his phone, muttering something about calling an Uber.

Pervis started to walk off but whipped around like a marionette on a string when Lita came back to the garage. "Lita, darlin', I'll be back!" he called out, giving her a double-guns finger point. "I'm going to convince you to go the symphony! It'll be the best night of your life! I promise!"

"No, Pervis!" she called back. "We'll call you in February—when the car is done!"

"February, right," he muttered, still grinning like a damned idiot. Pervis wandered off down the road, presumably to hail an Uber. It could be a long wait around here. Holliday Hot Rods was in a little bit of a desolate spot on Route 60, with no sidewalks, and no nice little cafes to wait in. The man was literally walking in a three-piece suit in the scruff on the side of the road.

Hopper and Ross watched him go, shaking their heads in wonder. "You think we should give him a ride into town?" Hopper sighed.

"After harassing Lita like that? Hell no." Ross glowered.

"All right then." Hop snickered. "But you have to admit that was a whole lotta cray-cray right there. I mean, have you ever seen Pervis act like that? I haven't! If you ask me, that little old lady *totally* put something in those cookies."

"Yeah, right." Ross snorted. Still not willing to admit anything was happening here.

Ross and Hop strolled back into the shop, and everyone went to their stations to dig into their day. Soon Hunter was back at his desk, drawing out designs for the custom grill plate designs their shop was known for. Hopper was busy attaching an engine block to an old Model T, and Lita was in the process of painting an American Eagle and Chuck Norris onto the hood of a restored Trans Am.

For his part, Ross was loading more of Hunter's drawings into the laser cutter. Or at least, he was trying to. Truth be told, he couldn't tear his eyes away from Lita today.

She seemed rattled. She'd dropped her airbrush gun twice now and had blasted herself with paint—something she'd normally be way too sure-handed to do. When she wasn't scowling, she was pacing and chewing her bottom lip ruby red. On a regular day, she would've been finished and putting the clear coat on by now. But she'd been spending so much time staring into space, she'd only managed to draw back over her guidelines.

There was no doubt about it. She was bothered by everything that had happened this morning.

And honestly, maybe he was too. There was no denying, between that mess with Pervy Junior and the weird tingling sensation he'd gotten when that old biddy had touched him, Ross was beginning to suspect maybe something strange was at work here. And then the business about him not being able to get his words out...

If that kept happening, things could get crazy around here quick. He shuddered.

Realizing he wasn't going to get any work done until he'd checked on her, Ross sauntered over to her station, dodging a couple of pneumatic paint guns dangling from the ceiling. Ross stood behind her, checking out the half-finished Chuck Norris.

When she realized he was there, she jumped in alarm. "Jesus!" she yelped and gave him a little shove. "Don't sneak up on me like that!"

Ross backed away and found a safer spot leaning against the car. "Sorry. Didn't mean to scare you. I couldn't watch you pacing around anymore. Hey, I get it. You're still wound up over that whole thing with the old lady, and Perv, and—"

She held up a hand. "No. I just am really sick of drawing Chuck Norris."

He laughed. "Bullshit!"

"How can you not see it?" She swept her arm in poor old Chuck's direction. "I've got his eyes so wrong he looks like an alien!"

He snickered. Okay, so the man's cheekbones were probably a little too high, but otherwise, it was still Lita's best work. She needed to get her head back into it. "Then he'll be the bad-assinest alien in two quadrants." Ross leaped into a bad crouching-tiger karate pose. "I laugh at your photon blaster."

She smiled ruefully, when she normally she would've laughed at the joke and probably said *pew pew* back to him. His own smile faded.

"Hey," he rubbed the tops of her arms. "You know you've got enough talent to beat this project into submission. You're the best there is. You're the most amazing woman I've ever met. You're incredible, actually—"

"Oh, *gawd*. Not you too," Lita shrugged out of his hold. "Just stop."

Ross felt that sting right in his gut. But after a second, it dawned on him what was happening here. She believed he didn't mean what he was saying. That *he* was hexed too.

Not wanting to confirm or deny that, he simply shook his head. "Lita. You know this isn't about me. Or Chuck Norris, even. You're letting all that weirdness with Perv get into your head. Come on, a man you don't like flirts with you, and now you're off your game for a whole day? Since when have you ever let the assholes get you down?"

"All right." She shook her head and held up her hand in testimony. "I'll give you that. This isn't like me. Any other day, I would've slapped some sense into that creep, right upfront. But I couldn't. You didn't see him as close up as I did. When he was looking at me, he was there but... I dunno. Was he? It was like he wasn't calling his own shots. You know what I mean?"

"No, I don't."

She opened her mouth again, like she was about to argue with him.

But he beat her to it. "Maybe he saw a beautiful woman and decided to make his move."

Lita snorted. "I'm not beautiful."

Ross snorted right back. "Seriously? You mean you can look in the mirror at all this—" he waved his hands in her direction, "—and not think, *damn,* girl!"

She grinned and gave him one of her little play shoves. "That's not what I meant! I mean, I'm not beautiful *to him.* Have you ever seen Perv with a girl who resembles me in any way? Every last woman he's dated has been blonde, tall, skinny, cultured, and from money. And then that bit about wanting me to go out in public with his parents on a first date? I mean, how crazy is *that?*"

Ross shrugged. "I dunno. It's a little intense, I'll give you that. But maybe he was trying to impress you."

"Ha! Everything Pervis does is to impress. But never, not once in all the years I've known him, has he ever looked my way. I don't care how long you stand there and tell me otherwise. You will never get me to believe Pervis would want to be seen in public with a girl with a nose ring and mermaid hair."

Ross suppressed the urge to growl. He hated it when she put herself down like this. Why was a conversation with that pretty boy bothering her so much? And what in the hell was he doing here, defending the man?

But then, he wasn't really defending Pervis, was he? He was defending Lita and the way she saw herself. He couldn't let her think she wasn't good enough for some dick like Pervis Langdon.

So as usual, he cracked a smile. "What—you weren't born with mermaid hair? I hear the pink-haired people of Mexico are the world's most legendary beauties. The chickarellas—sirens of the bodega."

She laughed and shoved at him again. But this time, she stopped, wrapped her arms around his middle, and totally shocked him with a hug.

Lita buried her face in his chest and squeezed. And for a second, the loud music didn't seem so loud, and there were no smells of grease or paint, only the smell of lavender and almonds that seemed to cling to her, no matter where she went.

Sweet Lita. He dropped his hands slowly around her back and swallowed hard. What he wouldn't give to be able to hold her like this, any time he wanted. He rested his cheek against the top of her head and let his eyes fall closed, reminding himself she'd only meant to give him a friendly hug. Still, she seemed to melt against him just a little, their bodies fitting together far better than he would've guessed. When was the last time she'd hugged him?

High school?

But she was all grown up now...

"Thank you," she murmured against him. "You always know what to say, Ross."

Because I see you. I've always seen you for who you are, Carmelita Rose Noe.

The words were crowding up in his mouth again, bursting to be said. And given his weird tendency to blurt shit like this out today, he wasn't in the mood to take chances.

He clamped his mouth shut long enough for the tingling to pass. "So." He grinned. "You really weren't born with pink hair?"

She pushed out of his embrace and stalked off for more paint, smiling and shaking her head. Her braids swayed as she went.

Someday, he told himself like he had a thousand times before. *Someday, I'm going to tell her...*

But it wouldn't be today.

CHAPTER 4

Lita parked her hot-pink 1968 Dart in the well-mani-
cured lot in front of Divalicious, clicked the ignition off, and
slowly put her head down on the steering wheel.

When she walked in the door, Mom and J would
inevitably ask her how her day was going. What would she
even say?

Somehow "fine" didn't seem to cut it.

First there'd been Pervis. Then, as she'd been driving
down the street, half the men on the sidewalk had literally
spun around on their heels to wave and smile and even
mouth *Call me*.

It hadn't stopped when she'd popped into the conve-
nient store for gas, either. Ricky, the afternoon manager
there, had left other customers standing in line to follow her
out to her car, tell her she looked like J-Lo, and ask her out
on a date to Hillbilly Hot Dogs and the local bowling alley.

She'd been almost too stunned to answer him. Ricky
had to be at least fifteen years older than her. Lord, she'd
seen him in here dozens of times over the years, and not
once had his attention been anything more than chit-chatty,
even fatherly.

Christ, the look on his face. Poor Ricky seemed starstruck or something. She hoped she'd let him down gently, but she could tell he'd been undeterred. Damn. Now she'd have to figure out another place to get her gas.

Grumbling, she got out of the car and came in through the back, careful not to attract any more attention than she already had.

When she pushed through the plate glass door, all those homey sights and smells greeted her...expensive hair dye and essential oils infusing the air, J's favorite disco/techno mix pumping through the speakers, paraffin wax hand moisturizer bubbling in its pot. For the first time today, the tension slid off her shoulders and her broody mood lifted.

It was like that every time she came to her mother's salon. She'd grown up here. It was home. Divalicious was an amazing place, a two-bedroom clapboard house Mom and Uncle J had painted pink and gutted to be an upscale two-chair salon. Fun and funky, they'd pickled the floors and the walls stark white, installed track lighting, and put up lots of Andy-Warhol inspired art—much of it based on Uncle J's best drag looks. The salon attracted everyone from wealthy retirees to millennials and even teens wanting glammed up. Many of them came to see Uncle J, who'd gotten a bit of a "queer eye" reputation, known as the makeover master of the Tri-State area. Some of their clients drove for hours get in the chairs here, and appointments weren't always easy to get.

Uncle J glanced up from the chair he was wiping down and beamed at the sight of her. "Carrmeliiitaaa!" He hurried across the salon to take her coat from her. "Your timing is perfect! I've been preparing for you all afternoon, mija."

He drew her into one of his standard bone-crushing

hugs, and she hugged him back, breathing in the scent of high-end hair product that could only be her sweet uncle. His face never failed to make her smile, because her uncle was always smiling. He was more full of joy, love, and artistic talent that anyone she'd ever met. He was perfection itself, as always, with his shoulder-length salt-and-pepper hair combed back just so from his forehead, and his thick beard trimmed up all precise and close to his chin. She pulled back and tweaked the end of the handlebar mustache he'd oiled up to a fine point. "Since when did you get one of these?"

"Oh, that." Mom rolled her eyes. "Your uncle has been twirling his mustache like that ever since he started following beardaholic on Instagram. Now it's 'beard oil' this and 'beard glitter' that. You're lucky he hasn't woven Christmas ornaments in his beard yet."

J cocked a hip and wagged his finger at her. "Girly girl, wait until I bring out the coordinated beard lights for Christmas dinner. I have a whole preprogrammed light show. You'll be jealous you can't grow one."

Mom shook her head but still grinned fondly at her brother as she busied around, sweeping up hair from what was probably her last appointment of the day. Lita scheduled her monthly hairdos at three o'clock for this reason. It took both her mom and her uncle to attack her braids, let alone do the color on her long, curly locks.

Mom had to be bone tired from being on her feet all day by now, but you'd never know it. She hummed as she busied around her station, sweeping and wiping and pulling out hair product. Somehow, she never had a hair out of place, either. Thick, gleaming black tresses flowed straight and full down her back. And she was wearing her normal uniform of a clingy, Divalicious branded sweater, tight leggings that hugged her perfect figure, and her favorite high-heeled silver wedges. With great bone structure and even better makeup, you'd never know the woman was fifty. Her mother was simply beautiful, inside and out. And she'd worked hard to make it look as effortless as she did. Honestly, Lita wished she had half that woman's energy.

Uncle J got her situated in her chair with her smock, while he disappeared to the back room to fetch his supplies. A few moments later, he'd removed the trim, red silk vest he'd been wearing, and had exchanged his tailored green dress shirt for a black Divalicious T-shirt. Lita watched him with resigned amusement. He'd always said doing her thick cascade of braids was like doing battle with Medusa. And he was suiting up.

It wasn't long before he'd tilted her head, braids and all, into his sink, scrubbed them down, and coated them in hair oil, making conversation about the crazy busy day they'd had at the salon. Then he spun her chair around, tilted her back again, and moved a little table behind the chair so he could fan out her locks on it.

As usual, J and her mom sliced off the bottom half inch of her braids and got to work unwinding them. It was something she'd had done every month for years now, and Lita had learned to find the labor-intensive process relaxing. She sank down into the chair, letting the the light tugs and two sets of expert hands on her scalp soothe her.

Before she knew it, her mother was shaking her awake.

"Miiiijjja" she sang out. "Did you enjoy your nap?"

Lita startled awake, but soon snickered with embarrassment that she'd let herself fall asleep in the chair. *Again.* "Ugh," Lita grimaced. "Please tell me I wasn't snoring. Or drooling."

"Hmmm, no snoring," her mother answered her. "But definitely mumbling about Ross. It was hard to make it out but you seemed unhappy about something. Did the two of you have a fight?"

Gah. It had been a confusing afternoon, hadn't it, with all that bizarre crap going on. Then half arguing with Ross, and that hug...

No wonder she was dreaming about it. That hug had felt...well, she didn't know how to describe the full-body experience she'd had. But it hadn't sucked. She'd hugged Ross before once or twice. But this time was different. Charged, maybe. With what, she couldn't say.

Or maybe she was just letting the cookies get to her.

She waved her mother's concerns away. "No. No, actually, it was the opposite. We just..." Her voice trailed off. She honestly did not have the energy to get into the totally insane things that were happening to her. They wouldn't believe her anyway. She'd never hear the end of teasing about it from J. "It was a weird day at work, that's all."

Mom stopped brushing for a minute and furrowed her brows. "There's nothing going wrong with your job, is there?"

"Oh, no-no. *Definitely* no," Lita countered. "It was only customer service stuff. No big."

The woman nodded, seeming satisfied with the answer. Lita was relieved when Uncle J swung back around to sit in front of her again. He was holding a big book of hair color samples and beaming from ear to ear.

He opened it up to the right page with an expectant grin. "I gotta tell you, mija, I'm super excited today. We got in some new extreme colors and I can't wait to try them out. See? They have an opalescent shimmery sheen once you do the built-in conditioning treatment. And these here? These are the new metallics. Aren't they amazing?"

Lita flipped through the pages but couldn't find herself getting too enthusiastic about any of these. Bright turquoise.

Burgundy and orange. Flaming bright purple. Candy apple green. Maybe a little more glittery, or more metal-like, but this was more or less the exact same colors she'd been putting in her hair for the last...dear Lord. What? *Fifteen years?*

Gah. No wonder Ross didn't know what her real hair color was. He'd never seen it! Nobody in Lewisburg had. She'd been that weird woman with the cartoon hair for so long, she almost didn't know who she was otherwise. And it kinda pissed her off, now that she thought about it.

What did her natural color even look like anymore? Did *she* even know?

She closed the book and handed it back to him. "These colors are cool, but what if I went back to my real hair color?"

A slow, wicked smile crept across his face. "I always knew this day would come!"

"Somebody call the newspapers!" Mom laughed. "You're finally gonna get to do it! You're gonna get to do those ombre tips on her."

"Yaaassss gurl!" J cried. "Ooh, we could do a center part too, with all those curls waterfallin' down. You'll look like a Botticelli painting!"

"Let me get this straight." Lita smiled. "You've been talking about taking my hair back natural for *years*, and you haven't told me?"

J shrugged. "We've talked about it ever since you've gotten out of high school. But I figured the colored hair was a personal decision, something you had to decide on. I didn't want to influence you one way or the other."

Funny thing was, J had, whether he'd been trying to or not. "Representing" for the salon was one of the reasons why she'd always chosen those bold looks. But now that J had freed her from all that...

It made her feel empowered. Grown, even. *Yeah, ombre*
—she liked that idea. Her natural dark brown, with gradated
blond right at the tips, would still be striking and allow her
to ditch those heavy braids.

"Let's do it!" She clapped, and J and Mom whooped
and high-fived.

This change of plan seemed to give Mom and J a big
boost of creative energy. And they'd need it, because the job
was going to require them to dye her hair white, color over
the white, give her a conditioning treatment, and a haircut.
All expensive treatments, but she wasn't concerned about
the price. They'd never dream of charging her, and she was
so frequently on their ads and social, they'd always said she
paid them back in publicity.

In the end, Lita took J up on his recommendation. He'd
thin out some of the bulk and trim up the back so it
tapered from her shoulder blades down to the small of her
back.

"Gurrrrrl, when we're done here, you're gonna have
every beautiful shade of honeyed brown in your hair. We're
gonna have something even Jesus can approve of." J made
the sign of the cross and pointed up. "And I do mean both
of us."

And so it went, Uncle J fussing and planning and
mixing up colors while Mom assisted. They'd been joking
and telling stories through most of it, but by five thirty they
were tired and bored and getting a little punchy. They'd
managed to get her braids out and were waiting for the
whitening treatment to knock out her color, before they
could do it all over again in brown.

Topics shifted, of course, to the Hairball. Not surprisingly, J hadn't shown Mom the outfit he'd planned for Lita.

When Lita held up her phone to show her, Mom made
a strangled sound. "Ai! Are you kidding me, brother? You'd

put your own niece in...what. Are you wrapping her in toilet paper?"

J let out an outraged squawk and held his hand to his chest. "Toilet paper? What do you take me for, an amateur? I figured y'all might object, so I've been sewing up an outfit I swear will keep all my beautiful niece's bits from falling out. Here. I'll show you!" He ran to the closet and came running back in with a flimsy outfit that was every bit as skimpy as Lita had imagined. She'd worn many a crazy outfit for her uncle's sake, but this?

Lita eyed it with more than a little suspicion. "That won't even cover my ass crack."

J scowled down at it. "Sure it will! I designed it to."

Lita jumped out of the chair, grabbed the hanger, and held it up to her. She tried, badly, to arrange it in front of her. She held it up to her hips specifically. "See? I'd be hanging out all over the place."

"Brother! You know I'm open-minded. But are you seriously planning on letting your niece walk down the catwalk wearing *that*? She'll be as trussed up as a little pink piglet on Easter day!"

"Hey!" Lita squawked.

"I can fix it!" J insisted. "I can make more of a panty. Is it my fault she's got all this junk in the trunk?"

"Hello!" Lita waved her hand. "I'm right here!"

Mom stamped her spongy wedge sole on the hardwood, and when that didn't make the dramatic sound she'd hoped for, she swore in a few nearly unintelligible Spanish phrases. "I draw the line at my daughter's ass crack!"

Uncle J opened his mouth to argue his point but was interrupted by an embarrassed cough coming from the reception desk.

They all turned around to see, *oh dear Lord*, a

uniformed UPS guy, standing there holding a stack of boxes. "Uhhh. Am I coming at a bad time?"

Mom spun around, immediately flushed with embarrassment, and nearly tripped herself. "Tino!" she called out, her voice unnaturally high. "We were talking costumes for the ball with my daughter. So, you're later than usual."

Brightening at the sound of his name, he broke out into a broad, engaging grin, and propped an impressively large forearm on her counter. "I waited until the end of my run. I've got some special deliveries for ya."

Mom swished off to the counter to meet him, hips swaying. "Really? You made a delivery after five, just for us?"

Uh-oh.

She *liked* this guy.

Lita glanced over at Uncle J, and he gave her a sly little nod of confirmation. Then an eye roll, for emphasis. Instantly, Lita went on high alert, wondering if she should intervene somehow so she could save the woman from herself.

Her mother had the worst radar for men she'd ever seen —favoring good-looking playas and deadbeats who'd end up leaving or disrespecting her in the end. She'd started out getting knocked up at eighteen by Lita's dad—a man who'd made it clear he loved gambling, get-rich-quick schemes, alcohol, and other women more than his wife and children. Even at six years old, Lita'd been relieved when Mom had kicked Dad to the curb. Since then, mom had followed up with one smooth-talking bad boy after another, not a single one of them staying around for more than a month or two.

Lita always wondered why. Her mother was a catch. Alessandra Ruiz was successful businesswoman, loving, funny, and smart. She was the kind of sexy that made most men sit up and say "Viva México." She could have any man she wanted.

Still, this guy didn't look a thing like the other men Mom had been interested in before. He was big—probably about six feet tall, muscular, and barrel-chested. But that was where the similarity ended. He was a bit thick around the middle, like a tank, and shaved completely bald. Still, he had a little graying goatee, which sculpted his face nicely. An attractive guy she supposed, but kind of...what? Derpy?

Her mom walked far enough away that she couldn't quite make out their conversation. But that was fine. Lita could always learn more from how a man acted than what he said. She sat back in her chair, not taking her eyes off them as her mother batted her thick eyelashes at the man and threw out shy smiles.

Uncle J nudged Lita's shoulder and handed her the customary glass of "while you're waiting for your hair to process" prosecco. "Seems like your mother is ordering a lot more stock now that we've got this new delivery guy. I'm tellin' ya, we've got enough product now to put half the town in drag," he murmured, low enough so they couldn't be heard.

"Who is he?"

"He's new to the area. Moved to Lewisburg when UPS shifted his route, but he's been a driver for twenty-five years. Went through a hard divorce a few years back. He goes by Tino, but his name is really Santino—Santino *Lasagna*."

Lita whipped around in her chair and let out a bark of laughter.

"Shh!" J cackled, holding up a finger. "She'll hear you!"

"You're making that up! There's no way his last name is *Lasagna*. Who's she goin' out with next? Tony Taco?"

"Gurl, I *know*. But I swear. He's, like, fourth-generation Italian American, with one of those big fa-la-la-la-la Italian families. And that's his born name. Can you imagine, going through life named after food like that?"

"Yeah." Lita hummed. "People would think you were cheesy."

"Or saucy." J grinned.

"Or, dare I say it, *hot*."

"Or meaty." J rubbed his hand up and down his chest and tsked. "Oh Lord, I wonder if he's the kind with lasagna with beef or the spicy Italian sausage."

They were both snickering outright into their wine-glasses now, trying and failing to spy without Mom noticing.

But Mom didn't seem to care. She'd come around to Tino's side of the counter and was smiling up at him like he was the only man in the universe, sidling right up in his personal space. Tino definitely didn't mind, and if she wasn't seeing things, the man was starting to preen a little bit, puffing up his considerable chest.

"Ut-ut-ut, look there!" J pointed. "She doing my favorite — the musical laugh-biting her bottom lip-twirling her finger on his shirt button combo! Awwww!" He sighed, holding his hand over his heart again. "I taught her that. And now Tino is blushing. Ai! I'm *so* proud right now."

"You like this one, don't you?"

J nodded. "'Fraid so, mija."

"Why? After all the guys she's run through?"

"Now don't you go getting on your mother's case. She's had her fun. But this one? I don't know. He acts so different. He's very serious and old-fashioned with her. He stops in here every day, bringing her little gifts and lingering to hear about her day. And he calls me Jesús."

Lita snorted. "So? That's your name."

"Yes, but I've let everyone call me J because it's easier on them. You know, all those Anglos squeamish about addressing you in the name of the risen Lord. But Tino not only calls me by my full name, and he says it right: *Hey*-sus. He squares up his shoulders, makes eye contact, and shakes my hand when he leaves too. It may sound like a small thing, but it isn't. He truly respects us, and your mother especially. It's, I dunno, *sweet*. And frankly, after a life full of salty, I think your mother could use a little sweet, don't you?"

As if to prove his point, Tino reached around and pulled what appeared to be two tickets out of his back pocket. Her mother squealed with delight, threw her arms around his neck and kissed his cheek.

"Somebody go find the party favors," J crooned. "The boy finally worked up his courage and asked her out to a show. I'm betting it's one of his."

"His?"

J gave her arm a playful shove. "Honey, the man is a musician in his spare time. He plays in a band!"

"What does he play?"

"Get this." J cupped his hand around his mouth and raised his eyebrows. "Accordion and bagpipes."

Lita's mouth fell open.

J held his hand up. "I shit you not. If I'm lyin', I'm dyin'. He's an Italian playin' in a punk Scottish band. His stage name is T, and he wears a kilt."

Before Lita could get out a laugh, her mother squealed and came out from behind the counter, carrying an enormous, insulated food bag. "Isn't it great?" She clucked, holding up the bag proudly. "Tino is taking me to a show! And he's made us some lasagna! This could not be better. I've been so busy I haven't had a bite since breakfast. Y'all want some?"

Lita smothered a laugh at how perfectly basic that was, but damn if that didn't sound delicious right now. She was starving.

While Mom worked on unzipping the bag and fetching paper plates, Tino wasted no time walking over to introduce himself. "Hi." He stuck out his big ham hock of a hand. "I'm Tino. You must be Lita. Your mother has told me so much about you."

She got up out of her chair to return his handshake, holding her breath for a beat to see if he had one of those strange magical reactions to her, like so many other men had today. He was single, after all.

But Tino kept pinning her with that forthright eye contact that seemed to say, *I'm here for your mother. I hope you're okay with that.*

Huh.

So serious. And totally not affected by her, or the spell. It could be that the spell was only a figment of her imagination. Or, it could be that Tino didn't consider himself single.

Whether it was from pure relief, or whether she was actually charmed by the man, she didn't know. But that thread of man-related anxiety permanently wound in her chest started to loosen a little bit.

Lita smiled at the man and found she really meant it when she said, "It's a pleasure to meet you, Tino. And I'm so glad you're taking Mom out. It's been forever since she's been to a show."

Mom squawked loudly as she spooned out the steaming fresh pasta. "Carmelita Rose Noe! Would you stop that? You're making me sound like a dried-up spinster!"

"No one would ever accuse you of that." Tino grinned. "*Believe* me. You're twice as pretty as Salma Hayek ever thought about being."

"Awwwww," J sang out, "all that, and he brings food too."

Tino started back toward her mother, but Lita caught his shoulder, gave him a raised eyebrow, and executed a two-fingered *eyes on you* gesture that her mother couldn't see. "Play nice. I'll be watching," she murmured.

He nodded, still grinning as if he was totally comfortable with that. "So noted."

And when her mother handed her a heaping plate of Tino's special recipe, so much richer and cheesier than what she'd usually choose, Lita's stomach rumbled in approval. After a long day, maybe it really was what they all needed.

CHAPTER 5

DOWNTOWN LEWISBURG

Ross HELPED his sister Tiffany down from their sleigh-bell-covered, horse-drawn carriage. She kicked her tiny feet with indignation as he lifted her out by her armpits.

When her boots landed back on the sidewalk, she shot him a dirty look. "Really, Ross? I'm pregnant, not a child. You couldn't hold your hand out?"

He grinned at her. "What can I say, short stuff? You're like a teacup preggo. I wanna wrap you up in bubblewrap."

And stand guard over her too, but he wasn't telling her that. She was his older sister by two years, but only four foot ten. And with her waddling along, eight months pregnant with her first child, he was having to refrain from the near-constant urge to carry her around on a pillow. But seeing as how she wasn't havin' that, he'd have to settle for keeping her from getting too cranky. Seemed like he wasn't doing *that* too well today, either.

His mom got out of the carriage next, smirking but shaking her head at them both. "Children, am I going to have to send one of you to the car? Must you always act up when we go out shopping?"

Tiff stuck out her tongue at him. "He started it." She giggled as he wrapped an arm around her shoulders, gave her a brotherly bear hug, and rubbed his knuckles on the top of her head. "Hey!" She snorted. "No messing with the hair!"

"Sorry." He held up his hands. "How soon I forget."

And it *was* easy to forget. Because when she stuck her tongue out at him, he couldn't help thinking how Tiffany hadn't changed much since they'd been kids. Even at thirty-two, a successful interior designer, happily married woman, and soon-to-be-mother of his first niece, her smile was like sunlight through the trees in autumn. She was tiny and curvy, like their mom, all freckles, wild auburn curls, and big brown eyes.

But damn, was she was a mess today. Not that he blamed her. Her height and the unusually big baby she was carrying made it seem like she'd swallowed a watermelon whole. Poor Tiff was at the stage where everything hurt—her back, her feet, her stomach. Throw in sleepless nights and anxiety over getting the nursery picture perfect, and you had a recipe for trouble. When Mom had recruited him to distract his sister with shopping , he'd readily agreed, even though it was hardly his thing. Somebody had to get her out of the house while Dad and her husband, Bernard, finished painting and assembling all the baby furniture.

Bernard, or "Bear" as they all called him, swore they'd be able to get the base coat up and the crib built by the time she got home later tonight. The man was one of the top architect/developers in the area. For his sake, Ross hoped he was able to do what he said. Tiff was getting antsy now that her due date loomed in January.

Because they'd "entertained" his sister so thoroughly, they were all starting to wear out. So far today, they'd hit three fabric shops, strung up Christmas lights, scarfed down brunch at Tudor's Biscuit World, and spent the afternoon in downtown Lewisburg, strolling in and out of the shops for the city's annual "Christmas in Lewisburg" celebration.

Tiff stood on the sidewalk, hands on what was left of her hips, scanning the streets for her next quarry. There was a lot to see, as many of the stores were having event-oriented sidewalk sales today. It was a beautiful day for being out— clear and crisp, with all the old-timey storefronts lined with painted windows and twinkling light displays.

Ross wasn't the type to browse around. Mostly, he'd get in, and get out, and be done with it. But today, downtown was the place to be. It wasn't so much shopping as a holiday feast for the senses. The clop-clop of the horse's hooves from the passing carriages, the happy bustle of people walking by all loaded down with presents. Mom nudged him and handed him the extra-tall steaming cider he'd ordered. He took a big drag, grateful that he finally had a chance to drink it. Was that cinnamon and ginger he tasted in there? Oh, *hell yeah...*

Mom tapped him on the shoulder, mid-sip.

"What?" he asked her.

"Stick your arm out," she said.

He shook his head, confused.

"Like this." She put one arm straight out in front of her.

He scrunched up his brows, but he did it. Then the woman smiled and looped all three fresh pine wreaths from their wreath-making class over his arm. Great. Now he smelled like a Christmas tree. He rolled his eyes at her.

Satisfied with herself now, Mom clapped her mittened hands. "Hooray! Now we're ready to shop some more."

Seemed like every store was doing something. There were readings at the bookshop, free food samples at the restaurants, games, and prizes everywhere. They weren't even close to exhausting their options yet. Together they decided to go up the hill a bit to where a food truck was parked, selling "thirty-six varieties of fudge." He could the sweet, creamy results of their candy-making demo from here.

But Tiff narrowed her eyes and pointed to a big crowd gathered on the sidewalk. "Isn't that Renegade Tats up there? Why are there so many people? I didn't even know they were open on Sundays."

"They're not," Ross answered her and started off in that direction, even without a consensus on where they were going next. Because Lita was up there today. And there was only one reason why a line of men snaked out of that shop—and he was willing to bet it wasn't the walk-in airbrushing she was doing. Some kind of crazy shit was going on.

A sharp shot of anxiety scrambled his stomach as he made his way up the hill.

Mom and Tiff exchanged a sly glance at each other but didn't say anything, just struggled up the street with him, weaving around a line that was two deep. When they got to the shop's plate-glass window, he finally saw her hunched over a table, airbrushing a sweatshirt.

Lita.

Goddamn, she looked...*perfect.*

"The sign outside says she's doing walk-in airbrushing." Mom clucked. "Isn't that a fabulous idea for Christmas? What a way to personalize a gift! No wonder she's so popular today!"

Ross stood rooted to the sidewalk as if he'd been planted there. He couldn't talk. Couldn't breathe hardly, the sight of her hit him so hard.

"Oh wow, check it out." Tiff hummed. "She did something different with her hair."

Ross smothered the urge to laugh helplessly. Cause that's exactly what he was right now. Helpless.

For the record, he'd always thought Lita was the most beautiful badass he'd ever met. She was the only woman he'd ever really wanted when it came right down to it. But he'd made this business of wanting something he couldn't have a daily thing. Something he'd gotten so used to, he'd almost forgotten how much it hurt.

But now? He was paralyzed by wanting her—this new, improved Lita he was looking at. She was a fuckin' vision. There was no other way to say it. Her hair was a gorgeous shade of honeyed brown, kissed by highlights on the end that he could see, even from here. She'd parted it in the middle and let it cascade down her back in wild, looping curls, freed from her usual braids. Not too surprisingly, Lita had Christmas-themed herself up. But she was way more dressed up than usual, wearing a little fuzzy midriff-baring sweater in neon green and a red, swingy wool skirt that nipped in tight around her waist and swished around her knees.

And then there were those hoochie-high red suede boots on her tiny little feet.

Joy.

To.

The world, baby.

How was it this woman he'd seen almost every day was suddenly knocking him flat like this? Was it the hair? Maybe. Or maybe it was *her*, revealing another beautiful layer of herself.

All he knew was, he'd never wanted her more than he did at this moment.

Lita waved at them through the plate glass, and Mom waved back. "She's always been a lovely girl. But she's a lovely woman now, isn't she?"

Tiff snorted. "Yeah and all the men in town have noticed. I heard rumors about men being so into her, they're following her down the street in packs. I didn't think it was true. But now I can totally see how—"

"Oh, dear." Mom interrupted, grimacing. "Is that Cam Longstreet up there with her?"

Tiffany sneered. "What does *that* manwhore want?"

"Everything," Ross grumbled. And he was gonna make damn sure the guy didn't get it. He quickly handed his mom the wreaths, and started pushing his way past all the guys in line, shoving and throwing a few elbows as he went. He didn't fuckin' care.

"Cam," Lita growled, pinching the bridge of her nose. "I *told* you. You can't be up here if you don't have something you want me to airbrush. There's a line."

But did the guy leave? Of course he didn't. No, he fell back on his old tricks, namely draping his finely sculpted ass right on the edge of her worktable. "Aww, come on, kitty cat. Since when have you not had time for *me?*"

Kitty kat—his old nickname for her. Did he really think that dumbassed trick was gonna work? Honestly, if it wasn't for this whole roomful of people watching her, she would've cussed him right back out on to the sidewalk.

But, reminding herself that she was a businesswoman and an artisan right now, she counted to ten. She leaned into his space and lowered her voice. "I believe the *not having time for you* thing started when I came over to your place for our date, and you were literally raw-dogging some redhead on your living room floor."

Cam shook his shaggy blond head and knitted his eyebrows for a moment, like he couldn't quite remember. "Humpf. I must've double-booked."

Really? *Really*, tramposo?

She stepped back a step and threw up a hand. *"¿Por qué me molesté con tu trasero infiel?"*

His shoulders slumped. "I-I don't know what that means."

"It means, *why did I ever bother with your cheating a*ss, that's what," she barked, loud enough for the whole room to hear this time.

A murmur went up from the mostly male crowd.

A few *oooooh, I heard that*s and *she told him*s pinged off the walls.

Lita considered this packed room of hopeful men—all of them ready to contribute to her craft hustle and her bank account. She should be energized by the opportunity. But she just felt tired, down deep in her bones. Defeated too. Would it be too much to airbrush some crap for people? *God!* She'd had no fewer than twelve guys ask her out this afternoon. Cam was number thirteen. And she'd let him get to her.

"Cam," she ground out as evenly and calmly as possible, "either give me something to airbrush, or leave."

"Okay, fine," he sang out. "But remember you asked for it."

And then, to her shock, the man proceeded to peel off his hoodie *and* the tight black tee he had on under it. Rippling chest now bare, he slapped the shirt down on the table. "There." He pointed. "Airbrush your new phone number on that, and we'll call it a day."

She blinked at the man, so pissed at so many things that honestly, her brain short-circuited for a minute.

That he really thought she'd give him her number again.

That he'd been calling enough to realize she'd changed carriers.

That he'd strip in here.

That he'd somehow believe the sight of his six-pack would somehow bend him to her will.

That he'd disrespect her business like this.

But she suppressed the urge to slap that smirk off his face. Lita whipped the T-shirt up off the table instead and threw it back at him. It bounced off his head and into his hands. "Get out, Cam," she growled.

And then the damnedest thing happened. Cam frowned, all hurt and confused now, and blinking back tears like some kind of lost little boy. "Aww. Come on. Don't be like that. Would it help if I said please? *Please*, Lita?"

Somehow, he'd managed to shock her again.

Cam Longstreet wasn't the type of man to beg. He'd never asked for anything, and never had to. His towering physique and easy charm meant half the female population in this area had thrown themselves at his feet, at one time or another. She'd never seen him display an honest emotion in his life.

And he sure hadn't seemed sorry to see her go, way back when. He'd even rolled himself off that chick, calm as you please, and had told her "it was bound to happen" and he "wasn't feelin' it" anymore. That was his only excuse. His only explanation. For Christ's sake, she'd seen him walking down the street with his latest conquest only a week ago, and he hadn't even turned his head in her direction!

The man had to be hexed. It was the only explanation. A small part of her felt just a little bit sorry for him.

But not too sorry. Because at the moment, he was trying to worm his way back into her space, and she wasn't quite sure what she was going to do about it.

He wrapped a big hand around her shoulder and squeezed. "Please, K," he whispered, right in her ear. "Please say yes."

Rather than melt at the heat of his breath on her neck, her wits came back online in a rush. She swatted his hand off. "Get out, Cam."

He grabbed her again. "But baby—"

"I said *get out!*"

Cam moved to touch her again, but before he could make contact, he went flying backward over the table with a jerk. Another yank, and he was flat on his back on the cold, hard linoleum.

Ross.

It was Ross, off the sidewalk and in the right place at the right time today. For once, she didn't mind the man's meddling. He got between her, the desk, and Cam, and put his foot down, right on Cam's chest. "I believe you heard the lady. So why aren't you doing what she said?"

The room erupted in applause, the rest of them glad to get rid of the competition, apparently.

Cam looked around wildly, like he had no idea where he was. "Dude!" he cried, holding out his hands. "What the fuck? What'd I do?"

Ross grimaced at him like he wanted to punch the guy but thought better of it. He swiped Cam's clothes off the counter and tossed them down to him. But Ross smashed his foot down a little harder on Cam's chest, to make his point. "Let's not get into that right now. Here's what you're gonna do. You're going to face the door, pull on your clothes, and walk out of here without looking back. You're not to come back here. Got it?"

Ross kept his foot right there until Cam finally held his hands up and shook his head. "Awright, man! Awright! Whatever!"

Ross stood back then, careful to block Cam's view of her. The crowd murmured and gossiped some more, but they fell back to make room while Cam dressed, brushed himself off, and stomped out the door.

Ross checked on her. "You okay?" He frowned. "You're a little pale. These guys have been bugging you all day, haven't they?"

Lita threw up her hands. "I told you why, Ross, but you won't believe me. You believe me now?"

"C'mon man," a voice rang out from the back of the room. "We've been waiting for hours! You really think you can get all macho and jump line?"

Ross growled and ground his teeth, but he kept his eyes on her, locked in with care and concern, instead of the strange l'amour she'd been dealing with all day from these idiots. She felt herself relax a bit, like she always did in his presence. The real Ross was with her, like always. The magic wasn't hitting him, apparently. Or maybe it was hitting him differently? Maybe he didn't consider himself single? Or attracted to her?

Ross had always been cagey about his sex life. He never mentioned anyone he'd been with by name. As far as she knew, he went out to bars in neighboring towns or did one-time-only Tinder hookups. But she supposed he could be seeing someone he just didn't want to talk about.

"You had enough of this?" he asked her. "Because I really think you should call it quits. I still don't know what the deal is. But maybe if you go to the back, they'll all come to their senses and get out of here."

She felt the reflexive urge to argue with him, and any man who came in and tried to tell her what to do. But Ross was right. She was done here. She nodded, defeat and embarrassment tying her tongue. Dammit, she was planning on banking what she'd earned today, and making a big deposit to her "buying your own place" fund. It's like she was watching that money go *poof* into thin air. She handed

Ross a stack of business cards for her Etsy store. "Give them this."

As she headed for the breakroom, she heard Ross yelling out to the crowd. "Okay, y'all. Show's over. Lita's packed in her airbrush for the day." Angry shouts broke out as Ross circulated in the crowd, but they abruptly stopped when she went to the back room and shut the door. Completely drained now, she collapsed on Tank's ratty old couch. If only Tank had been here to help at his shop today, maybe none of this would've happened in the first place. Trying to be nice and give her more space, the man had allowed her to use the shop on his one day off for this. And foolishly, she'd thought she could handle it.

She dropped her face in her hands and massaged her forehead. *What the hell is happening to me? And how much worse was this going to get?*

At the sound of the door opening, she raised her head. Ross' mom, Sherry, and his sister Tiffany came scurrying in. "Oh my goodness, Lita honey, are you alright?" Sherry sat down beside her on the couch and grabbed her hand, giving it a motherly squeeze. "That was scary out there!"

Am I alright?

That was a very good question, wasn't it? She blinked up at Sherry and her sweet smile and kind eyes, in a flowered corduroy print dress she'd probably made herself, and wondered if she'd ever get her to understand. Ross' mother was such a normal-as-apple-pie kind of person, how could she ever explain what they'd seen out there? Hoo, the woman would probably cart her off to the psychiatrist.

Tiffany, for her part, flopped down on the other side of the couch. "Okay, girlfriend. Out with it! Everybody in town is talking about how men are following you around. Your new hairdo might be pretty awesome, but it's not *that* awesome. What are you doing? Emitting some high-frequency radio wave that hypnotizes them?"

A rueful laugh bubbled up from Lita's throat. "No."

"Okay, you got some kind of new perfume then," Tiff answered.

"No."

"A team of social media experts, lining you up on dates?"

"God, no."

"Are you paying them to—"

Lita rapped Tiff on the leg. "Um, noooo."

"What is it then?" Tiff narrowed her eyes. "And don't tell me you don't know, or it's nothing. Because it's definitely *something*. I've seen grown men out there I've known my whole life acting like you're Aphrodite walking among us. Men who've known *you* most of your life too, and not acted like that before. So you want to tell me what's going on, or do we have to drag it out of you?"

Sherry gave Lita's leg a reassuring pat. "Best you answer her, dear. You can't resist two of us at once. It's a Mason family trait."

Lita flopped backward on the couch and rubbed at her eyes. "Ughhh. I could tell you. But you'd never believe me."

They both solemnly swore not to tell her she was crazy. So slowly, surely, she started to spill her guts. The day at Corn+Flour, the strange old lady. What the woman had told them. The glowy cookies. And then the men asking her out. Being irresistible and all that.

When she finally came to the end of her tale, Sherry and Tiffany looked at each other for a long, disbelieving beat, then burst out laughing.

"Oh my gawd," Tiffany wheezed. "Magic cookies! I'm so relieved! I was afraid you were gonna tell us you'd drugged their coffee!"

Sherry laughed so hard, she had to wipe a tear from her eyes. "And to think, I was ready to go for the 'paying them off to make Ross jealous' theory!"

What? Why would she think that? Had Ross said something? Lita decided to file that tidbit away for later. That was definitely a thread that needed pulling. "Sure, guys, go ahead. Laugh at my pain." Lita sniffed. "But know this—I don't have any extra money to buy anybody off. That's why I'm here in the first place. Trying to earn some. And as for Ross, there's no reason for me to make him jealous."

"Right," Ross answered, suddenly filling up the doorway. "Because we aren't a thing, right?"

She was probably waiting a beat too long to answer him, because she was trying to decipher the intense look he was giving her. There was something about the soft way he'd said that, and the way his eyes flashed right now that seemed...disappointed. Maybe even a little hurt. Like he *wanted them* to be a thing.

And that kinda took her breath away, for just a second.

And she...maybe she wanted...

She scrubbed her hands over her face, nearly succumbing to the sudden, overwhelming urge to cry. Because she had no idea what to think or how to feel. About any of this.

It was probably just a trick of the light, or her reading way too much into things, like she always did. "Right." She cleared her throat, which felt strangely thick. "We're not a thing. Of course."

"Awww, honey." Sherry leaned over and gave her a one-armed hug. "We don't mean to laugh at you, really. It's only that it's such a ridiculous story. You know how odd that sounds, right? If you want my opinion, I think you've come into your own, and all the men in town are finally getting to see how amazing you are." Lita opened her mouth to argue with the woman, but Sherry held up a hand. "Let's have a thought experiment here and assume the woman did have some kind of magic powers. She said it was just for the season, right? From what you're telling me, all you'll have to do is be extra careful between now and New Year's Eve or maybe New Years's Day. Don't go out by yourself. Walk around at least in pairs. And don't start up anything serious with anybody. Should be simple, really. You've simply got to wait it out."

Wait it out. Maybe it really was that simple. She'd just have to be extra careful, right?

"Don't worry," Ross weighed in. "I don't know what's happening here any more than the rest of us. All I can tell you is I'm here. I'll make sure nothing happens to you. *Always*, Lita."

Lita searched his face any sign that he might be under some kind of spell, or simply telling her what she wanted to hear. The gaze she got back was determined. Real. He was making her a promise he intended to keep.

A promise he'd always kept, hadn't he? He'd always been there for her—when she was up, when she was down, when she needed any little thing...

She'd never appreciated that before, had she?

There was so much about this whole mess that she didn't understand. Was Ross under the spell too, and just fighting it? Or was he just under a different kind of spell? He had been saying some awfully nice things to her lately.

And that look he gave her just now...

She really didn't know, did she?

Either way, she was just glad to have a friend who was putting up with her crazy right now.

Lita found herself getting up from the couch and walking across to him. She threw her arms around his middle again and squeezed him tight. She hummed a bit as she buried her face in his sweatshirt. For the first time today, she felt safe. Maybe even understood. "Thank you," she sighed.

She dug her fingers in the back of his coat, breathed in his familiar, calming scent, and wished she could say so much more than that. But for now, it would have to do.

CHAPTER 6

Public Notice:
From now until January 3rd, Holliday Hot Rods will not be
allowing any deliveries, gifts, calls, or personal visits for
Carmelita "Lita" Noe. We appreciate your help in keeping
our workplace a distraction-free environment. Thank You!

Ross FINISHED TAPING the sign to the shop's door. He'd
gotten it approved by Hunter, laminated it, and now it was
hung up in big, bold letters for every motherfucker to see.
He only hoped it kept the weirdos at bay. After that afternoon at Renegade Tats, Lita was still a bit shaken up.

As if he'd summoned her with his thoughts, Lita
appeared at his shoulder. She scowled at the sight of the
poster. "Okay, so *that's* not embarrassing at all. Are you guys
sure you couldn't come up with a better solution?"

"What do you expect? Snipers and concrete
barricades?"

"Fair point," she grumbled, "but you know right now,
the barricades sound like a good idea."

They exchanged wry smiles. Yeah, he could see what she meant. All day there'd been a constant stream of men in and out of here, dropping off gifts. Movie tickets. Candy. Flowers. Jewelry, even. Lita'd had to send them all away, their gifts unopened. Thank God, they'd all been very respectful. But she hadn't been able to get a thing done for all this mess, and it was setting them both seriously off schedule. Hunter'd had to come out from behind his AutoCAD to run interference. And that wasn't cool in anyone's book. By four o'clock, they'd gotten things calmed down enough so Hop and Hunter could leave for their estimating appointment for a new customer in Richmond.

So, as it stood, he was Lita's only backup if there was any new drama. This sign had better work. They had a lot on their plate today. He'd been so busy admiring his handiwork, it took him a second to realize the sniffling sound he'd heard was coming from Lita's direction. *Ah, hell.*

Her eyes were shiny and her nose was getting red on the end, like she was barely holding her emotions in. In all his years of knowing her, he'd never seen her like this, even once. The woman had made a religion of not letting people get to her. A pang of sympathy registered in his chest. Lita wasn't crying exactly, but her chin was wobbling a bit. "I hate being irresistible."

Ross chuckled and wrapped an arm around her shoulders. "Awww, c'mon. I believe the word the old lady used was 'sweet.' And you, Carmelita Rose Noe, will never be sweet. No matter what magic is involved. It's maybe the best thing about you." He stopped for a minute, kinda frozen, because once again, he'd blurted out what was on his heart without thinking.

But like usual, she took it as a joke. Lita shoved him off, grinning. "Damn right. At last! A man who finally sees me as I am!"

Something, somewhere inside him rebelled at that. He was struck by the sudden urge to be serious. To his surprise, he put his hand over hers on the crossbar. "I'm the guy who's always seen you, all this time. And I've liked what I've seen. Every single day." Ah damn. Everything inside him cringed. Yeah, he was definitely on a blurting spree. And sounding creepily desperate, probably. Which was pretty much the opposite of what Lita needed today, even if what he'd said was a hundred percent true.

He half expected her to slap his hand away and mutter at him in Spanish about being an idiot.

But she didn't.

Lita looked down at their linked hands and back up at him, searching his face for hints of, what? Magical influence? Bullshittery? He wouldn't be that guy. He decided to own it.

And what he saw staring back at him...

Was he seeing this right?

He could swear something flashed in her eyes that seemed a lot like...holy shit. *Interest.* For one hot minute, color rose to her cheeks, and her eyes grew dark. His heart kicked up its beat, and he watched her, breathless, waiting to see what she'd do or say next.

But it didn't last.

Lita shook her head a little bit, like she was trying to dismiss the thought, and gave him a patronizing pat. "You've always been a good friend to me." She sighed. "The best, really."

His heart fell to his knees. *Yeah, that's me*, he'd wanted to say. *Good ol' Ross. Ol' buddy. Ol' pal.* But he had that lips-clamped-shut tingling again.

He nodded and managed a "You're welcome" as he sauntered back through the door.

Disappointment settled like a stone on his chest. He

wasn't sure why, exactly. Why shouldn't this be like any other day? He wanted her. But she'd brushed him off again.

But dammit, this had been different. The current between them hadn't been one-sided. He'd felt the circuit complete this time. He wondered what that meant. All these years, he'd figured she didn't see him that way. But maybe...Jesus, had he been wrong?

His heart surged with hope. But his gut churned with confusion. And his whole damn body seemed to be crackling from the energy that had passed between them just now. Was this what it'd be like to be with her? That...*combustible?*

Or is this all in my head?

He couldn't answer that, could he?

Whatever that was, he couldn't dwell on it now. Their job for this afternoon was removing the interior of this 1940s Ford truck, piece by piece. Over the next couple of hours, their job was to clean out the interior of this thing so he could fabricate new pieces for the dash, and she could rebuild and reupholster the seats. It was a hard, dirty job, but one they'd done so many times together, it was like second nature.

And today was no different. In no time, they'd removed the gearshift box from the middle of the floor and, after dumping a ton of WD-40 on the rusty, fussy screws, they'd finally managed to pry the dashboard loose. They were backing it out of the car when the unmistakable sound of rapid fire texts chimed on Lita's phone.

"You need to get that?" he asked her.

"Nah, given how fast they're coming in, it's probably Mom and Uncle J."

He started to set down his end. "No, really, you can get it. It could be important."

But she stepped a foot out of the car and kept pulling.

"Trust me, it's not. You know, I debated about whether or not I should tell them about this whole hexed-cookie business, and I didn't, because I figured there'd be no end to the teasing. You know what? My instincts were right on the money. Uncle J had a person in his chair yesterday who saw what went down at Renegade Tats. And he spilled the whooooole story. When Mom called me, acting all concerned, I had to tell her what happened at Corn+Flour. Now, she thinks it's the funniest thing she's ever heard. Mom's sure I'm morphing into a fairy, and Uncle J is blaming my new blond highlights. Anyway, they're both acting like they're getting to watch a live-action telenovela starring me."

He snickered a little at that, thinking about the five-alarm frenzy this little story must've started at Divalicious. Knowing her crazy family like he did, it was a pretty fair bet Lita wasn't exaggerating.

Together, they arranged the dash down on the clean tarps they'd set out. "I know it's annoying, but you should count your blessings," he told her. "Your family is fun, and funny, and nuts about you. They're up in your grill because they're part of your life. I've got that, you've got that—not everyone is so lucky."

She let out a disgusted *humph* as she scrolled her phone. "Whatever you say, Ross." She held up a finger. "To give you an idea of what's on my screen right now, Mom and J are placing bets on who will contact me next. So far, Mom is ahead. And J is demanding I take both a picture of the prospective beau and the gifts he's brought before I send them away. Like mug shots or something. So they can do...*value tallies*? Oh no." She snickered as she handed him her phone. "Check it out."

He couldn't help cracking up at what he saw. "You've

gotta be shitting me! They made a grid! Like a Super Bowl pool or something! Man, they're taking this serious."

"As a heart attack. Honestly, I'm surprised they're not selling the squares off to their clients. But right now, it's only the two of them, putting their money on certain squares. Whoever guesses the most men correctly has the highest total. And the person with the highest total by January third wins a spa day at the Greenbrier."

Ross shook his head as they both climbed back into the truck. He slid into his usual position, with him sliding onto the floorboards, and her kneeling on the seats. "I dunno. This looks like my chance for a payday. Maybe I should get in on this."

"Right." She snorted. "Like you'd go to a spa."

"Hey! I could totally get into being massaged all afternoon with cucumbers on my eyes."

"Well, well, well. You think you know a person, and then you find out they've got all these proclivities." She threw a smile back at him over her shoulder as she worked, and he couldn't help but appreciate the view of her bootylicious ass from down here. She was wearing his favorite—her purple high-waisted leggings and a loose, off-the-shoulder top, a fashion choice that had been torturing his daydreams all day, like a low-grade hum of arousal that had taken up residence under his skin.

He grinned up at her. "You know, I'd be happy to introduce you to my proclivities anytime."

Lita snorted again. "Nice try, dog."

He laughed but didn't answer her. That strange tingling had taken up residence in his mouth again, and he didn't quite trust himself not to blurt out something like, *Lita I'm so serious I've wanted you every day for more than a decade please do me.* So, he clamped his teeth together tight.

· · ·

Ross got awful quiet as he worked, sprawled out on his back, loosening the seat legs. But Lita didn't mind. Sometimes she liked the silences between them as much as the talking. Guess that was part of being friends for so long and spending so much time in each other's company. You could just be, and that was enough.

The two of them set into a demolition rhythm, one they'd refined from years of practice. They crawled over the truck and over each other, taking the interior apart bit by bit. Hunter often bragged he had the fastest demo crew in the business, and she wouldn't doubt it. They'd gotten so used to working these things together, it'd become like a dance. They knew when to sit, when to stand, where to put a foot, when to pull, when to push, and what tools to use.

Lita kept at the business of loosening the seat back from the metal skeleton of the truck. She often took this task, as the upholstery expert. Her slim fingers were better for getting into these tight spots. It should be easy, but this seat was a real beyotch. Trucks this old tended to have seat backs that were flat and bolted into the metal truck wall behind them. And no matter how much oil she poured over the rusted bolts holding them in, they weren't budging.

She pulled out the crowbar, wedged it between the seat and the metal wall, and with some mighty yanks, was able to pull the seat away from the wall about an inch. The rest, she'd have to do with brute force.

Wedging her fingers into the cracks, she pulled with all her might. Whew! There went one side. But when she went to the opposite corner, she ran into resistance. She shimmied and struggled, finally deciding to pull backward on the diagonal with all her weight.

And that was the problem. Because when the back gave way, she went flying, bouncing off the dash frame before she landed right on top of Ross. *Hard.*

He shouted awfully loud, and she panicked.

Lita scrambled over top of him. "Oh, God! Are you okay? Did I put a knee somewhere I shouldn't have?"

They were stomach to stomach, nose to nose, splayed against each other from head to foot. Ross tried to stifle a cough. "No," he wheezed. "Just knocked the wind out of me."

She still didn't like the sound of that. Frantic, she started patting him down, even though they were smashed in there like sardines. "Ross, I'm *so* sorry. I pulled too hard. You're sure there's no cuts or anything?"

He grabbed her wrist and pulled her hand up against his chest. Suddenly she realized how much she'd been feeling him up, just now. And how good it had felt, to touch him like that. His heart beat under her hand, hard and fast. "Hey-hey. Stop worrying," he told her. "I'm fine. You didn't hurt me. Just surprised me, that's all."

"Oh. Okay, good," she murmured. Lita set her knees on either side of his hips, and raised her arms over her head so she could lever up the seat, which had fallen down on top of them too. She was able to loosen it, but when she tried to push it off, her head yanked back and a fierce, painful pull registered on her scalp. "Ow!" She stopped and rubbed her head.

"What's wrong?" Ross asked.

"I think I'm caught on something." She pushed again, harder this time, and pain shot through her head like her scalp was about to come off. And then it hit her. There was all kinds of old glue, hooks, sticky staples, and... "Shit-shit-shit!" she yelped. "It's stuck on my hair!"

"*What?* No, that can't be." Ross gently lifted the cushion up with his knees and worked both hands into her long curls. Of all the damn days not to put it back in a ponytail. Tying her hair back was part of her routine at work, a practical way of keeping her hair out of the paint. But she'd been enjoying the lightness and the freedom of having her hair unbound, and now she was paying the price.

Ross' breathing picked up while he stretched and strained, his chest rising and falling underneath her. But finally, he huffed out a "There it is." He paused. "Lita darlin', I have good news and bad news. What do you want first?"

She groaned. "The good news."

"It's only one hank of hair that's caught, but it's wound too tight. I can't get it loose. Still, it should be a simple matter to cut this one piece off, here at the end."

"And the bad news?"

"You've got me pinned, so you're going to have to get my pocket knife out of my pants."

Lita grumbled and banged her forehead against his chest a couple of times. "Ahhhhh. Fuck. Me!"

Ross laughed, and the sound resonated through his whole chest. "Oh, Lita. How long I've waited to hear those two little words."

She snickered. "Leave it to you to think of sex at a time like this."

"You gotta admit..." He skimmed his hand over her hip, gently pressing in his fingertips. Then he snuck a look at her from underneath his lashes. "It's hard not to."

Just like it had at the door a few minutes ago, the electric shock of his touch raced up her spine, catching her off guard. And all at once, it occurred to her how small this space really was. How his warm breath skated over her neck. How solid he seemed underneath her. How this wasn't creepy, or unpleasant, even if it was awkward. Because it was Ross.

He was her friend, wasn't he?

But this? This didn't feel friendly. This felt charged. Real.

Ross was the kind of guy who was always joking and flirting. She'd always assumed he was messing with her. But what if he had *meant* it?

"Very funny," she managed to choke out. It was her official reply. The reply she needed to give to set this whole crazy thing to the side. With the stupid way men had been acting around her lately, how did she know he wasn't affected too? Were his defenses starting to crack?

But here was the thing.

Her heart was hammering away in her chest at the thought of it. And yeah, he'd put the idea in her head, of them together, having sex. And now it was like the bell that couldn't be unrung. Now everything felt upside down, as if this relationship they'd always had wasn't what she thought it was, at all.

Telling herself she was making too much of Ross' standard-issue banter, Lita tried her best to concentrate on getting the damn knife.

But she couldn't help noticing Ross wasn't nearly as skinny as she'd assumed he was under his baggy clothes. Had he been lifting weights? Under the guise of trying to find the right path to his pocket, her fingertips had a mind of their own, taking the long route over fascinating terrain...his smooth pecs, and each and every ridge of his lean, tight abs, pulled taut from their awkward position. Maybe this little spelunking expedition for his knife was really what she'd been wanting to do all along. She bit her lip and tried to conceal the fact that he'd left her breathless.

Damn. Was his skin getting hotter under her hands?

Hers was. There was no hiding it. Sweat was starting to pool on the small of her back. Clothes that had felt comfortable minutes ago now were constricting, and in the way.

Her breath hitched as she wedged her hand between them, down past his belt. And for just a moment, her head swam with the sensation.

"There," Ross winced, sounding breathless, too. "Right there."

He shifted under her, swallowing hard, closing his eyes, and setting his jaw as if he was barely holding himself together. And as she carefully slid her hand down into his pocket, she understood why. He was hard. The edges of his erection were right there, skating along the backside of her whole hand. Holy shit, it was big, rock hard, and pulsing with a heat that was no match for his thin pocket lining.

Her mind blanked, forgetting why they were here and what she was supposed to get. She found Ross watching her, focused intently on her, searching her face. Her cheeks had to be blazing red. She knew they were, and he would see it, even in the dim light.

Had he let himself get all hot and bothered so she'd...

No, this wasn't some skeevy maneuver on his part. His surprise was unmistakable, even in this dim light. His expression was tense, wide-eyed, like he was helpless to see what she'd do next. His cocky, teasing mouth must have abandoned him.

So had hers. And the hell of it was, as her fingertips hit the bottom of that pocket, she didn't know what she was going to do. Because on some deep, elemental level that she didn't want to examine, she wanted to curl her hand over all that thick, straining masculinity, and squeeze. She wanted to know the contours of him, the weight, the heat...

He's hot for you.

She had evidence now. The realization arced through her, racing along every single nerve ending in her body. And she...

She was way too close to just unzipping his zipper, and having her way…

Lita gritted her teeth to keep from swearing.

The knife. *Right.*

Worming her hand around, she finally located edges of his Swiss army knife, and she shifted enough so she could grab it. She pulled it free and gave it to Ross with trembly hands. "Found it," she squeaked in a voice that didn't sound anything like her.

Ross raised an eyebrow in her direction, but took it without comment. He started to work on her hair. "Okay, so, could you lay your head down on me so I can see? I don't want to cut the wrong thing."

She did as he asked, burying her nose in his shirt and flattening herself out completely against him, ruthlessly blocking out the near primal urge to roll her hips against his. His heart was beating fast. She could hear it. And he smelled, not too surprisingly, like motor oil and dirt. She probably did too, for that matter. But there was something about the combination, the familiarity of it, and how she could trace the elements of his day somehow in that scent… how he'd drained an oil pan on that Cadillac earlier this morning, and how he'd spilled part of his morning coffee right here.

And there was something else too. His body heat, bellowing out the pure, elemental scent of his skin, somehow still clean-smelling even though he was sweaty. His shuffling and shifting underneath her was getting to her. Making her too warm. Too shaky. She shimmied a bit to the side, to give him space, and that only made it worse. Damn he was so hard, he was pressing against her belly, almost all the way up to her ribs.

Mierda.

So fucking hot.

So fucking *big*. She couldn't stop thinking about that. No wonder he'd "had a rep with the ladies." His tool belt was rather impressively equipped. And if ol' P-snap was just as good with his tongue...

Jesus. She closed her eyes, and the filthy possibilities played out on the backs of her eyelids. How could she have missed all this masculinity, right under her nose? She couldn't *believe* she was having these thoughts. But then again, it had been so long since she'd...

The snap of her hair pulling loose brought her little sexual fantasy to an abrupt stop. Ross kicked the seat away and suddenly, the bright light made it all too clear. She was laying on top of her best friend. One who was probably under the influence somehow, like half the other men in this town.

She couldn't read him right now. Ross was quiet, and tightlipped. Her heart sank. Here she went again, reading more into things than was there. Ross was a man whose body was reacting to a woman rubbing all over him. Almost reluctantly, she pushed herself back off him and back up onto the seat.

"Thank you," she sputtered, pulling her hair around and coiling it in her fist. "You're sure you're okay? Totally, like, not bleeding or anything?"

"I'm fine. Really. You'd better go check out your hair. Make sure I didn't scalp you."

Lita didn't have the faintest clue what to do or say right now. Ross was flustered. Flushed. From the determined set of his jaw though, he wasn't going to take any of it back. But he wasn't going to say anything, either.

So she was going to take the out he gave her. "I-I'll be right back," she told him, and scampered off to the spartan single-stall woman's shower Hunter had installed when she'd started here eight years ago. She'd outfitted it with her favorite stuff, since she was the only one using it, and scrubbed the debris out of her hair, trying not to remember the way Ross' simple touch had branded her skin like no other man before. Because that was just...ridiculous. That's what that was.

In no time, she'd towel-dried her hair, pulled it into a high ponytail, and gotten herself into a fresh sweatshirt and leggings. She walked out front again, taking note that Ross had moved to Hopper's inventory workstation so he could retrieve the new engine they were gonna need for the truck. Working with that system was not Ross' strong suit, as Hopper had been the one to design it. It was a bona-fide logistics masterpiece, as it allowed them to hang their big parts—the engines, the transmissions, the body panels—from hooks on a motorized chain. Find the piece you needed in the spreadsheet, hit a button, and the pulley would activate until the item slid down to a special docking system, right by the door.

Thing was, Ross hated searching the spreadsheets, and it took him forever. She was about to go over there and help him when the door chimed with a customer walk in. And it was Cam, dammit.

She set her jaw and marched up to the door to head him off at the pass. "I thought Ross told you not to come around me."

Cam shrugged and unrolled one of his practiced, sexy smiles. "I saw your stupid sign, okay? I'm coming here for totally legit reasons." He pointed a thumb back at the rust-riddled, piece o' crap 4x4 he'd nearly driven into the ground. She could see the enormous hole in the driver's side door, even from here.

"What'd you do? Hit a mailbox?"

Cam shrugged. "It's rust, mainly."

Lita pinched the bridge of her nose. Men who didn't

take care of their vehicles were a special kind of man-child to her. Especially Cam. He had a decent job as a coder. He could've afforded to prevent that. Why own a car if you were going to treat it like crap? How long had he been driving like that? Forever probably. But now he suddenly cared about his car maintenance? She decided she wasn't playing along with whatever game he had going. "You're gonna have to wait until mid-February, Cam. We don't have space for non-emergencies."

"But it is an emergency!" He reached out for her, grabbing her by the hips, of all things. "I have to tell you I'm sorry for that crazy business at Renegades. I-I shouldn't have made a scene like that and…I want another chance, Lita."

She slapped his hands off her. And that's when she heard a ferocious growl from behind her. Ross had spotted them.

"Hey—asshole!" he called. "I thought I told you to stay the fuck away!" Ross took two steps to charge over to them.

But he never made it. Because the engine barreling down the pulley system had gotten to him first, four hundred pounds of American-grade steel clocking him right on the head. And now her best friend was in a heap on the ground, out cold.

Maybe concussed. Maybe worse.

The scream that came out of her sounded like it had come from somebody else. And before she knew it, she was on the ground, bawling so hard she could barely see. "Ross!" She shook him. "Ross, wake up!"

But he didn't move.

"Cam!" she shrieked. "Call 911! Now!"

The man seemed dazed for a second, but he finally reached for the phone.

She laid her head on Ross' chest and felt an overwhelming relief to hear his heart still beating, and his slow, steady breaths.

She wrapped her arms around him, determined to listen to every beat until the ambulance came.

Because this was all her fault.

CHAPTER 7

BEEP.

Beep.

Beep.

Beep.

Light, steady pings brought Ross' mind back online. Dimly, he realized it was the sound of a heart monitor. Whose monitor? *Mine?*

It must be, right? A crisp bedsheet had been tucked around him, and a blood pressure cuff tightened automatically around his arm. He tried to say something, but he couldn't quite get his lips to move. Fuck, his eyelids must weigh a thousand pounds or something. His head screamed with dull, throbbing pain.

But then, a delicate, warm hand curled around his. Ah, the unmistakable scent of almond and lavender. Lita. She was here. He would've smiled if he could've gotten his lips to move.

He drifted off before he could say anything, lost in some dark, murky dream state he couldn't quite swim out of. But when he heard the sound of footsteps on linoleum, his ears, at least, woke up again.

"Are you his wife?" a male voice asked.

"No—uh, no." Lita pulled her hand away. "We're really good friends. Coworkers too. I was there when it happened. His family should be here any minute."

"I'm Dr. Martinez," he told her. "I'm a surgical neurology resident working here, working on Mr. Mason's case. I should probably wait until the family arrives to update—"

"No!" she whined. "I can't wait for—" But then she stopped and cleared her throat. "He got clocked with a very heavy truck motor because I distracted him. I need to know. He isn't going to need surgery, is he? Is he going to be okay?"

The doctor chuckled. "Him? Oh, yeah. He'll be fine. I sewed up the cut there on his jaw. The MRI and vascular scan showed he'll get out of here with only a mild concussion. I think the shock of the impact sent him offline, you know? So don't worry you killed the man. He should be snapping out of it soon."

Lita let out a whoop and grabbed his hand again, this time pressing it up to her cheek, and raining down several happy, quick-fire kisses there. He would've whooped too if he could have. Because even though this situation was pretty messed up, it felt good to have Lita here for him, holding his hand.

"Oh, thank God!" he heard her cry. "I couldn't have handled it if something had happened to him. My prayers have been answered!"

"Oh, wow. You guys must be pretty close after all, then," this—what was it?—Martinez guy said to her. Ross didn't have to have his eyes open to see what the man was getting at. He was checking her out. While Ross was defenseless in a hospital bed. *Prick.*

Lita lowered his hand down to the mattress. She

paused. "I'm not sure what your definition of close is," she drawled, "but if it's what I think you're asking, the answer to that question is no—we're not close like that."

That did it.

Ross ground his back teeth together and wiggled his fingers. This Martinez person laughed in this vaguely wolfish kind of way, and that was all it took for Ross to come roaring back to full consciousness.

"Well," Martinez paused. "I don't make a habit of this, but maybe we could talk a—"

"*No.*" Ross managed to get out a weak whisper. "No, don't—" His monitor went crazy with the beeping, and with a mighty effort, he pried his eyes open. He managed to move too, practically shooting out of the bed.

"Ross!" she cried. "There you are!"

"That's right," he rasped. "Here I am. So we don't need you, doc. You can go and doctor things somewhere else."

Rather than respond to the barb, this dude laughed. Laughed!

"Ross!" Lita cried. "Don't be a jerk! The man's trying to help you!"

"And help himself to you," he grumbled, feeling the sudden urge to bite off his own tongue. He was blurting again. And there wasn't much chance he'd be able to control it in his current state, either. He wasn't even sure he wanted to.

Lita reddened up with embarrassment as she met this guy's gaze. The two of them shared a little glance, and Ross wanted to friggin' howl. The guy was pretty sharp. Mr. Clean-Cut all decked out in his starched white, mono-grammed doctor's coat. About their age, he was tall and fit, with wavy dark hair brushed back from his forehead, all perfectly trimmed, of course. Big, dark Latin eyes too. The type of guy who probably knew how to make his grandma's posole and perfectly roll his Rs. *Goddammit!* Why did Ross have to get the hot resident? *Why?*

Dr. Martinez held up a hand, somehow managing to be both smug and magnanimous. "Oh, believe me, I've heard a lot worse from patients waking up with head injuries. He'll probably be a bit volatile for the next forty-eight hours or so. That's totally normal. We'll keep him here overnight for observation, then let him out. He should be good for work in two days, with some Tylenol."

"Hey!" Ross barked, a bit louder than he intended. "I'm right here!"

Dr. Perfect Asshole smirked at Lita. "See? Volatile. Like I said."

Lita grinned at the man, and Ross growled. Between throbs, his head was spinning with all the ways he'd love to stuff this guy's head up his ass. But before he could act on it, the door to his room opened. His mom, dad, and Tiff piled in.

"Goodness!" His mom clapped her hands. "You're awake!"

With the way the noise sliced through his aching head, he almost wished he wasn't. Lita jumped up and gave his sister a seat. His family fired questions at him so fast he couldn't answer them all. And while he was being smothered with family concern, the jackass doctor excused himself, saying he'd back in for an update once his family got settled in. And all he could do was sit there and watch the man lead Lita out into the hall, grinning like he couldn't wait to get to know her better.

Ross closed his eyes for a second as a wave of nausea and vertigo slammed into him. He gingerly laid himself back against the pillow, resigning himself that he was in no shape to fight off Dr. Dentyne.

At this point, it was hard to tell what was making him

sicker, the damned injury, or watching Lita walk off with this guy.

But hey, it wasn't like this situation was anything new, right? He'd been watching other guys come on to Lita all week...hell, the whole time he'd known her. He only hoped she had the good sense to tell that prissy little shit to get lost. But in a fair fight between him and the good doctor, he wasn't exactly guaranteed to win. And that made his head hurt more than it had before he'd come to this place.

Lita figured the doctor would head off to his rounds when they left the room. So, she was surprised that he'd motioned her out to the waiting area, instead. "Your friend is lucky," he told her. "If he'd been turned a bit the other way, things might've been different."

She nodded. "Yes. I know. Thank you, doctor, really. I'm so grateful."

"Call me Victor." He held out his hand to shake hers, which she did, readily. "You know, I don't think I even got your name."

"Carmelita," she found herself telling him. Which was odd, because she always went by Lita. "Carmelita Noe."

"Carrrmeliiita," he purred. "Let me guess. Is your family from Argentina?"

She smirked. "Interesting guess, but no. I'm only half Hispanic. My mom's side—the Ruiz family—is from Mexico. I'm second generation. My grandparents came here to pick peaches in Georgia and got their citizenship. My dad's side came here from Scotland in the early 1800s."

"Hmmm. Mexican-Scottish. That's a spicy combination."

She chuckled. "So I've been told."

"I'll bet." He nodded. His chin tilt was cool, but the way the corners of his mouth curled up was all masculine play.

Well now. Maybe Ross was right. Maybe the good doctor really was flirting with her. She wasn't used to guys being so subtle. What a concept!

She shuffled on her feet a bit, and her nerves jittered like she'd had too much coffee. Except she hadn't had any coffee. So that left only one explanation. She was having the "talking to a cute man" jitters. And Victor *was* pretty cute, after all. He had a wide, easy smile and soulful eyes. His broad shoulders didn't hurt, either. In theory, she should really like the guy. She stood there waiting for that pull, that excitement to come. It didn't.

Victor cleared his throat, apparently catching on to her distractedness.

"What about you?" she chirped, desperate to fill the silence. "With a name like Martinez, I'm guessing you didn't come here on the Mayflower."

"Mi familia vino aquí desde Puerto Rico justo antes de que yo naciera," he answered, putting his hand over his heart as he did.

Lita wanted to roll her eyes but didn't. The man had taken a risk, assuming she knew Spanish without even asking. She did, of course. She knew he was saying that this family had come here from Puerto Rico before he'd been born. But there was something about that display that grated her nerves. Was this an intelligence test, or maybe even a heritage test, and he was waiting to see whether she would pass?

Should she answer him in Spanish? It certainly would be well within her wheelhouse. She'd always loved the musicality and simplicity of Spanish, and loved speaking it too, when the time was right. Growing up, Spanish had been a big deal in her house. After all, her mom had been determined her kids would group up bilingual.

And maybe for that reason, Lita didn't like the idea being all show about it. Spanish was more personal than that to her. It was the language of her family, not something to speak for bragging rights. So no, she wasn't going to talk in Spanish to this guy, even though she couldn't say she disliked the man.

She smiled and nodded at him to let him know she understood, but for the life of her, she couldn't figure out what to say next. Dammit, now shyness was creeping up her neck, and she twiddled with her hands like some awkward teenager.

Luckily, Mom and J came barreling down the hallway, coming to her rescue. "Lita! Oh, mija! I'm sorry it took me so long to get here. But I had an appointment run long. We got here as fast as we could."

J hugged Lita and walked all around her, checking her up and down. "You sure you're okay? No cuts? No bruises?"

To be honest, she was pretty sure she'd bruised her knees from her tumble in the truck earlier. And she may have scraped herself, skidding onto the floor when Ross had had his accident. Lord, she didn't know she was capable of being so frantic. "I'm fine," she told them. "Really." Lita crossed her feet so she'd cover the rip in her leggings, down by her ankle.

Mom turned, as if she was only now noticing Dr. Martinez. "You must be Ross' doctor."

"Yes." The doctor brightened and stuck his hand out. "I'm Dr. Martinez. Victor, actually. I've been enjoying my time getting to know your beautiful daughter here."

Mom cocked her head and slid him a surprised smirk. She stuck out her hand rather daintily to shake his. "I'm *so* pleased to meet you, Victor."

J, for his part, was just as dainty, throwing out his hand and his hip, and flipping his hair for good measure. "I'm J, the crazy uncle. But you can call me Jesús."

"Now now." Martinez grinned. "You don't seem all that crazy to me, Hey-sus."

Ugh. Her uncle was grinning from ear to ear, checking out the man's perfect hair, trendy Italian-looking dress shoes, and million-dollar smile. "Oh, I *like* you," J told the man, and gave him a playful shove on the arm.

Gah. The subtext here was so thick you could cut it with a knife. *Oh, look at this eligible bachelor, Lita, this nice, respectable guy. What a catch for a girl like you.*

Determined to change the subject, Lita steered the conversation to the safer ground of Ross' condition. They spent some time catching up on the facts, and she had the chance to tell them all exactly how the accident had occurred. Her call to them earlier today had been so rushed, and she'd been crying her eyes out. She didn't even want to think about what kind of shape her mascara was in.

Of course, Mom and J didn't let the conversation stop with Ross. They hardly let the boy come up for air, peppering him with questions about when he'd moved here (two months ago) about his family (relatively poor, in Chicago), where he'd gone to school (Northwestern, completely on scholarship), how he'd ended up in West Virginia (again scholarships, requiring work in an under-served area), and his favorite tamale (anything with pineapple).

Lita didn't get too suspicious until they started in on the tamale business. Mom always had a tamale party on Christmas Eve and made it her business to make everyone's favorite flavor. Did she really expect him to be there? For God's sake!

No doubt, Mom was acting weird. Now the woman had

buried her head in her phone while J was busy charming Martinez with his trademark witty banter.

But the good doctor didn't seem to mind all their pushing. He excused himself, pulled Lita aside. "So, um Lita, before I break away here, I wanted to tell you how much I've enjoyed meeting you. And I was wondering if you'd like to get a bite to eat with me, just you and me. I don't know a lot of people in town yet, and it'd be so great to keep this conversation going."

Lita stared at him in disbelief, not realizing she'd furrowed her eyebrows until her forehead pinched. "When? Like, right now?"

"Not exactly. I've been on rotation since yesterday with no sleep. But the weekend is coming right up. And when I started here a couple of months ago, I got this big welcome package that included a voucher for a dinner for two at the Greenbrier. It has a bunch of other perks thrown in. I hadn't known what to do with it, until I met you. Could I talk you into going out with me on Saturday? No pressure, you know. Just two people, getting to know each other."

Lita hesitated again, and in the second of silence, she heard the photo shutter on her mom's phone click.

Lita whipped around, and so did J.

OMG. *She didn't.* Did that woman just make a Martinez square for their betting pool? "Mom!" Lita yelped. "Seriously?"

"What?" The woman batted her eyes innocently. "A mother can't get excited when a hot catch shows interest in her daughter?"

J glanced up from a celebrity magazine he was paging through. "Wait—what's happening?" But then realization dawned. He narrowed his eyes and reached for his phone. "Alessandra!" he squealed. "You are one stone-cold opportunist!"

Poor Victor, for his part, took all this cray cray in, still managing to maintain a confused smile.

Lita held her hand up. "Mother dear, could you come with me?" She walked her mom down the hall, well out of earshot. "Seriously?" Lita hissed. "Is this what it's come to? You're taking bets on my love life...parading me around like I'm some kind of...*prize chicken?*"

Mom hid her cackle behind her hand. "Baby girl, if you want to get technical about it, wouldn't he be the prize cock?"

"Mother!" Lita yelped. "Would you please, please for one minute be serious?"

"I am!" She grabbed Lita's hands. "I so totally am, darling, but you have to realize, your hot doc over there is the black swan that could win me the whole shebang. J couldn't have seen him coming. He'll never catch up!"

"You'd have me go out with him so you could get a free massage? Are you even for real right now?"

"An actual date does double my points, according to the rules. And anyway, it's a massage and a *pedicure*, Lita!" She pulled her stockinged foot out of her rainbow crocs, for a theatrical touch. "Have you even seen my man feet right now? How can I go to the Hairball looking like a primate? You'd seriously deny me this? Just so you won't have to go out with that smokin'-hot, very nice, highly accomplished doctor over there? Did I not raise you to seize the day?"

Seize the day, yes. Seize the doctor, no. Truth be told, she'd never, not once in her life, dated someone with advanced degrees. And she'd never eaten in a place anywhere near as nice as The Greenbrier. She had no idea what doctors even talked about, let alone wanted. "You're kidding me, right? He wants to take me to the Greenbrier, Mom. You know, America's Resort? Only one of the fanciest places to eat in West Virginia, if not the whole country. Not a single stitch of my clothing would be appropriate for that place. I wouldn't even know how to act!"

"Carmelita Rose!" She wagged a finger. "You are not some feral child who's never been out in society. You know how to talk and use a napkin and a fork, for crying out loud! And if it's your clothes you're worried about, let me take care of that. You know I've got all kinds of formalwear in your size. Shop my closet. I'll even do your hair and makeup for free. How's that?" Determined to drive her point home, Mom grabbed her by the shoulders faced her in the good doctor's direction. "There now. See the way he's drinking you in, Lita? There's a man who wants to take you out on the nicest date of your life. Don't you think you owe it to yourself to find out if there's any magic between you two?"

Magic was what she was worried about. Could he be under the magical influence? Martinez was so naturally smooth, it was hard to tell.

But if he was hexed? Honestly, she didn't know what she'd do. She didn't have it in her to start going out with some guy, end up really liking him, and then have him come to his senses and run for the hills come January, when the pixie dust wore off. And it would wear off, wouldn't it? Sherry's logic had made pretty good sense, after all.

Then there was the matter of not having much in common with the good doctor. There weren't any sparks happening, at least from her, anyway.

And what about Ross?

There had been sparks with him—enough for a whole fireworks display. Could that have been magic too? Magic or no, that whole situation in the truck had become flat-out embarrassing. Ross'd acted like he was really into her, just for a minute. But then he'd barely been able to look at her afterward, like he refused to acknowledge that whole attraction had happened. And that'd hurt, a lot more than she wanted to admit. Lita squeezed her eyes shut, willing away the memory of the heat, the closeness between them.

When she opened her eyes again, she took a hard look at the doctor, like Mom had asked. Even at a distance, sparks danced in his eyes when he looked at her. There was a man who wanted her for sure, at least right now. She could feel it.

Her mother must've sensed her starting to crack, because she took her hands in hers, and went for the kill. "Sweetheart, if you don't want to go out with him, then don't. Don't do it on my account. But before you send him away, ask yourself this. Where are you gonna find another guy like that, a fantastic guy who seems to be totally into you? And who's *worthy* of you. It doesn't have to be a big thing. Go on the date. Have a great meal. Laugh. Make eyes over the candlelight. Don't you think you deserve that, when so many others haven't taken you seriously?"

There it was. The *coup de gras*. She had to go out with him now, and "enjoy" didn't she, if for no other reason than to give a middle finger to all the guys who'd dumped, gaslighted, or ghosted her this year. So, without a word, she marched back up to Martinez.

And she told him yes.

CHAPTER 8

By the time Lita stuck her pretty head back into his room again, his parents were walking out. The doctor had come back in and given the Mason family a report, and detailed information about everything they needed to do for his "care" these next two days. Which basically included sleep, no sudden movements, no work, and Tylenol.

Shit, he could've told them that himself.

But still, his mom had taken it as license to be his nurse caretaker until the rest period was over. And as much as he loved the woman, the thought of being mothered to death made him even crankier than he'd been before.

Martinez held the door open for his family to leave, all courtly and gallant like some kind of Disney prince. When Lita walked in, the man reminded her, "Visiting hours ended, Lita. You'll have to make this quick. So—I'll see you on Saturday. Is six okay?"

Her mouth curved into a flirty smile. "I'll text you my address."

Dr. Dentyne smiled back. "Can't wait."

Ross saw it all.

And he felt it too, right in the chest. Like some kind of

dropping sensation, as if his heart had been removed from its engine and thrown in the scrap heap like a used-up part.

Was he being dramatic? Maybe. But he'd known Lita a long, long time. He'd seen her entertain promposals. And group dates. And booty calls too, for that matter. They'd never gotten to him like this one. He didn't need a knock on the head to know that this guy was a threat to him. That Martinez was *better* than him.

Ross hadn't even started to fight for Lita yet. And wasn't this the story of his life? Every time he started to get his courage up, she'd do or say some kind of friend-zoney thing that would shake his confidence. Or, more likely, some other guy would swoop in. Over and over again.

But this one?

This could stick. It could.

How ironic that Martinez would appear out of the mist, the very day Ross had gotten any inkling of hope. That sizzle between them, back at the truck...holy shit. She'd wanted to go farther.. She'd hesitated far too long with her hand in his pocket. Her heart had been beating fast, and her nipples had hardened up against him. Hell, he'd smelled the spice of her, rising with her heat in that enclosed space. You couldn't fake that kind of arousal. He'd been waiting for her to say something, to confirm what every single one of his senses had been screaming at him. *She wants you.*

How wrong he was. And that wrongness was right in front of him, slapping him in the face.

Still, Lita sidled up to his bed, popped a hip up onto the mattress, and grabbed his hand. "Hey, how you feeling?"

"Like shit," he simply said. And it was true.

She patted his hand. "You should be improving by the morning. Anyway, it's time for me to go now. I'll check on you tomorrow after work. How about I bring you pizza, or maybe cinnamon rolls? Maybe we could hang out and watch a movie."

How nice. Like pals! Should we braid each other's hair and paint our toenails?

He wanted to say it. But his mouth was tingling again, warning him. He yanked his hand away instead. "Don't bother. Mom's insisting I stay at her place until the forty-eight hours is up. And Martinez backed her up. Prick."

Lita raised her eyebrows. "Lay off the doctor, Ross. I haven't seen him do a damn thing here but his job."

Except take you from me.

He wanted to say it. But he couldn't. The magic probably wouldn't let him. He was too angry. So he crossed his arms over his chest instead.

Lita blinked at him. "What?" she finally sputtered, throwing up her hands. "What the hell is your problem?"

"He's taking you on a date, then?"

She crossed her arms too. "Yeah."

"Where?"

She narrowed her eyes. "It's none of your business."

"*Where*, Lita?"

"If you must know, he's taking me to dinner at the Greenbrier. Carriage rides, Christmas cocktails, and the whole nine yards."

Wow. That dude is going for broke trying to impress her, isn't he?

It was the second time today he'd felt like he'd had all the wind kicked out of him. Ross was totally blown away—not by the fact that some dude would ask Lita out on Barbie's dream date. *That's* nothing less than she deserved. No, it was the fact that she'd be so quick to go with this guy she'd just met.

That she'd *want* to go.

Was this what she'd been waiting for, all these years? A guy to sweep her off her feet and treat her like a princess? Ross knew he couldn't compete with that. But here was the thing. She'd always been a princess to him. A warrior princess. The kind who had engine dust on her shirt and paint under her nails.

Another wave of nausea rolled over him that he suspected had nothing to do with his knock on the head. He was losing her. Or maybe, he'd never really known her like he'd thought he did. Maybe she'd never taken him seriously because he couldn't offer her what she needed. Money. Ease. An Instagram-ready husband on your arm. International vacations and kids in private schools.

And it could happen. It really could. If this Martinez figured out how incredible Lita was, he'd lock that shit down, for sure. And Ross could kiss any sliver of a chance he'd had with her goodbye.

He laid back on the pillow and closed his eyes, hoping the horrible tingling in his mouth would subside. Because right now, he felt like he was being pushed by tiny fairy cattleprods to say the very things he shouldn't.

You're the only woman I've ever really wanted, Lee.
Please don't go.
Just this once, choose me.

But he couldn't say any of those things. Because that would sound totally psycho at this moment. And he still had his pride, after all.

When he finally opened his eyes, Lita stood there, scowling at him. "Are you sure you're okay, Ross? You're a little off kilter. Do you want me to call the doc—"

"No," Ross ground out. "Please don't." Then he clamped his mouth firmly shut, like Fort friggin' Knox. No blurting allowed.

Lita sat on the side of the bed, checking him over.

"You're sure you're not gonna throw up, and you don't need anything. You're gonna be alright."

He nodded.

She narrowed her eyes and studied him again for another long, long moment. "You're really not gonna say anything about my date? No jokes? No jabs? No *order enough for seconds and get a doggy bag, Lee. You never know when you'll be back.*"

Yeesh. She'd just done a pretty good impression of him. Did he really sound like that? He racked his banged-up brain and came up with a memory of saying that exact thing to her a few months ago, when Cam had taken her out to Hill and Holler pizza. He'd meant it as a dig against Cam, not her, as that dumbass was well known for asking a girl out and "forgetting" his wallet. "What, do you want me to say something?" he finally managed.

"Don't you always? You've had something to say about every guy I've gone out with."

"You were too good for them," he blurted.

She rolled her eyes. "And Martinez? I'm too good for him too?"

"Yes," he told her, because he knew it was true, in his bones. "He could never appreciate a woman like you."

From the look on Lita's face, the comment hadn't landed like he'd intended. Her head snapped back like he'd slapped her. "A woman like me? What's that supposed to mean? What, am I not sophisticated enough? Too country? Too loud? Too Anglo? Not enough degrees? *What?*"

Words crowded on the other side of his teeth. Yeah, Lita Noe was a lot of "toos" he could think of:

Too unforgettable
Too sexy
Too original
Too perfect

"You're too..." sneaked out. He bit his tongue real quick to keep from flat-out embarrassing himself. Owww. Shit, okay, maybe hit bit his tongue a little too hard. It hurt, but not as much as his heart would hurt if he put it out there to get crushed right now.

And again, his restraint didn't appear to be winning him any points. Lita twisted her face into a rueful smile. "Ah. So there it is. The real story comes out. I'm just *too much*. Too many inconvenient emotions. Too much work. Too much trouble. Go on, Ross, you can say it. Every other guy has!"

He swallowed down a nervous yelp as dismay swamped him. This was fucking torture. There were just about a hundred things he could say to that. But every single one of them would out him for the lovesick fool he was.

He didn't answer her. He couldn't. His mouth was tingling so bad it felt like he'd swallowed firecrackers. He was gonna blow any second now. So he just let all those wrong-headed ideas of hers stew in the air like some kind of toxic brew, while he laid there in a head-pounding, stomach-churning panic.

Lita was getting that red-faced, teary eyes look again, dammit. *Dammit!* "Okay then." She nodded. "After all these years, I guess it's good to know what you really think of me." She scooped herself up off the bed. "You're just like the rest," she muttered as she headed for the door.

"Lee!" He sat up, head swimming. "No! That's not what I—"

But she held up her hand. "Stop it, Ross. Don't worry. I got your message loud and clear."

Then she marched out, just like that. No take-backs. No second chances to explain himself.

And when the door clicked shut, he knew she was gone.

CHAPTER 9

I'M AN ASSHOLE. A big, greasy, hairy hole on the ass of an ogre asshole.

Ross threw his arm over his eyes, hoping he could block out the morning sun peeking through the Star Wars curtains in his childhood bedroom.

Okay, okay, he was blocking out the sun *and* the sight the desperate apology texts and voicemails he'd sent to Lita over the last day and a half. No way could he let her go around thinking those things about herself. Or that *he* thought those things. His phone sat on his chest, branding him there, still hot from all his pointless scrolling and checking.

There'd been nothing but silence on her end. And what the hell else should he expect? He squeezed his eyes shut, but nothing could stop the endless loop playing in his head. He'd tried to protect himself, but in the end, all he'd done was hurt Lita. His silence had spoken volumes more than his words ever could. *That she's too much to handle. That no guy would want her. That she deserved all the treatment she's gotten.*

He was sick with remorse. And now here it was, Saturday morning. Tonight, she'd be putting on a pretty dress and going on her dream date. And it wouldn't be with him.

Because you're an asshole. And a coward.

That was really what it came down to, wasn't it? None of this would be happening if he'd had the balls to tell her the God's-honest truth—that she was it for him. Full stop. Yeah, there'd been hookups. But his sex life could best be described as marking time, a random Tinder date here or there to let off steam. And this past year, there hadn't even been much of that. He hadn't had the heart for it. Maybe he was getting old.

Old enough to want more, maybe.

He took a couple of deep breaths, but it did little to get rid of the tightness in his chest. Yeah, "ridiculous" didn't even begin to cover the mess he'd made of his life. His best friend, the woman who meant more to him than anyone, now hated his guts. In the space of one conversation where he'd barely even talked, he'd managed to fuck up the best, longest-lasting relationship he'd ever had outside his family. And the hell of it was, it wasn't like him. Lita and him, they horsed around and had their mock fights. But they'd never really argued, not once. And then this.

He ground his teeth and stuffed an extra pillow over his face. His pain reliever had worn off and once again, he felt like he'd been hit in the face by a four-hundred-pound engine. But that wasn't anything compared to the heaviness that had settled over his whole body, a bone-aching, energy-sapping misery he couldn't shake.

Three soft raps on the door caught his attention. "Come in," he grumbled.

His mother leaned her head through a discreet crack. "I

thought I heard you rattling around in here, sleepyhead. It's ten a.m. already! How you doin', punkin'? Your stomach hurting?" She came over and pressed a cool hand to his forehead.

"Mom, really, I don't have fever or stomach pains. I don't have the flu, for cryin' out loud. I only need more Tylenol for this headache."

She pulled out a bottle from the pocket on her apron, and a bottle of water too. "Your wish is my command." She grinned.

He took them from her gratefully. "You know, you really are pretty good at this mom thing."

She ruffled his hair and smacked his shoulder. "And as your mom, I'm telling you to get up. Time's a-wastin'. Besides, I've got a job for you."

"Hey! I thought I was supposed to be resting!"

"You will be. But you'll be sorting through all your childhood junk while you do. Your father and I are over this shrine to your teen years. We want to bring the treadmill up from the basement and make this an exercise room."

He flopped back down on his pillow. "Okay. But I need a shower first."

Mom wrinkled her nose. "No kidding."

"Argh." He threw his arm over his head again. "It's just dawned on me. I don't have a change of clothes! Maybe I should go home and get a few things like—"

She let out a loud bark of laughter. "Nice try, boy-o! I know all your tricks. You're staying right here until the job is done. Besides, there's plenty of clothes here. You left a ton behind. And I need you to go through the drawers. The shower's all stocked up with fresh towels and a new razor." Then she stopped, picked up a hank of his hair, and pulled a yuck face. "You might try some of my conditioner. Seriously. It's like black straw. Don't you ever use conditioner?"

He smacked her hand away. "No."

She snorted. "That explains a few things. Anyhoo, get up and get going, child. I'll bring in something for you to snack on while you work. See? We're full service around here."

"Riiiight." He snickered as she scurried off.

The door closed behind her, and he slowly sat up in bed. The twin bed he'd grown up in but no longer fit. He took a good look around at the place. *Yeesh.* It was like some kind of crusty time capsule of his childhood. Mom was right. He really should've cleaned this place out by now. Why hadn't he?

He'd had a good childhood, one surrounded by friends and family. But it wasn't some kind of wonder years utopia keeping him from throwing out his old Lego sets. Had he really thought he'd come back for this stuff?

Jesus, this room. He was fond of it, but the place was a wreck. The walls were still covered floor to ceiling with peeling posters that careened from one interest to the rest. Hot girls on classic cars, of course. But also music bands from across the decades—The Cars to GooGoo Dolls, Chuck Berry to Foo Fighters and Guns & Roses. Harry Potter. Japanese Anime. Classic superhero art. Come to think of it, he was lying here under a pilled, nasty comforter he'd wanted for Christmas one year because it had a skull, a rose, and "live free or die" scrollwork on it.

He shuddered and threw the covers off. *Ugh. It's a cringe-fest in here.*

Deciding this cleaning project might be what he needed, Ross swung his legs over the side of the bed and scrubbed his hands over his face. He took one last look at his phone and debated whether he should try Lita again.

No. He wouldn't. At this point, she'd probably think he was trying to derail her date. But he wasn't. In the cold light of day, he could see how much she really deserved to go. He wouldn't upset her beforehand. All those text and voice-mails had made his point for him. He'd have to do some first-class groveling when he saw her at work and hope like hell she'd see how sorry he really was.

So he left his phone on the nightstand and went in for a long, steaming shower in the family bathroom. He'd forgotten how nice it was to have a big, walk-in shower. He pulled down the shower nozzle, sat down on the shower bench, and aimed the spray at the back of his head. The heat soothed his headache, and he was happy to scrub off the last of the garage dirt. He stood in there for a long time, and by the time he'd toweled off, he'd rejoined the land of the living. He caught sight of the four-inch, sewed-up gash on his jawline in the steamed up mirror. It didn't hurt anymore, and he didn't hate it. After all, he'd gotten it trying to help Lita, and it had gotten Cam off her case. Every guy needed to have a few scars, right?

He dried himself off, wrapped a towel around his waist, and sauntered back to his room. When he caught sight of himself in the mirror, he swore.

His hair. He looked like a red skunk. He picked through the mess, inspecting the damage. What was that, an inch and a half of flaming orange roots? He'd been putting off coloring it and had been spraying on temporary color in the meantime. And now he'd washed it out, without anything on hand to fix it.

Yay me.

He started rifling through his drawers, trying to find anything that wouldn't be too embarrassing to wear. Finally, he settled on a pair of threadbare gray sweatpants that were a bit too short and a Harry Potter polo shirt, black with a diagonal yellow stripe.

He stood in front of his full-length mirror and shook his head.

Slytherin House.

It had the word "shrewd" screen printed on it, and if Ross could've figured out a way to successfully punch himself in the face, he would've done it right now. He'd asked for this shirt for his sixteenth birthday, thinking it'd make him a badass. Looking at himself right now, at twenty-eight, "shrewd" was pretty much the last thing he'd call himself.

A wave of clarity hit him hit him so hard, it nearly knocked him down. He didn't want this shit. He didn't want *any* of it. He spotted the cleaning supplies and garbage bags Mom had left for him, as well as a sandwich and milk on his nightstand. He whipped open a garbage bag, stuffed the sandwich in his mouth, and started shoveling his childhood baggage by the drawerful into overstuffed hefty bags.

And it felt...good. *Damn* good.

Whether it was the sudden epiphany or the pain meds kicking in, he didn't know. But his head wasn't hurting anymore. He got kinda giddy as he ripped the posters down and tore them into pieces.

Bye bye, Motorhead.

So long, Miss Hot Rod Hottie USA!

Bye bye, Katy Perry, and your sexy-ass fireworks!

Sayonara, Dragonball Z! Don't let the door hit you in the ass!

In minutes, he'd had the walls clean and his shit sorted, mainly by choosing to not sort at all. Yeah, he liked the way this looked, like he'd blown the dust off his life. Just to be sure he'd gotten everything, he started opening and closing drawers again. And he'd missed one, this bottom drawer here. So, he opened a new bag, tipped the drawer over, and heard a hard thud.

Fishing around, he finally found the culprit.

His senior yearbook. It was the only year he'd bought, mainly because his mom had insisted he'd want to remember it all someday. Yeah, right. He'd skated through high school, more content to mess around on his car projects and help his dad with his vet practice than to study for some stupid test.

Yeah, there was only one reason why he'd walked through the front door of Greenbrier East High School every day, smiling.

Lita. Go, Spartans!

He flipped to her senior picture and couldn't help staring at the confident tilt to her chin, and the gleam in her eye that seemed to say, *let's have fun.* Her hair had been mint green back then with a big pink streak, right down the front. Administration had made her take out the matching green rhinestone hoop she'd worn in her nose for the occasion. She'd been pissed. He smiled at the memory.

There was plenty under her picture. Track team. Student Council Treasurer. Art Club. "Most likely to have her own art show." She'd been pretty and popular, and generally regarded as one of the coolest girls in school. So it went without saying that she'd had more than her fair share of candid shots in here. There was Lita, flying down the track, knees up for a hurdle, her braids whipping behind her. Lita, setting up the decorations for the prom. Lita and a group of kids laughing and cheering at a football game. He'd been in that one.

Curious now, he flipped to his senior portrait. *Ugh.* There was nothing there but a name, and a picture of a guy with a stupid haircut. Which, he was quick to notice, wasn't all that different from the way he wore it now.

Memory tickling his mind, he paged to the inside back cover. And that's where he found it—Lita's inscription. He'd never been into that stupid tradition of having all your friends sign your yearbook. He had friends, of course, but the whole "how many people can you get to sign" thing had always seemed like a stupid popularity contest to him. But when Lita had asked him to sign her yearbook, he had. Then she'd insisted she had to sign his, even if she was the only one. It said:

To Ross—

The soon-to-be tattoo king. Here's hoping you leave a mark on life, and life leaves its mark on you. It wasn't easy moving here sophomore year, but you made everything okay. You always had a joke for me, or an idea of something fun to do. You helped me get to know and love this place. You've shown me the meaning of home. I've never thanked you for that, have I? Thank you, Ross. You're the best friend a girl could ever have. On life's long road, I hope I never have to live without your smile.

Yours,

xx- Lita

Yours. He couldn't stop staring at the word. He wanted it to be true, more than anything he'd ever wanted in his whole life. And it was time he started acting like it. He needed to man up and start telling her how he felt. No more immature jokes. No more hiding. No more fear. The only way to get what you wanted in this world was to work for it. And he was ready to start working for her. For himself. For a future for them, together.

He had to fix this. No—he had to do more than fix this. He had to make it absolutely clear what he'd thought about her all this time. That she was special. Worthy. That he loved her exactly like she was.

Then he had to show her what could be. He had to show her his love was something worth wanting.

Ross stared at himself in the mirror, and realized he knew exactly where to start.

He was calling J.

CHAPTER 10

LITA SHIMMIED into Mom's little red loaner dress and tied the ankle ribbons on the matching red peep-toe pumps. When she saw herself in her full-length mirror, she stilled.

She hardly recognized herself. The dress was clingy, bright, and run through with tiny metallic threads that caught the light. It had a deep vee in the front that exposed the globes of her breasts, and a tall slit that showed off her thigh to perfection. She pointed her toe. Hmmm. Not as muscular as her track days, but leaner. Sleeker. She turned to the side and almost choked. The way this dress hugged her booty was borderline obscene. She gave herself a shake. *Not too bad, chica.*

She spritzed J's special oil in her hand and tweaked the ends of her curls for what felt like the thousandth time. Mom had parted her hair on the side today, so some of it would tumble into her face a bit, and that made her self-conscious. She looked pretty tonight. Beautiful, even. Mom had gone all out with her makeup for this ensemble, with false eyelashes, precisely matched red matte lipstick, and contoured blush so perfect Kim Kardashian should take notes.

But she couldn't help feeling like the girl formerly known as Lita. *Trussed up, like that prize chicken.* She only hoped she wouldn't embarrass herself. She'd gone online today to review which fork to use and which glass to start with in these formal service settings. Casual restaurants where you could put your elbows on the table were her usual thing. This was...different. Harder, maybe. She'd have to be thinking about how the candlelight was hitting her face. Whether she laughed at all the right spots or acted interested when the conversation got boring. Whether she'd edited herself down enough...

She pressed a shaky hand to her stomach. Yeah, all these nervous jitters wasn't doing her appetite any favors. It didn't really matter how much she ran through appropriate conversation topics and reviewed dining room etiquette. She was going to a place she'd never eaten, with a guy she didn't know, in clothes that didn't even belong to her.

But hey, I can handle it, right?

Right.

Of course, I can.

She took her nose ring off and considered replacing it with a fake diamond stud. Then a super-slim gold hoop. In the end, she opted for none at all, for the first time in years, and was surprised to see she really didn't miss it. After trying on several different necklace and bracelet combinations, she ended up going with a dainty gold necklace with a teardrop rhinestone that dripped right between her breasts, and a collection of thin gold bangles around her wrist. She'd even painted sparkly gold polish on her nails—something she never did, because *hello*, auto shop.

She checked the time on her nightstand clock. Victor was picking her up in fifteen minutes. Lita paced around in her heels a bit, willing the butterflies in her stomach to settle the eff down.

But a tooth-rattling blast of Bob Marley tunes blared through the apartment speakers, stopping her in her tracks. *Goddammit, not again!* "Moooooooose!" she yelled over the din.

Of course, that *idiota* couldn't hear her.

She stormed out into their living area, straight into a haze of smoke. She coughed. It was Saturday, and her roommate's live-in boyfriend, Moose Barkley, was into his weed stash again. She found him sitting on their lumpy, stain-ridden futon, his long blond hair hanging over his bong, which Pansy Highgarden, her flighty, earth-mother, artsy-fartsy roommate, had painted for him in Christmas colors. How festive. She almost laughed.

Lita clicked off the music. "Moose!" she cried. "Dude, seriously? You couldn't wait a minute? My date is coming to pick me up any second now!"

Moose sucked down a big toke and emerged, smiling, in a freakin' cannabis cloud. "I'm sorry, Caaaar," what he often called her when he was too high to manage her whole name. "I didn't know."

She took in his bloodshot eyes and his big goofy grin, and found she couldn't be too mad at the guy. He hadn't been warned, after all. "Next time, start the party after I leave, 'kay?"

Pansy swished through the useless bead curtains separating the kitchen from the living room and set the music to a much lower volume. She flounced down in a striped maxi dress she'd knitted herself and grabbed her boyfriend's bong. "And party we shall, right, honey?" She gave Moose's thick neck a nip. "When do you think you'll be back?"

Lita checked her phone. It was almost six-thirty now. Their reservation was at eight. "I don't know. Ten-thirty? Eleven?"

Pansy's big blue eyes seemed to get even wider. "You're

wearing a dress like that, and you're not staying the night?"

"No," Lita answered, right away. She didn't even have to think about it. The last thing she needed to do was throw herself at the guy, just because he'd gotten her a nice meal. But it was more than that, wasn't it? She didn't *want* to, though she couldn't figure out why.

"I'm sorry we stunk up your outfit. You can try some of my perfume before you go. It's on my dresser. I mixed it myself. It's patchouli and ylang ylang essential oils. Super yummy."

Lita cringed. It was a kind offer, but she wasn't going to trust herself to another one of Pansy's poorly mixed concoctions. The last time Lita had tried one of these potions, she'd ended up walking around all day smelling like ass. "It's okay," she told her, reaching for dressy wool coat she stored in the closet for times like this. "I'll go stand outside. The breeze will blow the smell off by the time he gets here."

Pansy elbowed her boyfriend. "Again, we apologize— right, Moose?"

He coughed up another cloud and nodded sincerely. "Yuh-huh."

"Besides, you won't have to put up with us for much longer anyway." Pansy clapped her hands. "We've made an offer on a house! You'll have the place all to yourself now! Isn't it great?"

Lita spun around, her mouth hanging open. *Great?* Was she even serious right now?

"Aww, look at you!" Pansy crooned, never one to pick up on social cues. "I can see from your expression how happy you are for us. It all happened so fast, I couldn't really believe it. So—you know I've been working nights down at the hotel desk, right? They decided to make me manager for the *day* shift! Can you believe it? My career in hospitality is finally taking off!"

"That-that's great, Pansy," she managed to sputter. "Congratulations!"

"Oh, but that's not the best part! So you know how Moose has been barista at the Bean House for, like, *so* long. Now he's found out, he's getting made assistant manager! When Moose's memaw offered to sell us her house for cheap, out of the blue like that, we couldn't refuse. And we're getting marriiiieeeeed! Look!" Pansy stuck out her hand. "He designed the ring for me and everything!"

Lita took her hand and bent it to the light. Moose had given her a beautiful and very unusual ring—a big oval moonstone with two tiny garnet stones beside it. Seeing it on Pansy's hand choked Lita up a little. Happiness. It suited her roomies. Lita couldn't resist bending down to hug them both. This was huge—the breakthrough this couple had been waiting for. And Lita was thrilled for them, truly. She only wished she knew what the hell she was going to do about the rest of the lease.

Lita had moved into this ratty apartment with these virtual strangers two years ago, for one purpose only—to save money. The apartment was a shitbox, to be honest. They lived on the top floor of a skinny, two-story downtown storefront. On the first floor? A shoe shop—home to noxious fumes, an entry door with bells attached, and surprisingly loud machines that ran morning, noon, and night. The place was drafty, noisy, leaky, buggy, and had the smallest kitchen known to man. But her share of the rent had only been three hundred dollars a month. And she'd saved a ton on gas, being able to walk to everything downtown.

Her less-than-desirable living arrangements were present pain for future profit. That's what she told herself every time she felt like the walls were closing in on her and her roommates were driving her nuts. Living here was a part of a grand plan to save every dime she could get her hands on. She wanted to buy a condo or a small house she could fix up. Maybe even take some classes to finish her art degree without taking out loans.

And though Holliday Hot Rods didn't skimp on her pay, it still wasn't enough for her to get ahead like she needed to. Not really. That's why she'd been running side hustle after side hustle for years now. Custom tattoos by appointment. T-shirt and sticker stores on Etsy and Redbubble. Custom murals. Painting store windows and arranging displays. But she still was a good two or three years away from her goal.

And now this.

She wanted to scream. Or throw something.

But she couldn't. *Of course*, she was happy for them, but as she stood there, gaping at the pair, she couldn't help the dismayed disbelief creeping over her. They were sweet people, but not the sharpest knives in the drawer. Pansy floated through life like she didn't have a care in the world, charms dangling from her blond dreadlocks. She thought Mothman was real, for Christsakes.

And Moose? He was a six-foot-five, three-hundred-pound lunk who didn't know how to pick his underwear off the floor or find the word "ambition" in the dictionary, for that matter. Or so she'd thought.

How crazy was this? When Lita had heard this room was open, she'd moved in with the two of them because she figured they'd never leave this place. And now *she* was the one stuck—not them.

"This is great for you guys," Lita told them, slipping on her coat. "But honestly, I don't know what I wanna do. You know anyone who could move in?"

Pansy crinkled her forehead. "Oh. I figured with all your extra jobs, you'd be able to afford the rent by yourself. I didn't think."

"I can afford it." Lita sighed. "But the whole reason I moved in here was so I could save up. I've got plans for that money."

Pansy brightened. "Ooh. I've got an idea! Why don't you ask Ross? He'd probably be happy to get out of that studio at the shop. And I bet he'd jump at the chance to get closer, you know? That boy is soooo into you, Lita."

"What?" Lita waved a hand. "No, no, no. We're friends is all." And after their big blowout at the hospital, she wondered if that hadn't been blown to hell too.

Her "friends" comment earned a round of giggling from the two of them. "No, you're not." Moose laugh/coughed from his seeming inability to inhale and laugh at the same time. He waved some smoke away. "You know how many times he's come into Bean House, bright, early, and bushy tailed, buying your morning coffee? He's done it for *years!* 'Hey, Moose,' he's always askin'. 'Has Lita eaten breakfast yet? You think she'd like this new coffee? New muffin? New bagel?' Sheeiiit. Ain't no man who does that just for a *friend.*"

The suggestion stopped her in her tracks. "But," Lita sputtered, "I *pay* him. Every time!"

"Yeahhhh, well," Pansy purred, "*you* didn't see his face the day he came over here to pick you up. You know, the day your car was in the shop, and you'd bought those new purple leggings? Omigod. The man practically swallowed his tongue. I think he's having a secret love affair with your ass, Lita."

Moose leaned back against the cushions, giggling. "Oh yeah, oh yeah. I remember. It was kinda like that old Jim Carey movie we saw the other day. You know, the one where he's wearing that zoot suit."

Pansy snapped her fingers. *"The Mask!"*

"Right!" Moose crowed. "That's it! The one where he

saw the pretty girl, and his eyeballs bugged, like, two feet out of his head, and then his tongue unrolled all the way down to the floor and rolled right back up into his mouth. Like that!"

"No way!" Lita gasped.

"*Way*, honey." Pansy grinned. "Open your eyes."

The thought stopped her argument cold. Could they be right? It would explain a few things. Why he always spent so much time with her. Why he was so considerate. Why he'd despised all her boyfriends, even before they'd fucked up. And why he'd been so awful about this date she was having...

Suddenly, their argument in the hospital made a lot more sense. Was this why he'd been afraid to answer her? Was this why he couldn't get his words out? He had real feelings for her he was afraid to say?

All her breath left her in a long exhale. "Oh."

Pansy giggled again. "There it is. Now you're gettin' it."

"Okay, okay. I see what you're saying." Lita admitted. "But *why*? Why wouldn't he *say* something?"

Moose snorted. "Geez, Caaar, you gotta give the boy a sign or somethin'. Let him know his play might be welcome. I mean, you're real good friends, right? What if he moved on you and you, like, slapped his face or somethin'? You sure wouldn't be friends anymore, I'll tell you that. And then you'd be right there, working with each other day in and day out and day in and day—"

"Okay, okay, okay." Lita interrupted. "I get it." She laid a hand over her stomach, which had graduated from jitters to a full-on riot. The realization had hit her like a Mack truck, and now she could barely hold herself up in her high heels. Warmth flooded through her. He'd been into her all this time?

That meant that moment in the truck...it had been *real*

then, not magic induced. If he'd been into her for so long, it had to be.

Man, the look he'd given her after that truck incident, like he didn't know what to do with himself. She'd thought maybe he'd been upset. Or embarrassed. But that didn't make any sense. If it didn't mean anything to him, he would've made a joke about it, right? He would've played it off, saying his dick proved his super-virility or something stupid like that.

But he'd been so intense, and kinda wide-eyed. Heat rose to her face just thinking about it. He'd wanted her. But he'd been afraid to mess things up between them.

Her phone buzzed in her pocket. Shit—Victor! She fumbled for the phone.

At your address. A shoe shop? Is there a spot to park? Where's the door?

Lita trotted over to the window facing the street and spotted him sitting in the loading zone in a late-model, blue Toyota Prius.

Don't bother, she texted him back. **I see you. Be right there.**

Jesus, she didn't have time to process this thing with Ross right now. It was too much of a mess for that. Too much left unsaid, too much left unspoken on both their parts. She'd have to figure something out.

She said goodbye to her roommates, squared her shoulders, and headed for the exit, trying her best to mentally prepare herself for what was to come. Because if these last couple of weeks had taught her anything, it's that she didn't understand men at all. And it when it came to relationships, anything could happen. Anything at all.

CHAPTER 11

J sat Ross down at his station, faced him to the mirror, and clucked disapprovingly as he picked up one dull strand after another. "Dios mio, child. If I'd known it was this bad, I would've called the paramedics. Ugh, it's like your hair has fallen and it can't get up!"

"Okay, okay I get it!" Ross grumbled "I know it's really bad."

J snorted derisively as he picked through his roots. "Bad? Bad is forgetting to condition for a couple of weeks. This, is...this is like, *I've-been-living-in-a-post-apocalyptic-hellscape* bad. But honey, the zombies aren't coming, okay? You could've taken the time for some conditioner and a decent haircut. Who does your hair?"

"Me."

J snickered. "No, really. Who?"

"I mean it," Ross said. "It all started when I was about sixteen. I decided I wanted goth hair, so I went out and bought black hair dye. I liked it, but it shocked the shit out of Mom, though. The whole family is red-headed, as you know. So she said as long as I insisted on having stupid hair, she wasn't going to pay a dime to get it cut or dyed. So I improvised. I used a Flowbee at first—you know that thing that's like a hair dryer, but really sucks your hair in and cuts it?"

J shuddered and screwed up his mouth into a queasy face. "I'm *aware.*"

"As I got older and my hair grew out, I figured out that I could hang my head down and use a straight razor to—"

"Zz-Zzz-Zzzt!" he yelped, holding up both hands and staggering over to sit in Alessandra's chair. "No, no! Don't tell me anymore! Oh-oh my Lord. I can't even. Seriously, I may hyperventilate."

Ross couldn't help chuckling. It really was pretty awful, wasn't it?

"All right now, let me see if I've got this straight." J held up a finger. "You cut your own hair. You only ever used cheap shampoo. You dyed it with the cheapest over-the-counter crap on the market. You never used any kind of conditioner or styling product. You routinely let the roots grow out like friggin' Howard Hughes, and you'd fill in with temporary hair color spray every time you washed your hair, which made the already dyed parts even dryer, and darker. Do I have the right?"

Ross cringed, suddenly sheepish. "It does sound pretty bad now that I hear it out loud like that."

"It's a hairdresser's worst nightmare, that's what it is." J sighed. "But lucky for you, you've come to the best there is. Uncle J can wave his magic wand and make this all go away. But I gotta tell you mijo, it's not going to be fast, easy, or cheap. Here's what I recommend." J showed him a picture on his phone of a red-headed guy with a hella cool cut. "See all that sexy you've been covering up? Lord, there is nothin' like a red-headed man. See how versatile this cut is? It's short up over your ears and on the sides, but there's enough hair here to sweep down over your brow or..." He scrolled to another picture. "You can slick it back. Either way, you can bring all the girls to the yard."

"Great!" Ross rubbed his hands together. "Let's do it then!"

J winced. "That's what I wanted to talk to you about. You've got about an inch of viable red hair. I can do you something up with that, but you'll be pretty scalped after having shoulder-length hair for so long."

Ross grimaced. "What do you recommend then?"

J gave him an explanation that kinda made his eyes cross, with terms like color remover, color fillers, and intensive moisture treatments and protein packs. The translation? He was gonna be here for hours. But at least he was getting the friends-and-family discount.

Ross listened to all this, stunned at what it was going to take to correct all the shit he'd done to his hair. But he knew J wasn't blowing smoke up his ass. Divalicious had its reputation for a reason. He was damn lucky to have someone with J's skills willing to work with this mess. So he stuck his hand out, and they shook on it. "Whatever you wanna do, J, go for it. I trust you."

And he'd meant it too, whatever it cost him. He'd been saving his money for something important, and this was important, right? He let J put that smock around him and enjoyed the man's cheerful chatter while he shampooed. And shampooed. And combed. And then slathered this weird, smelly goop onto his hair.

And Ross had to admit—he kinda sorta loved it. It was nice getting fussed over, and with his headache from the accident starting to recede, all the massaging was exactly what he'd needed. Divalicious was such a cool, calming oasis, but edgy enough to give you a sense of possibility, like you were doing something adventurous.

Ross supposed he was. He was getting rid of all the crap

he was hiding behind. Starting with his hair. *"Everyone will see how sweet you are,"* the old woman had said. Maybe he wasn't so afraid of that anymore.

"Boyyy," J crooned. "I know this is messy and awful but take heart. Even a butterfly has to become goo in its cocoon before it can emerge as its new self."

"Come to think of it," Ross muttered from underneath a hot towel, "I am so totally like goo right now."

"Then I'm doing my job." J laughed. He pulled the hot towel off. "Hmm. The exfoliating and hyaluronic skin treatments are doing wonders for your face."

"I have no idea what any of that is—" Ross grinned, "—but it sure sounds good."

"I swear, you have the most amazing skin. Ivory pale, but with a hint of a ruddy, masculine glow. Pair that with your freakin' fabulous natural hair color, and all those arty black-and-white tats, and you, my child, are going to be my masterpiece. Ooh, it's gettin' inspiring up in here!" He drummed his fingers on his chin and narrowed his eyes at him. "Tell you what—Imma mix you up a bit of custom everything—shampoo, conditioner, pomade, gel, and even moisturizer for your face and body. My treat."

"What?" Ross grimaced. "No! I can't ask you to do that! I'll pay you!"

J snorted. "Oh, honey. You can't afford all that at once. People pay top dollar for this stuff. I import the base in from an artisanal, organic supplier, all my own formula. And I mix up a unique scent for each customer. But if you like it, I'll let you have a free supply for life. You, my child, are a walking, talking billboard for Divalicious. You let me take some photos of you for the website when we're done, and you'll never pay for grooming supplies again."

Ross grinned at the offer, and that was all it took for the man to swing into action. Ross was thoroughly entertained watching J go, arranging all his empty bottles like he was about to teach a potions class. J opened up what he called his "scent bar," a big-ass wooden table he rolled out on casters. He flipped open half the top, revealing what must've been fifty big dropper bottles. He gathered several different kinds of creams and gel bases.

Then J started waving bottles under Ross' nose to see which ones he liked best. And there were so many—*so* damn many. He tried all kinds, from standard scents like sandalwood and coconut, to "manly" scents like sawdust and pine essence, fruity ones like mango and blood orange, and even crazy ones he'd never even heard of like frangipani and bergamot and plumeria. Man, this essential oil thing was crazy! In the end, they'd narrowed it down to his favorites—not surprisingly, sandalwood, leather, and campfire.

"Okay, I can work with this." J clapped his hands and did a shimmy. "Ooh, this is going to be so good!"

While J mixed and muttered and hummed away, Ross settled in to wait on his...what was it? Color filler? He'd had so many things lobbed on his hair at this point, he couldn't keep up. Getting bored, he pulled out his phone and started scrolling through the headlines. But he'd barely gotten started when a text from Tiff popped up.

Hey, where is everybody? Bear threw me out of the house again. Went to Mom and Dad's and the place is deserted. Aren't you supposed to be there resting up?

Dad had an emergency call. Horse is foaling at one of his client's and having a difficult time.

His assistant is off until New Year's so Mom went to help out. So why did B throw you out?

He's doing a plaid whitewash over top of the rose-gold paint he put up last week in the nursery. I would've done it myself. But Bear says I have to stay out late until it's dry. Why aren't you at Mom and Dad's?

I'm at Divalicious getting my hair did.

LOL. Very funny.

He snapped his picture with all the foils and things hanging off him. The string of emojis she sent back cracked him up. Fireballs. The scream. The happy face with the hearts for the eyes.

OMG I have to see this!!!! When will you be done?

Prolly not for another hour and a half or so. Been here all afternoon.

You hungry? Why don't I bring you some dinner? I've got pregnancy cravings for Road Hogs.

. . .

Ross snorted at that. She always had cravings for Road Hog's barbecue, like everybody else he knew. He relayed her plan to J, who wanted some too. She made plans to stop by with the food, which was good, because for the first time since his knock on the head, he was well enough to be hungry. Maybe even hopeful too. For once he was starting to see why so many people liked to go to a nice salon. He already felt a lot better now than he had walking in.

J, however, was still hard at work. He'd finished up making the products, which were setting up nicely, and to Ross' surprise, smelled sexy af when mixed together. The timer went off for his color filler, and J washed it all out, cutting off about three inches of length so it'd be easier to manage later. Then he put on some fancy-ass conditioning product that had to set up under the hairdryer. It felt weird being under a dryer like some 1950s housewife. Real weird. But hey, if he could have foils on his head for an hour, he could do this. At least there were no curlers involved.

When J washed out the conditioner and ushered him back to his chair, Ross was dumbstruck. His hair was red again. It shouldn't be a shock, but it was. This hair he'd always hated so much now looked fantastic—distinctive, even. Mom had always said he'd grow into it. But he hadn't believed her.

Honestly, Ross couldn't remember a time in his whole childhood that he hadn't felt weird—like he was an alien or something. He was always too thin, too jumpy with ADHD, too pale, with features that never seemed to be in proportion to his face. A mediocre student at best, he'd always struggled to sit still and conform to expectations at school.

He'd been having a particularly rough patch sophomore year when Lita had shown up and instantly become his ultimate, unattainable dream girl. He'd gone through a growth spurt so sudden that summer it had made his bones ache constantly. He'd been hungry all the time, but no matter how many milkshakes he'd drunk, he'd still looked like a freakin' matchstick—all bones with ferociously orange hair sticking up at every cowlicky angle.

He'd sat there in class with Lita only a couple of seats away, but she'd never noticed him. Until the day he'd decided to dye his hair and start with the baggy streetwear. It had given him the little boost of confidence he'd needed to say hello to her. The two of them had found out they had a ton of things in common, liking all the same shows and bands and activities. And before he knew it, he'd been folded into her circle of friends. High school had become bearable, because of her. He wondered if she understood what she'd done for him, all those years ago. She'd thought he'd been the generous one, showing her the ropes about Lewisburg. But she'd never needed him. If anything, it was the other way around.

He'd been so zoned out, lost on his trip down memory lane, he hadn't realized J had stopped cutting, and was slicking the pomade back through his hair. "And there it is, boyfriend! Your new look. You've gotten awfully quiet. What do you think?"

Ross stared at himself in the mirror, and for a moment, his brain was stuck in some kind of does-not-compute loop. He looked so incredibly different, it was almost like having an out-of-body experience. His flaming orange hair was cut short for the first time since, what—middle school? Which would be weird enough. But this cut was hot. Sophisticated, even. J had slicked it back, but let a hank fall like a boss over his forehead. He ran his fingers through his hair to make sure his arm movements really were attached to his reflection in the mirror. Damn, the texture of his hair—it was smooth and thick, and seriously silky under his hand. Ah, so *this* was what healthy hair felt like! "I think you're a goddamn miracle worker, J."

"And I think *you're* looking like a professional model now, kiddo. No magic cookies needed."

Before he even had the chance to laugh at that, Lita's mom came barreling through the door, giggling, in a short red mini kilt and a black rock T-shirt. A big bald guy also in a kilt was right on her heels, probably the new boyfriend Lita had told him about. When she saw the place was occupied, Alessandra stopped short, her gaze going back and forth between then two of them.

She stamped her combat boot and fisted her hands on her hips. "Jesús Domingo Ruiz! You sneaky sneak!! You're totally trying to blow up my grid!"

J snorted. "Sister, I'll have you know *he* came to *me*, completely out of the blue today. So what? I decided to come in on my day off for a few treatments to give the boy a fighting chance. Not that you weren't trying to do the same thing with Lita!"

"Me?" Alessandra sniffed. "I was adding one layer of temporary glitz. But this? Ross. Seriously. You look like a new man. This is next-level sorcery, J." She walked up to the chair and sniffed Ross' hair. She clucked. "Dios Mio! You broke out campfire. You *know* women can't resist campfire."

J chuckled evilly and twirled the end of his mustache. "I put in a couple of drops of the ginger too, 'cause I'm saucy like dat."

"Wait." Ross held up a hand. "I'm not sure I understand what's happening here. I thought the grid was made up of people you that thought would hit on Lita. Are you saying you put *me* on the grid?"

Alessandra sighed. "Ach, no. I didn't. You two have been friends too long. But J? He did." She stabbed an accusing finger at the man. "That boy put you in for all the marbles."

Ross squinted at her. "Which means...?"

"It means he is letting his points on the others count for less, so your square counts for more," she explained. "He'll triple his points each time you jump over a hurdle. More if you get her to go out with you, even more if you get her to commit to being a couple by January third. See?" She walked over to her station, pulled their grid out of a drawer, and shoved it in his hands.

The big guy ambled over and snuck his head over his shoulder so he could read too. "I'm Tino, by the way. Nice to meet you, man," he said, sticking out his hand. Ross gave it a hearty shake, liking the guy and his big broad smile immediately. Tino nudged Alessandra. "Hmmm. If you're the pink squares on here, honey, you've got a substantial lead."

J let out a disgusted tut. "And yet she's still gilding the lily for this date tonight. That red dress. You might as well have sent the girl out in shrink wrap!"

She squawked. "And making Ross ready for the cover of GQ isn't cheating?"

"I have two words for you, sister," J spat, waving his finger angrily. "Airbrush. Makeup. What, you think I missed that photo you posted on Insta?"

While J and Alessandra bickered about who was cheating whom, Ross quietly opened his Instagram app and pulled up the picture in question on the Divalicious feed.

"Shew!" Tino exclaimed. "Look at her. No wonder they're placing bets."

Ross studied the picture and, honestly, he couldn't quite tell how he felt. Oh, she was gorgeous, no doubt. That dress alone was already making his pulse quicken. But there was something that bothered him about it, way down deep that he couldn't shake. He had the sudden urge to rip the dress off her, scrub off all the makeup, tangle his hands in her hair, and suck the perfume right off her skin. To have the real Lita, right there, under his fingertips. Skin to skin. Real.

Guilt twisted in his chest. *Am I seriously that much of a caveman? Nothing more than a possessive, jealous creep?*

He sat there, silently searching his heart.

No, the answer came back.

And he realized it was true. If this Martinez guy treated her right and gave her new opportunities and all that, he'd be happy for her. But something about this photo was all wrong—the big doll-baby eyes, the candy apple cheeks, the pushup bra.

But that wasn't it either, was it? It wasn't the makeup. It was Lita's expression. She didn't appear joyful or empowered, like you'd expect someone all dressed up to be. Her eyes had lost their shine, and the way her eyebrows were scrunched up, she seemed unsure of herself. And honestly, that was an expression he'd never seen her wear. Was she really that worked up over this date tonight? The thought of Lita feeling nervous or inferior made him grind his teeth. The fact that she needed to go this far out of her comfort zone to please this guy...

Shaking his head, he stuffed his phone back in his pocket, peeled off his smock, and stood up to brush all the hair off him.

The brother-sister smackdown volley of brinksmanship still continued, but finally Alessandra threw up a hand and stomped off to the coat closet. "I don't have time to argue with you, mijo. I stopped in here on our way to see Tino play." She fished around in the closet. Finally, she squealed. "Ah! I knew I'd left this here!" She pulled out a short, black leather moto jacket, which somehow managed to top her look off perfectly. "What do you think?" she trilled, turning around in a circle. "Do you think I could pass for Scottish?"

Tino laughed. "No, baby. But you're still the prettiest lil' lass I ever did see. Mm-mm-mmm!" He sidled up behind her, wrapped his big arms around her waist, and squeezed.

The giggle that came out of Alessandra made Ross smile. She sounded free. Happy. Appreciated. All the things he wanted Lita to feel, if only he could figure out how to do it. And let's face it, he was definitely out of his depth in this area. He'd never had that kind of relationship in his life. But as Ross stood there, seeing the effect Tino had with his simple acts of love, he realized he wanted that. Maybe more than he'd ever wanted anything.

The happy couple scurried off to the door with blown kisses from Alessandra and a "nice to meet you Ross" from Tino. But before they could leave, Tiffany came barreling in with three sacks full of barbecue. And her eyes locked on Ross.

She screamed now for real, the food forgotten on a chair, and went running over to him. "Is this my brother? Is this my *brother*? Oh my *Lord*!" she squealed as she circled around him. "Oh, Ross!" she got all teary-eyed and fanned her face. "I don't believe it. You're the hottest guy in town now, hands down. Except for Bear, of course. But you get what I'm saying. I knew it! I always knew you'd look amazing if you'd take care of yourself. Jesús Ruiz—" she held her hand up in testimony, "—you are the second coming, as far as I'm concerned."

"That's what he said," J quipped as he put his bottles away. They all cracked up.

Tiff snorted at the sight of his Slytherin shirt. "Let me guess. You didn't have a change of clothes. You haven't worn this since you were, what, seventeen?"

"'Fraid so." Ross sighed.

Tiff tsked, patting down his pecs and pinching his biceps like she was sizing him up. "At least this tight shirt shows off your assets. When did you get all beefed up?"

Ross shrugged. He wouldn't exactly call himself beefy, but he'd gotten a barbell and a pull-up bar for his apartment to kill time. He'd put on a bit of muscle and gotten a little definition—nothing too crazy. So yeah, he wasn't some skin-and-bones kid anymore.

"That does it!" Tiff started snapping her fingers real fast, like she does every time she's up to something. "I am not letting you go out with all this—" she waved her hand at his face, "—and all this—" she waved her hands at his body, "—while you're wearing all that. So once we've finished up the 'cue, you and me, we're going shopping. I'm going to help you buy a whole new wardrobe. This town won't know what hit them."

Ross opened his mouth to argue. That's how you're supposed to act when your bossy sister tells you what to do, right? But it dawned on him that this might be a seriously good idea. He was dumping all the rest of the juvenile shit out of his life. Why not his clothes too? And with his sister's amazing design eye, she was the one person he might trust to do this. "Okay," he found himself saying. "My wallet is yours to command, Tiff."

Tiff squealed and gave him a huge hug. "Omi*god*, we are going to have so much fun, brother."

Alessandra groaned as she stood in the doorway, taking it all in. "And that, my friends, is the sound of my certain defeat. But for the record, Ross, I think I might not mind losing. My brother needs to get his brows done by a professional, after all."

"Ack!" J squawked. "Get outta here already!" The damp rag he threw at his sister hit the door, just as the woman slammed it behind her, snickering again.

Ross hugged his sister back, thinking about how this was so much more than a game to him. This was everything. And maybe for the first time in his life, he was in it to win it.

CHAPTER 12

"AND FOR YOU, MISS?" A very proper waiter stood there in his Greenbrier uniform, pen poised over his order pad.

Lita scanned the menu. A creeping mild panic threatened to close off her vocal cords. It wasn't like her to be scared by a freakin' menu, but the entire thing was in French. Everything was translated, of course, and she could have ordered using that. But with the adoring, expectant way Victor was looking at her right now, she could tell he was hoping language number three would trill right off her tongue.

Everything on here sounded hella good. Even the royal fume, whatever that was. How was she even supposed to pick? The options swam in front of her eyes.

Victor reached out and touched her hand with a solicitous touch, like you would a small child. "Would you like me to order for both of us?"

She nodded with relief, and a bit of the tension she was holding slid off her shoulders. "Yes. That would be great," she told him.

"Okay, so if you don't mind, I'd like to change my order," he told the waiter, handing him their menus. "We'll take the Chateaubriand pour Deux. And how about the Terrine de Fois Gras with two plates, so we can share. Why don't we go ahead and get the bottle of the Beaujolais my lady is drinking here for dinner. Sound good?"

"All excellent choices. I'll get your fois gras out right away," he said, popping off a curt nod before he slid away on silent feet, back to the kitchen. Lita couldn't help watching the waiter go. The man was so buttoned up and professional, he was exactly what she'd expect an English butler to be like, if butlers had southern accents.

It had been one of a continuing string of surreal moments for her that had gone all the way from Pansy's revelations, to the magical carriage ride around the property, to cocktails at the bar, to here, in the main dining room. Everything had been so beautiful, so perfect...

She'd been out here once or twice ice skating and walking around the property. But she'd never gotten to experience the Greenbrier full on like this. There was a reason why people called it America's Resort. The property went on for acres and acres of pristine West Virginia wilderness. The architecture here was Georgian, built at a time when the founding fathers could have visited. Thousands of Christmas lights twinkled as they'd ridden around the property. And here in the main dining room it was as old-school as it got, with crisp white tablecloths, fancy brocaded curtains, and mirrored columns to catch the candlelight on every table. Waiters brought out perfect platters under silver domes.

She was now experiencing the perfect romantic evening. But Lita couldn't help feeling like she was watching herself from outside her body. Like this really wasn't her life, and she was wearing someone else's clothes.

Oh, yeah. I am wearing someone else's clothes!

Victor held up his tumbler of twenty-five-year-old

Scotch, snapping her attention back to him. "I'd like to propose a toast." She raised her glass too, of course.

"To Christmas," he said, beaming at her. "And a beautiful night with the most beautiful girl in Lewisburg."

She raised an eyebrow. "Lewisburg isn't a very big place, Dr. Martinez."

"Yes, but it's prettier with you in it," he replied.

Lita clinked and drank, peering at him worriedly over the top of her glass. Part of the reason she'd agreed to this date was her mom. The other reason was Martinez himself. He'd seemed normal to her back at the hospital, treating her like any other pretty girl he'd met and wanted to take out on a date. He hadn't been slavering to get at her, like so many of the other guys who'd been hitting on her since the cookie incident. In other words, he'd seemed totally in charge of his faculties. But he'd seemed like too cool a guy to blather on with a ham-handed compliment like that one. Could it be that he was more affected by that hex than she'd realized?

Figuring she should steer him to safer topics, Lita went for the one thing guaranteed to make a date go well—getting the guy to talk about himself. "Victor, tell me again, what made you decide to come to a place like West Virginia when you grew up in Chicago?"

"It really wasn't my choice," the man answered, shrugging. "Look, my parents never made a lot of money. Dad was a low-level mechanic who came home covered in grease, and never managed to earn more than minimum wage at some oil change place. Mom was a cleaning lady who juggled two or three jobs and was never home. There wasn't any money for college, or much of anything else, for that matter. But I had fantastic grades at a big urban high school, and that earned me a minority scholarship at Northwestern. Then when I went to med school, they made me sign an agreement that said I'd go wherever they sent me for my residency, whatever underserved area needed me most. And Lewisburg?" He snorted and shook his head as he took another big sip of his Scotch. "It probably would've been my last pick, honestly. But I would've moved to any backwater they told me to, to keep from having two-hundred K in student loans. Now I'm here, in this one. Lucky for me, it'll only be for four years, so..."

He shrugged again and gave her a knowing look like, *amirite?*

She sat at the table, grinding her teeth now. What did he expect her to say? That she hated it here? She *didn't.* Lewisburg was her home, and she loved it. She loved the land. She loved the people here. And you know what? They *loved her back.*

Honestly, Lita was blown away. In, like, literally one paragraph, he'd told her everything she needed to know about him. He was prissy, condescending, and probably an opportunist. Here she'd thought he was Mister Altruism, all hardworking and kind. She wondered if his patients knew what he really thought of them. Of their home.

So much for Dr. Ken dream date here. She almost wanted to crack up laughing, honestly. How much stomach acid had she swallowed down, worrying about making the right impression on this guy? She sure as hell wasn't spending another second on *that* anymore. Now she wouldn't be worrying about whether she said the right thing, or accidentally smudged her lip gloss with her napkin, or reached for the wrong fork.

Luckily, the waiter brought their fois gras, silently sliding it between them, filling up her wine glass. She watched Victor as he spread it with some of the topping they offered onto a round of bread.

When she tried it, the explosion of savory sweet flavor in her mouth distracted her a bit from her jittery stomach—

and the fact that this chico pomposo seemed to look down on mechanics, people with more than one job, and Lewisburg, for that matter. "Hmm. Sounds like you don't like it here, then."

"Well," he hedged, at least attempting to be contrite. "Who cares if I like Lewisburg or not? It's just another stop on my journey." He reached across the table and linked his fingers with hers. "I like *you*, though. A whole, whole lot. In fact, I've never seen someone soooo perfect."

Ugh. So *that* didn't seem magically manipulated at all. She carefully unwound her fingers and folded her hands in her lap. This was going to be a long dinner. But by God, she was at least going to enjoy the food.

She asked him a few questions about his life back in Chicago. It had been tough on the mean streets, he'd told her, but he'd been lucky to have mentors. He went on and on about his medical rescue travels as the waiter took their plates and brought out the beef tenderloin filet and short ribs croquettes.

The chimichurri sauce was to die for, and there were all kinds of things on this plate she'd never had, like pickled ramps and black garlic. It was great, of course, that he'd done so many trips to the jungles and war-torn countries, assisting charity organizations while he traveled the world. This was all very noble, really. She should be dazzled. But she wasn't buying what he was sellin' now. She also didn't like how hard he pushed it all, like he was trying to draw underlines under his intellect, his bravery, his concern for the downtrodden.

Like he was unrolling a resume, or something.

Like he was trying to get something he wanted.

Into her pants, apparently.

She swirled her very lovely Beaujolais in its glass, considering him. The guy was a low-key dick, to be sure.

Whatever interest she had in him had pretty much fallen to zero. So there would be zero pants-getting tonight.

Besides, she was about ninety percent sure he wasn't in his right mind right now. But she needed more proof.

The wheels spun in her head, and she decided if she was going to be stuck here with this guy, she might as well do some experiments to see if she could break through the magic. She needed to give this date a mercy killing. As she watched Victor sitting there with his gleaming manicured fingernails and his fussy little cufflinks, swilling his fine whiskey like he was James Bond, or something, she got a few ideas.

Oh, ho ho yeah. She *definitely* got some ideas.

She suppressed a grin as the pieces fell together in her mind. This might actually be fun. Let the operation begin...

Lita took a big sip of her wine and executed a big, theatrical wince. "Ack" she grimaced as she swallowed, fanning her face. "Oh, that was..." She sat her glass down, and batted her eyelashes at the man, trying her best to act clueless. "Do you know anything about wine, Victor?"

He brightened. "Yes, a bit. I took a wine appreciation course for an elective in college. And I've been on a wine tour or two. Why? Is there something wrong with yours?"

"I dunno." She scowled at her glass, all puzzled. "It's off or something. Would you mind tasting it to see if it's spoiled maybe?"

She handed him her glass, but he held up a hand. "Oh, don't bother with that." He grabbed bottle to pour himself one.

"Oh, no!" She stopped him. "I can't tell whether this glass has gotten some cork in it, or if there's something wrong with the glass itself." She held the glass up hopefully, all wide eyed. "Surely with your superior knowledge and all, you could tell me what the trouble is."

He grinned dreamily at her. "You know I can't say no to you, Carrrrmeliiita," he purred. He took the glass, swirled it, sniffed it, held it up to the candle to search for debris, and gave it a good long quaff. He paused, then shrugged. "Tastes fine to me. It's very good wine."

"Oh, good!" She laughed, making sure to layer on a good snort as she took back the glass. "Whew! That's a relief! Must be that nasty case of mouth thrush coming back again. You know they say that can affect your sense of taste."

"*Thrush?*" His eyes were as round as saucers. "That's contagious! You actually— You're seriously telling me—"

"Oh, don't worry, doc," she said, running her tongue over her teeth. "I go on dates all the time with this. They say it's only transmissible when you've got the sores coming on." She rolled her tongue around in her mouth a little bit. "Hmm. I guess I've got a couple bustin' out, now that I'm checking. Wow. They're really oozy this time." She shrugged and popped a pate crostini in her mouth, whole.

His disgust-o-meter must've kicked on, because just for a minute, poor Dr. Martinez turned about five different shades of green. He quickly swilled his Scotch, tipped his head back, and started *gargling*. Right there, in the middle of the Greenbrier dining room.

Oh, no he did not.

She held her glass up in front of her mouth to hide her cackling as their waiter scurried over to the table. "Sir?" He patted Victor's back. "Are you alright? Is there anything you need from me?"

Victor spit his alcohol back into the cut crystal glass and handed it to the man. "Yeah," he croaked. "Gimme another one of these."

The waiter grimaced as he gingerly took the glass. "Yes, sir. Right away."

The disgust continued as Victor wiped his fingers one by one on his napkin. But then it was the strangest thing. As he made eye contact with her, all that disgust melted away, and he got this adoring, mushy vibe again. "As you were saying, Carmelita?"

She sighed. Oh, man. Poor guy. She almost felt sorry for him. Clearly, she was gonna have to try harder.

Lita squirmed a little uncomfortably in her seat. Then stopped and rolled her eyes as sweetly as she could. "Victor, baby, you wouldn't happen to be one of those old-school gentlemen who carries a handkerchief, would you?"

He slid her a satisfied grin. "As it so happens, I am." He pulled a crisp white handkerchief out of his impeccably cut suit jacket. "My abuelo drilled that one into me. He always said a real man always has a handkerchief and jumper cables handy."

Lita nodded sagely as he handed her the neatly folded cloth. "A wise grandfather indeed." She whipped the cloth open and fanned it out on the tabletop to fold it into thirds longways. Then she reached around to her backside, through the deep back vee in her dress, and stuffed the handkerchief down into her shapewear.

He gave her a quizzical smile. "Carmelita, sweetie, what are you doing right now?"

Handkerchief fully positioned, she leaned back and sighed a huge sigh of relief. "Ohhhhhh, yeah. Now that's better. You wouldn't believe how swampy it can get down there. You know what it's like with a cheap compression panty. Doesn't breathe. Especially with the rash."

His eyebrows flew up. "Rash? Like, what kind of rash are we talking about here?"

She scratched at her bottom. "Oh, geez. I see where you're going with this. I don't have an STI, if that's what you're thinking. No, I've got my roommate to thank for this one. I told her not to bring in that old, stained couch from the dumpster. Now that idiota gave us bedbugs! Can you believe it? Ugh, those red bumps." She scratched some more. "It does get weepy sometimes when you wear too much polyester. This little bit of cotton is a lifesaver!"

He swallowed, appearing worried. "You're saying you've got bedbugs? You know that can get in your clothes." He swallowed again, pulling at his shirt collar. "Your car..."

"What? Don't worry." She waved a hand at him. "I won't infest you or anything. We had it bombed and we threw all the furniture out. It's just gonna—" she twisted in her seat again, "—take a few weeks to—" scratch-scratch, "—go away." She reached over and poured more wine in her glass, unfashionably high, nearly to the rim. "Here's to you, man." She tipped her glass and took a sip. "For saving the day and all. You're a man among men."

She did the eye contact thing again and watched the concern and confusion drain right off his face. He reached out for her other hand, which she'd draped in a rather unmannerly fashion on the table. He took her hand and caressed it.

Lita sighed, knowing this was just going to keep going on and on unless she found some way to put this poor guy out of his misery.

"I'm sorry," he crooned. "I've been talking about myself all evening, haven't I? Now I want to hear about you. All you, Carmelita. All night long. Tell me everything. I want to knooooowwww."

Oh man, that was terrible. Lita pushed down the nearly overwhelming urge to bust out laughing again. This was really getting ridonkulous. If she ever needed direct evidence that this guy wasn't in his right mind right now, here it was. So she just decided to lay the cold, hard truth alllll out there.

"You want to know about me, Victor? Well, buckle up, buttercup." She grinned and took a big ol' slug of her wine. "My dad knocked my mom up when they were still teens. My parents divorced when I was six, and I was pretty much raised by my mother, who never had a college degree, and worked as a beautician and at any other side job she could find for most of my childhood. My dad gives the appearance of being this swaggery 'professional poker player' but he's really a gambling addict and a grifter who's constantly hounded by his bookies, and only comes around when he tries to bleed more money out of my mom. And then there's me, of course. I work in a hot rod shop getting greasy every single day, and there's nothing I like better than having auto paint under my fingernails. I have tattoos, and several side jobs, one of which is doing custom tat design at Renegade tats, here in town. The local Hell's Angels are some of my best clients. I only have an associate's degree. I've never been out of the country, and don't care if I ever go. Oh, and I took Spanish but I got a C, cause my teacher was some cracker jackass. There. How's that?"

She chugged down the last half of her wine in one swallow, burped, and snickered, feeling remarkably light all of a sudden. "Damn! That was some good shit!" Lita thunked her wine on the table, daring him to say something about it.

And she watched the conflicted emotions pass over his face. Surprise. Disgust again. A certain *what am I doing here?* expression. Then, tiringly, right back to that default adoring, wide-eyed wonder.

"Awwww," he crooned. "That's *so* cool. You are the cutest thing, Lita!"

Lita wanted to slap herself on the forehead and swear loudly in Spanish. But for the sake of her stomach acid and the good people here at The Greenbrier, she decided to let it go. Her gut had been telling her the truth all this time.

This whole evening was some kind of magical pantomime, the point of which she had yet to decipher. She simply had to get through it.

Luckily, they were mostly finished with the main meal, and the waiter came by to extoll the virtues of dessert. She waved the man off, patting her stomach and saying she had a case of explosive diarrhea brewing, and it'd be best if they took the shortcut home. She didn't, of course. Now that her jitters had disappeared, her stomach was totally fine. She just didn't want Dr. Martinez squeezing her too hard.

The waiter crinkled his nose up at the news, bless him, but he fast-tracked the processing of the gift certificate and his gratuity—no doubt on fire to save the fine jacquard upholstery presently positioned under her ass. The valets brought up the good doctor's car with all due speed.

Blessedly, the drive from the Greenbrier to downtown Lewisburg wasn't long, either, so she only had to listen to a short sermonette on irritable bowel syndrome, the early stages of ulcerative colitis, and ringworm. She nodded wisely at him, and they both openly speculated over whether she could have an allergy to goose livers. She wondered aloud if her stomach could be curdling as some kind of unexpressed trauma passed down through her DNA, as her great grandpap had died back in terrible rabid goose swarm of 1937. She shuddered. "They still talk about it hushed whispers, even today," she told him.

He totally bought it. And he put his hand on her knee, for comfort. Unfortunately, he kept it there.

"Oh!" She wailed, gripping her stomach, "The gurgling, Victor! The gurgling! Please— step on the gas!"

He did, of course. And Lita bit the hell out of the inside of her cheek to keep a straight face. It was almost fun.

When he skidded to a stop back in the loading zone outside her place, she tried to make a hasty retreat. But he insisted on "helping her" up her rickety stairs to her door, no doubt to deal with any piles she might leave on the steps. Still, she managed to get to the top of the steps, remarkably pile-free, and he took both her hands in his.

"It's too bad you're not feeling well tonight, Lita. But I want you to know I had a totally wonderful time and I think you're such a beautiful girl and..." He leaned in for a kiss, apparently totally forgetting about the whole thrush thing. Oh, gawd.

Not wanting to be too rude about it, she pulled back her head and went for his cheek instead, giving him an innocent little peck.

And that's when things really got weird. Victor snapped to attention and stepped away from her. And when he made eye contact this time, he was back to normal. No adoring sighs. Only total confusion. "Hang on. Whoa, where am I? And who are— Wait. Aren't you that girl who was visiting Ross Mason, my patient?"

Lita was too shocked to get a word out for a second. But then she realized what was going on. The spell—she'd discovered the antidote! All she had to do was kiss them! And not even on the mouth, either. Relief, elation, even giddiness coursed through her in an almighty rush. She would have fist pumped the air if she could have. "Yes!" She recovered herself. "I am! And you came up here to check to see how he was doing! He's totally better. Remember?"

"No, actually." He grimaced as he got a load of her shabby, dimly lit hallway. "Wow, it's like, I can't remember anything from the last couple of days. Just something about...*explosive diarrhea?*" Still frowning, he rooted worriedly around his inside jacket pocket, like he wanted to disinfect himself. "And where in the heck is my hand-kerchief?"

Lita almost lost it, right there. Yeah. That was one handkerchief he was never getting back. She put on her best concerned, solemn expression. "I don't know about the handkerchief, but yes, doctor. Ross had a pretty bad case of the trots when he first came home from the hospital. Thankfully those little white pills you told him to take fixed him right up."

"Little white pills?"

"Yeah." Lita wrinkled her nose and cupped her hand around her mouth. "You know, the *anti-diah-hreal*."

He nodded, still looking confused. "Right."

This night had been a mistake—one that had wasted this poor man's time and his perfectly serviceable gift certificate. But why be guilty about it? She'd gotten information she needed to break the spell, and that could help a lot of guys. This had been research in the public interest, right?

She took his elbow this time and led Victor down the steps, back to his regular life. She clapped her hands as she got to the bottom landing. "Yes, you know, doc, we're all good here. You can go. Really."

Opening the door and shuttling him out, she'd thought she'd gotten rid of him. He turned around and with his finger in the air instead. "Can you tell me why we're both so dressed up?"

She pasted on an innocent smile. "Now Dr. Martinez, you came in that way. As for me, I'm not in the habit of discussing my personal life with my friend's physician. Thanks for checking in. You have a nice night now."

She closed the door and leaned back against it, letting the laughter out that she'd been holding in the whole evening. Turned out, the night had been pretty entertaining, after all.

CHAPTER 13

Ross PULLED his rehabbed Trans Am into the back bay of Holliday Hot Rods, relieved it was out of the thick sleet that had been slapping at the finish. But though his favorite ride was out of the crosshairs of ice-stormageddon, he hardly felt protected.

Because Lita's car was here, right beside his. As he'd predicted, she was riding out this crazy Nor'easter at work. And he was gonna go find her and do something he'd never, ever done with a woman outside his own family.

Apologize. Face to face.

Sincerely.

He'd never been close enough to another woman to need to do this before. And honestly, he felt like he was playing for the whole pot or something. If this didn't go well, he wasn't sure what he'd do. He'd been so worried about it, he'd even poured out his heart to Tiff. She'd dispensed a lot of girl wisdom while they'd been draining his pocketbook dry, remaking his image. Like the big sister she was, she'd given him a checklist for "making proper apologies to a romantic interest." She'd even made an acronym, because evidently, he was thick enough to need one.

LOVER. It was stupid as shit, but damn if he couldn't remember it in his sleep now.

Look good
bring a peace **O**ffering
be **V**ery contrite
Explain the wrong you did, in detail
Really mean it when you say never again

This morning, he'd spent a lot longer than usual sifting through his new wardrobe, and he was pretty sure he had the L part down. He was wearing a new pair of brown, steel-toed combat boots, slim-cut Levi's that hugged his thighs, and a heather green thermal fitness tee that clung to his chest and showed off his arms. And thanks to the pomade tutorial from J, his hair was freakin' perfect, if he did say so himself. He checked his 'do in the rearview mirror and tweaked the piece or two that was curled over his forehead. Yeah. *Perfect.*

He hadn't wavered over the O-part, either. Ross had decided it was well worth braving the storm to buy Lita her favorite—a tall coffee and a cheese danish from Corn+Flour. He'd even managed to buy some flowers at the local florist before they'd battened down their hatches. And the best part? The ribbon around the vase had "I'm sorry" printed on it. It was as good an impression as he could make, all things considered.

Now he had to handle the V-E-R part. He wiped his sweaty palms on his jeans and tried to breathe through the anxiety currently clamped around his chest. *I can do this.*

Grabbing everything, he trotted into the shop, stopping only to hang up his coat. He said a prayer of thanks he wouldn't have an audience for this. Hop and Hunter had gone out to buy the last of the supplies for the Christmas party before the roads got too bad. There was no telling how this would go.

Finally, he caught up with Lita in the break-room. She had her head buried in the refrigerator, cleaning it out in advance of the guys' shopping trip. Ross stood across the room, wondering if he should come back. But he steeled his nerve. "Lita," he called out. "I think it's time we had a talk."

She jumped and banged her head on the inside of the refrigerator. "Dammit, Ross! Why do you always have to sneak up—" When she finally faced him, she stopped, shock etching every single one of her features. She swayed on her feet for a second, grabbing at the counter behind her for balance. The container of yogurt she was holding fell out of her hand with a splat. She didn't even notice. "You— Your hair is red," she sputtered, still digging her fingers into the counter.

He set down his armload on the breakroom table and took a step or two closer. "Yeah." He shrugged. "It's always been red. But I was a stupid teenager who wanted to be a cool goth. I'm over that now. Do you like it?"

"I..." She swallowed hard and grimaced. "I'm still mad at you," she told him. But as he took another step closer, he could swear he saw her eyes go dark. She was breathing harder too. Yeah, this new style of his seemed to be hitting its mark. He couldn't quite suppress his grin. *L—check.*

Lita's vise grip on the counter hadn't lessened. He pressed his luck, crowding her a bit as he reached for the roll of paper towels on the counter. Then he bent down in front of her and pointed to the mess. "Here, let me help you get that."

"Oh!" She rounded her eyes as she finally realized there was a mess on the floor. "Oh, yeah." She shook her head, like she was disgusted with herself, and got her own towels to join him down there. He leaned in close as he worked. Closer than he might have normally. She didn't move away. "You smell different," she murmured.

Wait, she'd noticed how he *smelled* before? And had thought about it enough to notice it now? He wasn't sure what to make of that. "The scent is J's doing. He mixed all new products for me."

"Oh." She tossed her head but couldn't manage to look him in the eye. "Makes sense."

Ross stopped for a second, trying to figure out the expression on her face. He'd never seen Lita act so awkward. And now the air was thick between them, like it had been that day in the truck. His heartbeat kicked up a notch, thinking about that day, about *her,* all curls and curves, pressed up against him in all the right places. He swallowed against his dry throat.

Lita jumped up and walked the dirty towels over to the garbage bin and rinsed her hands in the sink. He hesitated for a minute, wondering what he should say as he watched her dry herself off. As she stood up to go, he stopped and grabbed both her hands. "Wait, Lee—I have something I need to say to you." The movement felt strange, making him pause. Holding hands with a girl wasn't exactly his M.O., but right now, at this moment, he could see why it was a thing. It felt...*good.*

Was Lita feeling it, too? She kept her eyes down on their linked fingers, fidgeting a bit with her legs like she might walk off any second. He half expected her to worm out of his grip, but she didn't. So he didn't waste any more time.

"I said it in texts and voicemails, but I want to say it again to you here, because I'm man enough to own up to my mistakes. That whole exchange in the hospital room? It was wrong, full stop. Because I couldn't get the words to my

146

mouth somehow, I managed to leave you with the impression that you are less. You are not less, Lita. You, in every way, are an amazing woman. You'd make any man a great partner, even if it ends up being that damn Martinez guy. Because you know what? You deserve a real partner, not some hookup. You deserve someone who knows you, and gets you, and will treat you like the queen you are. If I made you think you weren't worthy, then I'm so sorry. Can you ever forgive me? Because Lee, I gotta tell you, you're, like, one of the most important people in the world to me. And it'd end me if I ever thought I hurt you."

Lita finally met his gaze for one long, breathless moment. She cupped his jaw, and circled her thumb lightly along his bruised jaw and new line of stitches. "You're forgiven, Ross. I can't stay mad at you, especially since I'm the reason you were in the hospital in the first place. And anyway, you were right."

"Right?"

She moved away and sauntered over to the table. She picked up the danish he'd brought, and bent down to smell the flowers. "Yeah, right about Martinez."

Hope surged in his chest. "I take it Dr. Perfect was a dud?"

Lita snorted. "Yeah. He was every bit as magically effed up as the other dudes. And boring too, the sort of guy who wants a woman to be in his orbit, like an accessory, you know? I had to pretend like I was getting explosive diarrhea to get the date to end."

Relief flooded through him, so powerful he almost had to sit down and give his knocking knees a break. He hooted. "Faking the squirts? Man, now that's what I can desperation."

"Yeah, well, desperate times, desperate measures. Dios mio, it was awful! And when he wasn't droning on about

147

how much he hated Lewisburg, he was all like, 'oh Lita, you're so cute, you're so awesome,' blah-blah-blah. Even when I told him the exact opposite of what he wanted to hear. He didn't make sense half the time. But here's the thing—I figured out how to fix it."

Ross raised his eyebrows at that, mainly because he was still trying to convince her he wasn't affected. "Whaddya mean, the so-called hex? How do you know he wasn't just really into you?"

"Trust me, he wasn't. And you wanna know how I know that? Because I figured out how to un-hex him. Yep! All I had to do is kiss him, and he snapped right out of it! The poor boy couldn't even remember where he was at! It's like it never even happened!"

Ross felt that in his gut, a little more than he would've liked. "So, wow. You-you *kissed* him then?"

She smirked at him. "Oh, please. Don't get so serious. It was only a peck on the cheek. But that was all it took to get him to come to his senses. You should've seen him! He had no idea why he was all dressed up, or with me. It was *so* wack."

A growl slipped out of him before he could stop himself. "Let me guess. Now you're going to go around kissin' on every guy who flirts with you?"

"Until the Christmas holiday is over, you got any better ideas?"

The thought of that...it tangled him up. He wanted to grab a big club and stand between her and every other guy in the world.

Jealous. It made him insanely, incredibly, point-of-no-return jealous. The sudden realization of it hit him sideways. Because this felt different than the useless pining he'd done, all these years. Pining was for boys.

This? This was a sizzle under his skin and a buzzing in

148

his brain. It was the desire a man felt when he saw something he wanted...no, *needed*, like air or sunlight. It was different this time, because he was ready to stand up, ask for it, and fight for it.

And this time he had a real shot with Lita. He could feel it in his bones—in his whole body, maybe, coursing through him like a shot of pure adrenaline and hope. Not quite sure where he was going with this, he pushed off the counter. He stepped one foot in front of the other until he stood right in front of her, toe to toe. "I don't like this plan, Lee."

He was up in her space again. And he saw that same flash of interest in her eyes, a spark she couldn't hide. He'd caught her blushing. "What's wrong with the plan? " she rasped. "It's a good plan."

"No, it's not," he answered her. "Any plan involving you kissing other men does not get my vote." And now his voice was sounding all raspy too. This business of standing so close like this was starting to give him too many feelings. Too many ideas. He couldn't stop himself from reaching out and brushing back a long, corkscrewy curl that had fallen in her face. When the pad of his finger touched her satiny cheek, electricity arced between them, so real it snapped through his whole body.

Lita trembled and stifled a gasp, and for a second she seemed like she couldn't look away from him. But like a beat that had passed, she stepped away. "That's too bad, Ross. My mouth, my decision." She took a bite of her danish, grabbed her coffee, and flashed him a shy grin as she walked out on the floor. "Don't you have work to do, Mason?"

I do.

It was all he could think about as he watched her walk her sexy ass away from him. Oh, yeah. He was going to work this. And he was only getting started.

CHAPTER 14

Lita attempted a confident sashay back to her paint station. But her quivering knees weren't making it easy.

In fact, it felt like her whole insides had gone shaky and molten. Ross' unbelievable transformation had really set her on her ass. He was now officially the hottest guy she'd ever laid eyes on. Like, work-the-runway meets classic-car-chic. Like the guy next door who had tats and muscles and the kind of piercing blue eyes that made you want to take all your clothes off. That kind of *hot*.

And it was *Ross*.

Ross!

That hair. Those pecs. Dios mio...that ass! She even liked that stupid, rugged, all-kinds-of-brave gash on his face.

Lita took a long, slow moment to coil her ponytail into a loose knot and secure it with a clip. It was the perfect excuse to ogle the man, who was currently screwing on the new grill he'd fabricated for that old Ford. Even from a distance, he was so combustible he practically singed her eyeballs.

How was it she'd never noticed the sexy way he moved before? Now that he was out of those baggy clothes, she could see he had a sinewy, fluid gait, with a muscularity that was completely unrehearsed, like everything flowed from his center. And yeah, she caught herself checking out his *center* too. Instead of his usual uniform of extra-large shirts, he was wearing a belt with a big, weathered bronze buckle, with a clingy thermal tucked in one of those just-in-the-front French tucks that reminded her of how much he was packin'. The way he filled those jeans out made her mouth water. A not-too-small part of her wished she hadn't missed her opportunity in the truck the other day. Boy, what she wouldn't give to squeeze...

She told herself she needed to concentrate on her work. But it wasn't working. Ross stood up and stretched out every muscle in his long, lean back, then popped the hood and bent over to check the carburetor. *Bent. over.*

She spun back around, feeling like all the blood in her system was being rerouted to her face, her lady bits...

Damn, had any guy ever made her this nuts? When she'd set eyes on him earlier, her knees had actually stopped working for a full two minutes. If it hadn't been for the counter, she would've fallen down, for sure.

And who does that? Exactly when did I become such a flippin' dork?

Getting pissed off at herself now, she poured cool water on one of her work rags and held it on the back of her neck until she got hold of herself. She didn't know why she was falling to pieces like this. It was just Ross.

But it wasn't "just Ross," was it?

Something was happening between them, ever since that day at Corn+Flour. He'd been different. Not so jokey. Not so immature. There'd been an awareness, a heat between them that hadn't been there before, at least on her end. But had it been there on his?

She couldn't answer that. But there was no doubt about

it, he was making an effort with her lately. Little gifts. Defending her. Now the flowers.

She'd deliberately not gushed over those, but she'd wanted to. No man had ever given her flowers. To be exact, no man had ever given her flowers that she'd accepted. It was such a basic thing, to get all squee about a simple bouquet, but she really loved them. They were going to be so pretty on her bedroom dresser. And every time she saw them, she'd be reminded that this man had maybe done more for her over the years than any other person, save her family.

And he'd given her something else she hadn't thought a man was capable of. *An apology.*

What did Ross mean by all this? Was he trying to get something started with her? She didn't know what to think. And then there was the issue of the hex. What if all this makeover business had to do with that? Could she stand it if she kissed him, and then he looked at her all blank, like Martinez? No, probably not...

But she couldn't dwell on that now. Her work wouldn't wait for her to sort her shit out. She'd promised Hunter she'd get the flames and pinstriping on the side of this custom Studebaker finished before three, before the party preparations started. She'd transferred the outlines last Friday so it would be quick work to get this done. She pulled down one of her extra-small paint nozzles and hit the spray valve, but it coughed and sputtered. She bent to check it, only to have it blast a giant glob of sticky paint right in the center of her sweatshirt. *Dammit!*

Luckily, she'd worn a thin thermal underneath, so she peeled it over her head and stalked off, muttering, to find two buckets—one for her shirt, and another for soaking her paint nozzles, which were obviously crusty as crap. Why the heck hadn't she checked it before she'd started? It wasn't like her to forget an important step like that. She ground her teeth. What else was she going to drop or ruin because she was all rattled by a man?

And now she couldn't do anything for another hour while the nozzles soaked. While she waited, she decided she'd paint an extra backdrop for the holiday party they were planning for their foster families. Surely it would be dry before the kids arrived, excited for their visit from Santa.

This party was her favorite event all year, and her backdrops, painted on simple muslin suspended by a scaffold, made the magic happen. This year's event was "winter wonderland" themed. Which was perfect, because they still had the twinkling LED lights and enormous origami snowflake spinners from Hop and Lila's wedding a couple years back.

But as she considered the finished backdrop sheets, she did some mental math. This event had gotten bigger every year. Would there truly be enough scenery to go around? Did she want to take a chance that there wouldn't be? A freeform art project might be exactly what she needed to get her mind back in the game today. One more ten-foot sheet. She could do that. She had stencils and could paint on some simple trees and snowflakes with her rollers in the time it'd take for those nozzles to unclog.

Lita trotted off to one of Holliday Hot Rod's many storage rooms—the one that had become reserved for their fabrics, leathers, trims, and the scattered seats and springs from more than a few interior carcasses. She flipped on the dim, flickering overhead bulbs, and propped open the door, hoping to get more light in this windowless space. She couldn't help but stand there in the doorway, shaking her head.

The old rule that "stuff expands to fill the space it's

given" couldn't be more true here. Hunter often referred to this dusty old hidey hole as "her" room, because it housed the materials she needed to do her work. But lately, the floor had become a magnet for everybody else's clutter—unopened deliveries, interior parts ordered for projects to be done in the next year, vintage auto advertising, and gas pump tops—you name it. She had to squeeze past a mountain of crap to get to her organized fabric shelves.

But after a quick inspection, she realized those were disorganized too. When Hop had offered to put away her muslin rolls the other day, he'd put them on top of the pile on the very tippy-top shelf—easily twelve feet in the air. Somewhere they had a ladder that tall, but she didn't have the first idea where the guys had put it.

Luckily, it was only one thing she needed, and she was good at climbing. She'd have to get up there and get it, that's all.

In no time, she'd scaled the layers of shelving and made it to the top. With one hand wrapped around the top shelf and her toes wedged on one of the shelves below her, she barely grabbed the end of the roll. She locked her fingers around the muslin and yanked. And yanked. Ugh. It was caught on something, probably one of the rolls above it. She reached out wide, dangling out far enough to give it one honkin' almighty pull.

And then—*oh, shit!* Everything slipped.

Her feet.

The roll. The pile of rolls on top of it.

Her hands.

Her body...everything tumbled down as if she were in slow motion. She screamed, and grabbed at the air, and tried to throw her hands out. But she just fucking fell, bouncing over boxes until she finally toppled right down into the bottom of one.

Ugggggghhhhh. So *this* wasn't humiliating at all. She was quiet for a second. Something soft had hit her back. Batting, maybe? She laid there, silently checking herself. No sharp pains, only a dull ache from where her arm had hit the side of a box, or whatever it was she'd fallen into. She could barely see anything but a small sliver of light. And it seemed about four feet away. Squirming, she realized she was in one hell of a position—bent in half at the middle, butt first like this damn tubular mailing crate was trying to deliver her breech.

Lita tried to bend her legs underneath her so she could stand up, but she was sandwiched in place. There was no way she was getting out of here without help. A spike of adrenaline curdled into panic. She struggled and rattled around. Nothing worked. She started screaming again, but this time, she was screaming Ross' name.

It only took a second before she heard the drumbeat of Ross' footsteps. "Lita!" he called, sounding about as panicked as she felt. "My God, girl! What happened?" He paused. "Where'd you go? Are you on the ground?"

"No!" she hollered and banged around in the box as much as she could.

Soon she saw his grinning face, blocking the last shard of light. And she heard the sound of the storeroom door shutting with a decisive click.

"Great!" Lita yelped. "Now you let the door shut. I had it propped! We won't be able to see crap now!"

Ross snorted. "Sorry. I wasn't watching. I must've kicked the wedge. But hey, I got enough overhead light to see you're folded up like a letter in there. How in the *hell* did you—"

"Fitting into small spaces, Ross." She sighed. "It's one of the many problems of going through life snack-sized!"

He gave her a comical leer. "Maybe not snack-sized as much as fun-sized—"

"Would you stop it!" she groused. "This isn't funny!"

"It kinda sorta is." He snickered, then stopped himself, his eyes going round. "I mean, you're not hurt, right?"

"No. Just embarrassed."

"Aww, c'mon, Lee," he drawled. "If you can't be embarrassed in front of me, who can you be embarrassed in front of? Alright now, let's see if we can get you out of there."

As this box was already stacked on top of other boxes, Ross carefully tilted it to the side. They debated about whether he should go get a box cutter, but she was wedged so tight, he was afraid he'd hurt her if the knife slipped. He tried and failed to tear through the reinforced cardboard. So, Ross simply grabbed her hands and feet and started yanking and tugging and pulling. Lita found if she flattened herself out as much as she could, things went faster.

When she finally unfolded herself, Ross was there to help her down to the last square foot of open floor. He grabbed her by the waist and lifted her easily, even from his awkward position. In this tightest of spaces, she slid down his body, inch by hot, hard inch, until the balls of her feet met the concrete.

They were pinned, hemmed in by the boxes. Outside, the storm was really kicking up. The wind howled, and rain and ice slapped against the metal roof, sounding ominous. The lights swayed a bit and flickered. Ross wrapped his arms around her reflexively. And just like that, the last of the dim overhead lights fluttered off.

"Damn," he muttered. "There goes the power."

That was the understatement of the year. Getting out of here was going to be a minefield now. It was so dark in this room, you couldn't see your hand in front of your face. Of course, the only thing in front of her now was Ross' pecs.

Then they heard it. A faint beeping, and the decisive sound of metal tumblers locking into place. They both swore under their breath. Because they both knew what that sound was.

Lita tipped her head against his chest. "That's the door, isn't it?"

"Yep," Ross let out a rueful chuckle. "'Fraid so."

Because of all the big trees around here, power outages weren't all that uncommon. Since Holliday Hot Rods was so huge, Hunter couldn't afford a generator that would run the whole place. But Hop, security fanatic that he was, had wired up a smaller generator that went only to the security systems. This room stored parts and other valuables, so it'd been one of the first to arm. There was no way they were getting out of here until Hunter and Hop came back from their supply run. That could be minutes. Or that could be a couple of hours.

"I guess we're stuck," Lita said.

"Looks like it."

"Together."

"You say that like it's a bad thing, Lee."

She didn't have to see the sexy grin on his face. She could hear it in the warm, wry amusement in his voice and sense it as his stubbly cheek rasped across her forehead. Suddenly, she was too aware of the steadying hands he held on her hips. Of the way his face tilted toward hers and his thumb drew lazy circles on her hipbones.

So, she did what she normally did. She shoved at him. Playfully, of course. Like it was all a big joke, and she wasn't pressed right up against single ripple and plane of his body. But he didn't budge. He couldn't. The space was too tight.

She shoved at him again, and he laughed, a low, sexy chuckle. "You're enjoying this, aren't you!" she growled.

"Aren't you?"

"Oh, come on. This flirty-flirt business is your play, isn't it? The same schtick you've been rolling out in every bar in the tri-state area, dog."

There was a long pause. "You keep calling me that."

"Yeah, well, you telling me your reputation with the opposite sex isn't earned?"

"I'm telling you it's not true. Well, okay, it *is* true. But not anymore. Ask me how long it's been since I've had a woman in my bed, Lita."

She wanted to know. But she didn't want to know, or... didn't *like* that she wanted to know.

Ross didn't like the silence, apparently. He pushed her hips up against his and nuzzled her hair, her ear. She was a little shocked at that, that he'd be so bold. But she was more than shocked. She was turned on. The tickle of his breath on the nape of her neck made her all trembly inside, dammit. And she could tell, it was getting to him too. His body heat bellowed against her. And he was getting hard, harder...

"Ask me, Lita," he whispered.

Her breath tangled in her throat, and though she knew she probably shouldn't be, she was completely lost in this moment. In the crack of the storm outside. In his smoky, spicy scent and the possessive way he cradled her.

She...she nuzzled him back, drinking in his scent like a drug.

"Ask me!" he insisted, curling his fingers around her ass.

"How-how long?" she finally managed to get out.

"Almost a year now." He ran the flat of his hand up the column of her back, slowly, then down again. "Can you believe it?"

"No," she breathed, and bit her lip to keep from moaning.

"It's true. I ran out of steam. One day, I was banging any

girl who'd have me. And the next, I realized I wanted something more."

"Like what?"

"Like *this*. Like you." His voice sounded rough. Like it'd cost him something to admit it.

For one hot second, she was right there with him but then...nah. She shook her head. "You don't want me, Ross. It's the hex talking. Like it is for every other guy in town."

"Fine then." He wrapped his big hand around the back of her neck and tilted her head up. "Kiss me. And not some half-assed peck, either. Really kiss me."

Whether it was from the authority in his hold, or the way he laid it out there, her body reacted. Pure fire rolled through her, just thinking about it. She shifted against him, and her hardened nipples grazed his chest.

"Come on, Lee," he whispered. He ran his thumb along her bottom lip, dragging it hard enough to make her realize how plump they were right now. How sensitized. "There's only one way to find out if I'm hexed or not."

Maybe she was the one who was losing her mind right now. Because her knees started to shake again, and she couldn't stop herself from doing the one thing she shouldn't. The thing her whole body was screaming at her to do. She nipped at the tip of his finger, drew it into her mouth, and sucked.

A shocked hiss left his lips. Then a trembling groan. "Ahhh...*fuck* me."

And then they were kissing. Lita wasn't sure who moved first. But it had been like two pieces of a magnet, snapping tight when you held them too close together. An irresistible force. His mouth tasted like morning coffee and sugar, sweetness and sin. And she wanted it. She wanted him, more in this moment than she'd ever wanted any man.

It shocked her how much. She wanted to rip off his

pants. And hers. Right now. She circled her hands around his taut waist, his meaty back, all the while letting him take and take with his hot, insistent tongue. And then she wormed her fingers underneath that French tuck.

Hot. Smooth. Ross had lasered off his chest hair when he'd covered himself with tat art. He'd told her that much. But as she skimmed the waistline of his low-slung jeans, her fingertips grazed over wispy hair...the beginnings of his treasure trail. It was probably red too. And the images that conjured in her brain made a moan escape her throat. She felt hot all over. Slicked. Way too ready.

Ross broke the kiss. "Shit, Lee." He buried his head in her neck, nipping, sucking. "I don't know what kind of magic this is, but I don't wanna stop."

She didn't, either.

No way was this magic. It felt real. Realer than real. She had no freakin' idea what that meant, but she couldn't stop now. She returned the favor, raking her teeth over the pounding vein in his neck, sucking the smoky sweat from his skin.

He wormed his hand under her shirt and palmed her breast. "Fuck yeah," he groaned. "You feel *so good.*"

She whimpered and squirmed, arching into his hands. She couldn't help it. She let him roll her nipples between his fingers. Let him push his hands underneath her stretchy lace bralette and hold her in his callused palm. She let him tip her against the boxes. And she raised her legs up, opening them, wrapping them around his muscular hips.

He gave her ass a delicious, stinging slap, and she whimpered.

"Hell yeah." He palmed her ass again and rubbed at the spot and did it again, "I've always wanted to do that."

She giggled as he pressed against her, grinding the ridge of his erection right where she needed him. Then he smacked her again. Hard. Lightning bolts shot through her, pure hits of white-hot lust. And they both swore and shook.

And then there was the sound of rattling and beeping. Far away. It seemed too far away to care about as Ross rocked against her, faster. *Harder*.

But then the door swung open. "Hey, guys. You in here?" Hunter called.

The beam from a big mag flashlight hit them square in the face. And she could see Ross fully in the harsh spotlight. The ruddy slashes of color along his cheekbones. The lips she'd kissed until they were red and swollen. The splotches of red on his neck where she'd sucked the blood to the surface. And the patch of tat-covered skin at his waist, still exposed from his hiked-up shirt. They both gave each other shocked, breathless looks and quickly stood to right themselves, smoothing their clothes.

"Over here," Ross croaked.

"What the hell?" Hunter scowled as he climbed over boxes. "How did this place get to be such a frickin' mess? Did you guys get locked in?"

"Yeah, for a minute." Lita sighed, trying her best to sound like it was no big deal. She stood in front of Ross to give him a chance to arrange his shirt and run his fingers through his hair. "Oh man, I'm a mess. I fell from the top shelf while I was trying to get down my muslin. Bounced right down into this box over here, and I couldn't get myself out. Thank God Ross was here. I would've been stuck in there until I died."

When Ross turned around, shirt now pulled down over his bulging crotch, he grinned. "Yeah, that's me. Here I am to save the day."

Lita bit her cheek to keep from laughing at the thread of irony in that statement. She was trying her damnedest to make all this seem legit.

But Hunter, for his part, didn't appear to buy it. The man's eyes darted back and forth between the two of them, and a grin of amazement spread across his face. They were busted. Caught *en flagrante*. If it was even possible, more blood rushed to her cheeks. Both sets. She was still throbbing down there.

"Let's try to refrain from climbing while we've got an ice storm going, okay, Lita?" Hunter sighed as they all started moving boxes to create a path. "Now's not the time for a workplace accident. The storm's gotten pretty bad. They're saying the roads won't be passable for a few hours yet, and damn. The power is out almost everywhere. Downtown is totally down, too. There's so many outages over the whole Eastern seaboard, they say it won't be back on for about two days."

Two days?

The thought took the wind out of her. "Oh, no!" she yelped. "The party! What are we gonna do about the kids?"

"Don't worry about that," Hunter answered her as they all found their way back out into the breakroom. "I've got that one all worked out. The Carnegie Center has a generator and they agreed to let us host it on their stage tonight. So don't worry about painting any extra backgrounds, Lita. I called in favors at a couple of local churches, and they're arranging for parishioners with SUVs to go pick up the invited families who can't get out. It's gonna work out. Many of those families will need to spend the night in heated shelters anyway, so this will give them a nice night of entertainment before they have to bed down for the evening."

Bedding down. *Ugggggh.* In a flash, it occurred to her that the power had to be down at her apartment. The thought of shivering through the night in a dark apartment with Pansy and Moose didn't do much for her mood.

Hunter must've seen her scowling. His face lit with understanding. "Oh, wait. Neither one of you has warm place to sleep tonight, do you?"

She and Ross shook their heads.

"Ross, your parents, do they have power?" Hunter asked. There was no need to ask about her mom and J. They'd already shut down the shop and had gone to stay with Lita's sister Rosario in Virginia for a few days. And both of their houses were within walking distance of Main Street. There was no hope of them being warm, either.

Ross checked his phone. "Nope. My parents have piled in with Tiff. It's a full house over there. Mom and Dad and Tiff's in-laws are staying."

Hunter clapped his hands, and then rubbed them together like an evil genius. "It's all settled then. You two are going to get warm, and you're gonna solve all my problems while we're at it. So, as you know, tomorrow I'm flying out with the family to go to Vancouver."

"Right." Lita frowned, not sure where the man was going with all this. "You always go to visit your parents and your brother at Christmas."

"Yeah, and I always hire the Brody kids to come over and feed and exercise our horses. But *their* farm is out of power, even though Kathryn and the kids are nice and warm at ours. The Brody clan decided to decamp to a relative's house in Maryland. And while I totally understand that, they've left us high and dry, literally the day before we have to leave. So here's what we'll do. You and Ross can stay at our house."

"*Us?*" Lita cried.

"Yes *you*." Hunter grinned. "Ross knows horses better than those kids, anyway. I need your help. You need a warm place to stay. It's a true two-person job, but a bit of work at the beginning and the end of the day, and only until we come back on the thirtieth. I'll pay you, even. Surely you two can figure out a way to peacefully coexist under my roof for two hundred dollars each, can't you?"

Lita looked at Ross. And he looked back at her.

Two hundred dollars. She could sure use it. That was a whole lot of airbrushed tchotchkes she wouldn't have to make.

But then she'd be there, in Hunter's gorgeous house, with way too many big, fluffy, empty beds. With the new, improved, totally fuckable Ross—a man she barely recognized, no matter how honest that makeout session had felt.

And that was a problem. Because there was no way to be one-hundred-percent sure he wasn't hexed until after New Year's Day. He said he wasn't—but if he was, would he even know? Maybe the woman had put a different spell on him than the other guys. It had kinda sounded like that, at the time. Oh shit, maybe the spell made him want her.

But Pansy had said he'd always wanted her. And the way he'd smacked her ass just a minute ago...

This was so damn confusing, she wanted to scream.

But before she could tell Hunter no or make up an excuse, Ross answered, "I'm down." He hadn't hesitated. And now Ross wasn't taking his eyes off her, waiting to see what she'd say.

Lita paused. She shouldn't do this, if for other reason than she didn't know jack about horses. And then there was the issue of her own self-preservation. But her only other warm nearby alternative was a hotel, and she sure couldn't afford several days in one of those. It wouldn't be right to take one of those limited slots in the warming center, either, if she had other options.

So, she was going to give in, you know, because it was the right thing to do. She was *totally* being a civic-minded citizen.

164

"Okay," Lita found herself saying.

Hunter grinned at the two of them, like he'd executed some kind of master plan. And Ross grinned right back at the man.

Lita wondered what she'd gotten herself into.

The butterflies in her stomach were telling her she was about to find out.

CHAPTER 15

"You know, you really did make a very cute elf." Ross grinned at her.

"Ugh," Lita grunted. "A little too cute, I think."

Ross cackled. "Hey, it was your idea for the free kissing booth."

She plopped the empty cooler on the floor of the storage barn at the Holliday farm and threw up her hands. "All I can say is, it seemed like a good idea at the time."

And it had been. The party had been a big success, in spite of the weather. Maybe even because of the weather, because those families had been so grateful to have a warm, welcoming, Christmassy way to ride out an ice storm. In a funny way, the event couldn't have been better timed.

The kissing booth idea, though, had been a bear to manage, even if it was her best strategy for un-hexing the male population.

"You had some real characters standing in line, didn't you?" Ross grinned. "Holy smack, did you see the look on that one old man's face? I swear, when he saw you standing there I thought we were gonna have to break out the defibrillator. He was pretty wound up, you know?"

Lita snickered. "Oh, him? He was one of the great-grandpas of one of our client families. He told me he was ninety-eight, and he wanted me to call him Grandpa Sexypants."

"Hmmm. I think I like that. In fifty years, will you call me Grandpa Sexypants?"

Lita hip-bumped him on the way back to the car. "Don't press your luck, Mason."

While Lita did love sticking a pin in Ross' ego from time to time, secretly, she enjoyed his sly humor and easy laugh. And right now, he was one of the few people she could confide in about the hex, and how much it was freaking her out.

Ross may be teasing her about the kissing booth, but he'd been supportive tonight, and a big help too, lining up all the single guys and making sure they didn't get out of hand before she could give them their "antidote" kisses. And all of them, to a one, had been totally fine after she'd given them their peck on the cheek. Ross had seen to it, leading most of them away with the promise of free spiked tipsy cake for the adults. It was one of the main reasons the event had ended up so nice.

Like some kind of miracle, they'd managed to throw the event together in record time. They'd hung all the backdrops and the origami, and one of the local church organizations had brought in big plastic tubs filled with the fixins for holiday dinners. Holliday Hot Rods had organized all the sponsors for the gifts and—with Hopper dressed up in a red suit—Santa Claus. Lila had been Mrs. Claus, of course, while Lita'd been happy to play elf, helping to get all the right gifts to the right kids. They'd had sandwiches, hot chocolate, and Christmas cookies. Fifty-two families had been helped, and together, they'd managed to dish out a heaping helping of holiday spirit, even when the town was covered in two inches of ice.

And here at eleven o'clock at night, she and Ross were still at it, unpacking the last of the tables and party gear into the Holliday farm storage shed until this time next year. Lord, she was footsore, backsore, and headsore, in equal measures—the natural byproduct of taking on the organization of this party every year. She'd been working on it for weeks, so it wasn't exactly so surprising. But with Ross here, she'd had someone to decompress with. Someone who understood how she'd put her heart into it.

It was...*nice*.

Still, she worried that Ross was too affected by whatever Christmas magic she was throwing off. He'd been shooting her adoring looks all afternoon, and a couple of times, he'd acted like he wanted to drag her off into a dark corner again for more illicit nookie. If she were honest with herself, he probably wouldn't have had to do much in the way of dragging. She'd have found a closet, locked the door, and handed him the key.

But their situation wasn't nearly that simple, was it? He wasn't just some guy. He was *Ross*. Probably her closest friend, if she stopped to think about it, because all her girl-friends from high school had moved away.

Maybe that's why it all seemed so odd, so out of the blue. And with all the strange manipulations going on in their lives, how could she really be sure of anything that was going on?

She couldn't.

Had she been manipulating Ross this afternoon? Was she still doing it now? What magic was it? Maybe if she just kept watching him, she'd find a clue, like she had with Martinez. She already knew it wasn't the same spell the other guys were dealing with. But it had to be something.

There was no way he'd be this sweet, this romance-y and attentive. It wasn't him.

Lita glanced up and found Ross lingering his gaze over her again, like she was the answer to all his prayers or something. It made her tingly all over, dammit.

Then he came up behind her and began massaging the knots in her shoulders.

Again with the Mr. Perfect thing. The man was doing an amazing job too, even though he'd have to be at least as tired as she was. After all, he'd hauled more stuff. *Gah. Those hands of his.* They were everything. Somehow he'd magically found the knot at the base of her neck and loosened it right on up. She moaned with relief as the stress rolled off her shoulders.

"You know," he crooned, leaning right up in her ear, "stick with me, and you could get lifetime rights to Ross' magic back rubs."

She definitely didn't hate that idea right now. But *lifetime rights?* What was that boy smokin'? In her experience, Ross Mason never talked "lifetimes" with anyone, let alone her. Another clue he wasn't quite himself. She slid out from underneath his fingers. "Yeah sure, buddy," she answered him. "That's a great offer, but we've gotta get our cars put away for the night. We should probably cover them up too, in case the ice storm decides to make another reappearance."

She started to walk back to her car, but Ross stepped into her path. For the second time today, he grabbed both her hands in his. "I want you to know, Lita, how much I admire all the work you've done over the years, putting this event together," he told her. "Holliday Hot Rods couldn't have pulled off all this without you leading the effort. You really are an amazing, accomplished woman. And one of the most beautiful souls I've ever met. It's time you knew that."

Beautiful soul? Ross had started off the day with flowers, and now he was ending it getting all flowery again? She started to laugh, since it was such a romancey thing for Ross to say. But as she studied his face, she could see he really meant it. That he felt it, way deep down.

And that, of course, had to be yet more evidence. She pulled her hands from his grasp. "I think we need to take a minute to talk about that incident we had in the storage room earlier."

"Oh, honey," he drawled. "I think it *way* more than an incident."

"And that's the problem!" she insisted, throwing her hands up. "We're going to be stuck here in this house for, what—about eight days? We need to learn how to act professional around each other. Just because we're here doesn't mean the rules don't still apply."

Ross raised an eyebrow. "What rules?"

"We're friends, Ross. And that shouldn't change."

He slammed down the lid of his trunk. "Who said that was going to change?"

"Nobody!" she retreated behind the driver's side door on her old Dart. "It's that you keep pushing and giving me these looks and—"

Before she could even finish the thought, Ross had rounded the side of her car and was standing on the other side of the door. "Hey." He leveled her with a very direct, very determined gaze. "I see where you're going with this. This isn't hex business. You're not manipulating me. And I'm not manipulating you. Nothing's going to happen here that you don't want. That you don't *ask* for. Do you understand me?"

Lita could only see his outline in the ambient headlight.

But she didn't need to see his face to understand what he was saying. The force of it. The meaning. The sincerity, maybe. "I get it," she said.

And she did. The fluttery feeling in her stomach told her so. So did her heart, which was pounding awfully hard all of a sudden. She wanted so bad to believe all these sweet things he was saying.

Would it be so terrible if she did, just until she could figure all this mess out? Maybe he could get his real emotions out. Maybe she could figure some things out about him, while she was trying to figure things out about the spell the woman cast.

Or maybe Ross could wake up on January second and forget everything, like Martinez. She shuddered.

She sat down in the driver's seat and buckled herself in, not knowing *what* to do.

He tapped on the window. "Drive safe now. The road up to the main house has a twist in the end that's more slippery than you expect."

Right. And that was a helluva metaphor for her life right now. Smiling at his overprotectiveness, she drove up to the top of the hill, powered over the slippery patch with her snow chains, and parked in the graveled off patch Hunter usually reserved for guests. She went around to her trunk, pulled out her cover, and carefully tucked it over her car. Wouldn't want anything to happen to the paint, after all. Ross was doing the same.

He grinned at her, of course.

Lita had been to the Holliday homestead dozens of times over the eight years she'd worked for Hunter. But somehow, she'd never been at Christmas time. All lit up at night, the place was magnificent. A red brick Victorian farmhouse with copper turrets, windows transomed with stained glass, and a wraparound porch, Kathryn had decorated the house to enhance every architectural detail. Swags of lighted garland laced the spindled porch railings, and multicolored lights blinked from wreaths that were hung on every window. A ten-foot yard sign saying "Alleluia" twinkled on the front lawn in crisp white lights, flanked with lighted straw angels blowing long trumpets. With the house's commanding location on this hilltop, it could probably be seen a mile or two away.

Lita and Ross entered the house together and found the place far more hushed than usual. It was late, and Hunter's sons were nowhere about.

Kathryn padded down the steps to greet them, managing to be elegant even in a long blue night robe and fuzzy slippers. Her short blond hair was never out of place, and her slight, willowy form gave her an effortless grace. Lita admired Kathryn for her ability to take everything in stride. The woman radiated calm and competence, even though she had such a busy life as a mom and a psychologist at the local veteran's hospital. She must be ready for a break in Vancouver, and some grandparent coverage with the kiddos.

"Where are the little guys?" Lita asked her.

"Asleep, thankfully. They're getting busier every day." She smiled. And they were. Her son from her first marriage, Wilson, has his twelfth birthday last month, and Ethan, her son with Hunter, was three. "Wilson put his brother to bed while we were at the party. They both need their rest before we travel tomorrow."

"I'm sure you do too. We'll get out of your hair," Ross said. "Will it wake anyone up if I take a shower before bed?"

Kathryn told him that was fine and filled him in on where to find the guest bath, towels, and such. Saying she was hitting the hay too, Kathryn directed Lita to drop her duffel in the bedroom at the opposite end of the hall from the master. Ross made his way up the stairs, and so did Kathryn, but not before she'd showed Lita how to run the complicated tv remote in the living room.

Lita had asked to watch tv by herself. It'd been one hell of a day, and she was still punchy and restless.

The Christmas lights were on full blast—all on timers until one in the morning, as Kathryn had shown her. Lita found herself walking around the room, checking out every detail and appreciating the graphic design of it all. The room had balance. The Christmas quilt hanging on the wall over the couch balanced the weight of the enormous live Christmas tree in the corner, covered with old-fashioned tinsel icicles. The oversized snow globe was the right visual anchor for the coffee table. While warm colors graced the walls throughout most of the house, Kathryn had pickled the original beadboard paneling in this family room, and a new barn red and blue hooked rug graced the floor. Together with the craftsman furniture in this room, it was all very Americana chic.

A couple more years. A couple more years, and she'd have enough of a down payment for a place of her own. Maybe one of those old, dilapidated farmhouses she'd been eyeing for years. Something with history. Something she could call her own, and fix up with her own artistic vision. No friggin' beaded curtains or bongs in sight. And her own Christmas tree, someday...

Yeah, she could definitely get inspired in a place like this. Maybe hanging out here for a few days wouldn't be so bad after all.

Lita stretched out on the couch, fanned her hair out over the quilted Christmas pillows, and started scrolling through the offerings. Classic Christmas movies. Superhero cartoons. Documentaries on Irish history. HGTV house makeover shows. All of them were things that would interest her on a normal day. Yet, somehow, none of them seemed quite right. And even her go-to, all-purpose choices like *Rust Valley Restorers* or *The Great British Baking Show* didn't appeal.

Finally, she scrolled through a couple of the sweeter channels. Maybe a Christmas romance might be more her speed today. She clicked through the queue of new releases, all of them darling confections like "Christmas with the Prince" or "Love on Holly Mountain" or some such. Normally, these adorable films were the perfect feel-good fare for her, as comforting as a warm blanket and a cup of hot cocoa. An escape into a total fantasy, where the women were the right amount of pixie hot mess, the men were strong and worthy, and everything always worked out in the end.

Except that wasn't how it worked out, was it? Real life wasn't like that. People were complicated. Men weren't always strong. Women weren't always cute. Sometimes they changed roles. Sometimes they never conformed in the first place.

Sometimes they lied, and didn't keep their promises, and hurt you, on the regular. The only way to ensure your happiness was to build it for yourself.

At least, that had been her experience, anyway. Lita stopped and caught herself. Was that really true? It wasn't like she didn't have examples of true love around her. Rosie and Darius. Hunter and Kathryn. Hopper and Lila. Ross' parents. And Uncle J and Jim. Who wouldn't want a marriage like those two had? They'd worshipped the ground each other walked on for nigh on twenty years now.

So maybe it was just her then. She was the one who couldn't seem to pick the right ones. Yeah, in her world, there weren't any meet cutes, or any royal hotties or randy billionaires waiting to take you to the Christmas ball. Hell, she'd been living in a small mountain town half her life. She'd yet to find a charming lumberjack that made her want to revisit her life choices because he knew how to shake her tree.

Unless that lumberjack happened to be a certain red-headed mechanic...

She shut off the tv with a disgusted click. Clearly, this wasn't going to help her wind down enough to get to bed. Or get that crazy whatever-that-was with Ross out of her head. And she most definitely needed to stop thinking about that.

Definitely.

Like, *right now*.

Because that thing between them in the storage room? It'd been magically fueled insanity. A total fluke, right? Yeah, he'd said some things. Words that had made it sound like she was some kind of prize to him. But she'd been right there rubbing up against him. And she knew from experience, T and A could make a man say anything.

Or more likely, it was Ross reverting to type. How many times would he be with her? Once? Twice? Enough to end his dry spell, probably. Maybe since they were such good buds, they'd make it to four or five times before he pretended like it didn't happen. Like it was no big deal.

And she was done being disposable. So. Fuckin'. Done. An image of Cam on the floor with that girl swam in front of her eyes for a second, and she cringed from her head to her toes. Honestly, how could she have been so stupid? It wasn't even that she'd been in love with the guy. Far from it. But people had seen the two of them around town together, like they were a thing. And she'd felt so...so *disrespected*. The thought of that happening to her with Ross, of all people, was really more than she could handle.

So she wasn't going to think about how Ross had felt up against her. Or the way those magic hands...

No. She grimaced, willing those fantasies back into their corners.

Have some self-respect, chica.

And besides, hadn't Hunter asked her and Ross to meet him at the barn at seven a.m. to discuss the horses? She needed her sleep. Deep, sound, man-free sleep.

Grumbling, she took her shoes in one hand and padded up the curving walnut staircase in her stockinged feet. When she got to the top step, she stilled. Because the old Victorian handle rattled on the bathroom door at the end of the hall. And Ross emerged in a cloud of steam, wearing nothing but a towel.

Her grip tightened on the stairway finial, and just like that, her heart was pounding right out of her chest. And she'd only looked at the guy.

If she was a better person, she'd cover her eyes. Really, she should. But she wasn't sure she was even capable of blinking right now.

Oh yeah, Ross might be putting on the greatest show on earth, and he didn't even know it. It was dark in the hall, but thanks to the generous bank of windows along the staircase, the moon bathed him in light. And never, maybe in the history of men, had a body ever been better suited to a moon bath.

Dulce Jesús, sálvame...

His pale, smooth skin glowed like an alabaster statue. Like he'd been hewn by the masters of the Renaissance. And those tats...

They were a miracle of shadow and light. All black and grayscale, fine-grained outlines and exquisite shading work. She'd only seen them in bits and pieces. He'd shown them to her one at a time as he'd gotten them done, usually a brief glimpse as he'd lift up one of his baggy shirts.

But the effect of them all together took eye candy to a whole new level. On his chest was a spiral staircase covered with vines and flowers that went straight up his middle from his belly button to the hollow between his pecs. It ended in an anatomically correct heart. On the top of his right hand was a clock face, all distorted, like it was warped through space-time. When he leaned back in to kill the bathroom light, she saw the whole timey-wimey system it was connected to. His right shoulder was draped with a melting clock face that looked like it had dripped down his arm and landed on top of his hand.

She grinned in the darkness. It didn't get more surrealist than that, did it? All together like that, they were the most beautiful, artfully designed tats she'd ever seen in her life, done by a nationally known surrealist tattoo artist Tank had recommended in Washington, D.C. With world-class ink like that, Ross should be walking down Main Street shirtless every chance he got.

Yet, Ross had always acted a bit circumspect about his tats. Never had he taken his shirt off in her presence, not even at the shop, in the blazing summer heat. She'd always assumed he'd been trying to be respectful and promote a healthy, harassment-free work environment. But some-where in the back of her mind all these years, she'd wondered if maybe it was only her that he was shy around. That he felt like he had to hide himself under all those too baggy clothes, because he thought he was too thin, or somehow "not enough."

If he had, it was a damn shame. Because *she* hadn't thought that. But she hadn't exactly let it come up for discussion, had she? She'd never given the boy even a sliver of an opening. Until today. If Hunter hadn't walked in, she wouldn't have been able to stop herself. She was that far gone.

Now here she stood, ready to act on all her worst impulses. She desperately wanted to tiptoe back out of sight again, but it felt like little elves had stapled her socks to the stairs. And anyway, before she could move, Ross spotted her.

His eyes were round as he locked his gaze with hers, and he froze for a second. But as Ross searched her face, his shoulders loosened, and he rubbed his hand over his mouth. A wild grin played at the corner of his lips as he sauntered over to the banister and leaned his arms on the railing.

Oh, shit.

"Evenin', Lita. Out for a stroll?"

Lita kicked up her chin, determined not to let her screaming ovaries get the better of her. *"I'm* going to my room, Ross, while *you're* parading around naked in the hall."

"Pardon me. I didn't pack my silk robe." His grin widened. "But you knooooowwww, if I didn't know better, I'd swear you were over here, hiding in the shadows like a pervert, happy to watch this parade go by."

She let out a whispered squawk. "I'm not a pervert, Ross!"

"Really?" He unfolded his big frame and stepped a foot down onto the stair pad below hers. His face was right there, right up in her space. "Well now. I stand corrected." He hummed. "Maybe not a pervert. A curious, red-blooded woman, then. Someone who wants to see how low these tats go." He ran a finger down her neck, over the slice of collarbone her shirt didn't cover, making her shiver. "Or maybe a woman who wants to trace them with her finger—" he leaned over to whisper in her ear, "—or her tongue. Or her *teeth.*"

Lita gasped at the contact of his stubble against her cheek and his wet hand around the small of her back.

Gasped, like an idiot.

She barely recognized this man—this confident, sexy Ross. Was this the charm he'd turned on other women all these years, but not her? Or was this something new for him —a bigger risk maybe—putting himself out there like this?

Either way, it was working for her.

Big time.

Heat prickled to the surface of her skin at the closeness of him, every nerve on fire to rub herself up against his hot, wet nakedness. All that concealed his body now was a single tuck in that towel. One flimsy, low-slung towel...she couldn't put the thought of pulling that tuck loose out of her head. Like she had no self control at all. But she did have some, didn't she? She wasn't even one-hundred-percent sure why at the moment, but she had to find it.

She put a staying hand on his slippery chest, and Ross stopped there, hovering. His heart hammered under her hand, the little tremor under his skin telling her he wasn't the cool, controlled player he was pretending to be. He was shaking like a leaf. So was she.

And what that meant, she had no idea. But she knew she'd better get out of here before she pinned the guy to the stairs with her body or something.

She pushed herself back a bit and saw he was flushed again—a fact she could see even in the moonlight. His eyes burned with flat out, full on desire. But there was a tinge of vulnerability there, a thread of honesty in his expression that moved her. Captured her. And made saying no almost physically painful.

Lita swallowed against her dry throat. "We-we have to be up for the horses tomorrow," she finally managed.

"Yeah..." He nuzzled her ear again and slid his hand on her hip. "But think how much better you'll sleep when—"

"*Ross,*" she cut him off, "please..."

The sound of warning in her voice was enough to make his smile dim. He gave her a slow, respectful nod and moved out of her way. She hurried by before she changed her mind. When she got to her bedroom door, he called out her name in a half whisper.

She spun around.

He opened his mouth, like he might say something else. But then he paused and gave her a wave instead. "Good night, Lee. Sleep tight."

"Good night." She nodded. "See you in the morning."

Lita slid into her bedroom, closed the door, and braced herself against the wall, trying to calm the *just-do-him hormones* that had hijacked her system.

Yeah.

It wasn't working.

This was going to be a long, hard Christmas.

CHAPTER 16

LITA SHOVELED out the last forkful of hay and wiped her forehead, wondering how she'd ever gotten so out of her element. She didn't have the first clue how to deal with horses and found them kinda scary, to be honest.

A big horsey nose nudged her from behind, confirming her notions. The beast had sent her hopping forward a foot.

"Hey, do you mind?" she told Starlight, Hunter's massive black bay.

The horse snorted, brushing her aside as he got to his hay.

Ross chuckled at that as he rounded the side of the barn.

"Oh sure, laugh it up, country boy," she called. "Not all of us got to grow up around these enormous, muscular, smelly—"

"Hey now," Ross protested as he ambled up. "Don't insult Starlight. Horses understand every word you say." He walked right up to the horse, patting its neck affectionately, and it nickered. "You're not smelly, are you, girl? Nawww, of course you're not."

Lita clucked her tongue. "Yeah, right. If it's not the horse, where's that ferocious stink comin' from?"

Ross shrugged sheepishly. "Oh, yeah. That's my bad. That's the manure pile you're smelling."

"The-the *what?*"

Ross cackled. "You see, Lita, when a half-ton animal eats, eventually they have to—"

"Would you stop it?" She hit him on the arm. "I know what manure is! Why is there a pile? And why didn't it smell like this when we were with Hunter this morning?"

"What do you think I've been doing out here all day? I've been going through the pastures picking up manure. Cleaning things up. Making it nice. Hunter has a manure box going already, and he uses it for all kinds of projects around the property. He'll need all that come spring."

Lita shook her head fondly at the man. Horse patty service hadn't been on Hunter's list of instructions for the week. But that was Ross, always going over and above for the people in his life. The man loved farm work—something he'd learned at his father's knee.

She'd envied him, really. She'd felt totally out of her depth this morning when Hunter had gotten them up at the butt-crack of dawn, handed them both some strong coffee, and had gone over everything the horses would need. She hadn't been prepared for it. The mucking. The raking. The brushing. The saddle polishing. The hoof picking. The feed. The exercise. Where they could and couldn't graze. How to work the solar array that kept the water trough from freezing up. She should've asked for more than two hundred for all this. Her back was aching already.

Stumbling through the chores with Ross this morning had been, well...a chore. But he'd gone all "thank God I'm a country boy" on her and had decided to stay outside with the animals. She'd opted to make herself useful by hitting the store for any special food they'd want that Hunter didn't already have. She'd wrapped Christmas presents, his included, which he'd brought along to give to his family. He was shit at wrapping, and he always admired the way she hand-decorated paper with her own drawings and stamps. She didn't mind.

Lita put away the pitchfork in the paddock tool rack. "While you were piling up horseshit, I was wrapping your presents. And I made you some Texas chili. It's in the crockpot."

He grinned and sidled up to her, leaning on a fence rail. "Aww. You goin' domestic now? Thanks for that. You didn't have to."

She knew she didn't. But she'd wanted to. It was Christmassy and intimate and homey, to do this for him. She'd made him happy. And it was...*nice*. While she was feeling all warm and squidgy about it, she made the mistake of locking eyes with him again. The sparkle of appreciation there drew her in.

But she shrugged off the warmth of that sensation and rolled her eyes. "Well. Don't get used to it." She smirked at him. "Aren't you standing awful close for someone who's literally been slinging crap all afternoon?"

Ross held up both hands. "I'm clean! I swear! I got washed up in the barn sink earlier. See? Even my fingernails are spic and span." When she narrowed her eyes at him, he did a circle. "Come on. If you don't believe me, you're welcome to smell me." He stopped dead in front of her. "Come on. You know you want to."

Lita shook her head at that, and walked back to the barn smiling, but muttering "En tus sueños." *In your dreams.* That boy...

When Ross followed her into the barn, he grabbed the

183

saddle for Kathryn's horse, Wellington, threw the saddle blanket over his shoulder, and started walking out with it.

"Hey, where are you going with that?" she asked him.

"Whaddya mean? I'm saddling her up. I've got the others saddled up too."

"That's obvious. But why? It's the end of the day, and they're in the paddock. Shouldn't we be bedding them down already?"

"Yeah, but we haven't gone on their daily trail ride. Remember what Hunter said this morning? He said if they didn't get their trail ride in before work, he always took them around the property at the end of the day. Last time I checked, it's the end of the day."

Lita's eyes got wide. She couldn't ride a horse and had actively resisted every time he'd begged to teach her. "How do you propose we do that? There's three horses and two of us. And I don't count. You know I'm useless on the back of a horse."

"And we're gonna change that. I'm teaching you how to ride."

Mild panic skittered over her spine. "What? *Now?*"

"Yes, *now*. It couldn't be an easier situation for a new rider. We'll tie all the horses together so we can go single file. The horses will follow my lead. You can learn how to balance and find your seat. Easy peasy."

In all the years he'd known Lita, Ross had always thought of her as pretty fearless. Mouthy. Opinionated. The sort of woman who didn't give a flying fuck what other people thought about her. But right now? She was clearly scared outta her mind.

It was almost cute. She stomped her foot and gave him all kinds of excuses that ranged from a bogus horse allergy

184

to an equally bogus story about a pony ride gone awry when she was little. Finally, he walked over, grabbed her by the waist, and threw her onto Twinkie, a sweet butterscotch pony specifically for Hunter's boys.

She bitched and complained and tried to cry off, but he'd saddled that horse up for her, and he wasn't gonna let her get out of it.

He stood in the way of her dismount. "You're gonna sit there and tell me that you, a grown woman, are afraid to ride the same horse that Hunter's kids ride every day?"

Lita squirmed around in her seat and glared at him. "It's just that I'm so far off the ground. What if she throws me? And I don't know how to do all those things with the reins."

"Don't worry about leading the horse. I'll be doing that from the front. And this horse couldn't be any calmer. Really. Like, grandma calm. Isn't that right, Twink?" The horse nuzzled his neck to prove his point. "See, Lita? Horses want to be your friends."

She growled at him in response, and he knew he'd won this round. She always gave out this growl when she wasn't sure about something but couldn't think of comeback. He hid his grin of triumph as he roped the horses together. He explained that the trail circled this property right on the perimeter and was about one mile for each loop. They'd go around three times. He'd been on this trail before with Hunter. There were a few rocky bits, yeah, but the horses were so familiar with the route they were taking that there shouldn't be any problems.

At least, that was what should've happened.

But as soon they got up the trail a bit, he began to worry this immersion therapy for Lita's horse phobia wasn't working. He kept stealing glances at her. It wasn't pretty.

"You okay back there, Lee?" he called.

"Fuckin' peachy, Ross," she called back.

He tried not to snicker. The poor woman was hunched up over the saddlehorn, clinging on for dear life. He would've stopped. But they were too far out now. "Okay, we're getting ready to go up over a steep stretch. The horse will know what to do. Hold on, okay?"

"Like I'm not?"

He didn't have an answer to that, so he spurred Starlight up over this rocky outcrop. The horse placed every foot right, and he was almost up to the flat hilltop when he heard a shriek from behind him. Twinkie had stepped into a divot at the same time that a possum had scampered out right in front of him.

The horse startled, not rearing exactly, but prancing to the side and tossing his head. Her ears were pinned back. *Oh, no.*

Lita was sliding around in the saddle and losing her grip. Exactly what you *didn't* want to do in this situation—irritating the animal. Then the possum hissed, and the horse jumped up, startled, its front feet leaping a couple of feet up off the ground.

Lita screamed out his name, and his chest tightened with anxiety.

If something happens to her because of me...

Twink wasn't getting any calmer. "Jump off, Lita!" he called, unable to get to her. The pressure on the ropes was starting to upset the other two horses too. She struggled, getting stuck in her stirrups for a second, but she finally managed to swing herself around and jump off. Lita landed hard—too hard—rolling off into the tall grass on the side of the trail.

In a flash he'd dismounted too, kicking the possum out of the way while he grabbed Twink's reins.

Danger now averted, Lita rolled herself to her feet, apparently fine.

"You're okay, right?" he called over to her. "Please tell me you're okay."

She grumbled as she brushed the dirt and weeds from her clothes. "Yeah, no thanks to you. I told you this was a bad idea."

It had been. And he was grateful it hadn't become disastrous. "Come on now, Lee," he shrugged, trying to lighten the mood. "You would've jumped at a hissing possum too."

"From now on, I'm going to stay on my own two feet, thank you very much."

Ross raised his eyebrows at that. "And how do you propose to get back? You'd have to cross a stream on foot and scrabble up those hills."

Lita crossed her arms over her chest, her chin getting that defiant jut that came on right before she'd dig in her heels about something. "Fine then. I'll cut across from one side of the trail to the other. There's no law saying I have to make the loop."

"Yeah. But you'll get lost! It's really dense woods with not even a path. You'll come out lost and covered with briars."

"I don't care. Ross, there is no effin' way I'm getting back on that horse—or any horse—ever again." Her mouth flattened into a thin, determined line. But as they stood there, locked in this standoff, her chin wobbled, and her eyes were too shiny with suppressed tears for his liking.

Holy shit.

She was really, honestly freaked out. And Carmelita Rose Noe was never one to get intimidated. Hell, Lita was just as likely to crawl under an oil pan as she was to tat up a Hell's Angel.

So, in a lot of ways, these reactions didn't seem like her. She was showing an outsized amount of fear for a short jump from a short horse, at least on the Lita scale. She didn't even seem badly bruised.

But a horse wasn't a car, was it? A car you could control. But you only had an illusion of control with a horse, who could spook over anything from a strange shadow to a bullet, and everything in between. And it dawned on him, all at once, that this might be problem. To ride a horse, you had to give up your safety, your control, to another living thing. *Trust.* It all came down to that, didn't it?

She didn't trust the horse.

But she'd trusted *him* enough to let him bully her into this. And now...look at her. His stomach twisted at the thought of what an ass he'd been. He'd pushed and pushed and pushed her. About the horse. About getting physical with him...

He swallowed at the bile rising in his throat. "Jesus, Lee. I'm sorry. I should've never gotten all up in your face about riding like this. I should've listened to you when—"

"Wait." She held up a hand and paused, blinking at him in disbelief. "Did you-did you say the S-*word* again? That's, like, the second time in less than a week!"

Ross shrugged a shoulder at her and stared at the ground. Regret ate at him. And not only for this, either, but for every single bit of dumbassery he'd managed over their entire relationship.

He kept his eyes on the dirt, because he didn't want to tell her the truth—that the hex had taught him something. The tingling and blurting, and shutting down his first, worst reactions. It'd showed him how much he'd used his humor as a shield. He'd been running from his feelings, like some kind of scared little boy. And he didn't want to be a boy. No, everything about Lita made him want to be a man.

All three horses had settled now, so Ross let Twink go. And he stepped right up to Lita, bringing his hands to rest on her shaky shoulders. "Yeah. I said I'm sorry, and I meant it. I've been pushing you to do a lot of things lately. I mean to get better about that, and a lot of other things too. And you know what I need to get better at? Actually teaching you how to ride. Will you give me a chance to do that? You could sit up on the horse with me. I'll be right behind you, showing you what to do. We'll all get back to the barn safe that way. You have my word—if you're still freaked out by the horses after that, I won't ever ask you to get up on one again. Do you think you can do that?"

There was something in the way Lita regarded him right now that made him feel unsteady. Exposed, maybe, like she was trying to find some flaw, or proof that he was shitting her. There wasn't any. And after a long moment, she gave him a miserable nod. "Come on." She sighed. "Let's do this thing."

Smiling now, he led her over to Starlight. The horse was big enough tower over her—about eighteen hands, with the kind of gleaming coat and muscularity that would put Black Beauty to shame. The horse shook his head in acknowledgement as Lita approached, and with a boost to help her get her first foot in the stirrup, she easily climbed up.

Starlight was too big a horse for Lita's short legs. They dangled, Starlight's girth making it difficult for her to get a good grip with her thighs. Fortunately, that was no problem for him. Ross popped up into the saddle behind her, wedged his boots into the stirrups, and settled in.

And he immediately realized he hadn't thought this all the way through. He'd been so concerned about calming Lita down that he hadn't thought about what it'd be like to have Lita's exquisite ass pressed up against him on a rolling, bouncing horse. The fantasy of a lifetime, of a million teenaged and not-so-teenaged jackoffs, was literally right here wedged up against his crotch.

And, like some kind of Christmas gift, she was wearing those thin jeans that fit like leggings. Every last curve and swell was right there, pressing, rubbing. Heat radiated off her skin wherever their bodies met, contrasting against the bite of the wintry wind.

Awww, hell...

Yeah, he was hot alright, and itchy in his layers all of a sudden, like all his senses had been placed on high alert.

Lita looked back over her shoulder at him. "You've gotten awfully quiet back there."

"Yeah, right," he answered her, clearing his throat. "I was trying to figure out the best way to show you how to direct a horse. The only way you're going to get it is if you can learn it, as we do it."

"Okay...?"

He almost laughed at the questioning sound in her voice. "Don't worry. It's simpler than it sounds. First things first." He circled his arms around her and wrapped his hands over hers, holding the reins. "Lesson number one, these reins aren't signals that tell Starlight where to go. They're really more for pulling up, to stop. So don't think you just tap his neck when you want to go right or left. He won't understand that. Steering the horse is something you do with your whole body."

"What do you mean, your *whole body?*"

"Here, let me show you." He splayed a hand flat over her smooth, tight stomach. "There. Now sit up high in your seat, with your back arched a bit, like me." She did as he said, and he took the reins from her. "I want you to put your hands on my thighs now and keep them there. I need to show you something."

Lita snorted. "That's what *he* said."

He chuckled. "Don't tempt me." She slid a hand on each thigh, stabilizing herself. "Okay now, if you want to the horse to move forward, you squeeze with both your thighs, like this, and give the horse a nudge with your feet. Like this."

When the horse began a slow walk, Lita yelped. But she smiled back at him anyway. "That was easy."

Easy. *Right.*

He gritted his teeth. Shit, he was getting harder with every step this horse took. This was getting to him...the whole thing was. The rhythmic sway of Starlight, clip-clopping below them. The way her windswept curls tickled his face. He gave himself a mental shake and tried to focus on how beautiful it was out here to keep himself from getting too wound up.

And it was beautiful. Breathtaking, even. Pine forests rose in neat, fragrant rows all around them—the remnants of when Hunter's grandparents used to run this farm for timber. The ice storm had been a mess, but it'd been a beautiful one out here. The trees glittered like fairy dust, and now, as the sun was just starting to dip low, the ice shimmered with all the reds and pinks and oranges in the sky. Like the heavens above were reaching down to touch them.

But there was no piney mountain's majesty that could take his mind off the heat building between his legs dammit. And it was spreading all over his body. His heart was fucking racing.

He ground his teeth together. *Horse riding. Right.* Wasn't he supposed to be teaching her?

When there was a turn in the trail, he talked her through how to press in one leg and loosen the other. He loosened the rein out on one side, drawing it wide. Starlight of course understood perfectly. And now, so did Lita.

She beamed at him. "I get it! This isn't hard at all!"

"Told you!" He couldn't help grinning back.

She pulled her hands off his legs and grabbed the reins

191

from him. "Okay. Now put your hands on my legs, and make sure I've got it."

Lita pulled up on the reins, and he pulled her back in her seat a bit so Starlight would stop. And then he did what she said. He ran his hands over the sweet, sweet sinews of her leg. She tensed her thighs hard, her muscles coiled to spring under his hands. He slid one hand over her stomach again to check her form, realizing too late that he'd slipped under her fleece instead of over it. His fingertips met bare skin.

But she didn't complain or shrug out of his grasp. No, she sat up taller, pressing everything tighter against him— her ass, her back, her gorgeous, tumbling curls...

She spurred the horse on with a giddy excitement he hadn't seen from her in a long time. "I think I might like this," she squealed. "It's awesome up here—kind of like you're king of the world"

Ross wasn't sure if she'd thought about what she was doing when she leaned forward in her seat to stroke Starlight's neck, but she tipped her ass up and over him, rubbing herself against his rock-hard cock nearly root to tip as she readjusted her position. Then she sat back down, and her breath caught, and she stiffened.

She had to have felt that.

He sure had. For just one second, he'd gotten an up-close-and-personal preview of what it'd be like for her to ride him. The heat. The give of her flesh. The way her ass made this perfect heart shape...

And the way her breath hitched—so much like a moan, it seemed to hang in the icy air all around them. His heart-beat kicked up more, if that was even possible.

He held his breath, waiting to see what she'd do. She didn't say anything, and he closed his eyes, wondering if his body had, once again, sent him over the line with her. Shit, it was so fucking good, it'd made him dizzy, like all the blood in his body was being rerouted to his groin, and away from his brain cells.

That was the only explanation for it. Because if he wasn't mistaken, Lita was loosening up under his hands. Rolling with the horse. With him. And she'd wedged herself tight against him now. *Mercy...*

He teased his hands against the bare skin of her stomach and goosebumps rose under his fingers. God, she was killing him. But she wasn't saying anything.

He wasn't, either. No, Ross hung his head over her shoulder and let the wind whip long, tickling strands of her hair against his face. The scent of almond and jasmine rose from her today, no doubt from the soap Kathryn had left in the shower. It smelled good on her. Too good. It made him want to breathe deep and lose himself...

Losing himself. That's what he was doing, wasn't it? And he wanted to be gone, wanted the world to narrow to this sensation, right now. He dipped his hands lower, over the smooth, thin denim still warmed from the heat of her skin. Lita had definitely found her seat, and the looseness in her lower back that she needed to meld her body to the sway of the horse. He should be proud, but all he could think about was what it would be like to make love to her, and have her rolling over him. He tightened his hand against her, curling his fingers over her hip and nuzzling his face against her neck.

Were they riding? He was glad Starlight knew this path, because he wasn't paying nearly enough attention. His whole focus was on the patch of warm skin here on her neck. Before he'd even made a conscious choice, his mouth had landed there, nipping and sucking, the sweet taste of her making him dizzy again. Because she tasted like everything, all at once, like almond and sweat and flowers and sunshine and the cold winter wind.

Lita's sharp intake of breath echoed in the silence that surrounded them. And so did the quiet, shaky moan that followed it. Her head tipped back against his and now he moaned too, probably a little too loudly, letting it out like the steam out of a boiling kettle.

It didn't seem to bother her. Lita arched against him, like a cat, like she had in the storeroom yesterday, grinding herself against him hard. She wanted him. Any fool could see it. And he sure as shit wanted her. He touched and kissed and nipped, exploring first one side of her silky soft neck, then the other. Around the bend, over the back course, they kept going, his hands roaming over her lithe muscles and Lita leaning into his embrace. The touch of her was like nothing else.

But then the horse stopped.

"We're here," she said. And dammit, the note of surprise in her voice had pulled the plug somehow. The electricity between them sizzled away with a snap.

He found himself sitting there on Starlight, dazed and surprised, too. But it wasn't the fact that they were already back in the paddock. It was the way Lita pushed herself off the horse as fast as she could. No smile, no acknowledgement of what had happened, no waiting for him to help her down. She simply landed on her feet and stomped off to the barn.

He was confused and pissed and, hell, he didn't know what. How was he supposed to take that? Was she mad at him? Had he overstepped?

The sounds of loud, deliberate banging and rattling in the barn answered his question. Annoyance spiked through him. What did that girl *want?* One minute she'd look at him like he was good enough to eat, and another, she'd be all like "we're just friends" and "let's be professional."

And now they were basically making out again and she was...*mad?*

What the hell?

He'd never in a million years want to force himself on Lita. But dammit, he knew her, maybe better than he did anyone else. And he knew full well he wasn't alone in what had happened on the back of that horse. Or in the store-room. Or in the truck. Shit, the electricity between the two of them was so thick you could hardly breathe the air.

And he was sick and fucking tired of pretending it wasn't there.

He followed her to the barn, but she'd walked back out again, stomping around as she carried the brushes back out to the paddock. She unstrapped Twink's saddle, and when he came around the side of the horse to confront her, she simply shoved the saddle in his hands. Shaking his head and grinding his teeth, he dutifully took the saddle back and threw it over the sawhorses where it belonged. When he hustled himself back out again, she shoved Starlight's saddle at him.

When he'd put that away, he grabbed a brush and started working on Starlight. She brushed poor Twink, who was probably getting a way too vigorous rub-down, but the animal wasn't complaining. The only sound was the crunch of their footsteps on the ice and the soft scratch of the brushes.

Finally, he couldn't take it anymore. "Really?" he snapped. "This is what we're doing now? You're not going to talk to me?"

She glared at him and didn't say anything.

And he glared right back, also giving Starlight a probably too-vigorous brushing.

The silence between them snapped tight.

He counted to ten. Then he counted to ten again. Then he tried to think of this from Lita's point of view.

Yeah, no.

He was still pissed. Probably definitely furious. He couldn't say why this thing had made him so upset. Except that the last few minutes had been pretty much the mother of all mixed signals. And he was done, done, done playin' around at the edges. They were gonna face up to this attraction, and name it, and do something about it, one way or another.

By God, after a lifetime of pining after her, Lita was gonna have to tell him whether she wanted him or not.

He stewed on that as he finished up with Starlight, and she put the brushes and equipment back up in the barn. Oh no, this shit was gonna end right here, right now. One way or another. And when she moved to go back outside, he stood in her way and backed her up against the barn wall. "We can't keep doin this."

She'd defiantly met his gaze at first, but then her attention moved to her feet, and she fidgeted. "Doin' what?"

He let out an outraged squawk. "Doin' what? Seriously, *doin' what?* You get me so fucking turned on I've got a goddamn brick in my pants. You let me kiss you. You encourage me. And now you're acting all pissed and won't even acknowledge my presence? This is fifty shades of bullshit, Lee."

She didn't answer him. Couldn't even raise her head up to make eye contact. She got red in the face, all flustered or embarrassed or who knew what. But she still didn't open her mouth.

Wasn't that tough shit? He wasn't leaving this barn until he got an answer. "You wanna tell me what I did wrong?"

Lita bit her lip like she might say something, but she

pushed off the wall and walked around him instead. Or tried to, anyway.

He caught her from behind, wrapping his arms around her waist. "No! It isn't right, you shutting me out like this. This—" He pulled her tight, grinding against her. "This right here. We did this together, Lee! Freely and consensually. And you damn well enjoyed it!"

She growled. "It's not you, okay? It's me. I—"

"Oh, no. Really?" He growled. "After all the years we've known each other, you're gonna give me the *it's-not-you-it's-me* crap? No. I need you to tell me right now. Why the hell does this make you so m—"

"You didn't make me *mad*, okay?" she hollered at him, going rigid under his hands. Her warm breath puffed out in short bursts in the cold air, her chest rising and falling.

He let the quiet hang between them for one beat, two beats, three...

Finally, she let out a disgusted huff. "You didn't make me *mad*," she repeated, this time so hushed and soft, he almost didn't hear it. "You made me *wet*."

There it was.

She said it. No takebacks. No going back to the relationship they used to have—at least, not for her. In a few short days, Ross may not remember this.

But she'd never forget.

She looked over her shoulder to meet his gaze, and what she saw there... *Dios mio.*

A flare of surprise, but then heat. Pure, feral.

Focused. His mouth had fallen open for a second, but he closed it into a thin, determined line. "You want me to do something about that?"

She swallowed against her thick throat and gave him a nod.

"The *words,* Lee. I need to hear the words."

"Yes! *Yes,* okay? I want you to f—"

She didn't get to finish what she was saying, because his mouth was on hers. Hot. Insistent. Devouring. Kissing her like if he didn't, she'd disappear. But she wasn't going anywhere. Not when a man could kiss like this. He backed her up a couple of steps and pinned her against the wall for real this time.

Ross was shaking again. She felt it as she roamed her hands over his back, and wrapped her legs around his hips. His movements were frantic and rushed, like he wanted to do everything, fast and all at once.

Maybe she wanted him to. Hot, tingly excitement surged through her, fueled her, like she was letting out the throttle on a gear she'd never known she had. Her toes curled in her boots as he rocked the long, hard ridge of his erection against her, the denim rubbing her right where she needed him most. One hand curled around her ass, he used his other to cup the back of her neck and tip her face up to his, deepening his kisses with every scorching sweep of his tongue.

She shuddered, wrapping her arms around his neck to get more, faster. This wasn't simply sexy-times kissing. Ross kissed her hard—desperately—like he was mounting an invasion and conquering everything he'd ever wanted.

And she was gonna let him have it. She couldn't help herself.

It was freezing out today, not that she could tell. All she could feel was Ross, tangling his body with hers. Grasping hands and growling moans, hot mouths on heated skin, and their heavy breaths mingled together in the cold air.

She was so dazed, it took her a second to realize Ross

had carried her over to a tall bank of haybales and placed her on her knees, facing away from him. And he was on her then, schooling her in the wisdom of this position, like he had on the horse. She pulled her hair around to the front to give him better access to her neck, and his mouth landed at her nape, sucking hard. And she groaned, not giving a flying fuck that it would surely leave a mark.

He pushed his hand under her fleece again, tweaking her nipples through her sports bra until her breasts felt swollen and heavy in his hands. And then his hand migrated to the waistband of her jeggings, hesitating at the button, as if he were waiting for permission.

"*God,* yes," she whispered, frantically fumbling with the heavy metal stud until it popped open. The zipper rolled down as Ross shimmied his hand under the lace of her panties, and straight to her hot, slippery center.

She hadn't been lying when she'd said she was wet.

"Fuck, Lee," he groaned when his hands met their target. She groaned too. Maybe even yelled a bit as his hard, calloused fingers slid through swollen, sensitized flesh, sending a crackle of oh-my-God racing down every single nerve in her body.

So good, so perfect... His hands went to work, one kneading her breasts and the other stroking her slow and strong. She'd never been one for quick orgasms, always taking a long time to warm up and usually not coming at all. But with Ross, it was so different, it barely resembled her encounters with other men. She couldn't even explain why he'd turned her inside out but damn—one touch, and she was responding. Writhing. Begging. So out of her head, she was begging him in Spanish to make her come.

She thanked the sweet Lord for their crappy Spanish teacher right now, because Ross'd understood every word. She heard a muffled "*hell* yeah" behind her. Before she even knew what had happened, he'd peeled her pants down to her knees and pushed her forward onto her hands. Cold air met her hot, exposed skin.

So did Ross' hand. He hissed in a breath as he stroked over every curve. He teased a finger under the string of her pink lace thong. "You always wear these?"

"Every day," she answered him. And it was true. He let out a strangled chuckle, but when she went to throw a teasing grin over her shoulder, the sight of him practically made her go up in flames. He had one hand on her, one hand rubbing at the enormous bulge in his pants. He was fevered. Frenzied, even. He'd undone his belt and untucked his shirt, because the tip of his cock had pushed past the top of his pants. He pulled it out, and pumped it.

Omifuckinggod. She couldn't tear her eyes away. Couldn't even breathe.

He ran one thumb up her seam, dragging it through her folds. And then he slid in one finger, two, three, watching them, rapt, as they appeared and disappeared inside her. Oh hell, so good...his fingers knew just how to press, how to fill her up. Her legs began to quiver with the pleasure, and she widened her stance, leaning into his hand.

Ross let out a moan and dropped to his knees behind her, and the sweet slide of his mouth on her nearly short circuited her pleasureboard. Her legs started shaking with it full on, and then her arms, and soon her whole body. White sparks erupted behind her eyelids. She was coming— coming so hard, and he had barely touched her.

But then he'd stopped, and there was the sound of rustling and tearing foil. And he was inside her, just like that. Making the pleasure go on and on. Pounding her so hard, she wasn't sure whose cries were whose anymore, and she didn't care. She just had to have him.

Him.

Ross.

She felt the moment inside her when he stiffened, then poured himself into her in hot pulses. He let out an incoherent shout. That was all it took to send her screaming over the edge with him again. Together.

Was this what it felt like, to do this together? Simultaneous orgasm. Oh man, did it ever live up to the hype...so wonderful, and powerful...she'd never felt so sexy in all her life.

Ross had given that to her. He pulled her backward then, up against him. They were both still shivering, and it wasn't from the cold.

"Lee," he breathed in her ear. "Shit. That was...that was..."

She gulped for air but managed to chuckle. "Yeah. You said it." He was inside her, thick, hard, and throbbing, even now. And that made her strangely happy, to be held like this. It was the kind of sex that felt like it could change your life, like somebody had flipped on the lights and the world was in color. But she couldn't trust that sensation, could she?

She'd been trying to find clues. But so far, the only clue she'd managed was that Ross was straight-up the best lover she'd ever had. Full stop. He'd made her come so hard, she'd nearly lost her mind, and he was only getting started. But if life had taught her anything, it's that men didn't take sex seriously, no matter how mind-blowing it'd been.

She had to figure out a way to keep her heart in check.

But then their gaze locked again, and she wondered whether that would even be possible. There was so much there in his eyes—warmth, affection, even friendship, shining steady and bright. Her *friend*... Oh hell, Ross. What was she supposed to do with the way he cupped her face in his hand, and gazed at her like she was his everything?

She kissed him again, falling into the deep of it. It was so sweet, so fucking ideal, like some kind of dream…But finally she found the strength to push herself off him. And he grinned at her as he shuffled off to clean himself up.

She grinned back as she tugged her leggings back up. She couldn't help her stupid, stupid self. When they'd finished washing up and piecing themselves back together, they walked back down to the main house, holding hands. She smiled at the sight of their linked hands. Had any guy she'd been with ever held her hand like this, just for the sake of it? She couldn't recall.

But this felt different, anyway. *She* felt different. But she felt good too. Warm. Cared for. It was all a bit much to take in, honestly, but there was no place she'd rather be.

As they walked together, swinging their hands between them, Lita was profoundly grateful Ross kept their banter light—the forecast for snow tomorrow, what kind of coffee she'd gotten at the store, whether he liked chili better over spaghetti or rice, or just by itself.

Everything was so perfectly normal. But somewhere down deep in her heart, Lita knew nothing would ever be the same.

CHAPTER 17

Ross BLINKED against the light of dawn that streamed through Kathryn's frilly lace curtains and regretted not pulling down the shades before he'd gone to bed last night. But he'd been too distracted to notice, in all the best ways...

By Lita.

After declining his earlier invitation, she'd knocked on his door in the middle of the night and had asked to sleep in his bed. And he sure as shit wasn't gonna say no.

He propped up on an elbow to watch her, the little spoon still deep in sleep curled beside him. It had taken him twenty-eight years to finally sleep the whole night in bed with a woman. But he was glad he'd waited until this moment.

Because this took his breath away. Straight up.

The sight of her made his chest squeeze tight. Sunlight stole over her glossy brown hair, making the blond highlights glow like fire in the morning sun. Was this what it felt like to be lovestruck?

Yeah, it must be. He let it wash over him, happy to go along with that current. Careful not to wake her, he coiled a single long curl around his finger.

God, this girl is so fucking beautiful...

He stroked the back of his hand along her hair, letting the length of it tickle his knuckles. All these years, he'd wondered what this would feel like, to tangle his fingers in these silky strands, and twist it around his fist. Now he knew.

How *that* was all finally happening, he couldn't say. Every time he thought she was trying to resist him, she'd reach out to him instead. Like they were seesawing back and forth between what they were and what they could be. Last night had been like that.

After that explosive session of theirs in the barn, they'd reverted back to friend mode. They'd stuffed themselves with chili and had crashed on the couch to watch a History channel documentary about Christmas traditions, or something like that. He'd been too sleepy to process it. When they'd both managed to shake themselves awake, he'd invited her to share a bed with him. She'd turned him down flat, and he'd taken that no for an answer, figuring it was best not to get greedy.

So he'd been pretty surprised when she'd crept into his room at one in the morning. She'd told him the winter thunderstorm outside had kept her up, and she didn't want to be alone in someone else's house. She didn't have to ask him twice. And when she'd crawled under the covers in the pitch dark, it had only taken a second for him to realize she was totally, completely naked.

Memories of it lived on his skin. The storm had flashed and raged outside, but they'd reached for each other in the dark, a slow, sensual experience that had felt so different from any sex he'd ever had before. Maybe it was the moves. Maybe it was getting to play out his fantasies, without time limits. But maybe it was simply her—and the fact that he wanted to be with her so, so bad.

His dick wasn't the only thing that wanted her. But somehow, that didn't scare him. He knew this girl inside and out now. This mole here on her shoulder. The sprinkling of freckles she tried to hide with makeup. Her stubbornness. Her humor. Her drive. And he wanted it all.

Something about Lita made him curious. He wanted to know all those hidden layers—the doubts, the fears, the parts she hid from the world. He leaned down to inspect a little mark he spotted behind her left ear. *Huh! Check that out.* She had the tiniest tattoo he'd ever seen back there, a miniature magic wand with stars coming off it. Like a teeny fairy had left it behind. He smiled.

All these years she'd never mentioned it, and he'd never been close enough to see it. He hoarded that knowledge away like a treasure. For a woman who made pretty good coin on the side doing specialty tats, she'd always been remarkably closemouthed about her ink. She'd always told him she had them, but she'd never said where. It was one of those weird, push/pull things about her he'd never understood.

But now, lying here with her like this, he got it. This tiny tat was hiding in plain sight. But you had to be close enough to see it, to appreciate it. It was sweet, and so like Lita. She'd never admit it, but the girl *was* sweet. You just had to earn it.

And hell yeah, he was in the mood to put in the work.

As if on cue, Lita's big green eyes fluttered open. She rolled onto her back, stretched, and gave him a groggy smile. "You spying on me in my sleep now?"

"Hey now, as I recall, it was *you* who crawled in here with *me*."

Lita stretched again and rubbed the sleep from her eyes. When the sheet slid down her chest, he saw the moment where her brain kicked back in, and she remembered they were both naked under these sheets together. Her gaze darted around the room. *Hah.* He'd never seen her act so cringingly shy before. It was cute. Lita grabbed the sheet and primly tucked it under her armpits. "I, uh, *well.* I suppose I'd better go brush my teeth and stuff."

Hunter had told him he could sleep in the master once the family had left, so Ross had taken the man up on his offer. "Master bath is right over there, babe." He pointed. "You're welcome to it. I've already been. New toothbrushes are in the second drawer on the left."

Lita cast a longing look at the bathroom door, and bit her lip. "Okay, well, I'm gonna get out of this bed. I need you to hide your eyes. Can you cover your eyes or something?"

"Cover my—" He barked out an incredulous laugh. "Are you serious? We've had sex! Twice! And let me remind you, *you're* the one who started this sans-pajamas thing."

She gave him a sheepish shrug. "Yeah, but it was dark, and there were covers an' all."

He trapped her in a playful embrace. "Liiita. Are you afraid to be all naked with meeeeeee?" He tickled her ribs and was delighted to find out she was ticklish too. This morning was full of wonders, wasn't it?

She squawked and squirmed, starting to giggle with him. "Would you stop it?" she wheezed. "Don't squeeze me and make me laugh at this hour. I gotta pee."

He let her go, holding his hands up in surrender. And sat there in amazement as she yanked at the big king-sized sheet until she'd untucked it completely. She folded the sheet up under her arms, and scooted to the edge of the bed, wrapping it around until she'd made a sleeveless gown of it.

"What in god's name are you doin', woman?"

"Preserving my dignity." With one last sweep, she picked herself and that enormous white sheet up off the bed. She stomped off to the bathroom, like Cleopatra, queen of the thread count. The fabric formed a long train behind her.

Lita disappeared around the corner for her morning constitutional, probably not realizing that he could still hear the tinkling. Noticing that the Christmas quilt he was under was now slung low on his hips, he arranged himself as provocatively as possible, popped his hands behind his head, and waited. Lita reappeared again and scrabbled around in the sink drawers for a toothbrush. And she brushed them too, a bit more aggressively than was good for her gums. He studied her as she spit out her toothpaste, then splashed soap and water on her face.

When she finished toweling off, Lita came up scowling at him. "Honestly. I'm brushing my teeth, and you're finding this entertaining?"

"Best show in town." He sighed.

She crossed her arms over her chest. "*Why* are you doing this?"

"Why are *you?*"

"I'm trying to fly high and travel light. Isn't that what you always say? Keep things light?"

"And I'm full of shit. Haven't you figured that out yet?"

She snorted. "I have, matter of fact."

"Yeah, well. I'm not kidding around about this. Not now."

She moved to the doorframe, still pulling at her sheet like she didn't know what to do with herself. And trying not to ogle his bare chest, which was freakin' adorable.

He cracked a smile, watching her shuffle on her feet. "You don't believe me, do you?"

She sighed. "You're not you right now. You've transformed yourself into some kind of—I don't know. Some kind of dream guy I don't recognize, okay? And then there's that whole hex thing."

He slapped a hand over his eyes and sat up in bed. "You keep saying that! I'm not hexed! And if you're searching for some dream man, I'm right here." He jumped up to his feet in all his naked glory, cock straight out and bobbin' in the cool morning air. It felt weird, exposing himself and his unannounced morning wood like this. But there was no going back now. He was puttin' it all out there, literally. He did a slow circle, holding his hands up. "This is it. This is *me*, just as I am. I want you, and I'm here for this thing that's happening between us, one hundred percent. Aren't you?"

Her eyes widened and she stilled for a minute, takin her good, sweet time inspecting every inch of his bared flesh. They stared each other down like a test of wills to see who'd crack first. It was Lita who blinked. She tried to storm past him, but he stepped in her path.

"Awww. Come on. You mean to tell me you're going to leave me hanging here?" He swept his gaze toward his crotch. *"Literally?"*

"Stop tempting me, Ross. We have work to do, don't we?"

He cracked another sly grin. "Don't you go blaming the horses for this. They've got hay and water. They'll wait." He gave a pull on the sheet, but she held it in a death grip against her.

She growled at him as he gave the sheet another playful tug.

"Okay, okay. We don't have to have sex right now if you don't want to. But why won't you let me see you at least?"

"Because!"

"Because what?" He started to tickle her again. "You got a third boob under there I don't know about?"

She laughed and squirmed as he tried to pin her. "No!"

"You're really an alien then. Sent down to populate the earth with hot women."

"Ross!" she giggled. "I don't want you to see..."

He managed to get his hand on the piece of sheet she'd tucked to keep it together. They were both laughing now as they got into a playful tug of war over it. "See what? Gills? Tentacles! It's tentacles then!"

He'd backed up, pulling at one length of sheet while she pulled in the other direction. Finally she narrowed her eyes at him and let go. On purpose. He staggered backward, tangled his leg in the sheet, and fell flat on his ass.

Lita stood tall in front of him, hands on hips. *"There. You happy now?"*

"Happy" didn't even begin to cover it. This woman was so ridiculously gorgeous, he might die, right here, and go straight to heaven, because there was nothing better than this.

He didn't need any magic tingling to tie his tongue. The sight of her had made his throat too tight to work properly. *God, Lee...*

The morning sun radiated from behind her, pouring in from the bank of windows. It lit her whole body up with fire, glowing up her golden skin. Her hair was parted down the middle, waist-length curls framing her like Venus herself, rising from a friggin' clamshell or something.

But that wasn't the thing that really got his attention. No, it was her tats that had him staring. She did have them, after all. And where she had them....

Jesus, take the wheel.

She had tiny feathers—a sprinkling—as if they'd dropped in a single trail from the side of her ribs straight down to her...

Her *pussy*.

Holy hell.

She was bare. Smooth as the day she was born. And right there on her mound was the fucking sexiest thing he'd ever seen. A tat of the head and shoulders of a big-eyed angel, winking over her shoulder. All black-and-white line work, like his, tucked into a perfect V-shape, right where her hair might've been.

Lita stepped up and tapped him on the shoulder. "Ross? You okay?"

She cocked her head at him, looking concerned. Not too surprising, really. God only knew the expression on his face right now. His mouth watered, looking at her. He was afraid to blink so he wouldn't stop seeing this.

He finally gained enough control over his faculties to run his hand up her sweet, smooth leg. "This," he choked out. "This was why you'd never tell me where your tats were."

She didn't answer him, but he reached out anyway. Jesus, he was so worked up, he was shaking like an idiot again. He ran his trembling fingers lightly over the design, mesmerized.

And when he finally met her eyes, she smiled a smile so soft, so real, it made his chest ache. Emotion swamped him so hard, tears pricked at his eyes. So this was what people talked about. This sweet, scary, falling sensation, like the ground was no longer underneath you.

"You're the most beautiful woman I've ever seen, Lee," he whispered, sounding so hushed, so full of awe that it hardly even sounded like his own voice. It'd just slipped out. The magic again, no doubt. But he found he didn't mind that he'd said it.

He saw her disbelief and skepticism. Yeah, no. He couldn't have that. Because this—this was big.

So he doubled down, in his own words this time. "No

one else could be this amazing." He caressed his thumb in a circle on her thigh. "You get that, don't you?"

Lita smirked. "Yeah, yeah, yeah. I'm all that and a bag of chips. My milkshake brings all the boys to the yard. What else is new?"

"Don't."

"Don't what?"

"Joke." He fell deep into those gorgeous green eyes of hers. "Not about that. There's nothing random about this. You're everything, Lee."

He means it, doesn't he?

Lita had heard about everything you could imagine from guys over the years. Except this. *Sincerity.*

Her mind blanked. She had no words, no comebacks, no easy defenses.

Only the overwhelming need to touch this man, right now.

Silently, she slid to her knees, straddling him, and cupped his face in her hands. It felt odd to do such a thing, to look a man so straight in the face. But something inside her needed to do it, to really *see* him. Ross met her searching gaze straight on, without so much as a twitch.

His growing beard rasped under her fingertips, deep auburn strands against his pale skin. His bright blue eyes had gone dark with desire, and splotches of red colored his cheeks and collarbones. His quick, hot breaths made a quiet, staccato sound in the morning silence.

Maybe she was breathing hard too. She tried to suck in air, but her lungs were vise tight. Yet somehow, the rest of her body had gone warm and loose. Ross cupped his fingers around the small of her back, and his simple touch made her arch and roll as his hand traveled up her spine.

An unspoken command her body obeyed without question.

A taste of minty toothpaste met her tongue as she leaned forward to kiss him. But as their tongues played together, she soon tasted the raw elements of the man, his pure masculine spice. Lita didn't know if it was the searching, sensual kisses or the way his hard hands roamed over her heated skin, but she felt more alive, more feminine, than she ever had.

His mouth was on her neck again, her collarbone, her breasts, each taste leaving sizzling sensation in its wake. And in this moment, this man was all she'd ever wanted.

Dammit, he was kissing her, only kissing her, but the slide of his mouth on her skin made the whole world spin. She swayed in his arms and he caught her, growling his approval.

Swooning—that's what she was doing. Gah. *Honestly*. She wasn't some stupid-ass *swooner*.

Except she was.

When his hot mouth met her nipple, she moaned, and when his teeth grazed her tip, she may have cussed in Spanish. His eyes flew open and he grinned triumphantly against her breast. He'd figured out how much she'd liked that last night. And now Ross was figuring out how to play her, storing up information for the next time.

Or maybe he cared enough to remember.

She couldn't sort it out in her head right now. All she knew was she wanted more of whatever this was. His heat, his taste, the sensation of him, skin to skin. She reached behind her and pressed his cock tight against her seam, rocking slowly and getting him good and slick without letting him in yet.

She curled one arm against his neck as she kept it up. And his already hard cock got even harder in her hand. The knowledge of that seemed to trip every pleasure wire in her brain, lighting her up with fire, making her need him so bad, she could feel her own pulse pounding between her legs.

His full-body shudder was hard to miss. Ross hissed. "Shit, Lee...*fuck! So* amazing."

It was more than amazing. It was perfect. *Right*. This was one of her favorite things, a favorite move.

And by the way his eyes were rolling back in his head, Lita guessed this might be, for Ross anyway, *novel*. Like he'd never...

"Oh, I get it now. You've never had a bare pussy before, have you?"

He sucked in a deep breath. "I've always been wrapped up."

She gave out a little hum of concern, but she still rolled her hips. "You're clear, right?"

"Always," he answered. "And you're—?"

"Clear. And covered. An IUD, you know."

"Ah," he panted.

Lita batted her eyelashes at him and understanding dawned on his face.

His eyes widened. "You-you want to..."

"Yes, Ross," she hummed.

"And you're going to—"

"Uh-huh," she breathed "Right now."

He let out a shocked, happy-sounding huff. But instead of just having his way, he grinned from ear to ear, grabbed both sides of her face, and kissed her. Deep kisses, tender kisses that explored instead of demanded.

His kisses, they took her breath away. It was shocking how much. And dammit, she was almost weepy again. She needed him, in every way a woman could need a man. Beside her, inside her...She wrapped one arm around his neck and tipped him in with the other.

"Leeeee…" He shuddered, his voice a reverent whisper. "God*damn.*" He leaned back against his hands so he could see them joined together, moving together. He let out an amazed, breathless chuckle, and she grinned.

She met his gaze, nose to nose, and kissed him again. But he nipped her bottom lip between his teeth and sucked. *Ohhhh…*

That was it. Whatever brain cells she had left had switched to the off position. She shoved him onto his back. When she lowered herself down on him, all the way to the root, and rolled herself against him, he shouted out a couple curses. Or was that her? She could hardly even tell anymore. He filled her up so completely, it was like he'd rolled right past all her defenses.

Ross grabbed her ass in both hands and held her there for a second, breathing hard. Then he gave her a stinging, wicked smack and started pumping.

Or was that her again? It was hard to tell who was doing who right now, and maybe that was the point. They traded thrusts as she pounded against him. Her hair had somehow gotten flipped over her head, making a canopy all around their faces. And in that little cocoon, she could see everything she was doing to him. Every rhythmic moan, every flash of desire, every whispered plea—it was all there on his face as he locked his gaze on her.

Neither of them was going to last long like this. But it didn't matter. They were on the same track, giving and getting. Almost like they'd made a motor of each other, trapped in a drive train that was pulling them to a destination she desperately wanted to get to. Faster, faster… And she was there, then, quicker than she'd expected, screaming out his name and swaying, her knees gone slack. She was coming. And so was he, pumping himself out hot, thick, and slippery inside her.

So good...

So good...

He held her tight. One arm wrapped around her waist, the other hand cupping the back of her head, tipping her forehead to his as they struggled to catch their breath. Flying high. And coming down together.

"Lee," he uttered again. And it was almost like another language that only she could understand. Just one little syllable, but in it, she could hear a world of thoughts and emotions—how satisfied he was, how full of wonder.

She'd made him happy. Not just sated, but *happy.* Maybe she was too, because this felt a lot like swallowing sunshine. Ross swept his hand around her head, pulling the thick curtain of hair away so the light could hit her face. And he covered her face in kisses—on her cheeks, her forehead, the tip of her nose...

When he finally made his way back to her mouth, he kissed her in that deep, searching way that always smoked her out. Kept her from hiding. And for right now, she didn't want to hide. She wasn't even sure she even remembered how.

Eventually, she curled on top of his chest, still unwilling to let go of the sensation of him being inside her. He stroked her hair, her face, not wanting to move, either.

She tipped her head up. "How was that?"

He gave her a rusty, breathless little laugh and traced a finger along her cheekbone. "Let's just say, Lita, it's another of the five thousand ways you've ruined me for other women."

Lita shrugged a shoulder at that, not willing to let Ross know how much that'd pleased her. No man had ever said such a thing to her. Ever.

Dammit, there was that lump in her throat again. Her ridiculous heart. It was telling her things.

Things like...*you're falling for him.*

You want him all to yourself.

He's the only man who could make you feel like this.

But that stupid heart of hers, it was a liar. Because she knew—she *knew*—this was too good to be true. Whether this lasted until New Year's or not.

Lita slid off him, picked the sheet off the floor, and tossed it in the hamper in the walk-in closet. She took a second to clean herself up too. When she came back out, Ross was still bare-chested, but he gave her another one of his devastating smiles while he buttoned up his jeans. Oh, the sight of him—she wanted to sigh like a love-drunk idiota. But she didn't and headed for the door instead. Ross caught her as brushed past and wrapped his arms around her waist, hugging her back tight against him.

He took a deep breath, and she swayed back and forth. "Mmmmm. Morning snuggles. I could get used to this."

She could too. But she didn't say that, either.

Oh, I really am in trouble.

But as she stood there sheltered in his arms, she realized she almost didn't care.

Almost.

CHAPTER 18

THE ANNUAL RUIZ FAMILY TAMALE HOLLY PARTY, MOM'S HOUSE, CHRISTMAS EVE AFTERNOON

Lita grabbed the plump, steaming tamale with her tongs and wiggled it at Ross.

He regarded it with real, honest-to-God lust. "Oh, mannnn. That's the last strawberry tamale, isn't it?"

"Yep. And if you snooze, you lose." She tipped her head at him, silently saying *you want it?*

He gave her an enthusiastic nod, and she plopped it on his already bulging plate.

Mom had her back to them as she and Tino were mixing up mimosas, but Lita could still hear her squawk loud and clear. "*Carmelita Rose Noe!* Are you stealing Ross' tamale? You know I save the strawberry ones for him!"

"No, Mami," Lita called back. "I'd never dream of stealing Ross' tamale."

Uncle J snorted beside her and leaned down to her ear. "I'll bet Ross would like to steal *your* tamales." He snickered.

Lita didn't exactly want to tell the man Ross was already well acquainted with her tamales, so she elbowed him in the ribs. "Would you *stop* it?"

Her mom rounded the kitchen island, grabbed Ross'

head in a headlock, and ruffled his hair. "Good!" She gave him a big, smacking kiss on his temple. "You know I only make those for you. Don't forget the strawberry sauce and the cream right over there."

"Yes, ma'am!" He grinned back at her.

Lita could only shake her head at the two of them. When Mom went to circulate with the rest of the crowd, she elbowed Ross this time. "*Suck-up.*"

Ross raised his eyebrows. "Lita! You think I need Alessandra points or something? No no, honey. The woman already loves me or she wouldn't have bothered making these. Honestly, it wouldn't be Christmas without your mom's tamales. Oh, man." He waved the plate under his nose. "Come to papa!"

J chuckled and pointed. "Mija, if you want to enjoy them properly, you'd better grab those two chairs over there, before they're gone."

Heeding her uncle's advice, they shuffled through the crowd and sat down. Ross tore into her mother's famous charred strawberry tamales before his butt had hit the seat. He made the same series of ecstatic food noises he made at this party every year. First the rounded eyes. Then the looking up to heaven and nodding appreciatively. Then the *Mm! Mm-m-m-MM!* Then the sign of the cross, even though he'd never been in a Catholic church in his life. Then the ceremonial kissing of the fork. "I've waited all year for this, and it was totally, *totally* worth it." He dug in.

Lita had to smile at the man. He wasn't kidding around. Nobody loved Mom's tamales like Ross. It had all started when they were sophomores in high school. Mom had been making the fillings and wrapping them nice and neat in the corn husks the night before, so all she'd have to do was steam them when their guests arrived the next day. Ross had been over that night, hanging out. When Mom had found out Ross had never heard of a tamale, she'd been determined to set him straight.

Ross had gotten so interested in Mom's speech, he'd even offered to help her. She'd shown him how to make the soft corn masa dough, and how to mix the flavors for all their varieties—fried pulled pork, chicken, shrimp, seared serrano/goat cheese. He'd gone nuts for every single one. And that was it—as far as her mother was concerned, Ross was family.

So it was only natural that he had a standing invitation to their Christmas Eve tamale party every year. All their friends, neighbors, and clients did.

Mom's house wasn't that big—just a small, pink, mid-century brick ranch with an eat-in kitchen. But people piled in anyway, and cars lined both sides of their neighborhood street. Mom' decorating style could best be described as second-hand chic—an artsy, colorful mish-mash of eclectic furniture that somehow made everyone comfortable. And nowhere was that better illustrated than at Christmas. Her guests fanned out from one end of the house to the other, perched two at a time on the old, recovered armchairs, crowded around the expansive buffet, and lined up at the folding tables Uncle J had set up all over the house. Over the years, Mom's tamales had gotten quite the reputation, and with all the crazy Christmas decorations J had helped her put up, this party had evolved into a community open house.

And of course, that meant there were plenty of single men here she hadn't had a chance to kiss yet. *Gah*. Lita had barely gotten two bites in her mouth before they started lining up like needy puppy dogs.

First there was Ron Jenko, the middle-aged mailman who delivered to Mom's house. Then preening Jimmy Peters, one of J's hair clients, who ran a hair supply store down the way. Then there was Lon Stevens, their long-time neighbor down the street who was easily old enough to be her dad.

Swearing a bit under her breath, she stood up and plunked her plate on her chair. But she pretended to be happy to see them all and opened her arms wide for hugs. She gave them each a kiss on the cheek, and they all eventually wandered away, confused but contented.

Lita's sister Rosario slid into the chair that had emptied beside her and lowered Lita's two-year-old nephew, Gabe, onto her lap. *"Wowwwww."* Rosie clucked her tongue. "I thought Mom was making all this up. But it looks like you really do have the Pied Va-jay-jay."

Ross choked on his tamale but didn't disagree with her. He hid his secret, fiendish grin behind his cup, and gulped down his cranberry margarita.

"I don't know what it is that I have, but I hope I lose it soon." Lita sighed.

Rosie tsked at her. "Are you even *serious* right now? I can't imagine how awesome it would be, to have all these men falling all over you."

"Hah!" Lita came back. "As if! Half the guys in high school asked you to prom. You practically had to fend the guys off with a stick!"

And it was true. Her sister Rosario was the classical Mexican beauty, the spitting image of their mother—petite and perfectly curvy, all radiant, golden skin, high cheekbones, and thick, straight, ebony hair so shiny, she could rep for Pantene. Her sister had great fashion sense too, with a wardrobe that emphasized her amazing, curvaceous figure, while still being sophisticated. Rosie had finished her degree and was a high school art teacher now. So her flawless design eye helped her stand out. But Lita knew the truth—it was because her sister was the pretty one in the family. That girl could make her own magic.

Lita could never make the woman believe that, though. Rosie shrugged her shoulder. "Yeah, I had a few good years. But those are long gone."

"Tell that to Darius." Lita tipped her head in the direction of her brother-in-law, who'd managed to pour himself another soda while simultaneously wrangling Rafe, Gabe's twin. The man felt eyes on him, and he turned. When saw it was his wife checking him out, he flashed her one of his devastating grins, and tipped his cup in her direction. His gaze danced with mischief while he took a lingering sip.

"Yeah, well." Rosie shook her head while she smiled right back at him. "The man isn't exactly objective, is he?"

Yeah, you could say that again. Darius was beguiled, besotted, all those fancy words people used to describe men who loved their spouses. He was one of those rare unicorns in the world of men—a catch. A Virginia state trooper, Darius was a proud, black man—tall, fit, and broad-shouldered, with the kind of sly, million-dollar-smile that put Taye Diggs to shame. When he'd pulled Rosie over for a busted taillight years ago, the poor woman hadn't stood a chance.

But it wasn't just his off-the-chain charisma that had impressed Lita. It was the lovely, cherishing, even protective way he treated her sister. He centered Rosie's crazy, impulsive qualities, and her fun-loving ways seemed to brighten his world. They were better together than they were apart. And she gave him hella respect for that.

And it didn't hurt that they'd made the world's cutest babies together, either. Gabe and Rafe were two perfect cherubs, with golden, glowy, mahogany skin, raven curls down to their shoulders, and the most striking hazel eyes you'd ever seen. Lita was about to succumb to the urge to pull Gabe in for auntie kisses when he pointed at Ross.

"Red! Red!" he cried.

Rosie smiled down at her son. "We've been drilling the colors with the boys."

Ross loved kids. Always had. So it was no surprise when he put down his plate and gave his buddy Gabe a comical, confused smile. "What's red? My cup?" He scowled at the cup in his hand, which was green.

"Noooooo." Gabe giggled.

Ross scanned the room and finally pointed down. "Oh! Is it my pants?"

"No! Not pants!" Gabe squealed.

Ross rolled his eyes real big and pointed at his feet. "It's *gotta* be my shoes then."

"No, silly!" the boy shouted. "Your hair!"

Ross chuckled and pulled a piece of hair down to his eyes, studying it. "Huh! I guess you're right." He held out his arms. "Now come on over here and give your buddy Ross a hug."

But Gabe's eyes immediately rounded in panic, and he shrank back in his mother's arms. "Nooooooo. You not Ross! Ross not Red! Ross is black!"

They all laughed at that. It took them several minutes to explain that Uncle J had changed Ross' hair color, and that's the kind of thing that went on at Divalicious, and sometimes people wanted to change their appearance and, in Ross's case, he'd been born with red hair.

Gabe still cast doubtful glances at the man, clinging to Rosie, until Mom's shih tzu, Whoopie, scampered by, snuffling under the chairs for bits of dropped food. "Whooooop-piiiiieee!" he hollered. "Wanna play with Whoopie!"

Lita could see why. Whoopie was an awesome little fluffball, super friendly and kid-tolerant. Today, Mom had pulled some of the dog's floor-length hair into a big sequin bow that had flashing red-and-green LEDs woven in it. The dog pattered over, put its front paws up on Rosie's knees, and licked at Gabe's tiny stocking feet. The boy shrieked with laughter.

Ross shoveled in his last bite of tamale and held up his hands. "Tell you what—why don't I take Gabe and Whoopie out to the screened-in porch? The yard's too muddy right now, but there won't be anybody on the porch and lots of space for them to run around."

Rosie smiled gratefully at Ross and bent her head down to her son. "Whaddya say, Gabe? You wanna go?"

Gabe almost jumped out of Rosie's lap as he held out his arms to Ross. Ross gathered up the boy, grinning, and gave him a high-five. Then he scooped up a wriggling Whoopie under the other arm. On his way out, he caught the attention of Darius, and together they wrangled the boys out of the party's fray.

As they walked away, Rosie clucked her tongue. "He's a keeper, that one. I hope you're paying attention, sister."

Lita snorted, eager to throw her sister off the scent. "You do realize this is Ross we're talking about, right?"

"J's convinced he's gonna win the pool," Rosie told her. "And when I came here, I was expecting Ross to have a different haircut. J had texted the before-and-after pictures. But I hadn't expected him to *act* different."

Lita scowled. *"Different?"*

"Yeah." Rosie shrugged. *"Different.* Like he's all grown up. And man, the way he looks at you, you'd swear—"

"Stop it." Lita held up a hand. "It's not like that."

Rosie rolled her eyes. "Isn't it, though? And before you try to tell me it's not, you haven't seen how he can't take his eyes off you. If you're not doing him, honey, you'd better get started. The pheromones in here are so thick you're gonna choke the rest of us."

That was easy for Rosie to say. Everything had been so simple for her. Rosie'd always had nice boyfriends. And everything with Darius had been so perfect and uncomplicated, they'd sailed to the altar in only three months.

"When it's right, you know."

Rosie had told her that, back then. But as Lita sat there, trying to put her predicament into words for her sister, the only thing she could come up with was a lump in her throat. Yeah, she'd had a lot of those lately, mainly when her emotions got too big to swallow down. And the helpless way it made her feel? It fucking *sucked*.

Lita opened her mouth to say something, anything, to get her sister off her back. She needed a story to give her and Ross space to figure themselves out—before they had to face all the expectations and opinions of their families. But she was coming up empty.

Fortunately, her mother's frantic waving at her from the front doorway cut the conversation short. "Lita! Sweetie! I think you've got a visitor," she called.

A *visitor?*

Here?

Lita wiped off her hands and dumped her plate in the trash. When she made her way to the open doorway, she groaned. It was Cam, of all people, standing there with a wilting poinsettia in his hands.

Not this again. She ground her teeth and stepped out onto the stoop. Cam stood there, eyes cast down to the concrete, acting more contrite than she'd ever seen him. "Lita, I'm not here to make a big scene or anything at your party," he rushed to say. "I knew you'd be here, though, and since you're blocking my calls, I figured I'd better apologize face-to-face. I don't know what's gotten into me lately, but it seems like I can't be around you without making a royal ass out of myself. Everybody in town's talkin' about it."

Ah. So there it was. *He's embarrassed.*

Lita held up a hand. "Cam, really, there's no need to—"

"No!" he insisted. "There really is. And I brought you a poinsettia." He shoved it in her hands. "Mom said I shouldn't go to a person's home empty-handed, so here you go. It's a Mexican flower, and you're Mexican an' all."

Lita cringed at that ham-handed whatever-the-hell-that-was, but she took the pathetic posey from him and set it down on the stoop. When she stood back up, Cam made eye contact finally. And right there in front of her eyes, his expression changed from remorseful to that crazed, *I-have-to-have-you* facade too many men had been casting in her direction.

She gritted her teeth. *Ah, crap. I haven't kissed him yet, have I?*

Poor guy. She knew he didn't really want her. And if he stood out here too much longer, Ross was gonna beat his ass. Considering that Mom was peeking through blinds right now, she'd probably be next in line. Lita held out her arms. "That was a very thoughtful gift, Cam. How's about a hug for old time's sake?"

The man lunged at her, but as soon as she kissed his cheek, he stiffened, as he realized where he was.

But before she could say anything to the man, there was a loud, masculine cluck coming from behind him. "Awwwww. Now isn't that sweet?"

Oh, no. She knew that voice. And when Cam stepped aside, her worst fears were realized.

Dad.

Or, to be more accurate, the guy who liked to act like her father exactly one day a year, usually around Christmas-time, so he could bilk Mom for another "loan." He stood there with his arms out, grinning fondly. "Hey now, since you're giving out hugs, don't you have a hug for me?"

Cam took in this scene, eyes wide and completely unhexed now. He winced, and she didn't blame him. Everyone in town knew how she felt about her father.

"I, uh..." Cam pointed at his truck. "Hoo, yeah, so I'm gonna go."

Lita gave him a half-hearted wave. "Alright, Cam. Thanks for stopping in. And thank you for the poinsettia."

Cam was occasionally was smarter than he looked. He gave her a curt nod and speed walked back to his banged up heap.

Dad raised his eyebrows as Cam blew by him but didn't comment. When he turned back to her, the man switched on his standard high-wattage smile. But Lita didn't buy it. She stood on the stoop, feet planted, staring him down.

Dad motioned toward the door. "So, Lita. Are you gonna let me in?"

CHAPTER 19

IT HAD BEEN three years since she'd seen her "dad," but he hadn't changed much that she could see. His curly blond hair was ashy with gray, but it still hung down to his shoulders. He still had the smarmy, manipulative smile. Yeah, he was still her dad, unfortunately, and he was definitely up to something. He always was.

The man had made an effort today. He'd slicked his hair back into a neat ponytail and had grown a cheesy goatee. Clearly, he'd been expecting Mom to have her annual party, because he was dressed all festive in a red-and-white houndstooth sweater, impeccably pressed black dress pants, and what appeared to be matching designer loafers.

Dad was the kind of man a lot of women would consider "a looker." Naturally broad-shouldered and muscular, he carried himself with masculine physical grace. His features were chiseled and perfectly symmetrical—like a middle-aged model in a magazine. Honestly, she was surprised he hadn't roped some other woman into another one of his scams. But Mom, apparently, was still his favorite mark. Probably because she was the easiest one.

Dad amped up his artificially whitened smile and held

up his hands. "Well? Are you going to keep me standing out here all day?"

Lita narrowed her eyes at him. "You're not invited."

"Says who?"

"Says me. I'm tired of you ruining our Christmas."

His smile fell. "Now, Carmelita, why do you have to be like that? I'm here to see my children and my grandchildren."

"Bullshit."

"It's true!" He tried to walk around her.

She stood in his path, blocking him. He tried again on the other side, and she stepped in his way, again.

"Child, you're being—"

Mom whipped open the door behind her. "Lita, baby, what are you doin'?"

"I'm saving your party," Lita ground out. "Dear ol' Dad didn't RSVP."

Dad tut-tutted, all innocence and good intentions. "You see what I have to deal with?"

Mom sighed. "When we got divorced, I promised myself I'd never be one of those moms who kept their ex from seeing their children. I'm not about to start now. Let him in."

None too happy about it, Lita stepped aside and let him pass. Mom could cling to her principles if she wanted to, but this wasn't going to go well. They all knew it. But they'd all have to play pretend, as usual, until he found a way to blow things up. It usually didn't take too long. Hours. Sometimes minutes.

Lita and her sister had been so young when Mom had walked out on Marshall Noe, neither one of them could really remember what it was like having him around. She and Rosie had some fuzzy memories of fights over money, and his drinking. Other women too. So it wasn't like anybody was standing around waiting for tearful reunions.

Seeming to sense this, the man melted into the crowd, heading straight for the buffet, and making pleasant chit-chat with everyone he met. He'd not had the guts to come up to Rosie yet, but overall, he was behaving like a perfect gentleman.

Still, this whole thing made her nervous. What was his game? Normally, Dad would show up every few years during their Christmas day dinner. It wasn't like him to show up when so many people outside the family were present. Was he using all these people like a shield so nobody'd yell at him? He could be crazy like a fox.

Deciding she wouldn't be responsible for any yelling for the moment, Lita hurried up beside Rosie, who was in the middle of telling a funny story about the twins to a couple of Mom's neighbors. Blessedly, Rosie'd had her back to the door and hadn't seen Dad come in.

Lita interrupted as politely as possible and pulled her sister aside. "Bad news alert," Lita murmured in her ear. "Dad's here."

"What?" Rosie hissed, but she finally spotted the man. She narrowed her eyes and growled. "After Mom paid him off that last time, he said he'd never bother us again!"

"He must've changed his mind." Lita shook her head. "He said he wanted to see his grandchildren."

"Yeah, right." She sniffed. "It's not like he sent a card when they were born. I'll bet he doesn't even know their names."

Dad headed over to the margarita machine and filled his cup up to the brim. She and Rosie exchanged a disgusted glance. The last time Dad had been here, he'd tearfully told Mom that he needed to go to rehab to kick his alcohol habit, but he didn't have the twenty thousand dollars it would take to go. As a "professional poker player," he didn't have insurance, and he desperately needed the help.

Like a fool, the woman had given it to him, truly believing he was trying to better himself. He'd disappeared without a word. No updates, no "thank you, I've finished the program." And then he had the gall to come in here and suck down margaritas? Like nothing even happened? Maybe he should sell off some of those expensive clothes he was wearing and give Mom her money back.

Lita growled, her blood boiling as she watched her dad sidle up to Mom again. Smiling. Laughing. Touching her on the arm.

"Where's Tino?" Lita asked.

"Mom sent him out to get some extra ice for the margarita machine. He should be back any minute," Rosie answered.

Good. That's good. It surely wouldn't hurt for Dad to see that Mom had moved on with a guy who was truly worthy of her. She only hoped the ensuing shitshow wouldn't be enough to run Tino off. Lord, talk about baggage...

She and Rosie kept a protective watch on their parents as they chatted. But when Dad directed Mom back to the master bedroom, and she followed, alarm bells went off for both of them. Every time the man had gotten their mother alone, he'd managed to bilk her for money. Five hundred dollars to tie him over to the next tournament. Two thousand dollars to pay off his back rent. Eight thousand dollars to keep his car from being repossessed. It was always a loan. But he'd never paid her back. Not even partially.

And now he was here, up to his old tricks. She and Rosie didn't even have to discuss it. They both headed straight for the bedroom to put a stop to this.

They jiggled the door handle, but it didn't budge. Her

father must've locked the door. Rosie pulled out a bobby pin from her hair, stuck it in the release mechanism, and it opened wide.

Mom stood staring out the window, arms crossed, and Dad still had his hand up, interrupted in mid-pitch. "Dammit, girls, haven't you ever heard of privacy?" he snapped.

"Too bad, *Papi*." Rosie waved a finger in the air. "Not when it comes to you. We figured we'd come in here before you'd emptied her IRA. What's the story this time? Fire? Flood? Tornado? Let me guess—an alien abduction?"

"None of the above!" Dad stood up proudly and pasted on his oiliest smile. "I've come here today with the chance for us all to earn back everything I've ever borrowed and more. It's our big break—a real can't-miss opportunity!"

Our big break? She and Rosie listened, slack-jawed, as the man outlined one of the most preposterous get-rich-schemes she'd ever heard. A "buddy of his" had cued him in to this up-and-coming company in China that had developed an alternative to bitcoin. Now his buddy needed investors to build his server farm, which would start producing the currency. It wasn't established as a method of payment yet, and the Chinese government hadn't gotten wind of it, either. But they were expecting people to buy in big and make them all millionaires. For the low, low price of fifty thousand dollars, she could get in on the ground floor of this opportunity. "Just write the check, Alessandra," he told her, "and I'll take care of the rest."

He'd *take care*...

Oh Lita couldn't *believe* this. Fury cracked over her, hot and quick. Since when had Marshall Noe ever taken care of *anything*? That this man would have the brass balls to stand here and make another big ask, after everything he'd already taken from this family. Like the nice memories of this party today, for instance. She curled her hands into fists so hard her fingernails dug in. It was the only thing she could do to keep from slapping that simpering, salesy smile right off his face.

Oh no, this little scheme of his would not be happenin' today, or any other day. She had about a thousand comebacks for this bullshit.

But Rosie let out a furious "Are you kidding me right now?" before Lita got the chance to say them. "Boy, what a creative beggar you've become. You've graduated from hitting Mom up with bogus sob stories, and now you've moved on to bogus business opportunities! You've given yourself a promotion!"

"That's right!" Lita spat, stepping right up toe-to-toe with her dad. She shoved a finger in his chest. "Seems to me like it's the perfect story too. You walk off with the money, and then you're all, 'oh, no! Those damn communists shut us down, what are we gonna do?' How about this idea, Dad? How about you pay mom back everything you owe her *before* you ask for an investment? How much are you up to now? Thirty thousand?"

Dad peered down his nose at her. "I don't see how that's any of your—"

"It's forty-six thousand, nine-hundred eighty-five dollars and forty-six cents, to be exact," Mom interrupted, finally moving away from the window. "You know, all these years, I thought I was really helping you, Marshall. That you were trying. Or, maybe...maybe it was my penance for getting knocked up too young. The literal price I had to pay. But I paid it, so you'd go away and not bother us. I didn't want you to be a terrible influence on the girls. It felt like the right thing to do at the time. But I see it now. Throwing money at your problems only made them worse. That stops now. The answer is *no*, Marshall."

For once, Dad let his mask slip. True panic flashed on his face, and a queasy kind of sadness seemed to transform his features. His shoulders drooped. "Alessandra..." he breathed. "You don't believe me?"

"No, Marshall. I never did." Her smile was soft as she gave his shoulder a gentle pat. "I've been your backstop— that hook that kept you from sliding over the edge for thirty years. I won't do that anymore. It's time for you to be a man."

His chin quivered and his eyes glistened with tears. "Alessandra, you don't understand. It's bad. I've got—"

"Stop. Just *stop*." Mom's voice got hard—hard enough that no one would doubt this was her final word. Lita felt a surge of hope in her chest as Mom stabbed a finger at him. "I don't care what bookie is after you, or who's repossessing what. If you want to walk through my door, if you want to see your family, you need to start paying me back. I want to see every dime from the loans. Until the day you can do that, you need to leave us alone."

Dad rounded his eyes in shock, and his face got all red. "Alessandra! Don't you get it? I can't—"

"Don't. You. *Dare*," Mom stopped him, real anger flashing in her eyes. "You think you're gonna get salty with me? That's your play? Go on and try it. One false step, and I swear, I'll hire a lawyer and sue your ass for the twenty years of child support you never paid."

Lita had never been prouder of her mom than she was at this moment. A wave of sympathy rolled over her too. All these years, she'd judged her mom, thinking she was too weak and blind to see Dad for what he was. The total opposite had been true. The woman had always known *exactly* what this was—what *he* was. She'd paid him off and let him think he was winning so she and Rosie could grow up in peace.

Her mother had saved them from years of disappointments and broken promises. And it had cost her—dearly—in every possible way.

For once, though, Lita couldn't help but wonder what this lifetime of mistakes had cost her dad. She'd never quite seen him like this. So cornered. So...confronted. He flattened his mouth into a thin line and stood there, shaking his head. "No. Ut-uh. You don't get to do this." He pointed an angry finger in Mom's direction now. "You do not get to tell me who I can and can't talk to. You do not get to tell me who I can't see."

"Yeah, buddy, I think she can." Tino stepped through the open doorway. "It's her house. Her kids. And if you won't listen to her, then you're gonna listen to *me*, boy-o."

Lita and Rosie both raised their eyebrows at that. They'd gotten so used to Tino being a big ol' softie, they'd forgotten how enormous he was. His muscles twitched under his silly Christmas tee, and he towered head and shoulders over Dad. Tino puffed himself up, chest to chest with Dad, crowding him.

"And who the hell are *you?*" Dad demanded.

"I'm with Alessandra," Tino told him, and it was impossible to miss the ring of pride in his voice. "I'm the one who's going to be here the next time you try shit like this. I'll be here next Christmas, and the Christmas after that, and the Christmas after that one. Because I'm crazy about her. And I'm not about to let the likes of you cause her one more minute of worry. Capiche?"

All Dad could do was stare back at the man. His face had gone slack, like the information was finally starting to compute.

Dad shook his head, scowled, and threw up his hands. He did his best to look both pleading and pathetic as he faced his daughters. A hail Mary pass, apparently. "Girls!

Are you hearing this? You're adults. Are you really going to let your mother tell you who you can talk to?"

"I'm with Mom on this," Rosie answered right away. "You on board sister?"

"Yeah. I am," Lita chimed in. "And don't stand there, father dear, and tell me all the things I'll be missing. Seeing your lying face for half a day every few years? Yeah, that won't be a sacrifice. God—is *anything* you ever told us true? Who are you, even? Hell if I know. And you know what, Dad? I don't want to. Not anymore. If you can't treat this family right, you don't deserve to be in it, not for one minute."

Rosie nodded, still glaring at their father. "Well said, sister. Well said."

Dad rounded his eyes and clamped his mouth shut into a tight, worried line. He scrubbed his hand over his face a little self-consciously. Yeah, he'd heard them. And from all his fidgeting, Lita could see the wheels spinning in his head. He was winding up his next story, his next pitch.

But before he could respond to any of them, Darius and Ross piled into the room with the boys in their arms. Darius spotted Dad and scowled. He handed Rafe to Ross and stood beside Tino. "You need any help here, T? Because I took the liberty of running Marshall's license plate before I came in here, and I'm seeing all kinds of open warrants."

That got Dad's attention. "Okay-okay!" he sputtered. "I'm leaving! Just let me see the boys before I go." Dad stepped over to Ross, who was balancing both boys on his hips. "Hey, buddies." He grinned. "Aren't you gonna say hi to your grandpa?"

Both boys shrank back, eyes wide.

Dad trotted out his charm again, widening his smile. "Oh, come on," he crooned. He reached out and nipped at Gabe's nose, and did the whole "got your nose" gambit.

Gabe only buried his head in Ross' shoulder. He tried to tickle Rafe's tummy next, but the boy shrieked and started to cry. Then Gabe was crying too.

Ross took a step backward. "Seriously, dude. You need to *leave.*"

Every eye on the room may be on Dad, but the man had lost his audience. He scanned the place, silently pleading for someone to take his side. But no one said a word. His face reddened up again, twisting up in an agony Lita had never seen him exhibit before. *Shame.* That's what it was. Maybe it was time he'd gotten acquainted with the concept.

Lita tried to muster some empathy for the man. But she couldn't manage it. The bill was coming due for all the things he'd done. And Christmas or not, it was time he understood that.

Dad took one last assessment of the room. The sound of his sobbing grandchildren rang loudly in the space. He didn't say another word. No "goodbye." No "we'll see about this." He hung his head and walked stiffly out of the room.

Lita walked behind him, not sure exactly why her feet had moved to follow him. Maybe she needed to watch her father walk down the hall, through the living room, and out the door. Everyone was having such a good time out there, they didn't notice the man walk by. Christmas music muffled the sound of the door as it slammed behind him.

She'd seen her father walk out that door so many times. But this was different. Bigger. More important.

It made her feel funny inside, seeing the door snap shut. Was this the last time she'd ever lay eyes on Marshall Noe? *Yeah, probably.*

That should be a good thing. Yet, Lita had a tingling, disconnected sensation as she shuffled back to the bedroom. Like this was all happening to someone else, and she was watching it from the sidelines. Like she couldn't quite believe this had finally, *finally* happened. She didn't really have a dad anymore, did she? Maybe she never had.

Mom, for all the strength she'd shown a minute ago, was a mess. Lita was a little surprised to see her mother fall into Tino's arms, bury her head in his chest, crying. She'd never seen her do that.

"I got you, babe," Tino murmured, rubbing her back.

By now, Rosie and Darius had moved to comfort her fussing sons, and Ross had stepped over to comfort her. He wrapped a warm hand around her shoulder and rubbed it. "Hey, you okay? I'm sorry I wasn't back here faster. That had to have been hard."

It *was*, now that she really allowed herself to think about it. Lita couldn't claim a close relationship with her father, or even any good memories of the man. But that wasn't what was making her heart sink. It was the loss—the loss of having a real father when she'd needed one.

Their family would never have a father figure, because of *him*. Mom hadn't had a good husband to share the load. Rosie hadn't had someone to walk her down the aisle. There had been one chair empty at the graduations. No bedtime stories, or kissing boo-boos, or a big, tall daddy to carry them on his shoulders at the grocery store. There'd been no grandpa to pass out cigars and candy bars when the boys had been born.

Lita couldn't quite get rid of the heaviness in her chest, and she definitely couldn't put into words the stupid, pointless sense of disappointment that always stole over her whenever she saw the back of Marshall Noe. But as Ross walked up to her with such sympathy in his eyes, she realized she didn't have to. "Come here," he murmured.

When he wrapped his arms around her, she let herself need him and every last bit of the comfort he was offering.

She took it like a greedy little girl, dry-eyed but still collapsing into his embrace.

A good man—she'd never had one of those. But maybe she could have one now.

Even if it was only just for Christmas.

CHAPTER 20

Ross couldn't help but smile at his dad while he roasted marshmallows over the fire pit. Only Rusty Mason would organize a patio party in the winter so they could make s'mores on Christmas Eve. Now they were all bundled up out here in blankets—his sister Tiff, shivering in her red velvet dress, her husband Bear, out of his contractor gear and in an ugly Christmas sweater, and his mom, of course, dutifully loading up roasting sticks for Dad.

And this time, there was Lita. She'd been to many parties out here over the years. Mom and Dad loved to entertain. But she'd never been here for their family Christmas celebration before. It felt different. Good.

Christmas Carols played through the patio speakers, while Dad hummed along and stoked the flames in the fire pit. Whenever he grilled, he got like this—all puffed up and happy like the dorky, middle-aged dad he was. His blue eyes sparkled, and his bushy gray mustache twitched with a smile as he watched that string of marshmallows brown up to a perfect crisp. Mom, never missing an opportunity to be extra about the holidays, held up a plate of red-and-green sprinkles.

Dad rolled the molten marshmallows in them then held out the stick to Lita. "Last chance for the glittery ones." He wiggled it, grinning. "You want it?"

"How can I say no to Christmas glitter?" Lita smiled at his Dad with a fondness and gratitude that made Ross pause. She'd had a helluva day today, whether she had relationship with her own dad or not. So he was glad he could give her a sweet, uncomplicated family Christmas.

Even if it was pretty cheesy. But that was the charm of the Mason family Christmas, wasn't it? Every year, his mom and dad concocted some fun, unconventional way to celebrate the holiday. Last year, they'd done a series of funny relay races in the backyard involving Christmas-colored silly string and shaving cream. The year before that, Dad had arranged for them all to go tobogganing. This year, because Tiff was so close to having the family's first grandchild, they'd gone more low-key, settling for having a white elephant gift exchange and sparkly s'mores on their brick-lined patio instead.

It was corny, grilling when it was forty-five degrees and getting dark. But it was fun and kinda cozy, The Mason family homestead was a simple four-bedroom ranch house, but the property itself was beautiful—eighty acres of forest, trails, and barns Dad used for his equine vet business. Tonight it was especially pretty, clear and crisp, and the moon hung low in a black velvet sky. Never one to do anything halfway, Mom had decorated the patio with Santa-shaped string lights, dragged out the outdoor heaters, and had even sewed matching fleece blankets for everyone to snuggle under.

Lita had assembled her s'more with a dark chocolate bar and graham crackers. She took a bite, but then broke off half and tipped it in his direction. She held it up for him to bite, and he scarfed it right down, licking his lips. Why wouldn't he? He'd been eating out of her hand, figuratively speaking, for years now. It felt stupidly good to do it now, for real. And having her here with family today connected him in a way he wasn't used to anymore. He wasn't the oddball adult, the single one, without anyone of his own.

He'd never believed in having a girlfriend for the sake of it, so he'd have someone on his arm at things like this. Maybe that's why he'd always been so adamant about keeping his love life casual. But then again, it hadn't been a love life, had it? It had been a sex life, one where everyone stayed protected, and nobody had any expectations.

It had all been so simple. Until it wasn't.

He'd gotten to the point where the thought of picking one more random chick off Tinder turned his stomach. How could he possibly want some hit-or-miss encounter when he could have Lita? He'd always wanted her, but now that he knew exactly what she felt like under his hands, how it felt to look her in the eyes...

He knew what it was now, to truly hand your heart over to someone else, even if he hadn't exactly said the words. And now that he had her, nothing else would do. He couldn't go back.

Just watching her lick the chocolate off her lips was enough to get him thinking thoughts...thoughts about how sweet she'd taste right now. Lita caught him ogling her and rolled her eyes. But she smiled too.

Yeah. She didn't want to admit it, but she was enjoying him as much as he was enjoying her. And he wanted to enjoy her some more. Very, very soon.

He was about to whisper that very thing in her ear, but his dad unrolled his lanky frame out of his camp chair and cleared his throat. "Okay, everyone, so as I told you earlier, I have a big surprise in store. It's time for y'all to gather up your blankets and walk with me."

Dad took them all around the side of the house and off to their main barn's paddock. When they rounded the corner, they were greeted with the sight of a big red sleigh, all decorated up with sleighbells, wreaths, and garlands.

Tiff laughed. "Omigawd, Dad, did you seriously buy a sleigh?"

"Didn't buy it. Borrowed it." Dad grinned. "There's a man up in the Snowshoe area who makes a buck or two giving horse-drawn sleigh rides. One of his horses needed treatment but he couldn't afford it, so—"

"You bartered for the sleigh over Christmas. That's pretty smart negotiating, Russ," Bear answered. "I checked into the whole sleigh thing for a date with Tiffany, back in the day. They can get pretty expensive."

Tiff raised an eyebrow. "And we didn't go, why?"

Bear wrapped an arm around her shoulders and slid his wife a sly grin. "I decided that weekend in the cabin was a better idea, remember?"

"Oh yeah, I remember." She shot her husband such a fond, wicked smile. And Ross watched them together, so happy and warm and intimate. He was so happy for them, but still, it made something needful ping deep inside him. He wondered what it'd be like to have that intimacy and history with someone. To be able to name it, and rely on it...

If only I could.

Eager to change the subject, Ross patted the side of the sleigh. "This is all well and good, Dad, but if you're wanting us to go on a sleigh ride, don't we have to have snow?"

"Not with this little baby," Dad crowed, and tapped a foot on the rails. "Do you really think capitalism would let a silly thing like lack of snow derail a moneymaking sleigh ride? We've got custom-built shock-absorbing rollers! What you have right here is an all-terrain sleigh. Come on, everybody, jump in! I'll get the horses all reined up."

Ross shook his head at his parents and their obvious joy over the holidays. They were incorrigible. And now that he really thought about it, he was surprised it'd taken the two of them this long to try a sleigh. Dad had always kept two Clydesdales as his own personal horses—literally calling them Clyde and Dale—because he believed were the most versatile breed, as good for pulling as they were for riding.

The man was right about that, of course. Ross could swear those horses were smiling as Mom fastened the bit and reins for the sleigh. He couldn't help admiring the sleigh as they piled in. This number was definitely built for speed, light and sleek, with a seat for two facing front for the driving team, and leather upholstered seats for two couples, facing each other in the back.

His parents proudly hopped into their driving row and whipped out top hats and scarves from under the seat.

Ross laughed. "Let me guess. You've been practicing all week."

"Of course I have!" Dad clucked. "It's great exercise for the horses!"

"Are they always like this at Christmas?" Lita murmured to him as they climbed aboard.

"This right here is the toned-down Mason family holiday," Ross answered her.

"You should've been here the year they decided they'd hide all our Christmas candy around the property." Tiff grinned.

"Oh, man!" Bear rolled his eyes. "I couldn't figure out why your dad laughed so hard when we found an ancient bag of candy canes during that shed reno. *That's* what that was."

"Hey!" Dad called over his shoulder. "Don't make fun of my enthusiasm for hidden treasure, or one day I might hide all your inheritances in Easter eggs and tell you to go hunt for it."

Ross snickered. He wouldn't put it past the man.

Plenty of Mason family zingers were exchanged as they rolled up the driveway. But once this surprisingly smooth ride hit the trail for real, everyone hushed. It was so pretty out here today, talking seemed like overkill.

It was pitch dark now. But that wasn't an issue for the likes of Rusty Mason. With his fondness for nighttime rides, the man had fitted up a couple of miles of solar arrays along the trail—enough to make it easy to stay on the well-beaten path. Clyde and Dale knew it by heart. The horses didn't mind the extra chiming sleighbells on their harnesses, either.

Ross tucked a blanket around him and Lita, and she smiled gratefully at him. He wanted to put his arm around her, the kind of easy, claiming embrace Bear had around his wife. But he wasn't sure how Lita would react to such an obvious, public move.

Tiff fit so well, tucked up under her husband's arm. The two of them were such a matched set, they reminded him of their parents. Tiff had long auburn hair like Mom's, and the same blue eyes he'd inherited from Dad. But she had crazy freckles. Bear did too, being yet another natural redhead. But that's where any passing resemblance to Rusty Mason ended. Bear was big, bearded and barrel-chested, with the kind of muscles that could only get honed from swinging a hammer for a living. His business building houses these days was booming, and the man had projects going in three states.

The man should be stressed out, but he wasn't. Tiff always seemed to calm him down. Ross took note of the easy set of the man's shoulders, the obvious pride he took in his growing family.

What would it be like to have that? Will I ever?

Just when he was starting to feel sorry for himself, Lita reached for his hand under the blanket and squeezed, all secret and sweet. Yeah, he'd take that right now, and the warmth that spread through him, because of her.

The trail was still muddy tonight, but it was cold enough that the ground was hardening up again. An occasional snowflake twirled in the cold breeze, and moonlight stole over the hills. The peace of Christmas was right there for the taking. This property was their cathedral.

They went around the farm twice, Clyde and Dale taking the gentle slopes with ease. And still, no one felt much like talking. There was too much to see for that. The trees laden with sparkling ice. The stars, shining bright in all their constellations. And Lita of course, profiled in the light of the moon, still holding his hand tight.

The ride had been long, but it seemed to have gone by in a flash. When they stepped out of the sleigh, everyone had a job to do to get the horses untethered and back in the barn for the night. Dad handed Ross the sleighbells and asked him and Lita to walk them up to the shed up by their second barn, as they were a family heirloom he didn't want accidentally going back to his client.

So the two of them headed out over the hill together. Once they were out of sight, Lita reached for his hand again, and they walked that way, together in the moonlight. Their conversation turned to chit-chat. She peppered him with questions. How the farm had gotten into his family (his great granddad), why he never became an equine vet like his dad (he preferred cars), where Tiff met Bear (Bear built her condo).

You'd think that after knowing each other for so long, they'd have nothing left they didn't know. But as he'd learned today at Alessandra's, Lita had layers. There was family history there. Things that made her who she was. Maybe he had layers too. Not so complicated as hers, most likely. But he was more than happy to let her start peeling, if it meant they could go down this road together.

Topics flowed easily as they put away the jingling harnesses and started to head back. He tried to make his answers entertaining so he could hear her laugh. It worked. Particularly the story about how Tiff had gotten herself wedged in her crawl space at her old condo, butt hanging out in the breeze, and Bear had been called to free her. Lita cracked up, giggling so hard she snorted. Probably because they'd been stuck in tight places too.

All these years, and he'd never noticed how musical her laugh was, how it rose and fell in such a joyful pattern. He stopped and pulled her to face him so he could hold both her hands. "It's good to hear you laugh, you know. You doin' okay tonight?"

"What do you mean? It's Christmas. Of course I'm okay."

"Come on, Lee." He gave their linked hands a shake. "You can't fool me. You pretend your father doesn't upset you. But I know he does. All the s'mores in the world aren't going to take that away."

She smirked. "I don't know. Have you tasted that red glitter?"

"I'm trying to be serious here."

"So am I. I really like s'mores."

Ross sighed. "Okay. I'm going to try this again. You've had a rough day, and I want to be the kind of guy who's here for you. Is there anything else I can do for you, Lita? Anything you want to talk about? Anything you need?"

Surprise sparked in her eyes, and she cocked her head at him like he was some kind of impossible creature she'd never known existed. "Just this," she breathed, and pulled him down by the scruff of his neck to kiss her.

She tasted so delicious—like sparkly sugar and warm cocoa. Hot sex and possibilities. Lita kissed him long and deep, her tongue playing with his until he'd tipped her head back in his hands and gave her more. He loved that she'd just grabbed him and kissed him like this. He wanted her to, anywhere, any time she liked.

There was nothing like this, like her. She wrapped her arms around his neck and pushed him back a couple of steps. His back met the scratchy stick of bark. And the suddenness of it made him stop.

Lita's smirk seemed to say, *what, hasn't a girl ever backed you against a tree before?*

Matter of fact, they hadn't.

He grabbed her ass in both hands now and hiked her in his arms until they were eye-to-eye. She moaned as she wrapped her pretty legs around him. Oh, yeah. It was *on now.* Chuckling, he flipped her around until he'd pinned her now. Turnabout's fair play, after all.

Was this what it meant to have someone? To always have them there, right at the end of your linked hands. To be able to reach out for moments like this, anytime you wanted. He growled and rolled himself against her.

He wanted her. He'd always wanted her. But now it was different. He was greedy. He wanted it all. Her sex, sure. But what he really craved was her attention. Her secrets. Her confidence. He was so close, and he wasn't stopping now.

One more kiss, Then another. Could she see how good they were together? He could, in every little thing—the way their bodies molded together perfectly. The way he could make her shiver and shake.

Like right now. He unbuttoned a few buttons on her

dress while he sucked and nipped at the delicious flesh along her bra line.

She tangled one hand in his hair and used the other to peel down the thin lace cups of her bra. "*God,* Ross," she murmured. "Your mouth is magic."

"You feel good too, baby. Like heaven. And I wanna go to heaven. Don't you?"

She snorted. "Gawd, I didn't know you were so cheesy, Ross."

He grinned back at her. "It's a family trait."

She rolled her back, presenting those glorious tits like the gift they were. He sucked at them, pulling them out to points with his teeth, exactly how she liked it. How he loved this, hearing the sounds she made, watching her bite her lip and hold his head down to his task. It wasn't long before she was moaning and fumbling for his zipper.

But suddenly, Lita stopped. She held her hand up in front of her face, blinking against brightness. It took Ross a second to realize it was a flashlight, trained right on them.

"Uh-oh," a feminine voice rang out. "I think I'm interrupting something."

He groaned. *Mom.*

Ross dropped Lita to her feet and stood in front of her, giving her cover while she buttoned back up.

The woman snorted, and even in the dark he could see she was delighted. "Yep. I'd say I definitely interrupted something."

"Mrs. Mason," Lita jumped in, sounding awfully formal all of a sudden. "I don't know what you saw but I want you to know that—"

Mom held up a hand, beaming. "Oh, you don't have to explain to me. Are you kidding? I'm thrilled! It's about damn time the two of you got off the fence. You've been dancing around each other since high school. I've never seen the like."

"It's not like that!" Lita cried. "It was a kiss. A one-time thing! I don't think of him like that! Tell her, Ross."

Her words hit him like a sucker punch.

Tell her?

Tell her what? *Whoops, there I go again, grinding on every woman I see and totally incapable of being serious about anything.*

That's how she wanted to play this? Like he was the big, bad lothario, accosting the one woman who...

Doesn't think of me like that.

Dismay rolled over him and his heart sank. In the harsh light Mom was casting, he saw Lita's panic. Her fear. She'd been caught and she didn't like it. They may not have talked about whether to take their relationship public, but was she really trying to send him back to the friend zone, after everything they'd shared these last few days?

Now he felt it too—the shame. The embarrassment. He'd thought they were building something real together. It had felt so good, so right. Had he been wrong?

He searched her face for something, anything. But Lita was all pokered up. Her eyes pleaded with him to back her up. She wanted him to stand here and lie to his mother about what she'd seen. Tell the woman it was a moment of insanity. *Ha-ha. Whoopsie. Won't make that mistake again.*

His heart ached in his chest—actually hurt. No, he couldn't say whatever words she wanted him to say. Shit, he could barely even breathe right now.

Ross did the only thing he could do. He walked back down the hill. Back to the house. Back to the stupidly empty life he knew. And Lita stood and watched him walk away, not saying a word.

CHAPTER 21

Ross had been so mad at her, Lita had taken the opportunity to hitch a ride back with Bear and Tiff. She'd tried to say goodbye to the man, but his mouth had clamped shut, and he'd refused to speak to her. He wouldn't even look in her direction.

Ross'd never been mad at her like that before...

But I've never hurt him like that before, either, have I?

She slumped back in her seat, more miserable than she could ever remember being. Exhausted and confused, the whole world felt like it was upside down.

Or maybe it wasn't upside down at all. Maybe she was just getting head out of the clouds and falling back down to hard, cold reality. Because it seemed to her like she'd lost two fantasies today. First, she'd lost the fantasy that her father would ever be in her life. And then she'd lost this fantasy relationship she seemed to be having with Ross, the sexy secret that could become so much more.

But maybe more than that, she'd lost his friendship, his trust. It was killing her. And she had no freakin' idea how to handle this. It wasn't like she could just go to the bookstore, browse the self-help section, and find *how to act when your best friend has been magicked into wanting you, but you might want him seriously for reals.*

She was so zoned out and miserable, Tiff had to snap her fingers to get her attention, and tell her they were nearly at Hunter's farm. Lita didn't know how she was going to face Ross now. And they'd have to feed the horses in the morning...

At the last second, Lita asked Tiff and Bear if they'd drop her off at Mom's. Yeah, it had been a sudden impulse, but it was probably the right one. Mom's house wasn't out of their way. If anyone could get her head on straight, it was her mother. Tiff agreed to the plan, and thankfully, didn't ask questions.

Lita slumped back in her seat again.

This was insane. She'd spent her whole day running, hadn't she? She'd run from the crazy at Mom's right into the mess she'd made at the Masons'. Now she was running from the Masons back to here. The way her heart was aching, her mom was the only person she wanted to see.

Lita leaned her forehead against the cool car window and closed her eyes, partly because she was tired, but mostly because of the way Tiff was giving her narrow-eyed looks. Tiff knew something had happened between her and Ross, some kind of argument. Lita admired the woman's restraint in not pestering her about it.

In one way, she couldn't understand why Ross had gotten so upset. She'd only done what she'd always done— held him off. Made light of things. Fallen back on the old friend trope. She thought that's what they'd agreed to. Only, everything had changed, hadn't it? And the disappointment on his face...even in the dark, it was plain to see.

She'd done that.

She'd betrayed her best friend in pretty much the worst way possible. Those s'mores curdled in her stomach.

When Tiff and Bear let her out of the car to a chorus of holiday well-wishes, she found herself standing there in the dark on her mother's driveway, hesitating. All the extra cars on the street were gone, and the only one left was Tino's. Mom was blasting Christmas music so loud, she could hear it from out here.

Ai, what was she going to be walking into? Mom had always had a healthy appetite for men, and she'd walked in on her once or twice, *en flagrante* on the couch or kitchen table with the latest bad boy of the week.

So, Lita gingerly opened the door and tiptoed inside, prepared to beat a hasty retreat and call an Uber if she had to. But the sight that greeted her was so sweet, so whole-some, she slowed her steps to a stop.

Mom and Tino were in the kitchen, the sink piled with sudsy water and serving dishes. Mom hummed along to "Jingle Bell Rock" while she did the washing, and Tino did the drying. But suddenly, Tino threw his towel over his shoulder and grabbed Mom, dripping hands and all, and started dancing with her.

It was some kind of couples' dance—the shag, maybe? Whatever it was, Mom fell right into step, tossing her head back and laughing. He spun her, even in the tight kitchen space, and she whooped. When he twirled her back, they swayed in each other's arms to the music. And Mom gave the man such a baldly adoring look, Lita's throat tightened in misery.

Because she wanted what they had so badly, her whole soul ached with it. She hadn't even realized what she was missing until Ross had shown her what was possible.

Except having Ross wasn't possible, was it, because it wasn't *real*.

Or was it?

Her mind wanted to laugh at the insanity of it, but her heart just felt like crying. And her heart was winning out. Dammit was her face wet now? She sniffled and wiped at her eyes with her sleeve.

Mom must have heard her, because she caught sight of her over Tino's shoulder. "Lita!" she called out. "What are you doing here? If you're here to do party cleanup, we've got that all covered."

"No, I—"she choked out an embarrassing sob. "I need to talk. Do you—do you have a minute?"

Mom furrowed her brows as she wiped her sudsy hands on her apron. "Of course, mija. Tino, can you?" She tilted her head at the sink.

"Course, babe. I'm on it." He nodded sagely, and discreetly went back to work.

Mom lowered the volume on the music, and led her back to her bedroom, closing the door. Lita propped herself on the bed among the velvet pillows, resisting the urge to burrow down under the covers and hide. Mom sat at the head of the bed with her, crossing her ankles. "This is a first, you coming over to talk like this." She patted Lita's hand. "And on Christmas Eve no less. So let me make this easy for you. I know that whole thing with your father was upsetting, and I'm so sorry you had to get mixed up in all that. But at some point, we've gotta let your dad's problems be your dad's problems, and not ours."

Lita slid down further among the shams. "I'm not disagreeing with you there, Mom. But I'm not here about that. I've got..." Her voice trailed off as she tried to describe the mess she was in. The way her heart felt like it was cracking in two. How angry she was, at herself, at the magic, at the whole stupid situation. And how, for the first time in her whole life, she felt like she was in completely over her head. "I've got boy trouble," she finally managed to say, even though she knew full well how weak that sounded.

Mom laughed. "Oh, mija! If this is Ross you're talking about, you don't have boy trouble. You've got *man* trouble. And that's the trouble, now isn't it?"

Lita raised an eyebrow at the woman. "What the hell is that supposed to mean?"

"The problem is you've known Ross for years. When you set the terms of the relationship, he was still a boy. Now, he's grown, and he's ready to take his life to the next level. He wants more from you. Don't you want more from him?"

Did she?

Yes.

The answer seemed to bubble up directly from her heart, without any of her brain cells involved. The fact that she'd reacted so quickly and viscerally to that question made her stop and turn the emotion over in her mind like a strange, beautiful treasure.

She could be happy with "this" Ross—this mature, attentive, loving, funny, loyal, sexy-as-fuck version of the man she was seeing right now. Lita thought about how he'd looked on the floor, flat on his ass, gazing up at her like she was the most amazing thing he'd ever seen. He'd called her a goddess, and he'd meant it too.

At least, she *thought* he'd meant it. But she still couldn't be one hundred percent sure. Hadn't the old lady said he'd be "sweeter than anyone knows?"

Maybe that was the spell—the special spell she'd put only on Ross. One that would make him forget about playing the field and magically morph into Mr. Romantic. Maybe his spell, like hers, was so strong it couldn't be undone with a kiss. Maybe the only thing that would undo it was the new year.

That made sense to her. Because she'd never seen him treat another woman the way he'd been treating her lately. He'd never cared whether they stayed or they went. And today? She'd hurt him, just for upholding the image he'd always had. Ross Mason: free agent. Now he suddenly felt offended by his own life philosophy.

Or maybe he's just getting serious about me...

The more likely thing was she was getting serious about a man who really didn't exist, and it was freaking her out. She was falling for a fantasy, some kind of Ross mirage.

But what would happen when the pixie dust, or the hex, or the whatever the hell it was wore off? She'd tried to fight it, but she was craving him now. When she was happy, she wanted to tell him. When she was sad, he was the one who'd listen. If she rolled over in the middle of the night, she wanted to rest her head on his strong, smooth chest and feel his arms curl around her. Even in the middle of a deep sleep, he'd pull her close, and you couldn't fake that, right?

Visions of being with him swam in her head, the thought of his hands on her, his mouth...

Even now, she shivered thinking about how amazing he was. No man had ever rocked her world like this. And it had to be *Ross.*

Mom tore away the sham Lita had stuffed over her face and grinned down at her. "I take it from your silence that I am *totally* not getting my spa day."

Lita stuffed a sham over her face again.

Mom laughed and yanked at the sham until she could pull it up by a corner. "Omilord. Are you blushing, Carmelita Rose? Is this even possible?"

"Stop it! This is serious!" Lita cried.

Mom giggled. "Oh, this is just too much. I knew this day would come. Ever since the tamales."

"Tamales? Are you kidding me? A man shows interest in tamales, and you—"

Mom put a finger over her lips. "Ach, don't be stupid. Ross was never interested in the tamales."

Lita snorted at that.

"Okay, okay." Mom held up a hand. "He did like the tamales. But he would've never been so into them if he wasn't into *you*."

"*Me?* He has a funny way of showing it! He's been making sexy happy times with half the women in Green-brier County."

"Okay, please know that I do this out of love, mija." Mom bopped her on the back of her head.

"Ow!" Lita cried, rubbing her scalp.

"And who do you think *you* are? The virgin Mary? It shouldn't matter how many women he's been with. It only matters how he is with *you. Right now.* Maybe he thought you didn't want him all these years. And he was getting his needs met until he got you to give him the time of day. Did you ever think of that?"

Jesus. Mom sounded like Pansy and Moose. Had the whole town seen it, while she'd been blind?

Lita racked her brain, rifling through her memories of their years together. Whatever he may or may not have felt for her, Ross had done a good job of hiding it. There'd been a couple of times, maybe, where she'd caught him checking her out from across the room, or he'd seemed like he was about to say one thing, then he'd crack some kind of joke. But there'd always been this vibe between them—an ease. A lack of drama. She'd enjoyed his company from day one, even their bickering.

But could that pass for love?

"I don't remember rejecting him," Lita told her.

"Maybe you didn't. Maybe you—oh, what do they call it these days—put him in the friend zone?"

Lita barked out a laugh.

But then she paused. *Had* she? She thought back to that time sophomore year, when her boyfriend had broken up with her right before prom. She'd complained about it to Ross. He'd said, "You could go with me." *Yeah, right*, had been her answer. Even a few days ago, at Corn+Flour, he'd offered to be her date to Hairball. Had he been *serious*? How many times had he joked about taking her out? A lot. It'd almost become a running thing between them.

What if it had never been a joke?

A strangled sound escaped her throat.

"Ah, *there* it is." Mom hummed. *"Now* you're getting it."

"But why now? That's what I can't get over. And he's acting so different, like Mr. Perfect. So lovey-dovey and stuff. How am I supposed to trust that, when every single guy in town thinks I'm all that and a bag of chips?"

Mom patted her cheek. "I suppose you won't know for sure until after the spell thing works its way out. But I gotta tell ya, sweetie, I don't think the way Ross is acting has to do with him being under the influence of magic. I still say the boy has been in love with you since he was fifteen. But hey, it probably doesn't hurt that he saw all these men chasing you, though."

Lita squawked and smacked her mom with her sham. "Is that the reason for the bet? For *Martinez*? You were trying to tweak Ross?"

Mom flopped back on her pillow, all pleased with herself. "I win either way, don't I? You either end up with Ross, or a nice doctor."

Lita snorted. "Mom, you know I love you, but your bets in the man department haven't exactly been on point."

"Hey!" She slapped Lita's leg. "I've got Tino. You like him!"

"Yeah! After how many years of players and deadbeats? How many of those men hung around?"

Mom shot up on the bed, and her eyebrows slammed down. "Carmelita! Don't go dragging my choices in men into this."

"Choices. Yeah, right," Lita muttered.

"Te escuché! What makes you think I wasn't making choices?"

Lita paused, reminding herself to have a little respect. Was she really in any position to drag her mom over her past? After all, her own love life could pretty much qualify her for membership in Bad Choices Anonymous.

But if they were gonna dissect her love life, maybe she could have the courage to ask her mom about hers. "Here's what I don't get, okay? Dad was such a disaster. And the men you dated after him? They were almost worse. They were always running around on you. Hopping from one woman to the next. Dumping you. Why did you pick these guys? You can't tell me they *respected* you, Mom."

"*Respected?*" Mom blinked. "Mija, I don't know where you're going with this."

"I mean, none of them ever treated you like you were important to them."

Again with the blank stare.

Lita sighed. "You know, they never acted like boyfriends."

"Boyfriends?" Mom laughed. "Oh baby I don't believe —" She laughed some more. "Did you really think they were my *boyfriends?*"

"Well, you were certainly doing—"

"Yes, Lita. I most certainly was. But I think I may have given you the wrong impression. See, I had your sister when

I was nineteen. And then I was stuck with Marshall, and..."
She let out a long breath. "When I finally got the courage
up to leave him, I decided no man would ever ruin my life
like that again. I didn't want anything serious. Then you
know, Grandma died, and J and I, we bought up the shop
and our houses, and to be honest, I didn't want a husband
telling me what to do. I only wanted someone to help me let
off some steam every now and then. And if you're gonna do
that, you might as well go with someone who makes your
heart race and doesn't have expectations, amirite?"

Now it was Lita's turn to sit there, blinking stupidly.
"Let me get this straight. You were making appointments
for the D all these years. You weren't the dumpee—"

"*They* were. That's right, honey."

The realization settled on her, and she was amazed.
Amazed. All these years, she'd taken her mother for a fool,
someone who'd let men use her over and over. She'd
assumed they'd broken her heart, when they'd just been
helping each other through the night. Alessandra Ruiz had
had her own thing going and had been happily, blissfully
commitment-free all those years. How could she not have
seen that?

She supposed it wasn't the sort of topic a mother often
got into with a teenaged daughter. But she wasn't a teenager
anymore, was she? She felt like the scales had fallen off her
eyes, or something.

"Okaaaayyy," Lita finally managed to say. "I see what
you're saying. So—when are you gonna dump Tino then?"

"Dump Tino? Oh no, he's a keeper."

Lita couldn't argue with that. But she couldn't understand why her mom had taken a left turn on her romance
M.O.

Mom curled the corner of her mouth up, her eyes
sparkling with amusement. "I can see you're not following

my logic. It's really very simple. When you girls were small, I needed a man who was serious and stable enough to be your stepfather. I never found that man, or at least, someone who was stable *and* I wanted to sleep with. Tino checks every box. And he's the kind of guy who makes me want to do nice things for him. With him. To him." She sighed dreamily and patted her heart.

"Auuugh. Stop." Lita grinned. "That's not a mental picture I want to have. But you know, if he's really as amazing as you say, why is he even on the market?"

Mom rolled her eyes. "His stupid ex-wife. He's been divorced for about four years." She paused for a long moment and nodded to herself. "Okay, Lita. I'm going to tell you something, because I think it's important for you to hear. But it's not to be repeated, all right?"

Lita nodded, wondering where she was going with this.

"Okay, so Tino was about thirty-eight or so when he'd married his first wife, and she'd wanted to have kids right away. He was on board with this, and they tried and tried to have kids for years. Finally they checked into it and found out T was infertile. His wife said it was okay at first, but when she found out how complicated it was going to be to adopt, she started picking fights with him all the time. Before long, she was having affairs. That's affairs with an *s*. The divorce really did a number on him. What people say, what they do—they can really derail your life, if you let them. Tino understands that, and I think that makes him treat what we have with greater respect than a lot of men would. And I have to respect that too, you know?"

Lita shook her head in amazement. "Wow, Mom. It sounds a lot to me like you could end up married to this guy."

Mom shrugged. "It's too early to tell. But I have to say, for once, the idea isn't scary to me. And you know what?

That feels *good*, Lita. I'm not running from that, and you shouldn't, either. It's the most wonderful thing in the world."

The most wonderful thing in the world. Yeah, right.

She was happy for her mom, straight up. But the fear Lita had on her heart was anything but wonderful. If she was running, she had good reason.

Lita poured out her whole story to her mom then—the PG-13 bits, anyway. How she and Ross had gotten together. The things he'd said to her. How he'd invited her to the Masons' and how they'd gotten caught. And the things she'd said in front of Sandy Mason...

Oh, hell. Her cheeks heated again, this time from shame. She couldn't explain why she'd flat-out panicked in the beams of that flashlight. Maybe because she'd felt like it was a point of no return. They'd be a couple officially, then.

If things didn't work out, *everyone* would know. Their friendship would be wrecked, for sure. They'd still be seeing each other on the job, and their families would probably be disappointed too. Lita would be yet another girl in a long line for him. Just another piece of ass. And she...

She couldn't *bear* the idea. Suddenly, images of Ross filled her head, waking up in bed with her on January second, all his boyfriend vibes unmagicked. He'd shrug, zip up his pants, and say, *"That was fun. See ya around at work, Lita."*

Her heart pinched painfully in her chest, just thinking about it. *Best feeling in the world, my ass.* "Mom, all I can tell you is he's acting so different. I'm not even sure he's in his right mind right now. How do I know he won't hurt me?"

Mom reached over and gave her a long hug. When she pulled back, she squeezed her shoulders. "Oh, mija. You don't know. You never can. And isn't that life for you?

Sometimes, all you can do is ask yourself, is it worth the risk?"

Yes.

Her heart answered the question again.

She could sit here and argue with herself all day, but it would never stop being true.

So yeah, she had some apologizing to do. She only hoped Ross would listen.

CHAPTER 22

Ross tossed the bale of hay into the feeder, untied the fastenings, and picked it apart with a pitchfork. He got a lump in his throat, like a stupid ass, as the horses happily tore into it. It was just like any other bale. But it had been *the* haybale—the one where he and Lita had...

He shut his eyes and swallowed hard. He really needed to stop doing this to himself. Lita had made herself crystal fuckin' clear.

She doesn't like me like that.

It shouldn't have hurt like it did. One way or another, she'd been telling him that during their whole friendship, right? It was him who hadn't been listening.

Well, he was listening now.

He'd moved out of the master and into another bedroom, so there'd be no confusion that he'd now be leaving her alone. He hadn't woken her to help him with the chores this morning, either. Mercifully, she'd slept in. And he was more than happy to be out this morning in the clear winter air, wallowing in his heartache by his own damn self.

Starlight nuzzled his ear. Ross laughed, thinking the horse was being affectionate. But then the horse nudged him in the middle of his back. He'd been standing right in front of the water trough.

Figures.

Ross went back into the barn, washed his hands, and took a few sips from his travel mug of coffee. He grimaced. He'd made it black this morning, from instant crystals, and it was cold and disappointing. Kinda like his life right now.

He went back to work, throwing around hay-bales to make a new stack configuration closer to walls of the barn. He didn't need to do it and hadn't been asked to take this task on. But he did it anyway. He wanted to work. Needed to.

You don't want to face her.

Yeah, that too.

But he was gonna have to, because Lita appeared just now at the bottom of the hill leading up to the barn. She was a freakin' vision with the morning sun at her back, but he steeled his spine. He couldn't be like this, so mixed up. Their lives were too intertwined for them to be all pissy with each other. He'd have to be an adult about this whole rejection thing, whether he wanted to be or not.

But damn, she was makin' it hard. She'd appeared at the door of the barn with a shy smile on her face, carrying a picnic basket, of all things. She'd worn her hair in a single French braid that went down her back, and a simple flannel shirt tucked into low-slung jeans. How cute. Wholesome, even. No one would suspect that she'd stomp on his heart, any chance she got.

"You didn't need to come up here, Lita," he told her. "I finished all the chores."

"And you didn't have to. Why didn't you wake me?"

He shot her a look, and it hit its target. Her smile got all pinched, and she cast her gaze to the floor. Now everything was all quiet and awkward.

"I-I brought you something," she finally said.

"I'm not hungry anymore." That's what he said. But his nose had gotten a whiff of sausage coming from that basket, and his traitorous stomach growled loud enough to hear.

Lita started to smirk but quickly hid her grin. "Really? That's too bad. I guess I'll have to eat both these biscuit sandwiches by myself." She straddled a haybale and sat down the basket. When she opened it up, his feet somehow moved on their own accord so he could see what was in there. *Awww, shit.* The unmistakable stamp of Tudors Biscuit World was on those wrappers. Dammit, she knew this was his kryptonite.

Lita held up that bundle of awesome and crinkled the paper a little bit. "I got you The Thundering Herd. You sure you don't want it?"

The Herd, named after nearby Marshall University. It was his favorite—sausage, egg, cheese, and hash browns, wrapped up in the butteriest, savoriest, fluffiest biscuits east of the Mississippi. Deciding right then and there that he didn't need to be a baby about all this, he swiped the biscuit from her hand and sat down. He unwrapped it, smiling at how the steam from its heat hit the cold air, and dug in. *Umpf.* So fuckin' good.

He glanced at Lita, and found her studying him as he ate. Satisfaction lit her expression as she watched him enjoy his food.

Ross frowned, wondering what she figured they were doing here this morning. What—did she think she could just make all this go away with baked goods? The idea made another stray shot of anger spike through him. But he glanced down in the basket again. Damn, she'd gone all out, braving the after-Christmas crowds at Corn+Flour to pick up his favorite danish too. If he were a stronger man, he'd tell her where she could stick those biscuits. But that would've been a terrible waste of a very good biscuit, and he couldn't have that.

They ate without saying a word, though, the only sound the occasional chewing noise or napkin wipe. He wasn't giving her the silent treatment exactly, but honestly, he didn't know what to say. His heart was too heavy this morning for small talk.

Lita finished her breakfast and primly stuffed all her trash back in the basket. She snapped it shut and gave him a very pointed, Lita-like look. "Is this what we're doing now? Not talking to each other?"

He didn't answer her, just trained his gaze to the horizon out the door, crunching his empty wrapper into a tighter and tighter ball. His anger bubbled up inside him for real now. And he needed to put a lid on it. It wouldn't help anything. She didn't want him, and that was that. Arguing would only make him seem like a pathetic, whiny little man.

But it appeared Lita wasn't going to let him get away with avoiding her for long. She sat there, boring a hole into him with that direct gaze of hers. What did she want him to say? Hell if he knew.

"You didn't need to do all this," he finally ground out.

"Why not? I've been buying you breakfast for years, Ross!"

He gritted his teeth at that. "Sure. Right." He nodded. "Because I'm your *friend.*"

Lita frowned and her forehead got all knotted up with confusion. "Yeah. Is there something wrong with that?"

He flinched. Actually flinched. He had to turn his back on her and hold up his hand as he walked away. He ground his teeth as he fiddled with the some of the barn equipment.

What's wrong with that?

Everything. *Every fucking thing is wrong with that.*

He felt the simultaneous urge to laugh and scream, but

he didn't do either. Good Lord, he couldn't believe her. Was that how she was gonna play this? Just pretend like all that incredible, life-altering wonderfulness between them never happened at all?

Yeah, those emotions of his...nothing could keep them from boiling over now. He felt every kind at once—grief, anger, and even stupid, pointless love, anchored like a sinking weight in his chest.

I don't want to be your friend, Lita. I won't go back in your goddamn box. He wanted to say it. Desperately. But his mouth...again with the tingling. He was so angry right now, it wouldn't even let him pry open his jaws.

Finally, it was Lita who spoke up. "I—" Lita let out a long breath. "I-I know you've got every right to be angry at me and... oh, I'm not good at this."

"At what?" he managed to say.

"Apologizing."

He made some kind of strangled, harrumphing kind of noise, mainly because that's the only sound he could manage. So he shook his head, pretending like that's what he'd meant, and kept banging away at the pitchforks and the shovels and the brushes as he put them away. The need to put his back to her was overwhelming. Because he didn't want to hear a single damn thing she was gonna say.

Apologizing.

Yeah. Sure. Why not? What apology would she pick? The *I'm-sorry-I-fucked-you-until-you-said-hello-to-God* apology? Or the *I'm-sorry-I-humiliated-you-in-front-of-your-family* apology? Or would she keep it simple and go for the *it-not-you-it's-me,* or maybe something more passive-aggressive, like *I'm-sorry-if-you-got-the-wrong-idea*?

Whatever excuse she had, he didn't want to hear it. Honestly, his stupid heart wasn't strong enough to take it. So he kept up his work, rearranging hay bales. Again.

Maybe if he ignored her long enough, she'd figure out he wasn't in the mood for this bullshit and go away.

It appeared Lita wasn't getting the message.

There was a long pause. But then her footsteps crunched in the hay as she stepped up behind him.

"Hoo." He heard her blow out a shaky breath behind him and let out a low chuckle. "This is scary. Did you know you scare me, Ross Mason?"

He snorted at that.

She grabbed his shoulders and spun him around. "That's right. I said it. And it's true, Ross. No one has ever scared me like you do. And you know why? It's because I have feelings for you. Real, honest feelings I can't ignore anymore."

What? He reared back, certain she must be punking him. But the sure, steady way her gaze met his told him she'd meant every word.

That must've been the magic key or pressure valve or something, because his anger slowly started to release its grip, even if his disbelief hadn't. His jaw unlocked, and his breath left him in a rush. "You sure about that?"

"I am." She reached out for his hand and twined her fingers in his. "This thing between us happened so fast. And-And I was afraid that when your mom found us, we'd hit the point of no return. You'd wake up one morning and be ready to move on, and then I'd lose your friendship too. And the thought of all that made me, I dunno, *freak.*"

Ross searched her face to see if she was giving him a line of bull. But she wasn't. This wasn't a bunch of words she was making up. Her neck was all blotchy like it got when she was upset, and her normal smile had twisted up in misery.

And he felt for her. He got it. He didn't want to lose her friendship, either. Ross cupped her face in his hands, gently, tenderly. "You really think I'd do that? That I'd bail on you like that?"

She bit her lip. "Haven't you done that with every other woman?"

He closed his eyes again as a sick kind of shame crept up his neck.

Shame.

He stopped himself at that thought. Maybe shame wasn't the right name for it. Because he wasn't ashamed, really. He'd never hurt anyone with his hookups, that he knew.

No, sadness was a better word. He was sad that his past behavior could make a woman like Lita doubt him. Because he could totally see why she would. He'd worn that whole casual-sex-only rule like his own personal screwed-up philosophy. *Two-fuck Chuck.* That's what his friends had called him, back in the day.

And this Christmas, he'd finally seen what a piece of shit her father was, and how her whole childhood had been a push-pull with his love. Everything clicked all of a sudden. He could see all his messin' around exactly like Lita would see it. He'd refused to take love seriously. So of course, she'd refused to take *him* seriously. Instead of fighting for her and proving to her how he felt, he'd made himself look like her dad, and every other dog that had come sniffin' round her family's door.

He winced. "Oh, Lee. Don't you know I could never, ever leave you like that?"

Her bottom lip quivered. "But—why? I'm like any other woman."

He chuckled. "You're nothing like *any* other woman. You're it for me, Lee. You get that right?"

Her eyes rounded. He'd surprised her, apparently. "What are you saying, then?"

Ross dropped his hands from her face and gathered her hands in his instead. "I'm saying I want you, and only you. And I want you to want me. And only me. Wherever that takes us."

Lita paused for a second before she nodded. "I told my family, you know."

"About us?" Hope surged in him, high and hot.

She nodded again. "I figured it was only fair. But they've been rooting for you anyway, so it wasn't any big shock."

He got that warm sensation in his chest again. That familiar, easy, happy, Lita feeling. He slid his arms around her waist and planted a jubilant kiss on her lips, swaying in her arms a little. "Your mom is *so* not winning that pool." He grinned.

"No, she's not," she answered him. Then she bit her lip and smiled the sexiest lopsided smile he'd ever seen. To his surprise, she stepped back a step and started...unbuttoning her flannel.

Hoooollllly shit.

He guessed they were made up now, because his heart was pumping out blood so fast to his extremities, he felt like he'd caught on fire. And damn if he didn't want to burn.

When her shirt fell open, he ran a shaking hand over his watering mouth. How could he get bored with the sight of these perfect tits? They were gorgeous—a bit bigger than his hands, with golden brown, upturned nipples that hardened when the cool air met them. He stepped up to her again like he was drawn by a magnet and slid his hands over her silky skin. Were those goosebumps from him, or the winter breeze? He didn't care, because this woman wasn't gonna be cold much longer.

He palmed her bare breast and kissed her. They were both shivering now. He should be used to it, how she made him shake from his head to his feet. But she always knocked him sideways. She kissed him, and he moaned. She swept her tongue deep into his mouth, and he growled.

Oh *fuck*, he wanted her, more than he'd ever wanted anything in his life. So he picked her up, threw her over his shoulder, and started running for the main house.

Lita whooped out a shriek. "What are you doing?"

"We're not doing this in the barn again," Ross answered as he bounced along the path. "I want to lay you out so I can lick every inch of your body properly."

She couldn't argue with that. Lita couldn't stop laughing as he jumped over rocks and hurried down the trail. When they stumbled through the door, he set her on her feet and pushed her shirt over her shoulders, onto the floor. And he kept walking her backward, backward, kissing and stroking. She didn't even know where they were going except further inside. And she wanted him so bad, all she could see was him, right there with her, with his hair and his skin and those freaking hot tats.

She had to get to them, see more of him. All these stupid clothes—she almost tore the buttons off his flannel before she could peel it off him. Her fingers were almost too shaky to undo his belt but, *oh*...when she undid his zipper and her hand overflowed with hot, pulsing...

She flipped him back against something hard. A wall? A couch? She didn't even know. Pure, unbridled cat-scratch lust had taken her over and narrowed her vision to him as she fell to her knees.

She pulled his cock through the gap in his boxer briefs, marveling at how incredible he looked in her hand. Pale skin gone ruddy and red, pulsing with need, right there in her palm. He was huge. Primed. *Delicious*.

When she ran her tongue from the root to tip, he moaned. When she circled the tip with her tongue, he swore. But when she took the whole length of him in her mouth, all the way down, he hissed.

"Fuck yeah, that's it."

She loved the way he tasted, like some kind of masculine sex cocktail of the woods, and expensive soap, and pheromones. Whether it was J's products or the natural taste of his skin, she didn't know. She just knew she had to have more. She had to hear him moan and hear that slapping flesh.

He wrapped his fist in her braid until it was tight against her scalp and started pumping. So dirty. So raw, she took every hot, slippery inch over and over again.

Her scalp tingled with every pull. She was tingling everywhere. Warmth flooded her, making her breasts heavy and her core pulse with need. Ross was above her swearing in a nonstop chant, but she hardly heard him...only focusing on him getting harder, harder.

Finally he yanked her head back. "Stop-stop-stop," he panted. "God, girl. That was... I'm not done with you. Not by a long shot."

He scooped her up then, this time wrapping her legs around his waist, and they clattered up the steps to the master bedroom in a haze of desperate gropes and kisses. Before she knew it, her bare back was hitting the soft bedclothes, and he'd shimmied her out of her jeans. In a flash he was naked too, ready to make good on that lick-every-inch-of-your-body promise.

But she was too far gone for that. She yanked his head up to hers. "I need you, Ross. Inside me. Right now."

He settled between her thighs and did exactly as she asked, plunging deep, as far as he could go.

She gasped at the sudden sensation of being filled. But

she wrapped her legs around him and held him there. Somehow, his heartbeat was everywhere, thundering where his chest touched hers, pulsing between her legs, hammering under the hand she held to the side of his neck. Or was that her heartbeat too, pounding in time?

Dimly, she wondered if this was what people meant when they talked about "two becoming one," because the raw power of them together took her breath away. He laced one hand with hers, then the other, and pushed them both above her head. He kissed her then, long and deep.

"I will never leave you, Lita Noe. Hear me." He pushed inside her again, hard. Harder. "Not now, not ever."

The devotion written on his face was so undeniable, it unlocked something deep inside her. She closed her eyes, soaking that in deep, and was surprised to find a tear trickling down her face. A happy one. He wiped at it with his thumb. And together they rocked up higher and higher. He kissed her face, her neck, covering her skin with sensation. So good, so perfect, he slid past all her defenses, harder, faster. And then they were coming together, like a sweaty, sighing explosion of everything good and right and perfect, synced in time. Like they were always meant to do this for each other, somehow. Like together, they were more. Maybe they were.

They laid there, spent and gasping. She stroked his back as the shudders finally quieted and they could breathe normally again. Ross stayed there, nestled in the hollow of her thighs, neither of them wanting to move or break the spell. And Lita knew, without a doubt, she didn't ever want to leave him, either.

They spent their afternoon lounging and watching movies together, tangled in each other's arms. But it was Christmas, and every Christmas evening, Mom hosted an intimate family meal and gift exchange. It would be time for her to get cleaned up and ready for it here in a few minutes, but she didn't want to go alone.

She lifted her head from its resting place on his chest. "Ross, do you think you'd like to come with me to Mom's Christmas dinner tonight?"

He stroked her hair. "You want me to be *with you* with you?"

She nodded.

"I'd be honored, babe. And hey, didn't I hear your mom say Tino would be cookin'?"

She nodded again.

"Damn, then I'm goin' for sure"

She snickered a bit as she sat back up on the couch and stretched. "I'm not gonna lie. The man can make a mean cannoli."

"Color me hungry. But you know what? Why don't we open our gifts for each other here? Right now."

"Wow. You still have mine, after I put myself in the doghouse?"

"Of course I do," he told her. "Let me go get it."

Once they both had retrieved the gifts from their hiding places, they settled down at the foot of Hunter and Kathryn's Christmas tree. She was all excited for him to open his first, so she started with the bigger shirt box.

He shook the box and furrowed his brows in confusion. "You got me clothes?"

"Just open it." She grinned. When he peeled back all her handmade bows and baubles and custom paper, he pulled out the shirt she'd made for him. He whooped. "Whoa, this is so fuckin' cool. This is your art, isn't it? But how?"

She'd experimented with a different technique, that's how. "As you can see, I started with this black long-sleeved tee. But instead of doing airbrushed paint, I tried blowing

274

on a bleach solution with my airbrush," she told him. "It took me weeks of experimentation and I had to make some custom stencils, but I finally got the whole bas relief thing going. Do you like it?"

"Are you kidding?" he crowed. "I love it!" He put it on, and she had to admit, she'd outdone herself. The tee clung to his body perfectly, outlining all his best assets. And the gear design was totally him. The whole front of the shirt was gears and pistons, like his skin had been peeled back and the steampunk mechanics were underneath—not too unlike his real tats, but with a warmer range of browns and blacks.

"You worked on this for weeks?"

She blushed. "Yeah. But now that I got the technique down, I may make it a new line in my Etsy store. You down to model it for my page?"

"Of course!" He puffed his chest out. "You want the pants on or off?"

"Ha-ha. Very funny. Now come on down here. I've got one more."

He raised his eyebrows in surprise. "Really? But we haven't been together long enough to do much with the gift thing."

"Yeah, well..." She shrugged. "I got this one this morning, when I went out for the biscuits." She handed him a square box.

He furrowed his brow again. "What in the world could this be?"

"Would you stop yappin' and start unwrappin'?"

He grinned back at her unrepentantly and peeled back the paper. When he cracked open the lid, his eyes got wide. "What? This is that watch I've been jonesing for in the store window. How in the world did you afford this?"

"What can I say? I'm a good negotiator. The guy who

owned that jewelry shop had come in asking for a tat, which I estimated at five hundred dollars. It was too rich for his blood at the time. But when I proposed a trade..."

Ross leaned forward and kissed her right on the mouth. "You got me a *five-hundred-dollar* watch. You, Lita Noe, are fucking amazing."

"I do try."

He put it on, and damn if it wasn't perfect, like she knew it would be. It was a beautiful Seiko—very sleek, with a chocolate brown starburst face and rose-gold accents. The brown leather band was a distressed too, with some blacking on it. It couldn't look better on him, the sort of fashion item that elevated whatever you were wearing and could be dressed up or down. Perfect for his new wardrobe. And every time he checked his watch, he'd think of her. What could be more perfect than that? "I'm gonna wear this watch for the rest of my life. Mark me on that."

"I'm glad you like it."

"I more than like it, Lita. That fact that you'd do this for me. It's-It's something that's all. And now I've got a present for you. A good one, I hope, but not so impressively wrapped."

He handed her a red envelope. It was thick. She opened it gingerly, careful not to tear anything. She pulled out a sheath of papers. On the first paper was two tickets to a street rod national showcase, in mid-February in Reno, Nevada. He'd made the reservation a couple of days ago. Then there were two plane tickets out there. One hotel room. And tickets to some really cool shows out there too. Four whole days' worth of stuff. A vacation. A real, adult vacation. She'd never gone on one of those, not by herself. And certainly not with a boyfriend.

A boyfriend. Ross was saying all the right things. But was that really what he was? Would he even remember that he'd bought these, come January second? She'd never seen him travel before, either. And she'd surely never seen him consider taking a woman with him, even to a nice restaurant. This was one hell of a leap.

But then again, so was getting a guy a five-hundred-dollar watch. She swallowed hard. Maybe they were both losing their mind, and they'd been magicked into behavior they never would've considered before.

She wished she could talk to that old weird old lady right now, because this was confusing as hell, straight up.

As she sat there, holding these papers in her hand, they felt a lot like plans. Promises, even. And promises, in her world, were almost never a good thing. They always hit right on the thing you wanted most in the world, dangled it so close you could touch it. But then life always, *always* snatched it all away. Promises were bullshit—a recipe for disappointment and betrayal. And yet, she curled her fingers around the pages, holding them in her sweaty fingers with the hope of a child.

Please, Lord. I don't ask you for much. But please, please, please, let this be real. Let me have this.

Ross reached over and rubbed her knee, concern creasing his brow. "You okay, Lee? You haven't said a word. Do you like it?"

"Yeah," she finally managed, though her voice sounded far more choked with emotion than she'd intended. "It's everything I've ever wanted."

And Lita knew in her heart, it was true.

CHAPTER 23

Ross HAD SPENT most of the ride over to Alessandra's hoping his arrival at Christmas dinner wouldn't be that much of a big deal. Wouldn't it be great if he could slide in there, the old family friend steppin' a toe into the relationship business? That was how he was going to play it, mainly out of respect for Lita's need to soft-pedal this whole thing. But one look at J's face when he opened up the door, and he could see that strategy was blown to shit.

J sized them both up, and smirked. He turned around with a flourish. "Oh, siiiiister dear," he sang out. "Look who got invited to diiiiinnerrrrr!"

Mom was setting out dishes on the dining room table, but she soon stopped. "Ross!" She crossed the room, wrapped him a warm hug, and actually *pinched his cheeks*. "I am *so* glad to see you here! Oh! This is fantastic!"

"I know!" J crooned. "I'm feeling positively victorious!"

Jim snorted from his position across the room. *"Tell* me about it. He's been going on and on about his pores ever since he gave Ross his makeover."

Lita gave her uncle a pinch with her hug. "Omigod.

278

Would y'all stop? What is it Grandma used to say—don't count your chickens before they hatch?"

J noogied her head in retaliation. "I'm not counting my chickens. I'm counting my pores! Some of them are getting so big I'm giving them names."

"I'd like to say he's kidding, but he's not," Jim called out. "He's called the one there beside his left nostril Troy."

J shrugged. "I'm not denying it."

Ross stepped over to the kid-sized folding table, where Jim was doin' his damnedest to make some kind of craft project with Gabe and Rafe. "Wow, what have you got goin' on here?"

Gabe looked up from his task, and his whole face brightened. "Ross!" the child hollered and jumped off his chair to come hug his leg.

"Hold up, buddy!" Ross caught Gabe seconds before his sticky, icing-covered handprints got all over his pants. He hoisted him up instead and grabbed a towel to wipe off what appeared to be white icing, red jimmies, and some kind of edible green glitter.

"We're makin' gingy-bed houses, Ross!" Gabe cried.

"Not exactly gingerbread," Jim corrected the boy. "Graham cracker houses. And I've been trying to build the Santa's village condo complex for the last hour, and they are eating my units as fast as I can put them up. Gabe, I'll have you know, demolished my marshmallow-and-icing snowman."

To prove the point, Rafe snatched off one of the roof pieces and stuffed it in his mouth too.

"Ugh!" Jim clucked at the boy. "Roof damage. You'll never get FICO insurance for that unit now. Oh well." He sighed. "Time to call the contractor!"

They must've been playing this game for a while now, because Rafe dove in the graham cracker box and pulled out another package of cracker. "Contac-tor comin', Uncle Jim. Beep beep beep!"

J shot Jim a fond, indulgent smile as he went back to work, shaking his head at Jim's shenanigans with the kids. Those boys loved Jim and hung off him like the man was a walking playground whenever he came to visit. The reason was obvious. The man was hilarious, and a joy to be around.

Jim had a very different vibe than his husband. The man was a regional bank branch manager, after all, very proper and professional. Jim was the real deal, sitting at his banker's desk—all cufflinked shirts, silk vests, shiny wingtips, and round horn-rimmed glasses for peering over. And the haircut J had given him—a 1920s-inspired undercut slicked straight back from his forehead—only made his features more dramatic.

From a distance, Jim was the kind of man who could seem prim and intimidating. But when J was around, Jim's eyes sparkled with mischief, and humor, and fun. They were the best case of "opposites attracting" that Ross had ever seen, a partnership twenty years strong. And Lord, when those two arrived, you knew the party had gotten started.

Rosario stopped arranging her appetizer tray and waggled her cheese knife at Jim . "Could you at least make a show of pacing yourself over there? The boys are gonna be too full to touch dinner."

Darius snickered while he manned the deep fryer. "Since when have we been able to get them to sit quietly and eat their dinner?"

Never. That would be Ross' bet. The little cutie hadn't any more gotten up in his arms than he was squirming out of his hold, waving his hands and squealing. "Tiiiino! Tino cooking! I wanna see Tino!"

Ross chuckled as he walked the boy into the hive of

activity that was Alessandra's kitchen right now. Tino had definitely made good on his promise to prepare them all an Italian feast. Ross had never seen so much delicious food in one place. There were big platters of fresh mozzarella slices layered with juicy red tomatoes and marinated with oil and spices. Giant bowls of Caesar salad. A big tray of what appeared to be fresh-made tiramisu, coming out of the fridge. Darius pulled the last of the calamari out of the bubbling oil, while Tino stirred the biggest pot of sauce he'd ever seen.

"Aaaaaaay, buddy!" Tino cried and held his arms out to catch Gabe. "There you are! I've been wondering how long it was gonna take you to get in here. I saved the most important job for you! Here. Come check out the bolognese."

He held up Gabe so he could see into the bubbling pot, and the two of them chattered away about how many tomatoes it took to make it, and how much brisket and veal. Gabe nodded intently. Lita came up beside Tino to see what they were talkin' about. Every time Tino would tell him one of his cooking facts, Gabe would shout, "Whoa!" Before long, every one in the kitchen was saying "whoa" all together, and giggling.

Tino grabbed a big fistful of fresh, chopped basil off his cutting board, and put it in Gabe's chubby fist. "Now it's your turn to cook, Gabe. I want you to take this basil here and put it in the sauce. Like this." He threw some in the pot with a snap of his wrist. "Boom."

"Boom!" Gabe hollered as he imitated him, and threw it in. He squealed with one of the cutest little-kid laughs ever.

Then Tino threw in more. "Boom!" Before you knew it, the two of them had boomed every spice in the kitchen, and the whole family was clapping and laughing.

From there the festival atmosphere set in as Tino started pulling everything out of the oven. They cheered when he poured the rich, wine-soaked bolognese over thick, curly homemade pasta. They applauded when he used a motorized grater to sprinkle fresh parmesan over the calamari. And when he pulled the cheesy, gooey garlic bread out of the oven and slammed on the last of the fresh oregano like a three-ring circus master, the crowd went wild. He took bows while everyone hooted and hollered.

Lita elbowed Ross in the ribs, grinning. "I hope he stays around. I think I like this Christmas tradition."

Ross hoped Tino *and he* stayed around too. He'd always thought Lita's family was rowdy and fun and totally awesome. He could totally see him doing this Christmas dinner, again and again. Hmmm. He liked the idea of being a new member in this tight group. Yeah, he definitely had room for two crazy families in his life, if Lita'd let that happen.

But he was getting ahead of himself. First, dinner.

Everybody piled their plates high, lined up at the table, and dug in without any ceremony. And because the boys had helped make the sauce, Gabe and Rafe both stuffed themselves with the pasta and cheesy bread. When it came time for dessert, Alessandra pulled out the tiramisu, and also Christmas cookies shaped like big red Christmas tree ornaments.

Lita picked up a cookie and took a bite. "Mmm. This one's good. Did you make these too, Tino?"

"No," Tino replied. "Your mom ordered them from Corn+Flour."

"Yes." Alessandra pursed her lips. "And that was strange too. I called Suzie up and asked them if I could have an extra order of those pretty cookies Lita had there a few days ago. But wouldn't you know, they said they don't ever sell Christmas cookies out of the case, even during the holiday. I described them to her like you'd told me, Lita, with all the cutouts and sugar work. But the price she quoted was more than I'd budgeted. So I had them make these."

Ross didn't even have to ask to know that Lita was thinking what he was thinking right now...

Were those cookies we ate really magic?

Lita sat at the family table, chewing on this perfectly good sugar cookie. But her appetite was officially shut down for business. *Holy crap.*

So—if Suzie's people didn't make those cookies, where had the cookies come from that they'd eaten that day? Had that strange old lady drugged them and brought them in the store, hoping to foist them on unsuspecting people? Maybe she's a witch or something who'd conjured them from the thin air... Had she bought it somewhere else and enchanted it somehow, right in front of them?

Her head spun out scenario after scenario. But they all came back to the same thing.

We accepted candy from a stranger.

Lita watched as everybody ate tiramisu and chatted. Clearly, no one had connected the dots that she'd somehow ingested some magic object. She had absolute proof now. That hadn't been some random cookie. Definitely not hungry anymore, she discreetly set the last of her perfectly normal, benign cookie on her plate.

Ross, however, didn't seem to have any such concerns. He ate one cookie and reached for another, acting bemused. *Ooh*, that man. He was enjoying this! She slapped his leg under the table, and he shot her a look that seemed to say, *what?* He leaned over and gave her a kiss on the cheek. "Ain't a thing we can do about it now. Might as well have your cookie and eat it too."

Lita wished she could be that calm about it. But it made

her wonder...all this time, she'd been worried about how the hex was playing out with other people. But how much had *her* thinking been affected? She wasn't exactly acting like herself, either. Jumping on Ross at his every beck and call, giving him expensive gifts, getting so serious, in days. *Days*.

Maybe *she* was the one who was messed up.

Seeming to sense her train of thoughts, Ross gave her hand a squeeze under the tablecloth. "You're alright. I promise," he murmured, just loud enough for her to hear.

But how could she know that? The simple fact of the matter remained, the woman had said whatever this was would last through the Christmas season. So until the morning of January second, all bets were off. Literally *anything* could happen.

And as if to prove her right, there was a knock at the door. When Tino got up to get it, who should be standing there but Dad, wearing a Santa hat and an uncertain smile. He had a big red sack full of, what—*presents?*

Like he was friggin' Santa Claus or something. Was the man even serious right now?

Dad swallowed hard as Tino towered over him in the doorway, scowling. He peeked around Tino's considerable shoulders and laughed uncomfortably. "Wow, Alessandra. Hell of a bouncer you've got there. You gonna let me in?"

CHAPTER 24

Lita didn't know what was a stranger sight—Dad being all contrite and off his game, or Tino turning from a teddy bear to a scary-as-crap bodyguard.

Tino squared himself up in the doorway, blocking Dad's path. "Yeah, see, I don't recall you gettin' an invite, Marshall."

Mom rubbed her forehead and wore a pinched, dismayed expression. She didn't exactly jump up to greet her ex. Nobody did. "Marshall," she called out. "If you're here to cause more trouble, you can turn right back around."

Dad's chuckle rang hollow. "Trouble? Now why would I be here to cause trouble on Christmas Day? Can't a man come to see his family?"

Tino glared down at Dad. "Family. What would *you* know about it, asshole? You've got the most incredible family in the whole world. You had a wife who was fuckin' amazing. Bright, wonderful girls. And grandchildren? Ohmigod, those boys. A joy upon this earth. But what would you know about it? You threw them all away. Now you come back here, all *family* this and *family* that. Like you've even earned the right to have the word in your mouth."

Dad held up his hands. "I see what you're saying, okay? I'm here to see—"

"Shut it *right now*, you manipulative little shit." Tino jammed a finger in Dad's chest. "You only have a family when it suits you. When you want somethin'. Not today, buddy. You can head right down that road and never come back."

"Alessandra!" Dad called. "Are you hearing all this?"

"Yes I am, Marshall," Mom called back.

"Aren't you gonna call off your dog?" he sputtered.

Mom crossed her arms over her chest. "I think it's *you* who's the dog in this situation, don't you think?"

Dad's face fell, and he sagged against the porch railing, all his fight gone. He cast his gaze to the concrete stoop, acting ashamed for the first—okay, maybe the second—time in his life.

Lita supposed the man wasn't used to blowback. Mom always opened the door for him, always listened to him, no matter how long it had been since he'd seen them all last. When they were kids, they'd be lucky to see him every two or three years, and even then only for an hour or two. He'd come trailing promises of trips they'd take together, or gifts he'd buy for Christmas or their birthdays. Or worse yet, gifts he *said* he'd bought, but were "tied up at home."

It'd taken her a few years to realize that Dad never, ever did what he said. But after a too many Christmases and birthdays spent watching out the window for him, she'd figured it out. By the time she was ten, she'd known for a stone-cold fact that her dad didn't care about them. Even when he'd lived with them, he'd never been the kind of dad to do bedtime stories or braid their hair. He wasn't even like the divorced dads she knew, who at least did a weekend or two every now and then and showed up for important events. No, when Marshall Noe showed up, the only thing he brought them was a headache.

"I get it, I do," Dad nodded. "Everything anyone has ever said about me is true. I've made a mess of everything in my life—especially this—with you, Alessandra. But I'm not here to try to win anybody back. Or ask for money or loans or investments, either. Not today. I have some things I'd like to give to *you* for a change. If you'll let me come in for a minute, I can do that, and I swear, then I'll be on my way. You can go on having a nice Christmas without me."

Tino narrowed his eyes at Dad, but checked over his shoulder at Mom. "It's your call, babe."

Mom exchanged glances with her and Rosie. "What do you think, girls?"

Lita crossed her arms over her chest. "Throw his ass out."

"I see what you're saying, " Rosie jumped in. "But I dunno. Don't you think you should let him in?"

Lita's mouth dropped open at that. "Why? So he can ruin another perfectly good Christmas? "

Rosie narrowed her eyes at their father. "I dunno. This feels different. Doesn't it feel different to you? I think we should hear what the man has to say. If we don't like what we hear, Tino can toss him face-first onto the driveway if he wants. I'm sure Darius would love to help him."

"I would. Definitely," Darius growled.

Mom let out a long breath. "Okay, Tino. Let him in. But only for a minute."

The family tidied up and tossed their dishes in the sink while Dad found a spot in the living room. Lita sat down on the couch with Ross as everyone shuffled reluctantly into the space.

Dad sat on an ottoman in the middle of the room,

nervously picking at the corner of the bag he'd brought. Lita couldn't help but notice how run down he appeared compared to yesterday. He wore saggy jeans and a faded Florida State sweatshirt, though he'd never gone to school there or followed the team. Scrubbing a hand over his gray, unshaven five o'clock shadow, he took off his ball cap, revealing a bald spot. Had he been wearing a toupee yesterday?

And why did he come here looking so raggedy? He knew full well the family came dressed to celebrate for Mom's Christmas Day dinner. Ross had worn a red cashmere sweater with his slim-fitting khakis, and she'd worn a green swing dress. Mom was in her favorite crushed velvet party dress, which matched Tino's Christmas vest. Rosie's whole family was dressed in matching red plaid. And J and Jim? They were dressed to the nines in matching neon green Christmas suits covered with tiny red Christmas trees. Her father couldn't have been more out of place.

Dad nodded toward Ross. "You introducing me to your boyfriend?"

Am I? Lita clenched her fists in the seat cushions for a second, but she gave in. "Dad, this is Ross Mason. Ross, this is the man responsible for my existence, Marshall Noe."

Dad held out a hand to Ross. Ross leaned forward and shook it, giving the man a quick nod.

"You don't look familiar." Dad said. "How long you known Lita?"

"Fourteen years come January," Ross told him.

Dad raised his eyebrows at that.

"Had you been around, you would've met Ross," Lita told him. "We've been friends since forever. And we work at the same auto shop, so we spend a lot of time together."

"Ah, friends. So it's not serious then," Dad answered her.

"Didn't say that," Ross cut in.

Serious. Lita tucked that adjective away for the moment, not wanting to fill in any of those blanks for her father. Her life was crazy enough without having to explain it to someone else.

There weren't enough chairs for everyone, so when Mom found a space to sit on Tino's knee, the family settled. "Okay, Marshall." Mom waved a hand at him. "Whatever it is you have to say, you have the floor. I suggest you make it quick."

Dad frowned with an expression far bleaker than she'd ever seen from him. Dad squirmed under their collective inspection, and it made Lita squirm a little too. But finally, he cleared his throat. "I know I've done a lot of bad things over the years. As Lita's pointed out, I've not been around, and not followed through on much. I don't know that I have an excuse for all that, except to say I was always chasing the next big win. The next high. The next chance to make it." He chuckled ruefully and wagged his finger. "And I'll bet you're all sayin' to yourselves—*wow*. Look at how far *he's* come."

Dad's attempt at self-deprecating humor fell flat. No one even cracked a smile. Lita almost felt sorry for him.

Almost.

"The truth of the matter is—I'm a failure," he continued. "And it's time I finally admitted it. I've spent my life drinking more than I should, womanizing more than I should, and living my life by the roll of the dice. I'm a fifty-two-year-old man with absolutely nothing to show for myself. I've got no home, no career, no legacy. All I've got is a bunch of gambling debts and a family that hates my guts."

"Marshall," Mom broke in. "We don't hate—"

Dad held up a shaky hand, and Lita was surprised to see real tears threatening. *"Don't*, Alessandra. I'm not here to sugar-coat anything. Yesterday was awful. But it opened my eyes to how many chances I've burned through with y'all. Of how many opportunities I had to be the person y'all needed, but I didn't rise to the occasion. Of how many chances I had to *love* you, but didn't."

That brought out a growl from Tino. "Where are you going with this, Noe?"

Dad pinched the bridge of his nose. "Relax, Tino. I'm not here to make a play for my ex-wife. I am smart enough to know when that ship has sailed, believe me."

That was a relief, Lita supposed. But Marshall Noe always had some kind of angle, some kind of play. Her dinner sat uneasily in her stomach now as she waited for the other shoe to drop.

From the way Mom was sitting there, clenching her jaw, Lita could tell she was thinking the same thing. Mom sighed heavily. "So why, Marshall, are you here exactly?"

"Wow. Well, okay." Dad scrubbed his hands over his face again. "When I finally figured out how y'all really saw me, it got me thinking clear, maybe for the first time. It was all right there on your faces—every consequence for everything I've done and not done with this family. My kids only know me for the trouble I drag in the door, not for doing anything good for them. My grandkids think I'm some weird, scary stranger. And the debt I've racked up with you, Alessandra, it's...it's not right."

J sniffed. "Yeah, well. You know how to fix that, don't you? The answer is green and comes in little rectangles with Ben Franklin on them."

"Right." Dad nodded at him. "You're absolutely right. So, I wanted you to know, I never intended to stiff you for those loans, Alessandra. I would get ahead, but then there'd always be the next lost hand, or the next wrong bet, and all hell would break loose. Enforcers would show up to demand their money. Or I'd get banned for counting cards. Or the electricity would get shut off, or some shit like that."

Finally, Rosie had had enough. "So what, Dad? Okay, so you made terrible life decisions, and now your family is refusing to be dragged down to hell with you. You're expecting us to buy into your sad story? Why? What's the big ask going to be this time?"

"Nothing. *I swear.* I'm not even asking for your forgiveness, because I haven't earned it. But I mean to start earning it, today." Dad reached into his bag, pulled out a bulging envelope, and handed it to Mom.

What in the world? What was that, monopoly money? They all exchanged shocked glances as he placed the envelope in Mom's hand.

Mom was speechless and wide-eyed, but she opened it. Damn, it was stuffed with bills. Her eyebrows went up even further as she ruffled through it. "There's a lot of money in here. Marshall? Are you trying to pay me back?"

"Consider it a down payment."

"But—" Mom sputtered, "—where'd you get all this? Aren't you supposed to be broke?"

"It's true—I didn't have any cash. So, I sold my car." Dad shrugged. "Well, traded in the lease, anyway. I was able to get six thousand cash out of it. And I figure that's a start. I'm going to pay back every dime." He looked around the room, but he got nothing but shocked, disbelieving faces. You could've heard a pin drop. "It's not a trick! *Okay?*"

Mom furrowed her brows. "Okaaaay."

Alright, that was crazy, right there. What in the world was Dad up to? Lita was so used to the man being horrible, she didn't even know what to do with this new Marshall Noe and his mea culpas.

Tense silence reigned in Mom's house—a place that was normally so full of sound and life and love. Even the twins were asleep in their parent's arms, and Whoopie was napping under a chair. Dad twiddled with the hem of that big cloth bag he'd brought, as if he were trying to make a decision.

Lita reached out for Ross' hand, and the riot of anxiety in her stomach seemed to settle a bit. As bad as these encounters were, she was glad he was here for her. He squeezed her hand, and she gave him a grateful smile.

Truth was, she'd never seen her father make these kinds of strange admissions. Surely, he'd do something. A business pitch. A rant. Another self-pitying speech.

But Dad did none of those things. Instead, he reached in the bag and started unpacking gifts, arranging them in neat piles. The boxes and bags were banged all to hell. The wrapping paper was faded, and some of the corners were rubbed through.

"Dad," Rosie groaned. "What are you doing?"

"I'm giving you your presents," he replied, still pulling out one box after another.

Rosie snorted. "I know you've got a lot to make up for, but isn't that kind of a lot?"

"It is," Dad told her, "for this year. But I've got presents here goin' back ten years, at least."

They all raised their eyebrows at that.

"Sounds nuts, right? Maybe it was. But see, every Christmas, I'd make all these plans. I was gonna fix things and have a nice holiday with my girls. I'd start months in advance buyin' stuff and storing it away. I'd get this story in my mind about how I'd come in here with these really considerate gifts, and I'd get to spend some time, and maybe you girls wouldn't think I was so bad."

Mom and J exchanged an exasperated eyeroll at that. But Dad didn't argue with either one of them. He simply handed his ex a long, flat box instead. Reluctantly, Mom tore back the crusty paper and opened it. It was a portrait of her daughters, when they'd been in grade school. Lita grabbed it from her. The drawing was really good—an original done in vibrant pastels, professionally matted and framed with non-reflective glass. The sight of it made her get a funny sensation inside, seeing her and Rosie, in all their kiddie-fied, gap-toothed glory. How much time had passed...

Mom, for her part, rubbed at the back of her neck, still looking confused. "Marshall, how did you do this?"

He pulled a faded photo of that exact pose out of his wallet. "Saw a woman on the street in Vegas doing portraits one day. I gave her this."

He carries our picture in his wallet? That wasn't something she'd ever imagined him doing. When Lita was that age, she'd always pictured him in some faraway place, having adventures and being glad to be gone. *But was he?*

By now, Rosie was starting to go through the stack of presents in front of her. As much as she could, anyway, still holding Gabe. She picked a big one off the top. When she freed the box from the paper and unrolled the delicate tissue paper, she gasped. Inside were baby blankets, or to be more accurate, small hand-pieced quilts with the boy's names appliquéd on them, and their birthdays. The dates were right.

"Dad." Rosie's voice broke. She shook her head and held up her hand, because she'd started crying now.

Stupid mom hormones. Lita scowled at her sister, and she scowled at the boxes in front of her. Was this some kind of manipulation on her dad's part? *Probably.* Hadn't it always been?

She didn't care if Dad gave her the flippin' Hope diamond, she wasn't changing her opinion of the man. Steeling herself, Lita started quickly tearing through the pile in front of her. Lucky guesses, all. Paintbrushes. One of those fancy laser cutter machines for crafting paper which, okay, *was* pretty cool. There were some nice, signed hardback books in there too, YA fantasies she'd been into a few years back. But when Lita came to the last box, she paused.

It was black velvet. *Jewelry.* She almost groaned. The big guns—the thing guys pulled out when they were really trying to win back your good graces. She wondered what kind of impersonal, Zales sale-of-the-month thing would be in here.

But when she opened the box, it was her turn to gasp.

There, nestled among the pink satin, was a gold necklace with her whole name—Carmelita—stamped out in cursive loops of rose gold. Over the A was a big pink stone.

"Rose quartz. That's the alternative birthstone for January birthdays, right?" Dad said.

Lita nodded dumbly at the man, still too blown away to speak. There it was again, that fullness in her chest. It was only a stupid necklace. She told herself that.

But it was like he'd found the one thing...

She shook her head and blinked fast, but tears still swam in her eyes.

Sensing her distress, Ross picked the box out of her hands. "Wow! Who'd have thought? You used to talk about this necklace all the time. Didn't Carrie Bradshaw have one of these, you know, from *Sex and the City*?"

Lita didn't answer him. The damn lump in her throat was too big. The fact was, this was one of those gifts she'd always wanted, but had never gotten. She'd gone through a Carrie Bradshaw phase about ten years back. It was a stupid, cringey detail about her life. She still had the whole *Sex and the City* series on DVD—her go-to comfort binge whenever she had a bad day. And honestly, she didn't know what was stranger, that Dad could've made this lucky guess, or that Ross would've known what the gift meant.

"How?" she finally croaked out.

"It wasn't hard." Dad shrugged. "Didn't you put it on your Instagram?"

She let out an incredulous chuckle and wiped at her eyes.

Yeah, she had. The one that very few people followed, mainly showing her artwork and art inspirations. But *he'd* followed her. All this time. Probably under an alias or something so she wouldn't block him.

She *had* mattered to him, after all. He'd just screwed his life up so bad, he couldn't show her.

Lita took the box back from Ross and unwound the necklace from its fastenings. In the din of crackling wrapping paper and conversation, Lita found her dad watching her. Hope, fear, vulnerability...they were so plain on his face.. It pinged her stupid heart again.

This gift didn't change anything. Her dad was still a crappy father. It didn't rewrite history, erase his mistakes, or unwind all the consequences that came with them.

But it was something.

Maybe even something important.

Lita unhooked the clasp and got down on the floor right in front of the ottoman where Dad was sitting. She held the necklace up to her neck and pulled her hair out of the way. "Would you mind putting this on?" she asked him.

Dad's smile was wobbly and his voice was hoarse when he said, "Yeah, honey. Come here."

She gave the man a hug then—the first one since she was maybe four or five years old. It felt...*good*.

When Lita looked over at her mom, she found the woman was fighting back tears too.

Mom cleared her throat. "Marshall, have you eaten yet? I could make you a plate."

The smile Dad gave her was surprised, and sweet. "Yeah" he breathed. "I'd really, really like that."

Mom popped out of her seat and headed for the kitchen. "Everything's still warm. Lucky for you, you're not too late."

CHAPTER 25

Lita never thought she'd miss those horrible, beaded curtains.

But as she stood here in her near-empty two-bedroom apartment, she found she really did miss Pansy and Moose. They were nuts, all up in the woo woo with their candles and incense, and not exactly good at cleaning their gross crap out of the refrigerator.

They were kind, and decent though, and good at coordinating everything here at the apartment. She should be rejoicing at the peace and quiet. But the sight of their keys and goodbye note on the table really bummed her out.

Our share of the rent is paid up and done. Take good care of the place. The roaches need a new mommy, LOL. If you need us to vouch for you for a new roommate, call. Don't be a stranger.

Hugs,

Pansy

For the entire time she'd lived here, all Lita had ever wanted to do was get some quiet, away from those two. But now that they were gone...

She sighed. Maybe this summer, when the weather got

nice, she'd invite them over to grill out on the roof like they used to do. *Chillin and grillin'*, as Moose always called it. Though, why they'd do that when they could roast a weenie in the yard of their new house, she had no idea.

The two of them were moving on, and she wasn't. But there was no sense cryin' over it, was there? She flopped down at her rickety kitchen table and shook her head at the sight of her dingy, empty living room. Maybe she could do something fun with the paint in here and buy something to sit on, at least. Something not too expensive?

Lita popped open a couple of online marketplaces to see if she could find any locals selling decent used furniture. She was surprised to find an authentic mid-century sofa that had been redone in some super-cool, Sputnik-inspired fabric. And then she'd found a fluffy bright blue shag rug. *Hmmm.* She could work with this. Tagging them as her favorites, she sent messages to the sellers and arranged to go see them. Hopefully meeting at their house would be okay. They didn't *sound* like serial killers, anyway.

That job accomplished, she had to move on to the part she dreaded most. Finding a new roommate. She could afford to pay for the whole place, but the thought of doing that made her shudder. Wasn't the point of living in this dump to save money? If she didn't find somebody to get her at least through the end of the lease, she'd be setting herself back a half year on her savings goals. And she'd likely be stuck here another year trying to play catch-up.

She laid her head down on her rickety Formica table and felt like crying again. But she didn't, dammit. Crying wasn't her thing, even if she was pretty overwhelmed right now. Why were all the things she wanted so far out of her reach? And now this felt like...

Like she'd gone one step forward and ten steps back. And it really, really sucked. Not knowing what else to do, she scrolled to the local roommate finder service, and hit the "post" button on the listing she'd saved.

New roommate needed for two-bedroom in historic old Lewisburg. Sublet until lease is up in summer, with opportunity to extend. Parking, electric, and gas included. Close to everything. Affordable.

She considered adding "and your roommate won't be too much of a bitch, most days anyway" on there, but decided against it.

Her stomach pinched with anxiety thinking about having to deal with strangers in her space again. And then there was the prospect of staying in this apartment for another year or two.

Gah. I could be spending my thirtieth birthday here...

She shuddered again.

Fortunately, her phone pinged at her, distracting her from this self-defeating pity party she seemed to be having.

The text, not surprisingly, was from Ross. He'd been texting and updating her a lot while they'd been staying at Hunter's, and he was beginning to sound a lot like he was her boyfriend, straight up. The kind who sent messages to her throughout the day when they couldn't be together. But this message was different.

Can you meet me out at the Palmer place?

Lita blinked in confusion, staring at it.

The *Palmer* place? It'd been abandoned for almost a year and was in really rough shape.

Why? she texted him back.

It's a surprise. I have something I want to show you.

That's what he said.

ROFL...no, I can show you that later

You need me to be there right now?

Please. I'll be waiting...

Not sure what you're up to, but I'm on my way.

Lita closed her phone, still wondering what he could possibly have going on. She wondered if he'd rented it for the afternoon or something, for them to have some kind of date. Though, she couldn't quite figure that out. That farm had to be fifty acres of nothing but thatch and wilderness. Why anyone would hang out there was beyond her. It wasn't even trailed out for ATVing that she knew of.

She hopped in her car and took the short drive out. Everything was a short drive here, but this farm was one of the few that lined Route 60 going into town. The house sat pretty far back from the road, but it was still visible, a crumbling white clapboard farmhouse probably held together by termites. When she pulled up in front of it, she smiled.

In high school, their school bus would pass this place every day. Junior year, she and Ross had gotten a rolling story going about the place that had lasted all year long. Every day, they'd tell an installment about the creepy old ruin, which at the time had still been inhabited by old Mr. Palmer, who'd been the town's crazy recluse. He'd never kept up the property. And in the two years it had sat empty after his death, it certainly hadn't improved any.

She got out of the car to find Ross bounding out of the house with his arms held wide, and grinning from ear to ear. "Well? What do you think?"

"I think the Palmer place is more haunted than it was when we were in high school. Is there a reason we're out here, Ross?"

Ross kissed her and seemed so pleased with himself, she couldn't help but smile with him. "Yeah, well. I wanted you to see the new Mason homestead. I've put the place under contract."

She laughed. "Yeah, right."

"No, I'm serious!" He raised an eyebrow at her. "What's the matter? Don't you think I can afford it?"

Wait—did she just hear this right?

Ross is buying a house? Not just a house, *a friggin' farm. What in the...*

Her mouth fell open for a second. But when she stopped to think about it, maybe she shouldn't be so shocked. She had to admit, maybe Ross *could* afford it. He'd always been better with his money than her. She'd moved out days after her high school graduation and had been scraping along ever since. But not Ross. He'd lived with his parents and had banked his full time pay for about four years. Then he'd shared a house with a few guys before he'd moved into the low-cost loft at the shop. He'd been restoring and selling one car after another too, and packing those profits away, which weren't insignificant. She did some quick math in her head.

Holy shit. Ross Mason had *money*.

He hadn't been holding out on her exactly, but—it was just something he didn't talk about. Maybe he *could* have put down half on this place. Who knows? With the shape it was in, he might've bought it outright.

Lita shut her mouth and shuffled on her feet a bit, contrite now for doubting him. "I didn't say you couldn't afford it, Ross. I'm surprised, that's all. I mean, it's so much —so big and all."

"And that's the best part!" Ross crowed. "Fifty acres! A historic house with four bedrooms. A barn perfect for my workshop. A man could put down roots here. Build a life an' all that."

All this time Ross had been saving his money, Lita had figured it was for his next new car project, or his next trip, or something. Not once had she heard him talk about all this "building a life" business. That had always been *her* dream. Hell, she'd been talking about restoring an old property ever since their days on the school bus.

What's gotten into him?

Lita was so stunned, she hardly knew what to say.

"Hey," he grabbed her hand. "I see that frown. I see you're skeptical. But this place isn't in nearly as bad of shape as you think it is. Come on inside, and I'll show you."

Lita let him lead her inside the place. The door creaked and rattled behind her, but once she stepped inside, all her expectations got flipped on their head. The spotless hardwood floors gleamed. The sturdy walnut staircase in the foyer gave way to a hardwood paneled hallway. All the entries to the rooms were rounded with wooden moldings several inches thick. As they stepped from room to room, she couldn't help but find one wonder after another. The whitewashed, exposed brick fireplaces. The built-in bookshelves in the parlor. The corner cupboards in the dining room. The scalloped cornice board over the farmhouse sink. The master bedroom with a bank of windows overlooking the pine-covered hills outside.

Sure, the kitchen and bathrooms needed to be gutted to make it ready for the modern day. But it was useable. And everything was so neat and prim inside. All it really needed was extensive landscaping and a maybe a redo on all that wormy clapboard outside.

Her heart started to pound, and she got that love-at-first-sight, butterflies-in-the-stomach sensation she had every time she went inside cool old houses like this. "How is it possible this place looks so good inside, when it's so terrible on the outside?" she asked him.

Ross shrugged. "Old Mr. Palmer never switched anything out. He still had the same shag carpet from the Seventies. When his kids pulled it up, the floors were perfect under there. All they really had to do was throw out all the junk he'd been hoarding and paint."

Lita was stunned. *Stunned.*

Sure, the place was cool. Beyond cool, really. But was it *Ross?* She had the sudden, overwhelming urge to talk him out of this. "Yeah—but the exterior! Do you know how expensive it would be to replace all that clapboard? Do people even do that anymore?"

"Bear came out and gave the place a once-over. He said the clapboard only needed to be scraped and painted."

"But the wires! And the plumbing!" Lita sputtered. "They have to be at least a hundred years old!"

Ross wagged a finger at her. "I can see why you'd be concerned about that. But you forget, old man Palmer was a plumber. Bear said the pipes were in better shape than most new construction. Now, the electrical will need a redo, but I figure I'll get into that when I redo the kitchen. And Bear agreed to do the reno at cost, so..."

Whoa. "A *reno.*" This was *Ross*—the same guy who'd dumpster-dived for half his furniture. And he was going to do a *reno?*

Who was this man standing in front of her? He was some kind of homesteader all of a sudden? Some HGTV candidate? This place was hella cool, but—what was going on here?

"How are you planning on pulling that off?" she asked him. "I can't exactly picture you with a bunch of design swatches and stuff."

Ross looped his arms around her waist and grinned as he swayed with her. "That's where I was hoping my beautiful, talented, incredible girlfriend would come in."

"*Me?*"

"Yes, *you!* Who else do you think I'm talkin' about? I want your opinion about everything. The paint, which trees to plant, what cabinets to pick, even the color of the curtains."

Her mouth dropped open for a second. *"Curtains*. You seriously want me to pick out *curtains*."

He grinned. "What, you got a thing against curtains?"

"No, it's just—" she sputtered, about to tell the man he'd taken leave of his senses. But he was so freakin' pleased and excited, she felt like she'd be kicking a puppy in the face or something. "Well." She sighed, deciding to demur. "You know how much I like fabric, and I do love a design project. But it's *your* place, Ross. Your decisions, not mine."

"Yeah." He sidled up to her and wrapped his arms around her waist. "That's the thing. I was kinda, really hoping this could be *our* place."

Our place.

She started to laugh again, but one look at Ross' totally open, earnest expression, and the teasing words simply dried up in her throat. She staggered back a step.

This is—this is nuts, isn't it? He's begging me to come play in my fantasy house. What is happening here?

"Whoa there." He reached out to her again and rubbed the tops of her arms. "You okay? I thought you might hit the floor for a second."

She might, actually. His words buzzed in her brain. She leaned up against a wall to steady herself. "Our place. You said *our* place."

"Yeah." He chuckled.

"As in living in this place *together*."

"That's right."

"But—I can't afford to pay half of whatever the mortgage would be on a place like this!"

Ross knitted his eyebrows together and scowled. "Who said anything about splitting things down the middle? Pay me what you can, Lee. That's not what this is about."

She blinked stupidly at the man. "What is it about, then?"

"Us, Lee. Don't you get it? I want this place for us. For our future together."

Our future together. He'd actually said that. Her heart squeezed in her chest, and she got that full feeling. That dangerous feeling that usually came right before she was disappointed.

"Future?" she breathed, like the world's dumbest parrot. She tried to laugh it off, but her titter sounded hollow. "What—you're becoming Rusty Mason all of a sudden?"

Ross shrugged. "Would that be so bad? My mom and dad got married young, but they've been happy together every single day. I'm not saying we should get married right away or anything, but..."

Fuck. Now her brain went on red alert status. *The M word. He said the M word.* She put up a shaky hand to stop him before he said anything else he couldn't take back. "Ross. Why are you doing this? Especially now. We've only been together for *days*."

"Because—" He let out a long breath. "I'd just started thinking about getting into the house market when this one came up. I remembered how much we'd always talked about the old place. It felt fated, you know? I had act. And yeah, it's fast, but it's not like we just met, Lee. And besides, by talking about this now, before the mortgage is final, I can get your name on the deed."

"*My name on the...*" She would have said more. Her head was spinning now, and she seemed to have lost the capacity to breathe for a moment. He'd seriously do that? He'd scrimped and saved for ten years, and then he'd put her name on a property, giving her half, just like that? She shook her head. "I don't have enough saved, Ross. Not like you. I have maybe fifteen thousand to my name right now."

He pulled her hands up to his face and kissed her knuckles so sweetly it almost killed her. "I don't care whether you have fifteen K or fifteen cents, Lee. I want you. I want us to have a life here. I can see it all so clearly. Big family dinners. Christmases. An art studio for you in the garage with lots of light. Fresh tomatoes from the garden. Your paintings on the walls."

Lita closed her eyes. And that was a problem. Because now, she could see it all too. Ross laying in a big, four-poster bed, with the morning light streaming over him from that bank of windows in the back. Making him tamales, and not just at Christmas. *Little red-headed children...*

Oh, no.

No no no. She couldn't do this.

She opened her eyes, and the expression on his face was so innocent, and hopeful, and sweet. Like there wasn't a thing in the world he wouldn't do for her, if only she asked. For a moment, Ross Mason had had her believing he was the sort of man who'd follow her to the ends of the earth, and never look at another woman, and would love her until the day he died.

Mr. Perfect.

How she wanted that. She wanted it with all the fierce burning hope of a kid putting out a list for Santa or the tooth fairy or something. But she couldn't do that to him. She couldn't lay all those stupid, pointless dreams at his feet.

Because this right here? This wasn't him. The Ross she knew saved, but never invested. He worked hard, but only for himself. His life was laughter, and lightness, and not getting too serious about anything or anyone. Especially her.

Honestly, she didn't know what had brought this on. Maybe it was that stupid magic cookie. Or maybe it was all that incredible sex they'd been having, frying his brain cells. Either way, she couldn't let him sign away his hard work and savings. Buying this farm was a huge commitment. Buying it with *her* was a life-altering decision.

"Can't we...can't we think about it?" she squeaked out, sounding far weaker than she'd intended.

Ross shook his head. "I know it's, like, some ridiculous turnaround. But the Palmer kids have to get the paperwork started tomorrow. They're only in town for one more day before they'll scatter back across the country. It's now or never, Lita. What do you say?"

She wanted to say yes—wanted one of those wholesome, made-for-Instagram moments where he swung her around and they laughed and kissed and thanked the stars above for their luck. But she knew what that was. It was a *fantasy*. And it was time she faced up to that.

"I-I can't," she finally managed.

His face fell. "Can't? Or *won't*?"

"Both."

"Bullshit. You don't believe in me. That's the problem."

Maybe not him so much as the whole situation. But he wasn't wrong. She pulled her hands away from his and started to go, but he held her to the spot.

"Lee...don't. Please." He tipped his forehead to hers. "I can't live without you. I don't want to be with anyone else. I *love* you. Don't you get it? I don't know how to do anything else but to love you."

Misery swamped her. All these years, she'd thought she knew what it felt like for her heart to break. But she realized now, she'd had no idea. Because right at this moment, she felt like she was being split in two, between what she wanted and what she knew she had to do, for his sake. "Oh, Ross, I don't know what this is, but it's gone on long enough," she said, only barely able to keep her voice from trembling.

He recoiled like he'd been slapped. "What?"

She marched toward the door as fast as she could, sure that every step took her closer to doing the right thing. The strong thing, even though she knew she looked like a coward about now. "I'm not moving in. Not now. Or ever. This has been fun, but all good things have to come to an end."

"Carmelita," he thundered. "Don't you dare walk out on me."

She stopped, right in the doorframe, not daring to face him.

"I know what this is," he told her. "You're scared. But I know you love me too. I can feel it. Can you honestly stand there and say there's nothing between us? That we've been playing house, friends with benefits and all that for these last few days?"

"Yeah," she answered him, winning the prize for world's biggest liar. "Something like that."

"I refuse to believe that."

Her poor heart felt like it weighed a thousand pounds, but she had to do this. She had to make him believe it. So she turned around and summoned the last drop of her will. "Believe it, Ross. There's nothing to this. It was just a little Christmas fun. Come on, you knew it had to end sometime."

Ross didn't answer her, but the devastation on his face did the answering for him. She'd hit her mark, and now pain reverberated in the air all around them. And she hate-hate-*hated* herself for it.

Anger swirled in her chest. At herself. At him. At the whole insane situation.

Damn you, Ross Mason. Damn you and all your pretty words and ridiculous promises.

He wasn't supposed to make all her wishes come true. But he had. And it was like some kind of horrible, cruel joke that he'd do it now, when he was clearly under the influence of something.

It had to be. He'd never given her any indication that

this was something he'd ever wanted. Love. A home. A life on a big farm. *Her*.

And now he was ready to spend every dime he had on a house *she'd* always wanted?

This didn't make even a little bit of sense.

She could tell him all that, but he'd only argue with her. Tell her all the reasons why he'd meant to do this. Blah, blah, blah.

But then it hit her.

What if she was the one who'd made him lose his mind like this? She had sat on the floor of Hunter's farmhouse and wished that "all this could be real."

Jesus. This whole thing, this temporary insanity of his... it was all her fault! *I've done this. Somehow I've called this magic down on his head.* And now, with every minute that she stood here, she was making him into a man he'd never intended to be.

So she really only had two choices here. Stay, and run the risk that he woke up January second with all his money gone and a house he'd never wanted, tethered to her in a way he'd grow to hate.

Or...

He could hate her now. And wake up blissfully ignorant on January second and go on as if nothing had happened.

Lita knew what she had to do.

So headed straight out the door without saying goodbye, before she could change her mind.

When the old screen door clattered shut behind her, she reassured herself that come January, Ross, like all the rest of the guys in this town, wouldn't remember this.

But there was only one problem.

She'd never forget a thing.

CHAPTER 26

It was New Year's Eve—one of Ross' favorite nights of the whole year, mainly because it was Hairball, and he'd get to dress up and party. Too bad he didn't feel like doing shit. He'd barely been able to eat or drink these last couple of days, after his big fallout with Lita.

And the hell of it was, he didn't even understand what he'd done. He hadn't been able to find her, let alone talk it out. Hunter had come back from Vancouver, so they'd not had a reason to be at the house together anymore. When he'd tried to visit her at her apartment, she hadn't been home, either. She'd gone radio silent on her texts too. He'd probably sent her dozens, making a total ass of himself. But he couldn't help it.

In all the years he'd known Lita, he'd never gone this long without talking to her. He felt the loss all over, like a full mind-body ache. Now here he was, goin' stag in this squeaky, sweaty outfit at Hairball, because there was a chance Lita might be here too. He threw back the last of the Christmas martini they'd handed him and grimaced at the taste. Ugh. Like a cranberry cough drop. Maybe he shouldn't have had this one. All this techno music was giving him a headache now.

He scanned the writhing mass of dancers and wondered how he'd ever see her in all this mess. The dance floor was packed with costumed, spangly people—an old factory they'd transformed into the rockinest night club this side of the Alleghenies. J had hired a nationally known DJ who was spinnin' the beats with a full-scale laser light show. Glowing drinks were served that blinked like fireflies through the crowd. J's beauty industry peeps from DC to Cincinnati had shown up, ready to compete in the event's hair and costume shows. Dozens of J's drag queen clan were here too, attracted to the fabulousness like moths to the flame. Alessandra had said they'd sold out all five hundred of their tickets, and he'd believed that.

Still, he peered into the cracks between people, hoping to see Lita rockin' that Leeloo costume. No luck.

Ross did, however, spot J, dressed like the blue-haired emcee from *The Hunger Games*. The man was about to go up on stage to make announcements, so Ross took his opportunity to grab him while he could. He rushed over and tugged on the man's sleeve.

When J spotted him, he gave out a scream of joy. "Oh my gawwwwwddd, child! I always knew this costume was made for you, but slap me now. Those tats and this patent leather. Keanu Reeves wishes he looked this good."

Ross was thankful it was hot in this place because he was blushing. He wasn't used to getting noticed for his sex appeal, even if it was J just being all fatherly about it. "Thanks, J. But the only reason I'm here is Lita. Have you seen her?"

"No! Can you believe it? That brat texted me today and said she wasn't coming. Something about not wanting to upset *you*. You wanna tell me what's going on?"

"I wish I knew."

"Come on. One thing I know about my niece is it's never nothing. You had to have done *something*."

Ross threw his hands up. "I didn't! I swear! If anything, it was the opposite. I told her I was buying a house and I asked her to move in with me. I told her I couldn't live without her! Isn't that what I'm supposed to do?"

J winced. "Okay then. So you *definitely* did something."

"Did I make a mistake? How could I not tell her what's been in my heart for years?"

J rolled his eyes. "You might've waited to profess your undying love until *after* all the men in town came to their senses."

"Yeah." Ross rubbed his forehead. "The thought did occur to me after I picked my heart up off the floor. But now I can't even find her. Do you know where she is?"

"About that. Rosie and Darius had to bail on their Christmas week at Snowshoe when the boys got ear infections. So Lita took their place. She's been holing up on the slopes these last couple of days all by herself."

A stray shot of worry hit Ross right in the gut. Oh no, she wasn't up there drowning her sorrows with some random ski instructor, was she? He wouldn't blame her. It's the sort of thing he might've done a year or two ago. "She's really not coming?"

"I'm afraid not." J gave him a sympathetic pat on his shoulder. "But you know what? Even if this thing with Lita is done and over with, I can't have you moping around here. Boy, it should be illegal to be that sad in patent leather. Why don't you get out there and dance? Come on, Ross Mason, I *know* you can dance."

He could. He was good at that bump-and-grind night-club dancing—a skill honed from years of seducing women he'd only just met.

J nodded toward a woman who was giving Ross very appreciative glances from over at the bar. "Look at her." J smirked. "I'd bet she'd love to trip the light fantastic with you."

From the way the woman's gaze lingered on his bare chest, J probably wasn't wrong. She was pretty—beautiful, even—a leggy blonde dressed in a skin-tight Captain Marvel costume. Just the sort of catch he'd have been all over in another day and time.

But he felt nothing. Not even a glimmer of arousal. "Honestly, J, I'm not up to dancing tonight. I just need to find a quiet corner or something."

J let out a disgusted cluck. "A *corner*? Looking like sex on a stick? Umm, *no*. That won't be happening. You're a walking, talking advertisement for Divalicious, remember? I need you to be *seen*. I tell you what. I won't make you dance with anybody you don't want to. But I have an idea that might remind Lita what she's missing and raise money for charity too. You game?"

"Do I have a choice?"

J grinned. "Not really."

"Fine then." Ross told him. "I'm in."

Lita didn't quite know what she was doing on this tiny sliver of balcony in the freezing cold. She supposed it was because there was so much racket outside, she couldn't watch HBO in peace. It was pretty out here tonight, even if it was noisy. It had snowed again—the thick, fluffy kind skiers loved. With all the lights and music and color, the sights kept her entertained enough. She'd bought herself a bottle of cheap wine and had toasted her own sorry-ass self every hour on the hour as it got closer to midnight. There was a festival atmosphere all over the mountain tonight and people were milling about, partying and dancing all through the chalets, shops, and bars in Snowshoe's resort village.

She'd watched them all from a distance from her tiny balcony for one, like she'd done this whole weekend. She hadn't exactly been in the mood for mingling, thank you very much. Ugh, the sparkling wine she'd bought was way more sickly sweet than she'd expected, but she was soldiering through. It had been ages since she'd drank something like this, and it brought back memories of the cheap swill she and Ross used to drink when they were younger. In another holiday and time, they probably would've been out in the cold, laughing in the bed of a pickup in the middle of the woods somewhere.

Now she was here, teeth chattering on her wine glass, "feelin' no pain." She snorted out a snicker at that. Who the hell thought that up as a description for being drunk? *Feelin' no pain, my ass.* Seemed like she was feeling every last bit.

"To another auuuullldddd lang syne," she murmured as she tossed back the last sip in her glass. Wasn't that stupid song about letting bygones be bygones?

At this point, her best outcome would be Ross forgetting everything she'd done and said. She'd never crushed another human being the way she'd crushed Ross. Now she felt like a monster.

And the hell of it was, she'd have to face Ross at work, bright and early on January second.

What I am I even going to say to the man now?

Her phone started to vibrate on the stand beside her, and she picked it up. A text, from Uncle J, with a few photos of the Hairball. Everyone was having so much fun and damn, the decorations...Mom and J had really outdone themselves this year with their cosplay theme. They'd managed to makeover an empty warehouse into the biggest nightclub in the area for one night.

There were photos of the DJ and the enormous crowd. She smiled. Oh man, there was Jim, now a total dead ringer for Doctor Strange. And Mom and Tino...they'd done a great job of throwing together Jamie and Clair costumes from *Outlander* on the fly. No doubt Tino had no shortage of kilts. That red wig Tino was wearing had J's fingerprints all over it.

And then there was...

Oh, damn. Ross, leaning on the bar. He was there after all, drinking a flashy Christmas cocktail and wearing that Neo costume. *Niiiiiicccceee.* Had the man just walked off a movie poster? Those tats, that hair, those totally lickable abs... Her mouth watered, and her ovaries practically had an armed revolt at the sight. Every last hormone she had was screaming at her to get her ass in the car and get to the party.

But she knew she couldn't. She'd never get there in time, and she'd had too much to drink anyway. Lita wasn't sure how much Ross had told J about their fight, but her uncle appeared to be rubbing her absence in her face with every picture he sent. And she scrolled through every one of them, masochist that she was.

There was Ross, laughing at a joke some girl had said.

Ross, standing in line to go up for the bachelor/ette auction...

Wait—what?

She fired off a text to her uncle. **OMG. J! Is Ross going to sell himself off to the highest bidder at this thing?**

He's single, isn't he? Did you not tell the man you weren't dating? J fired back.

She had—of *course* she had. Lita paused her thumbs

over her phone, any number of "yeah, but" type statements running through her head. But her fingers were frozen. What could she say?

For the record, I talked Ross into the auction, J added. **He stepped in for a guy who cancelled.**

Stepped in...the words on the screen swam before her eyes and her stomach churned. Was Ross being noble, and taking some guy's place so the food bank will get its donations?

Maybe. But she knew the more-likely answer. Ross was moving on without her. You didn't stomp on a guy like she had and then expect him to keep coming back for more.

A date...

She closed her eyes and clenched her fists. Yeah, anger and helplessness swirled around inside her like a toxic brew. Hello, jealousy. This must be what it felt like.

And how crazy was that? She'd never even felt a glimmer of it before. Even after all her terrible boyfriends, it had taken Ross Mason to take her to school on that subject.

Ugh, the idea of some random girl sitting across the table from him, kissing him goodnight...tracing her hands over the magnificent art on his pale, smooth chest...

Dammit, tears threatened again. She flipped the phone over in her lap and clicked the screen shut. She swallowed those tears down. *Down-down-down.* She had to. She wasn't going to sit her on this freezing balcony and cry like some crazy, entitled whiny-butt about something *she'd* caused.

If she hadn't rejected him, they'd be there at Hairball together. How much fun they'd be having, laughing and dancing the night away. Hell, he'd even asked her to go *before* the whole cookie situation.

What if she'd taken her head out of her ass and had said yes, back in that bakery? How would things have turned out then? There'd have been no fight, attracting the old woman's attention. There'd been no magic cookies, no nothing.

Just them. Easy and simple. If only she could wind the clock back and do it all over. But there was no doing that, was there?

Lita curled her fingers tight around the phone, unable to put it away.

J must be trying to torture her for not coming tonight, or for breaking his bracket or something. The man kept sending pictures of Ross as he waited with the other bachelors, laughing and joking. When Ross got up on stage, J really stuck in the knife. He sent a live video. And she clicked on it. Of course she did.

Music blared. Wow, Hairball had a huge stage this year. Ross slid on dark sunglasses and did a pretty damn convincing catwalk to the end of the runway, stuck his hands in his pockets, and pivoted, leveling his gaze on every person in the audience.

"This glorious redhead is one of my best customers," J crooned over the speakers. "Isn't he gorgeous? And those tats are one hundred percent real, baby. Ross Mason is twenty-eight, cisgender and straight as an arrow, folks. By day, he works at Holliday Hot Rods as an engine specialist, and a night, he's searching for that special someone who can rev his engines. Who will start the bidding?"

There was a long pause before several women and a few men stepped forward. The bidding started at five hundred.

Started at that. From some blonde in a Captain Marvel costume. *Who the hell is she?*

Then seven-fifty from a guy in the back...the numbers kept climbing.

Who in the hell *were* these people, that they had this kind of cash to throw around?

There was the blonde again...$1200...

The alcohol in Lita's stomach sloshed around danger-ously, and she felt a bit faint. Maybe she was too buzzed and miserable now for her own good. She sat down on the ice-covered metal chair on the balcony, not caring that it was soaking her clothes and burning her legs with the cold. And the numbers kept going up and up.

She'd seen bids go high in the past, but like this? It was all because of that Captain Marvel chick. The one in the front. The one who was prettier than her. Richer than her.

Someone who appreciated him and wanted to give Ross a chance.

And Lita hated her.

Hated. Her.

If she was any kind of person, she'd be happy that other people saw the real Ross. That he was coming out of his shell. That maybe he could have something real with someone who wouldn't hurt him like she had.

Was this how Ross felt when she'd gone out with Martinez? When all those other guys had come on to her?

Two thousand...

Three...

Ross took off his sunglasses nice and slow, and licked his lips. The crowd went wild. And the bidding kept going.

Oh, no...

For just one hot minute, she thought about bidding. She could do it. She could call one in. It wasn't like she didn't have any money in her account. She could empty it...she really could.

No, don't, she reminded herself. *You're staying away for him. For his sake. Remember?*

She had to be stronger than this.

Disgusted now, she clicked the screen shut again and decided to go back inside. She'd no sooner taken her coat off and brushed off the snow than her phone started to ring again. She considered not taking it, but it was Rosie. She flopped down on the couch and answered it.

"Feliz año nuevo querida hermana," Rosie sang out. "¿Tiene una fiesta para uno?"

Lita snorted at that. "*No*, I'm not having a happy new year, and *no*, I'm not having a party for one."

"Yeah, I figured," Rosie answered. "Have you seen how much Ross is going for on the open market these days?"

Lita decided she wasn't dignifying that with a response.

"Oooooh. Broody silence. So much better than an outright denial." Rosie clucked. "You wanna tell me why Ross is literally selling himself off? What did you do to the man?"

"Why do you always think it's me?"

Rosie snorted again. "Because I know you, and I know Ross. And only you are capable of effing up things so bad that you'd drink alone in a hotel room. And you are drinking, right?"

"Maybe. I've been working on this lovely bottle of sparkling Apple Spumante." She tipped the bottle up for a refill, but it was empty. Lita raised her eyebrows at that and tossed it in the trash.

"Ew. *Apple* Spumante? What is that even?"

"Beats me. It seemed like a good idea at the time."

"Five thousand!" Lita heard Darius clapping and whooping in the background. "The boy's on fire, y'all!"

"Is that the bidding for Ross?" Lita grumbled.

"Yep. Darius and I have been watching the stream on the Divalicious website. Ooh. Wait-wait! Whooooa. The bidding just closed at sixty-five hundred! That had to be some kind of Hairball record! Who made the bid, honey?" Rosie asked her husband.

"Some person on the phone. An anonymous donor," he answered.

Lita let out a silent *whew* as a wave of relief washed over her. So, it hadn't been lil' Captain Marvel. Still, she wondered who would've made that bid. "He's worth a lot more," Lita found herself saying. She hadn't meant to say it out loud, but there it was. She shut her eyes and cringed, embarrassed she'd just blurted that out.

"Awwwww, someone's sorry for herself. Seriously, sister, it's time you spilled the tea. I'd be derelict in my sisterly duties if I didn't find out what had you so wound."

When she opened her mouth, Lita had intended to say, "Nothing's wrong." But somehow, that wasn't what came out. Oh no, she poured everything out about these last few days to her sister. She told her all about the hex. The fights. Her disastrous date with Martinez. The antidote. The sex— holy shit, the sex. The mess at the Masons' house. All those breakfast biscuits and the whole bit at the Palmer place, with Ross saying he loved her—

"Wait, what?" Rosie squealed. "Ross said he loved you? And wanted you to move in with him, and be his *womaaaaannn?* Omigawd! Gurl! What did you *do?*"

"I told him no, of course!" Lita sputtered. "He was actin' all crazy and he was about to blow his savings tryin' to make me happy and—"

"Hang. On," Rosie interrupted. "What's the problem here? You think he's doin' this strictly because of you. Right? That he's not making his own choices?"

Lita paused. "Well, yeah. I guess that's it, really."

"You like the guy. In a he-could-be-the-one kind of way. But you can't be sure his grand offer is real?"

"Right," Lita agreed.

"Lita, what if I could prove he wasn't under the influence? At least about the house part anyway. Would that make a difference?"

"Yeah," Lita answered her right away. "At least some."

So Rosie went off on this story, telling her all about this pair of ATVs Darius had inherited from his uncle. Lita knew about them, of course. When Darius had gotten them from his uncle's estate, he'd asked Lita to swing by and give him an estimate so he could put them up for sale. They were prime, tricked-out four-wheelers, and they were expensive, probably worth as much as four thousand each.

"I don't get it," Lita grumbled. "What's so important about the ATVs? Didn't you find a buyer months ago?"

"Yes!" Rosie cried. "That's what I'm trying to tell you! The buyer was *Ross!*"

Lita stopped to consider that new tidbit. "He was probably just going to fix them u—"

"*No*, sister. Come on, you know they were perfect— there was nothing to fix. Ross wanted them for himself. He told Darius he'd been saving up for years to buy property, and he might be getting close to pulling the trigger. He bought the ATVs but asked Darius if he could make payments. We've been holding them here at the house until he was ready."

"What?" Lita blinked. "Why in the world wouldn't you have mentioned that?"

"Because he asked us not to, that's why."

Lita didn't have anything to say to that. Why in the world would Ross keep that from her? It didn't make any sense.

"Baby sis! Did I shock you? I swear, I'm not making it up. He asked me not to say anything, because he said he knew how bad you wanted to buy a house, and he didn't want to make a big deal about his savings success. A couple of days ago, he came and picked them up, and made the last payment on the down-low. He told us he was buying the Palmer place and he wanted to surprise you. He said he wanted to see the look on your face."

Her surprised face. Oh, he'd seen it, all right. She curled into a ball, feeling low enough to slide under the floorboards. Here he'd been ready to reveal this grand strategy, the big payoff for all his hard work. And he'd wanted her to share in it.

And what had she done? She'd totally yucked his yum. Pissed on his dream. Crushed him, and any other way you could think of sayin' it. She wasn't just a monster. She was the queen Kraken primordial mother of all monsters.

"It still doesn't prove that he loves me, though." Lita insisted. "Once all this magic wears off, he'll leave. Don't they always?"

Rosie let out a disgusted growl that probably would've been a lot louder if the boys hadn't been in bed. "Are you kidding me right now? How will you ever know if you don't give him a chance?"

"Rossssiiie! Would you stop? What would you know about getting run over by men? You always got the good ones! And now Darius–"

"Darius?" Rosie clucked. "Yeah, I've got the world's best husband, but do you really think he came out of the box like that?"

"Hey!" Darius sniffed.

"Awww, D." Rosie chuckled. "You know I love you, you sexy thing, but I'm trying to make a point. And the point is —I see you, sis. I see what you're tryin' to do with this whole 'poor me, no man will treat me right' bullshit. But you know what? Who chose those losers, even though they already had a bad rep? *You.* Who wasted time, hoping against hope that they'd realize your stuff is golden and want to change their ways? *You.* Who never asked them for what you needed? *You.* So don't you dare sit around and blame their sorry asses, or your childhood, or Dad, or any other damn thing. You want to know why this keeps happening? Look in the mirror. Because settling for the less, Lita? That's a *choice.*"

A choice.

Had she been doing that, choosing less, without even realizing it?

The realization crept up on her like a slow, painful burn. Disappointment. It had become her pattern, one she was all but guaranteeing with every choice she made. Just the thought of it all made her sick to her stomach.

How could she have been this stupid? How much of her life had she wasted, playing this out, over and over? Too long. But this pattern, she was the one who'd created it. And she was the one who could destroy it too. For the first time this whole night, Lita felt a tiny spark of hope growing in her chest. She had to cling to that.

But simply recognizing her own mess wasn't going to clean things up with Ross. "What if he doesn't choose me?" she whispered. She hadn't meant to say it, but it'd slipped out, escaped from some hidey hole where she'd locked away all her insecurities.

"You're killing me here." Rosie sighed. "I'm trying to lay down some truth, and now I'm you're making me all sorry for you."

"It's just that you make it sound so simple. It's not."

"Yeah, it is." Rosie laughed. "When love is right, it's the simplest thing there is. You either feel it, or you don't. You're either willing to work for it, or you're not. You've got to tell him how you what's going on with you sis, and what you need from him. If he doesn't want it, or isn't ready for it, then you'll know. You can pick yourself up, adjust your crown, and keep on goin'. No magic cookies needed."

Lita soaked this in, and even in her fuzzy state, those words clicked into place like tumblers in a lock. She was about to tell Rosie that when the sound of the boys crying erupted over the woman's baby monitor.

"Ugggggh. Those damn earaches," Rosie grumbled. "I gotta go."

Rosie was about to click off, but Lita interrupted. "Rosie Rosie Rosie—wait."

"What?"

"Thanks," she croaked, her voice sounding thick and raw and just about as beat up and emotional as she felt.

Somehow, Lita could hear the smile in her sister's pause. "You're welcome, boo. No go out there, and don't be an idiot."

She laughed as her sister hung up. *Don't be an idiot.* She couldn't make any promises about that. Because telling Ross what was really on her heart? That may be the dumbest thing she'd ever done.

But it was a risk she was willing to take.

CHAPTER 27

LITA ROLLED BACK into the outskirts of Lewisburg on fumes. Yet, when she stopped at her favorite gas station, she'd forgotten that Ricky was working behind the counters most Mondays. God, *Ricky*. It didn't dawn on her until she shuffled through the door that she hadn't kissed his cheek yet and "unmagicked" him. The bells made a huge racket when she walked in.

So much for walking out. Ricky would never miss her now. What would she get today? A marriage proposal from the guy?

She held her breath.

But Ricky adjusted the stack of cigarettes behind the counter and gave her a bland, businesslike smile, exactly like he had every other time she'd been here over the years. "Oh. Hey, Lita!" the man chirped. "Haven't seen you around for a couple of days. You have a good holiday?"

Ricky had greasy hair and an even greasier grin. But he was a good sort. And he'd never flirted with her in his life until this Christmas magic mess had kicked in. She stood there, staring so long his cheeks started to redden.

"Lita?" He frowned. "Everything okay?"

She shook her head a bit, embarrassed. "Yeah." She pasted on a smile and waved a hand at him. "Yeah, stupid me. Guess my mind's spinning with all the stuff I have to do when I get back to work, right?"

He rolled his eyes. "Boy, I heard that. It's hard to get back into the swing of things after so many days of parties and such." He took her gas money without comment, like it was any other normal day. Ricky apparently had not a single clue that he'd chased her into the parking lot a week ago, begging to take her out for hotdogs. And if he remembered and was trying to play it off, she'd know. Ricky was the kind of guy who got flustered. He'd be nervous by now, probably all sweaty and uncomfortable-looking.

But he wasn't. *At all.*

Huh. Did this mean the magic was over? *Could it be?* Another fresh round of hope stirred.

Lita paid for her gas and tested her theory on the drive in to work. She made sure she stopped at a light, right in front of a couple of distant acquaintances she knew for sure were single. Yeah, she hadn't kissed either one of them on the cheek yet, either. But both of the guys kept walkin' by, not even turning their heads in her direction.

Alrighty then. That's good, she supposed. Lita bumped up the volume on her radio.

The sun shone bright through the trees, and the morning sky was clear and blue, not the standard pale over-cast gray they usually got around here. The snow sparkled over every last branch and rooftop. Now that this curse or hex or whatever was gone, she should be cruising down this road without a care in the world.

Yet, when her wheels crunched to a stop in Holliday Hot Rods' lot, heaviness settled on her.

Hooooo. This is it.

She was gonna put it all out there. Roll the dice. And

she'd either win the love of her life or lose everything. All the way here, she'd told herself this was gonna be simple. But if Ross didn't remember...

How could they work together? How could they stay friends? How could she ever scrub the memory of his kiss from her mind? Heated memories pinged in her head—the barn, the storeroom, Ross emerging from the steam in that towel...

What if he laughed at her, and she never got to be with him again? Or worse, what if he remembered but couldn't forgive her? Lita laid her head on the steering wheel for a minute, worry paralyzing her.

She took a deep breath. And another one. *Stop it, idiot. Just stop.*

Forcing herself to sit up again, Lita considered herself in her rearview mirror. She didn't like what she saw. Yeah, her hair was done and her mascara was on, but her expression was just not her. She looked tired and scared and small.

And she refused, freaking *refused*, to be scared one more moment.

Blanking out every negative whisper in her head, she stared herself down until she'd wiped the fear off her face. Then she pushed herself out of that car, squared her shoulders, and took off for the shop before she could change her mind.

It was time she made her own damn magic.

Ross stood over the breakroom sink, sipping his coffee, spaced out and worrying about what was gonna happen when Lita finally appeared for work. She'd spent the weekend pretty much ignoring him.

Maybe this was it then.

Maybe this was all there was. Coffee and danishes, and

a laugh or two while they tore up cars for a living. But that was all he was gonna get. It was what he'd have to accept, right? Just another day at the office? The thought made him *sick*. He took another sip, but his stomach was too jittery for shit this morning. Pissed now, he peeled the lid off his coffee, dumped it down the sink, and tossed the cup in the recycle bin with a disgusted snap.

When he turned around, he was surprised to see Lita standing there, wide-eyed and rubbing her hands nervously on her jeans.

"Wow." She pointed to the trash. "I've never seen you throw out perfectly good mountain mud before."

His stupid heart surged at the sight of her. But for his own sake, he held himself back. He crossed his arms over his chest and leaned back against the counter. "Yeah, well," he grumbled. "Maybe I'm not in the mood for coffee this morning."

Her expression was tense and worried, but hell if he could tell what was on her mind right now.

"Lita, we need to—"

"Ross, we gotta—"

He stopped. They'd both talked at the same time.

Lita held up her hand. "Me first."

Ross nodded, and watched her fidget, and study the ceiling before she finally said, "Woo. Okay. So, I've had some time to think about it, and I think maybe I'm a terrible person."

He scowled at that. Okay, maybe that was going a *bit* far—

She held up her hand again. "Just-just let me do this, okay? I don't know how much of this you can remember, Ross, and I don't care. You need to know—I am a terrible person, because all these years, I called you my best friend. But I never saw you. I never saw that this thing between us,

it had always been more. And this Christmas with you..."
Her eyes started to well up now, for real, and she cleared
her throat. "This Christmas with you, those may have been
the best days of my whole crazy life. Maybe it was some
magic cookie that made you do it, but you showed me the
man you really are. And...I love that man, okay? There I
said it. I've loved you all this time, I think, and I maybe
didn't even know it. And I kept shoving you off, and making
light of it, and running away because...because I was
scared."

Scared?

There was so much to unpack about what she just said,
but his mind kept tripping over that. He supposed, with her
history, that this shouldn't surprise him. But it hurt his heart
all the same. "You're scared of me...because of your dad?"

"No, Ross." She shook her head and pointed at her
chest. "Because of nobody else but me. Because...because
you're the one, Ross. And if you just snapped out of it, or
decided to leave or, I don't know...found better choices or
something, it would break me, I think. So yeah, Ross. *You
scare me.* Maybe, in one way or another, you always did."

He nodded slowly, taking this all in.

She loves me. It was all he'd ever wanted to hear. Ross
wanted to cheer or throw a ticker tape parade or something,
because he felt that from his head to his toes. But instead, he
pointed to bags and boxes of Monday morning food sitting
on the table. "I brought you breakfast," he simply said.
"Have some."

"Seriously?" She threw her hands up in the air. "I, like,
open my whole chest and show you my beating heart, and
you're thinking about freakin' *breakfast* right now?"

He rolled his eyes, trying to suppress his smile. "Just
open the white box, 'kay?"

Lita pursed her lips and grumbled as she went over to

the box. But when she cracked the lid, she gasped. Marveling, she pulled out a big ornament-shaped cookie with a red Linzer heart, bright green icing, and swirls of silver-and-gold nonpareils. Her eyes were almost as big and round as the cookie itself. She seemed completely speechless.

He couldn't help chuckling as he stepped up to her. "You know, Lee, it was never a spell. Not for me, at least."

She stared stupidly at it. "How did you..."

"I drew a picture and took it over to Suzie at Corn+Flour. She'd told your mom she could do a special order, right? She said it was the most complicated cookie they'd ever done, but they were always up for a challenge. So am I."

The look on Lita's face told him his message had been received. Her eyes welled up with tears again as she took a small bite. She swallowed, shaking her head. "It even tastes the same," she whispered.

"That's because I could describe it. How it tasted in my mouth, how good it made me feel all over. I remember *everything, Lee.* Every single, beautiful detail."

Yeah, she knew he wasn't talking about the cookie. He took it from her hand and gently laid it down on a napkin. Ross cupped his hand on her jaw and stroked a thumb over her cheek.

"I don't want the magic to be over. But I'm telling you now, this thing between us—it was never a spell for me. I've loved you from the minute you showed up in sophomore homeroom, swinging that hot-pink ponytail behind you like you'd walked right out of my dreams. But you know what? I was scared too. Because I knew if you told me no, that would be it. Because there could never be anyone else for me." He looped his arm around her waist and was relieved when she curled against him and let him tip his forehead to hers. "But if that Christmas magic made you irresistible, it gave me courage. And every time I was about to use my jokes and jabs like a shield, it stopped me from speaking. I could only say what I really meant."

She thought about that for a minute, picking at the metal snaps on his work shirt. "Everything you said to me. It was true. It was really you."

"Yeah." He nodded, but then he rolled his eyes. "Especially that part about you being a goddess and all. Those tats. I mean...*damn,* girl!"

She laughed and gave him one of her smiley shoves. "Now I *know* you're back to normal. But I don't want to just go back to normal. Ross, I need you to know I never meant a word of what I said to you back at the house. I was just so afraid you were going to blow all your savings buying a house for me, when you really didn't want it."

He tipped his forehead against hers. The relief he felt was so overwhelming, he couldn't help snickering ruefully. "Ohhhh. That's good, because I signed the papers. The house is mine, Lee."

She gulped.

"Relax," he told her. "I've always liked the Palmer place. I bought it for me. But it would be more like home if you were in it with me."

She bit her lip, nodding slowly. A shy smile broke out over her face. "I guess I'm picking out some curtains then. But—can we give the moving-in thing a little time? I just wanna enjoy being a couple before we throw living-together into the mix. Can we do that?"

"Yes, Lee!" He whooped. "Definitely, absolutely, *yes.*"

He kissed her then. And damn if she didn't taste like that cookie...so beautiful, so sweet, he was about to become a sugar addict for the rest of his days.

When they finally came up for air, gasping, pulse

pounding, she had her hands on both sides of his face. "I want you, Ross Mason. Do you hear me? Right now. Just you and me."

He found himself standing there, smiling at her—well, grinning so hard, his cheeks hurt. He nodded slowly. "Just you and me."

She chuckled, low and soft, like she was making a promise. And then she kissed him back, so hard and fast, she actually jumped up in his arms. He caught her, happily curling his hands around that perfect ass of hers and wrapping her legs around his waist. They tumbled into the table, but he didn't care. There was only this, only her, everything he'd ever wanted, wrapped up in his arms like a thousand Christmas presents rolled into one.

He fell into the deep of it, holding nothing back. And it felt good to do it too. To let the joy wash over him, the heat.

But a discreet cough rang out behind them.

Reluctantly, Ross looked up. It was Hunter, standing there with a coffee cup in his hand, smiling like a man who'd known this would happen all along. "I guess we didn't discuss *this* in the employee handbook."

Lita hid her head in his shoulder, but he could see she was smiling. She tried to get down, too. Yeah, she wasn't going anywhere.

"Boss, I would officially like to put in the first vacation request for me and Lita this year. We'd like the rest of the day off."

"Granted," the man said, and tiptoed away.

Ross grinned down at her and hoisted her up over his shoulder like a caveman.

She yelped and laughed. "*Where* are you taking me?"

"Upstairs, to my place," he answered her and just kept walkin'.

"Ross!" she gasped, still giggling. "Wait-wait-wait. You forgot the cookies."

"Oh, yeah." He bent down so she could grab the coffee cups and he could snatch up their box of food with his spare hand.

As he ran past Hunter and Hop on his way up the steps, Hunter elbowed Hop in the ribs. "Don't make this a habit, Mason!" the man called out after him. "We've got a lot of work in the shop!"

"Sure thing, man!" he answered as he kicked open the door to his apartment and slammed it behind him. *A sure thing.* When he watched Lita set down their food, stalk toward him, and pin him up against a wall, he knew a sure thing was exactly what he was getting.

This was gonna be one hell of a great new year.

CHAPTER 28

DECEMBER 21ST, ONE YEAR LATER

LITA POKED her head out of the Impala body she was working on when she heard Hunter calling her name. "Hey, Lita!" He pointed toward the door. "Your dad's outside to see you!"

She waved at the man and trotted outside, using a rag to wipe the clear coat from her hands as she went. She caught up with her father in the parking lot as he was opening his ancient beater of a Toyota hatchback.

She shook her head fondly at the rusted-out heap. "When are you going to let me repaint that for you?"

He booped her on the nose. "When I can afford to pay you for your time, and not a moment sooner. Besides! I'm so happy to have a car again, I could care less about appearances."

It was true. Her father had turned over a completely new leaf since he'd decided to move to Lewisburg. He'd thrown out his toupee and had given up his life on the poker circuit for a job waiting tables at one of the nice white table-cloth restaurants downtown. Turns out, he was good at this high-end waiter thing, and he was making a killing in tips.

He was making real headway with the family too. And

though it almost pained her to admit it, it was *nice* to finally have a father figure around. Two father figures, actually, if she counted Tino.

"I brought your paint," he told her, pointing to the cans in his hatch.

"Oh, great!" she beamed. "Thank you so much for this. I told you, you were buying too much."

He shrugged. "I wasn't sure how much of this sage green I was gonna need once I covered up all the cracks in the wall. Turns out I only needed two coats. I'm glad you could use it."

And she could. She and Ross had been knee-deep in the reno since they'd gotten engaged this summer, and this color would be totally adorable in the walk-in pantry they'd finished building. Come to think of it, she might use it as an accent on the bookshelves she was painting too. Ross was right. That Palmer place was an incredible investment, and was turning into a place worth staying in, for sure. "This should be it for your painting projects, right, Dad? You won't have any more leftovers to send my way?"

"Yeah, this is it." He pulled out the last can and set it on the ground at their feet. "I think I've finally managed to get the old place habitable."

Habitable? That was being modest. Now that he'd moved into her ratty old two-bedroom apartment, he'd made it beautiful. It had all begun right after Christmas, when he'd agreed to be her roommate until the end of the lease. He'd needed a place to stay, and she'd been spending a lot of time with Ross, so it worked out for everybody.

And shockingly, he'd turned out to be the best room-mate she'd ever had. Dad had started by sweet-talking the landlord, telling her that if she'd pay for extensive extermi-nation services, he'd fix the walls and weatherize the windows.

Lita was shocked by how easily he'd gotten the landlord to work with them, when cheap, borderline-nasty woman had never listened to a single one of their requests before. Lita could say this about the man—he sure knew how to use his charm to make a deal. And, to everyone's surprise, he'd not only followed up, he'd gone above and beyond.

By the time the lease was up in the summer, he'd installed a new window air conditioner and replaced the faucets. Thanks to their landlord ponying up, they'd also had no bugs and a new stainless-steel refrigerator. With ice! By then, she'd moved into the Palmer place with Ross.

She'd really thought Dad might take off then. But he hadn't. And to everyone's surprise, Dad had stayed, signing a new lease so he could be close to family. Apparently, he liked staying in one place and building on something. He didn't need the car so much because he could walk to stores and work. And he'd gotten the decorating bug. He'd patched and painted every room including the cabinets, and had cobbled together an impressively chic collection of refinished, rehabbed furniture. Now the place wouldn't be out of place on HGTV. "Fixing broken things." That was what he called his design style. It fit him.

Ross peeked outside and saw the paint cans. He came trotting up to them, giving her dad a hearty handshake. "Hey! You brought the paint! Lord, it'll be so nice to get the shelves up in that pantry."

"Glad I could help." Dad smiled. "But honestly, I'm surprised you've got time for that right now. Isn't Alessandra running y'all ragged with the wedding?"

Lita laughed. The man wasn't making that up. Ever since Tino had asked her mother to marry him, the woman had been going through herself, coming up with one elaborate plan after another for the kind of huge wedding she'd never been able to have the first time around. "You're coming, right?" she asked him.

"Of course. Seems like everyone in town is contributing something to it. Did you know she threatened to make me a groomsman? I'm glad she's off that idea. I'm happy for her an' all. But that would've been...I dunno."

"Weird." Lita laughed.

"Yeah, weird." Dad shuddered. "Did she ever decide where she was having it?"

"You're not going to believe this. They've decided to do it during *Hairball*," Lita squealed.

Dad raised his eyebrows at that but agreed with her. The festival atmosphere at that party was the perfect place for a wedding. And Mom was such a beloved member of the community, it just made sense for them to do the wedding right in the middle of this charity event they'd organized, year after year.

Everyone they knew was going to be there this year. Even Tiff and Bear were coming, and putting in a brief appearance with the newest redhead in the Mason family, Ross' freaking adorable baby niece, Autumn Opal.

"Mom wanted a huge, fabulous crowd, and now she's gonna get it. The Divalicious community is over the moon about it. They may have to find a bigger venue. Ticket sales are already through the roof."

Ross shook his head. "I'll tell you one good thing about it. I won't have to wear patent leather."

Lita snorted. "You sure about that? I wouldn't put anything past them."

Dad barked out a laugh. "Yeah. *First* she floated the idea of me being in the wedding party. *Then* J wanted to make me the flower girl! I mean, can you imagine?"

They all snickered as Dad pantomimed that out, flailing around in a routine that would've given a professional comedian a run for his money. She shook her head. Her dad was a pretty hilarious guy, really. That was another thing she'd never known about him. But she was glad to be learning that now.

When they all calmed down, Dad leaned against his rusted heap and narrowed his eyes. "What did you guys decide to do about *your* wedding?"

Lita smiled down at the rose-quartz-and-diamond ring Ross had bought her.

But it was Ross who answered. "We've decided to let Alessandra have the bash. We're going to have a smaller affair here at Holliday Hot Rods, probably about fifty people or so with a justice of the peace. Hunter and Hopper both had their weddings here recently, and neither one of us could imagine having it anywhere else. We're planning it for Valentine's Day. You free?"

"Where else would I be?" He nodded. He seemed genuinely intrigued and excited as she explained their unconventional wedding plans. They were going to do a brunch-themed wedding with a tower of Tudor biscuits, a "wedding cake" made out of gourmet donuts and, of course, heart-shaped cookies. There would be more. Mimosas and fancy coffees and hot chocolates, and probably tamales, if Mom had anything to do with it. Corn+Flour was catering, so she knew it would be good, no matter what they picked. And Hopper's wife Lila was going to bust out her mad origami skills to make giant lacy paper heart lanterns to put on the tables and hang from the ceilings. It was going to be *gorgeous*.

Unconventional? Yeah, that too. But what they'd planned would be perfect expression of all their years together. She couldn't wait. And since they'd already taken that trip to Reno he'd promised, they'd be sitting their butts on the white sand in St. Croix for their honeymoon.

But she had one more detail to address. "So, Dad, do you think I could talk you into walking me down the aisle?"

The smile Dad'd been wearing disappeared, gone expressionless as he rounded his eyes in shock. He didn't say anything for a minute. "You-You'd let me do that? Even though I was never there for you?"

As she regarded her father, this man who'd meant so many different things to her, her heart felt full. At peace. She grabbed his hand and squeezed. "You're here for me now. Isn't that what counts?"

Dad's eyes filled with tears, and his nose reddened up. "Absolutely" He nodded. "You got it baby. I'd *love* to." He pulled her into a bone-crushing hug. "Omigod! I'm gonna have to get myself a new suit!"

Lita returned that hug, knowing Dad *would* be there, and he *would* buy that suit. And damn if it wasn't wonderful to see him become the kind of guy who would. It wouldn't make up for all the milestones he'd missed. Nothing would. But it'd be a start.

Lita and Ross didn't have much time to bask in that wonderful family moment, though. Dad said their goodbyes to them and was pulling out of the lot, just as a new customer was driving in. Make that two new customers—a man and a woman—riding in a black, tricked-out, brand new Land Rover. Lita furrowed her brows at that. It hardly resembled the busted-up heaps they usually dealt with here.

When the two passengers hopped out of the SUV, Lita gasped. She recognized the man immediately—the same black peacoat, the same military pants, the same trimmed salt-and-pepper hair and mysterious dark eyes. She nudged Ross. "Hey, isn't that the guy from Corn+Flour—the one who was with the old lady?"

Ross checked the man out. "Yeah. Yeah—I really think

so. What's *he* doing here? Didn't he say he wasn't from around here?"

"I don't know." She started off in the man's direction. "But I'm think we'd better find out."

Ross followed along behind her as she made her way across the lot. Hunter and Hopper had already come out front to greet them by the time she and Ross pulled astride. The man had never told her his name back when they'd first met, but she overheard him introduce himself as Michael Makepeace to Hunter. It was clear he'd recognized her and Ross right away. The man inspected them from head to foot. Ross draped his arm over Lita's shoulder and tucked her up close to him. She couldn't blame him. This was making warning bells go off for her too.

Makepeace gave them both a quick nod and a vague smile.

Hunter scrubbed a hand over his jaw as he considered Makepeace's engine. "You say it's making a noise?".

"Yeah. I think it might be the alternator. It's making a screechy putt-putt-putt kind of noise," Makepeace said. "Isn't that right, Cass?"

"That's right," the girl said, which was confusing. Because she didn't *look* much older than fifteen, though she had the bearing of a much-older person. This Cass person was tiny built, with a blond pixie cut with green tips that shimmered blue, or even pink, depending on how the light hit them. Lita couldn't help but notice the girl's striking constellation of tiny, flattened gold-and-silver studs, punched all over the cartilage shell of her ear. Her eyes were so big and green, they almost didn't seem real.

Whoever this Cass was, Lita had never seen her in these parts before, or frankly anyone who'd even remotely resembled her. She must've been staring at the poor girl, because when Cass stared back, her gaze was so intense, Lita almost jumped.

Lita stood there and listened with half an ear to the conversation with Makepeace, because she was watching Cass. The girl had jumped up in the car and turned on the ignition, as Hunter requested, and there was a noise, exactly as this Makepeace guy had said.

Bored with the conversation now, Cass hopped out of the car, wandered through the open bay, and stepped onto the shop floor. At first, the girl seemed to be walking around, entertaining herself by checking out the art, the cars, and the overall Holliday Hot Rods spectacle. But with one quick step to the side, Lita saw what Cass was really doing— making small hand movements, waving them over the space and muttering.

Was she...was that girl weaving *some kind of spell?*

Panic gripped her. Oh no, there'd be no more magic in this house. *Not again!*

"Hey!" Lita called out. She stomped over to her and yanked at the girl's hand. "Hey, what do you think you're doing?"

Cass blinked innocently at her and gave her a bland smile. "Doing? What do you mean?"

Ross, Hunter, and Hopper all lifted their heads from under the hood, where they'd been trying to diagnose the problem.

"There some kind of problem, Lita?" Hunter called.

"Yeah!" Lita answered back. But then she paused, searching for words that somehow wouldn't make her sound like a total lunatic. There were none. "She was," she sputtered, "she was trying to put the whammy on us or something!"

Makepeace laughed. "Somehow, I don't think *whammies* are part of Cassandra's skillset."

Lita narrowed her eyes at Cass, but the girl just kept up with the big, innocent eyes, though there was a thread of amusement there this time.

Hunter blanched. "I apologize for my employee, Mr. Makepeace. But in her defense, we have a healthy respect for all things magical around here in West Virginia. And let's just say we've had more than our fair share of strange happenings in these parts."

Makepeace shrugged. "No offense taken. And as for your employee, it's smart to be cautious. Once strange things happen around a person, it makes them sticky, you know? More strange things are likely to happen. When was the last time something odd happened to you that you couldn't explain?"

"Last Christmas," Ross answered, crossing his arms. "And there wouldn't be anything you could tell us about that, and the nice old lady who was with you then, is there?"

Ross and Hunter exchanged confused glances, but their eyes soon widened as they realized who this guy was.

"Oh, yeah." Makepeace nodded, trying to be all casual about it. "You're remembering your encounter with Maggie. She passed away soon after we crossed paths. But such is the way of old crones. You can't keep your magic forever." He stuffed his hands in his pockets and smiled apologetically. "And...well. This seems like a silly question, but nothing odd has happened since then, right?"

"Right," they all answered.

Makepeace clapped his hands. "Good!" He waved at Cass. "Everything good to go here?"

She gave the place one more look around and nodded at the man.

"Gentlemen, I suppose I'd better get back on the road. I try to keep track of all the goings on. You know, to chronicle Appalachian sightings and folklore and spooky stories an' all that. Maybe you can tell me your stories sometime." He handed Ross a card. "You'll call me if you see anything new?"

"Yeah, sure," Ross shook his hand, not sure what else to do.

Makepeace motioned to Cass, and she turned for the car.

Hunter held up a hand. "Wait! Don't you want us to get to the bottom of this problem with your car?"

"Oh." Makepeace shot Cass meaningful glance. From Lita's vantage point, she was the only one who could see Cass nod, make a swirling motion with her hand, and snap at the car. The noise stopped. *Abruptly.*

"Wow. Okay." Hopper threw up his hands. "The thing is purring like a kitten now."

Makepeace popped in the Rover, and so did Cass. He lowered the window as he gave it a couple vroomy taps on the gas. "Hah! Guess we dodged the bullet this time, gentlemen. It must be one of those things that comes and goes."

Hunter snapped the hood shut with a confused grimace. "I suppose it's okay to drive. But if I were you, I'd take it to an import dealer. They've probably seen this kind of thing before, and they'll have parts on hand. We're used to dealing with body repairs and older cars here. I can give you a recommendation. Where do you live?"

Makepeace shrugged. "Roundabouts. Wherever there's mountains and stories to tell. I promise, Mr. Holliday, I'll take good care. You should too. Merry Christmas to y'all."

"Merry Christmas," they all answered and waved as the back end of that SUV disappeared in the distance, kicking up sparkling snow it its wake.

Hopper shook his head. "Man, can you *believe* those two?"

"No." Hunter scowled. "And that's the problem. What do you think he meant with all those weird warnings?"

"Beats me," Ross answered him. "But check out his card. It says he runs a website called "Appalachia-creepy-and-unusual.com.""

Lita looped her arm around Ross's waist and gave him a squeeze. "I don't care what he meant. I'm glad he's gone back to wherever he came from. I think I have all the magic I'll ever need, right here."

Hunter chuckled at that. "Yeah, me too."

"Me three," Hopper agreed.

Ross slid the card into his back pocket and grinned when s slid her hand into the other one. He gave her a kiss. "What do you say we get back to work?"

Lita looked into his smiling eyes and knew in her heart there was no place she'd rather be. A soon-to-be lifetime with this ordinary man, no sorcery involved.

"Sure babe." She smiled back. "Sounds like a plan."

A perfectly ordinary plan. Nothing could be sweeter. And she could soon get a taste for that.

The End

SO, WHAT DID YOU THINK?

I'd he so pleased and honored if you'd review my work. It's easy, and you'll help others find me online!

(My Book)

(Or go to Amazon's search bar and type in: B09FZ26J4S)

A SPECIAL PREVIEW...

If you enjoyed *Sweet Like Christmas*, check out my next
series of steamy, angsty, Southern small town romances
coming out in 2022!

Sirensong Falls

By Liza Jonathan

After nearly being killed by a bucking bull, rodeo star Wade
"Dice" Deckers is more than happy to hang up his cowboy
hat, and never step foot in the arena again. He's fine with
riding off into obscurity, and healing his scars on the farm
he's unexpectedly inherited in the Carolina mountains. No
one will ever call him "the most reckless man in rodeo"
again.

Until he finds Jenna, the love he left behind, living in
the caretaker's cottage on the farm next door. Now, he's
feeling reckless, all over again...

CHAPTER 1

Jenna swore at the sight of her broken windshield wiper.

The stupid thing had finally snapped in half, biting it right in the middle of a sudden, sleety October rain. Yet another broken thing she'd not had time to fix. Now she was out here in the pitch dark, spinning her wheels on this muddy country lane, with about eight square inches of clear windshield to see through. She flipped on her high beams and gave the dashboard an encouraging pat.

"Come on, Flash," she crooned, as if her ancient, rusted-out Chevy Silverado might actually hear her. "You've got this."

The old truck shuddered and rattled, but popped back out of the rut like always, flinging gravel in its wake. *Atta girl.* Another turn through these hilly apple orchards, and she'd be home.

Home. God, her little five-room, clapboard cottage sounded like heaven about now. She rolled her aching shoulders. Did she have any wine left? God, who knew. She'd been on her feet since five this morning—an occupational hazard of owning Apple Addie's, Sirensong's favorite café. Normally she enjoyed the bustle of it. But after a day with a busted dishwasher and too many missed orders, she was as fried as a day-old fritter. All she wanted was a little solitude, and a little peace.

And maybe a long, hot bubble bath in her clawfoot tub to soothe her aching muscles. And some chocolate. Yes—definitely chocolate. She still had some chocolate kisses left in the bottom of the bag, didn't she? Maybe she'd light up her new scented candles too. Hey, why not? She might as well go for the whole dateless-in-your-thirties, Sunday-night package while she was at it.

Jenna huffed out a rueful chuckle and shook her head.

Dating. *Right.* As if there weren't worse fates in this world than not having a damn date. Yeah, she'd fought hard to get here, to this place, warm and settled in this small mountain community she loved. She wasn't going to let some man mess things up now. Lord knew, they always, *always* did.

She curled her fingers tight around the steering wheel as she bounced over the rough terrain, so tired and punchy she must be getting philosophical.

Yeah, this road was like a lot of things in her life—dark, bumpy, and surprisingly twisty. But hey, at least she was headed in the right direction, right?

Smiling at the thought, she pumped up the volume on her favorite country music station, popped the clutch, and kicked up the gear. Just one last little rise around the back forty of this property, and she could call this day done.

But when she made the turn for the access road to her place, the glare of taillights suddenly appeared ahead. She slammed on her brakes.

What the hell— Jenna skidded to a halt, stopping mere inches from the corner of a horse trailer jack-knifed in the road.

Jesus. Who in the— Why is somebody out here on my road? Are they lost?

Jenna blinked against the flashing red hazard lights, trying to calm her racing heart. She let out a shaky breath.

Okay, so maybe this trailer wasn't exactly jack-knifed. It was really more of a slide-off into a ditch. Whoever was wrecked here had money. Because that two-horse, goose-neck trailer was attached to a white, brand-new-looking truck—a Ford F-250 Platinum, no less—mired up to its grill in sudden runoff from the rain.

She clicked off the radio and cracked open her door to get a better look. Oh no, there was definitely a horse inside. The sound of scraping and panicked whinnying that came from inside the thing was unmistakable.

Sick dread filled her stomach. Jenna knew horses. And she knew even a minor slide-off could break a horse's leg, or worse. What was this *idiot* doing, hauling a horse trailer in this kind of weather, at this time of night, all the way out here?

Instinct had her jumping from her still-running truck and reaching for the trailer door. Maybe she could help. She hadn't squandered her early twenties as a rodeo stable hand for nothing.

But before her hand met the handle, a strong arm pushed her back.

"*Hey!* Dumbass!" a deep, angry voice boomed. "What do you think you're doin'? Are you trying to get yourself killed?"

Fuck off hovered on her lips. So did a colorful rant about how horses deserved to be treated.

But as she turned to face this entitled prick, something made her stop. Thunder rolled in the distance. And she could see this man, barely, in the flickering headlights. Broad shoulders bulging against a denim jacket. A flash of pale, stubble-covered features. A cowboy hat, dripping rain off its brim. Point-toe Justin boots, sliding in the mud. The outlines of one pissed-off cowboy.

But when the light caught his face, she choked on her gasp.

Because she'd never, ever forget that face.

"Wade?" she croaked.

He narrowed those steely gray eyes of his at first, then his eyebrows flew up. "Jenna." He let out a shocked exhale as he raked his attention over her. His mouth hung open, then clamped shut, like he didn't have a thing to say for himself. *Of course.*

Users are like that, aren't they?

Still, looking into his eyes made her heart race, dammit. Threads of a past she'd tried to forget wound 'round her.

She'd been his once, not so very long ago. Back when he'd been a rising rodeo star—and she was the girl who'd given up everything to follow him on the circuit. Once upon a time, there was nothing she wouldn't have done for this man.

But as Jenna stood there watching the cold rain pelt his face, the years seemed to stretch between them like a chasm.

She swallowed hard.

Lord. *Wade Deckers.* Of all the people to meet on a dark, stormy night. In many ways, he was the reason she'd ended up in Sirensong ten years ago. But how in the hell had *he* gotten here?

She didn't have the chance to ask. The trailer rocked, and the horse shrieked in fear. Their attention snapped back where it belonged, to the horse that needed them.

Wade threw open the double doors to a scary scene. His horse was upright but sliding—stamping, snorting, and unable to stand straight on the tilted floor.

Before Wade could stop her, Jenna slid through the side door and into the trailer.

"Jenna! *Goddammit*, don't!" he called. But she ignored him. Her small size made it easier to duck under the chest bar and wedge herself up close, where she could make a difference. Eyes white, hooves scrambling, the horse tossed its head, slamming her hard against the stall. She swung right in front of its nose anyway. Grabbing the dangling tie strap from its breakaway halter, she managed to calm the animal. Even in the dim light, she could tell he was a beautiful butterscotch-colored bay—a quarter horse, and a gelding, from the looks of it.

She stroked the poor boy's neck while he shuddered and eventually found his feet. "Shhhh. *Shhhhh,* honey. You're alright. We're going to get you out of here."

The horse seemed to settle just a bit, and his ears slowly unpinned themselves.

Jenna looked over the horse's withers to find Wade's gaze on her—piercing, intense, and far too familiar. In the shadows, she caught his wry smile.

"They always did listen better to you."

She looked away, not having a clue how to make conversation with the man.

To his credit, Wade took the cue, filling the silence with a search for supplies in the adjoining stall.

The horse whickered as she patted his neck with long, reassuring strokes. "Aww now, you're a sweet one, aren't you? Just a little scared, that's all. Don't worry, Jenna's got you." She couldn't help whispering and cooing. It'd been ages since she'd handled a horse. But some things you never forgot.

Jenna didn't have time to enjoy it, though. Because all at once, Wade's hand was on hers, stealing her attention again. The warmth of his touch set off an instant ping of recognition, an echo of memories still running loose in her mind. She almost resented the slide of his hard, calloused fingers over hers as he tugged the strap away...resented the way her breath caught and her hand tingled. She studied his still-athletic form as he snapped on a new lead and led the protesting horse onto solid ground again, soothing and reassuring all the way.

Not liking the stinging rain or the oozing mud, the bay huffed and tossed his head.

"You're all right," Wade murmured over and over while the horse slowly, surely lowered his head. Wade grinned with triumph, stroking sweet boy's nose. "There now, you're not scared, are you, tough guy?" When the man shifted back to her, he looked her up and down, losing his smile. "You're bleeding," he growled.

What? No *thank you for your help?* No *hey great to see you again, Jenna?* But Wade had never been one for social niceties. Why start now? She tapped around on her bruised shoulder, trying to assess the damage. Her fingertips met torn leather. *Great.* Now her coat was ripped, and probably ruined. Dammit, it had been a favorite, and a rare luxury–a vintage short designer trench she'd found thrifting. Her hand came back with a little blood on it, too. She must've caught herself on something.

He grimaced. "Look, we've gotta get to shelter, and your shoulder needs tending. You know any place where we can get out of this storm?"

"Yeah, this way." Jenna pointed. "See that little house on the clearing? That's mine. There's an abandoned barn out back that's unlocked. The new orchard owners moved out the farm equipment, but I think there's still some hay in there."

She jumped back in her truck and swerved around the wreck, parking her car the same time he'd made it to the barn doors with the horse. They opened the doors together, and she helped him find the switch to click on the ancient, flickering overhead lights in the place.

Without a word, they teamed up to remove the horse's shipping boots and blankets, the two of them performing a kind of workaday dance they'd done together hundreds of times. The bay was muscular and healthy-looking—just a simple farm horse. Without an ounce of attitude, he let Wade lead him into his stall. While Wade confirmed the horse was uninjured and set out a few forkfuls of hay, she got the rusty well pump to belch out clean water and filled up a trough.

The horse gratefully drank and drank. She grinned at the sight. The poor thing would be munching down that hay pretty quick too, she'd bet. Trauma had a way of making a horse ravenous.

Jenna peeled off her jacket and grimaced. Damn, she was soaked to the skin, her white button-down work shirt gone nearly transparent. Wade's attention lingered on her, but when her eyes met his, he quickly looked away. She poured a little extra water over her wound, taking her turn to watch him as he moved around the horse with measured, practiced movements.

He was soaked too, and the way those jeans were clinging to him distracted her, drawing her eye to his rangy, muscular body.

She tore her eyes away and fiddled with her shirt, disgusted with herself for looking too long. Oh no, she *would not* ogle the man.

God, she'd run so far to put this part of her past behind her, but now in the space of a few minutes, it'd all come hurtling back. Wade, horses, bans, and the girl she used to be.

Rodeo was a world she was never supposed to know—a

total twist of fate. The Wyoming Cavalcade was where she'd landed when she'd run away from her abusive home. It was one of the only places that would give her work, after all, and it came with a place to sleep. That job had saved her life, really. It'd given her a reason to get up in the morning with a smile. The horses had needed her. Between the big shows and the cowboys coming in and out, stabling their horses, there was always something to do.

And do it she had. She'd worked there for six years, from the time she was sixteen to twenty-two. By then, she'd worked her way up to manager and had done nearly every job they had—ticketing, accounting, mucking, raking, you name it.

They'd never paid her much, but she'd been wild and free. She'd been free to get a little wild with the cowboys coming in and out of their barn too. Back then, she'd never wanted anything more—until the day she'd laid eyes on Wade Deckers. There had been something about this bigger-than-life bull rider that had called to her. Wild to wild, like to like. Their relationship had been intense, combustible. When he'd asked her to go on the circuit with him, she'd happily accepted. The man had made her his rodeo princess, after all. Their year together had seemed like one big party, a ride-or-die adventure, until it all had gone so wrong...

Jenna closed her eyes for a moment, willing the memories back into their corners. After all, she still hadn't figured out how this man had managed to come crashing back into her life, had she?

She nodded over to the horse. "What's his name?"

"Scout."

She snorted. "What? No Diablo? No Renegade?"

He raised an eyebrow at that. "What? It's the name he came with. You got a problem with it?"

She shrugged. "Of course not. But it's not exactly the kind of horse I'd expect Dice Deckers to buy. Not wild enough."

"Nobody calls me Dice. Not anymore." He met her gaze full on, purposefully, like a dare.

And she saw why. He was showing her the scars from his accident. She'd wondered how long it would take him to get his courage up and face the light. Word of his accident had been big news in the rodeo world, high drama filling the pages of every major publication and news feed. She'd read all about it, of course. His fifteen-year run of incredible luck had ended with a gore to the hip and a hoof to the face. He'd nearly died. Now the right side of his face was mapped with thick, white lines, probably from an extensive reconstruction. His face was probably the least of his scarring.

The Most Reckless Man in Rodeo.

Yeah, she could see why no one would call him by that old nickname anymore. And it wasn't because of the disfiguring scars on his face, or the hitch in his step when he walked, either. It wasn't even the fact that he'd retired from the ring for good. No, something else was at play, something deeper than that.

Wade hadn't lost that direct, forthright way about him. But when he locked eyes with her, she couldn't even find a glimmer of the gorgeous golden boy he used to be. The wildman who'd mastered the world's most dangerous bulls was long gone. It was like all that crazy, go-for-broke confidence had burned away in the red-hot heat of fame. Now she couldn't name what was left there. Regret? Vulnerability?

Jenna wasn't sure how she felt about the little ping of sadness that gave her. But she was done trying to fill in those blanks. Wade owed her some answers. "Okay, mystery man," she called out, hands on hips. "You want to tell me why you're out on my road in the pitch dark? Because it only goes to the apple orchard, which is corporate now, or to the Pierce place next door. And old Mrs. Pierce is dead."

He smirked. "You've answered your own question. Mrs. Pierce was my great aunt. I used to spend summers up here as a kid, and I loved it. Remember how I'd go on and on about retiring to the Carolina mountains? Well, that was here. Great Aunt P never had kids of her own, as you probably know. So, when she died it-"

"It went to you." Jenna squeezed her eyes shut, and her heart practically rolled over in her chest. "Jesus, Wade, you're my new neighbor."

CHAPTER 2

Neighbors.

Well—that's fucking ironic, isn't it?

Wade would've laughed out loud if he had it in him. Because this? This was friggin' *nuts*.

All those years he'd spent looking for Jenna, only to find her right next door. The big man upstairs must really enjoy a bad joke.

There were so many things he wanted to say to her. But somehow, all he could manage was, "Neighbors. Yeah, it looks like it."

It was bad enough that he'd wrecked his truck and put his horse in danger. Now his broken-down ass was standing here in front of Jenna.

Jenna Coleman. Of all people.

And just like that, ten years of his life seemed to melt away. He stood here, all fidgety and tongue-tied, falling into her amber-brown eyes again. He was trembling, and probably not from the cold. Was she happy to see him? Or did she hate him still?

From the stubborn set of her jaw right now, he was

putting his bets on "can't stand the sight of me." And who could blame her?

The last time he'd seen her, he'd been drunk. He'd said some pretty stupid shit, too. The next day, he'd woken up to the mother of all hangovers and everybody talking about the big public scene he'd made, accusing her of cheating on him. He'd been wrong—*dead wrong*. All he'd wanted was to find her, throw himself at her feet, and beg her forgiveness. But it was already too late. She'd disappeared into the rangeland fog like she'd never existed.

She'd left him. And he'd deserved nothing less.

Now here she was, somehow more beautiful than she'd ever been. Her sun-streaked hair had faded to warm brown with blond tips, and her leggy, coltish figure had matured to lean, womanly curves all too visible in her soggy clothes. Yeah, he felt Jenna—felt her deep in his bones. Always had. But this tough, restrained woman in front of him was nothing like the rowdy, up-for-anything girl he used to know.

Jesus *Christ*, this had to be some kind of cosmic, sadistic torture, that he'd finally find her now, after he'd become a banged-up shadow of himself.

"So, what are you going to do?" she asked him.

"With what?"

She toed the ground with her boot. "What are you going to do with the farm?"

"Don't know yet," he answered, stepping closer to her. "There's not enough land for cattle. I might grow alpacas. Or Christmas trees. Or put in tiny houses for rental. I could do anything, really. I haven't worked it all out yet." He reached for her battered shoulder, but her eyes got wide and she flinched away. Skittish, not that he could blame her. "I-I was only trying to take a look," he rushed to say. "It's in a funny spot you can't reach. You should let me tend that for you. Do you—" He hesitated for a moment. "Do you have anything to treat this back at your house?"

She blinked up at him, chewing her lip as if weighing whether she wanted him invading her space. But finally she nodded. "I can't reach it, so—yeah, I guess I could use the help."

He let out a breath as relief rolled through him. At least she trusted him for that much.

Together, they bedded Scout down for the night and walked to the cottage she called home now, all painted white and covered with spokes and spindles on its porch.

When she opened the door, he whistled. "Wow, your house is incredible," he told her. The place was a far cry from the trailers and hotel rooms they used to share. The little four-square cottage was tiny, probably an old caretaker's cottage, judging by her position between the two neighboring farms. Always one to do more with less, Jenna had decorated it up perfect, with pickled pine walls, a kitchen the color of a robin's egg, and cheerful old quilts thrown over white couches. With tall, lace-covered windows and well-worn knotty pine hardwood, the place was sophisticated in its modest way. Welcoming and bright, just like her. She hadn't lost that.

"Thanks. I've worked hard on it." Jenna paused, crossing her arms and rubbing at them a a bit nervously. "I —uh. I suppose I should get cleaned up. You know, so you can get a better look at my shoulder. Help yourself to anything in the fridge, or use the sink if you want to wash up."

He nodded and gave her a little lame wave as the bathroom door snicked shut.

Wow.

He rubbed at his chest, feeling like there was a stone lodged in there. Yeah, he'd fucked up with her, and time hadn't made it any better. Now he didn't have a clue what to say or how to act.

Wade scrubbed his hands over his face and groaned. Wasn't this just the story of his life?

He'd been reckless with her, just like he'd been reckless with everything. He was Dice fuckin' Deckers, strutting around like consequences weren't for the likes of him.

Funny. Now his life was consequences central.

Looking back on it, losing Jenna had been the first of many, many setbacks and failures. Oh, he'd kept up appearances. He'd still dominated the circuit on pure adrenalin alone. He'd tried to move on with a string of different women, too. But after years of trying to fill the void, it took him lying in a hospital bed to realize that the void was in him. *He* was the void.

He'd built a life he hated, one where he'd become a star mainly to appease his father, his main sponsor. Wade had been terrible at school, and even more terrible at working in administration in the family ranching operation. But by God, having a son who was tearing up the arena was quite the feather in the cap for his Dad, a man who was known far and wide as one of the nation's biggest beef producers. And after his career-ending injury, Dad had been furious when Wade had refused to go back to Wyoming and back into the family business.

But his great Aunt Louise had left him her farm for a reason. Somehow, the woman had known he'd need this escape hatch someday. So, yeah, he was takin' it. He was dead set and determined to make Sirensong his home now. The fact that Jenna was here? Well, it was too soon to say it was fate, or serendipity, or whatever. But it was definitely the mother of all bonuses in his book.

Man, the squeak of her bathtub faucet and the sound of hot, splashing water...just the thought of her being naked on the other side of that door was exactly the punishment he deserved.

Could he fix things with her?

Wade ambled around, giving the place a cursory look. He didn't see any signs of a man in her life: no boots under the bed, no photos, no ring on her finger. It surprised him, honestly. Jenna was gorgeous—like, spin-you-around-on-the-sidewalk beautiful. And though she'd never pressured him at the time, he'd caught her once or twice talking about having a farm of her own and building a family—a big, happy one, with lots of kids running around.

But ten years later, she hadn't done any of those things. He wondered why.

Desperate for a distraction, he pulled out some firewood and got her wood-burning stove going. After all that sleet, she had to be as cold as he was. She'd probably be glad for a hot drink. A quick scan of the kitchen, and he found the coffeemaker and a little basket full of autumn spice coffee packets. He grinned. Definitely fancier than the greasy grog he usually drank, but he started it brewing anyway.

Catching a glimpse of his filthy clothes, Wade muttered a curse. He'd not taken off his caked-up boots when he'd come in, and now he was tracking chunks of mud every-where. He hopped out of his shoes and socks, swept up the mess, and took Jenna up on her offer to use the sink, rinsing off the mud on his jeans, shirt, and Henley. He'd gotten his pants back on but was still at the sink, barefoot and shirtless, when Jenna padded back into the room, dabbing at her long, looping curls with a towel.

The sight of her shouldn't have felt so big and overpow-ering. But it was.

Jenna didn't have a drop of makeup on. And the clothes she wore weren't designed to impress—just a simple pair of thin, black yoga pants and a lavender tank top with wispy spaghetti straps. She was every inch the Jenna he remembered, and yet, these last ten years had changed her. Her long, lean muscles were a bit more honed, and her complexion was creamy now without her wind-stung paddock tan.

She was flinty, yeah. But she was confident too, centered in a quiet, self-assured way she hadn't been before. He couldn't stop smiling as he thought about that. Her thirties looked good on her.

And damn, he couldn't take his eyes off her. How many times had he seen her like this—all fresh and glowing from a bath? Dozens? Maybe a hundred?

And yet, he'd never really *seen* her, had he? He'd never understood the gift it was.

There was a time she would've come out of that bathroom and taken him in her arms with so much trust and love. But now she gave him a wary look, reminding him of everything he'd lost. And that made him feel...well, it made him feel like shit, to be honest.

She raised an eyebrow at his shirtless state but didn't say a word as she padded into the kitchen. "Thanks for starting the fire," she nodded. Jenna regarded his chest, his face, and his fucking scary goring scar with her customary frankness. He'd never forgotten how those big, brown eyes of hers could pin him to the spot. Man, they were mesmerizing, velvety dark and soulful, with a hooded, sleepy look he'd always found incredibly sexy. But the moment didn't last. She pointed to the mug on the counter and grinned. "Is that for me?"

"Yeah," he murmured, sounding like some breathless moron. He cleared his throat as he poured them both a cup. "Cream and sugar in this, right?"

"No." She took it from his hand. "I take my coffee straight up these days."

He nodded and motioned her over to the table so he could get a better look at her shoulder. He sifted through the first aid kit she'd handed him and laid out the supplies. When he stepped up to the table, disinfectant in hand, she'd settled into the chair and had pulled her hair to the side so he could see the cut. The sight of it made him sick with remorse—a livid, purple bruise with a bloody gouge that bisected it, tracing her delicate shoulder blade. Not bad enough for stitches, but bad enough.

And it was all his fault. *His.* Even if she'd insisted on helping.

If he hadn't gone to buy that horse today, if he hadn't stopped at so many supply stores, he wouldn't have been out at that ridiculous hour. She'd be by the fire, alone. *Safe.*

Slowly, he began the work of cleaning and bandaging the wound, glad he could do that much for her, at least. And with a little effort, he was able to get the conversation going.

He wanted to know everything about her life here in Sirensong and, thankfully, she was in the mood to tell him.

She told him about the diner, filling him in about how she'd gotten a job with the woman everyone in town knew as "Apple Adeline" and how Addie had become like a mother to her. Jenna talked about Addie willing her the cottage, and the work she'd put into renovating it. She talked too about how she'd negotiated to buy the diner from Addie's nieces and nephews, since the woman had never married or had kids. Jenna said she'd paid them off in five years—five years ahead of schedule.

Impressive. But he couldn't say he was surprised. Nobody worked as hard as Jenna or was as careful with money. She was far more focused and level-headed than him. He'd always admired that about her.

Wade moved to the chair opposite hers, soaking up every detail like the parched earth soaked up rain.

When it came to his life and his world, he didn't have all that much to tell her. No, his story was an open book, splashed on every tabloid with headlines like *"Rodeo's Wildest Ride Comes to an End."* But finding out how she'd done, after all these years? It meant the world to him. He was happy for her. Proud, even if she decided she'd never speak to him again.

He nodded at her and smiled. "Looks like you've built a good life for yourself without me."

She stopped, cocked her head at him, and furrowed her brow. "Without you? What—does it bother you that I've done so well?"

"*Bother* me? Of course not! I just wish it hadn't ended like it did. I never wanted that for you, Jenna, to have to start all over again and strugg—"

"Stop it, Wade." She held up her hand, color rising to her cheeks. "As I recall, *you* were the one who ended it, not me."

"And I was wrong, Jenna. I found out the truth soon enough. I woke up, and you were gone. And there was no way for me to make it right or get you back or...I'd just blown it. And then you were out there, all alone."

She gave him a stony look. "I've been alone all my life. I'm pretty good at it by now."

Not quite able to stop himself, he caressed her satiny cheek. "And whose fault is that? *Mine.*"

Jenna stilled. He hoped she saw the regret on his face. The sorrow. Maybe even the need. But she pushed herself up to her feet and stomped off to the sink with the mugs. "You give yourself too much credit, Wade. You think I've been here, pining away for you all these years? While you've been doing God-knows-what with God-knows-who, I've been here building something real. For myself. For my future. I don't need you, or anyone."

But he didn't listen to her. He followed her. "And I don't see why you would." Deciding to take a chance, he stepped up in front of her as she turned from the sink. "But what if *I'm* the one who needs *you?*"

He cupped her face in his hand again. God, had her skin always been so soft? He looked deep into her stormy brown eyes and found she was doing the same, searching him for an answer.

"Wade," she breathed. "What is this?"

"This is me, wanting to make things up to you. It wasn't right. How things ended. They never should've ended, Jenna."

She shrugged out from underneath his grasp and stepped away from him. "But they did. God, isn't this just like you, thinking you can come crashing in here and have everything your way. I'm not some stupid twenty-two-year-old anymore, Wade. And apologies, and *trust?* They don't work like that."

"I know." He insisted, not willing to let it lay. "You have my apology, Jenna. I'll do the work to get that trust back. Whatever it takes."

She shrugged out of his grasp with a bitter laugh. "Work? What would you know about working at a relationship? You had a career, and I followed you around. I was at your beck and call, twenty-four hours a day. Like some kind of pathetic little puppy. When you treated me like trash and threw me away, I shouldn't have been surprised."

He made a strangled sound.

Jenna wanted to roll her eyes at that. *Theatrical much, Wade?*

But the look on his face was so pained, she realized he was having a hard time getting his words out. It-it caught her off guard. Pain wasn't something the legendary Wade Deckers ever showed.

He grabbed her shoulders and made her face him. "Is that what you thought? Is that really—" He squinted his eyes shut and shook his head. "The only trash in that whole awful mess was me, Jenna. Not you, *me*. I was the one who was drinking myself blind every night and getting up on a bull the next morning."

Indignation spiked through her, though she'd told herself she wouldn't let him get to her. She let out a disgusted squawk. "Ah, so there it is. I was wondering how long it would take before you trotted out the booze-made-me-do-it excuse."

"I haven't had a drink in a year, Jenna. I've got an AA coin to show it, and it's a start. But the alcohol? It didn't have that much to do with why I freaked out on you back then. I'd heard...I'd heard the other guys talkin' about you, okay? They were swappin' these lurid stories about being with you and putting their hands on you. And—I just couldn't handle it. Because Jenna, you were my one good thing. The one thing in my whole crappy, scary life that made sense. And I thought for sure they were takin' you away from me."

What—was she supposed to be moved by that? She ground her teeth, surprised the old anger was so easily accessed, right under the surface. "Dammit, Wade! You didn't *listen* to me! I told you that wild night had happened two years before we'd met. But my word meant nothing to you."

"I didn't know what I was doing. Hell, I never knew what I was doing back then. But I'm a different man now."

Jenna snorted at that and shook her head at the man. *That's a likely story...*

"You don't believe me?" He hung his head as he nodded at her. "I suppose I should've expected that."

If he was waiting for that hangdog expression of his to get her sympathy, he'd be waiting until hell froze over. "Oh, *I'm* supposed to believe *you* now?" she sneered. "Well, you know what, Dice? Different is as different does. And the way I see it, you've elbowed your way back into my life, spewing excuses and trouble. So you wanna tell me how that's any different?"

Wade stood there, blinking at her like he had nothing to say for himself. The color had got up a little in his ruddy skin, and his bare, hairy chest was rising and falling fast. His eyes looked a little watery too. That was new. It made her breath catch, and she found herself cocking her head at him in wonder. She'd never seen this look on his face before. So intense, so emotional. So broken down, maybe.

Hey, the man could cry her a river, but she wasn't planning on letting Wade back in now. Not when she'd fought so hard to get to this point of not needing anyone, or anything.

Needing anyone...

She drew a shaky breath. It'd been so long since she'd had a man standing in front of her like this, it was a shock to her system. Jenna realized they'd moved closer and closer to together while they'd been arguing, and her hand was on his bare chest. She supposed she'd put it there to push him back, but now she couldn't manage to move it, any more than she could stop her legs from shaking. Because he felt good under her hand, strong and steady, and he smelled like horse and autumn leaves.

"I am different," she heard him say, in a voice that sounded so small and quiet, it was nothing like the "Dice" she knew. Maybe losing his career and facing death changed him in ways she could never understand. Maybe he really was a better man, now that he was "just Wade." But that was a pipe dream, wasn't it?

"I won't believe it until you've proved it," she told him.

He raised his head. "You want me to *prove* it."

She kicked up her chin, refusing to break eye contact. "That's right."

He considered her for a long moment and swallowed hard. "Okay, then."

And then he—he curled his fingers around the back of her neck, and he *kissed* her.

She hadn't expected that. But she didn't exactly want to stop him, either. Because this? This was nothing like the fast, hungry kisses she remembered. And the shock of *that* left her rooted to the spot. Because this kiss was slow. Searching. Sensual. A tease of his surprisingly soft mouth against hers, warm and perfect.

And for just this one, weak moment, she gave herself permission to experience it fully, like the sun on your face after a long, cold night. She couldn't do a thing but lean into that sensation, and lean into his arms as he slipped them around her waist. She slid her arms around his neck before she could stop herself. Wade curled his fingers in the hem of her shirt, and the rasp of his calloused hands sizzled through her whole body.

This was how it happened.

This was why.

She'd been ready to follow this man to the ends of the earth, once. And now, he came in here with kisses so aching, so tender, they almost broke her heart, all over again. And she-she wanted more...

But slowly, her brain managed to send her a message. *He's still the man who hurt you.*

It was a small voice, but just loud enough to get through over the din of her raging hormones.

She managed to wedge her arms between them and give him a gentle push. "Wade," she groaned. "I-I just can't do this. You know I can't."

His eyes widened a bit, but he nodded, chastened and absently wiping his mouth with the back of his hand. "Yeah...I get it. I'm sorry," he told her, pausing as he looked around at his feet, his dirty shoes, his coat—anywhere but her eyes. "You know, it's pretty late. I guess I'd better walk up to my place before it gets much later."

He started to shrug his flannel shirt back on and grab his hat.

She sighed. "Wade, wait. You can't go up there in the middle of a rainstorm."

"It's better if I do," he told her as he started searching for his shoes. "I've already strained your hospitality enough for one night. I can come back and get Scout in the morning."

Jenna reminded him that his place was a good half mile up a muddy mountain road. And that road usually wasn't passable after a big rain, at least for a few hours. He wasn't getting up there on foot or by car for a little bit.

"Wait here," she told him, as she dashed off to her bedroom. She came back out with a pillow and a spare comforter. When she handed them to him, a lopsided, self-deprecating grin curled across this face.

She patted the arm of her couch. "This little loveseat makes a pretty good bed, believe it or not. It pulls out. There's a tab you have to pull, underneath the cushions. It's comfortable, I promise, and will be as good a place as any to ride out the storm."

He held the blankets to his chest, and gave her a look so earnest, it pinged her stupid heart again. "Thank you, Jenna, for everything tonight. It was more than I expected.

And more than I deserved. But then, you've always given me that, haven't you?"

She rolled her eyes, but secretly, she wondered if that little statement was more than just an obvious play. Either way, she wouldn't be getting the answer to that tonight, or anytime soon. "Good night, Wade," she told him.

He nodded at her in that way of his that made him look like he was tipping an imaginary hat. "Sleep tight," he simply said.

Her steps were light and purposeful as she walked into her bedroom and snicked the door shut. Jenna leaned her back against it, the heavy, hundred-year-old walnut door not doing a thing to keep out the thoughts crashing around in her head.

God.

Wade Deckers is here.

In her house.

On her pull-out bed.

By now, he'd probably be getting himself settled and stepping out of his jeans—a thought that tugged at the edges of her thoughts. She stood in the dark, letting out a quiet, breathy chuckle in the still of her room. *Jesus, this is insane.* In another day and time, there was no way she would've left that much hot cowboy all alone on the sofa.

But Wade wasn't just another cowboy. And this was now, not then. Legs still trembling a bit from that kiss, she resolutely walked over to her dresser, fished out her favorite ratty nightshirt, and slid under the covers. Alone.

Her head hit the pillow, and her bone-tired body took over. Sleep came easily, in spite of the coffee.

When she blinked against the bright morning light and rolled over to look at her bedside clock, she was surprised to see it was eleven a.m. Somehow, her body must've known this was her one day off a week.

She cocked her head to hear any tell tale sounds of Wade shuffling around.

Is he still here? Why didn't he wake me?

She shuffled out to the living room in her fuzzy pink robe, giving the place the once over. The couch was rolled back up and the bedding neatly folded on top of it. Wade was long gone.

Hands on hips, she stood there in the living room, swallowing down a strange, lingering sense of disappointment. It was stupid and irrational, of course. What did she expect—him standing in the kitchen making pancakes? History had taught her not to expect more, after all, and she'd learned her lesson well.

Deciding to distract herself with errands, she headed back to her bedroom, got herself cleaned up and dressed in her favorite jeans and sweatshirt, and tied her hair up in a braid. No muss, no fuss, no drama. Just another ordinary day.

She toasted a bagel for the road. Absently, she reached for the peg where she'd hung her torn jacket, thinking she'd take it somewhere for mending today. But she'd found a man's denim jacket there, instead. A note was attached.

Until I can buy you a new one—Wade

Before she'd thought better of it, Jenna slipped on the jacket. She grinned at how enormous it was, and how the arms flopped over her hands. Its scent cut a direct path to her memories, carrying the clean smell of Wade's sweat and hay. She had the sudden, irrational urge to curl herself up in it and wear it all day. But she quickly put it back up on its peg.

It was a nice try on his part, but it wouldn't do for her to be walking around in his jacket. They weren't a thing, after all, and in a small town like Sirensong, people would wonder.

As Jenna walked out and locked up, she noticed that the horse, the trailer, and the truck had been towed away while she'd slept, and a load of new gravel had been carefully raked into the road where he'd slid off.

Jenna was still grinning as she hopped in her truck. *Well, okay then.* She revved the engine, and the windshield wipers started wiping. The *new* windshield wipers, which were tied with another note.

Stay safe out there. I hope to share this road with you for a long time—Wade

That man.

She didn't know what he was up to.

But she had a feeling she was gonna find out.

For more second-chance romance with Jenna and Wade, stay tuned! Sirensong Falls will release in 2022! Sign up for my newsletter at lizajonathan.com, and stay up to date on all my new releases, get special deals and free book promos, and more!

This book is dedicated to my high school Speech, English, and Journalism teachers back in Fairmont, West Virginia. You told me I could, so I did.

ACKNOWLEDGMENTS

Nothing gets me in the Christmas spirit faster than writing a Christmas Romance. Here's hoping that reading said romances puts you in the holiday spirit, too. The world can always use a little peace, love, and celebration, right?

This book may be the last in my *Mountain Magic Christmas* series, and I must say a fond farewell to the fictional crew at Holliday Hot Rods. At a time like this, it only seems appropriate to give thanks to all the very patient, talented, and hardworking people who've helped this book become a reality. In particular, those thanks go out to Rhonda Merwarth, my editor who's been with me this whole series, and Kelly Martin of KAM Design, who worked with me on this and all the covers in this series. I couldn't get along without either of these fabulous ladies. Or my proofing posse, Stephanie Parker-Knott and Nan Cayton (who also happens to be my high school journalism teacher. She's a superfan now!)

I'd be remiss, too, if I didn't thank all the good folks of Lewisburg, WV, which I assure you is very real, and every bit as charming as I've described. The folks in the Greenbrier Resort Marketing department have been an enormous help to me, and have agreed to sell my books, as well. Suzie Hoffman, actual proprietor of Corn+Flour, thought this all was quite a hoot. She really does do an occasional custom cookie order, but can't guarantee anything more magical than their deliciousness.

Snowshoe Mountain Resort has been very gracious. You'l find signed copies of my books have become quite the draw in Another Page Bookshop in Downtown Lewisburg, I'm proud to say. All these Southern West Virginia delights are well worth your visit if you're in the area.

And by the way, if you've been through the Mountain State without having a Tudors Biscuit World biscuit, well then, you just don't know what's good.

I'd like to take a moment, too, to give a shout out to my cousin Darrell, the retired drag queen and VP for Aveda whose quick wit and superior knowledge of essential oils were the inspiration for Uncle J. Sadly, Divalicious and Hairball in the Holler are entirely my fictional creations. But they were made more real with the help of my hairdresser, Rachel Spring of Phenix Salons, who put up with my thousand and one questions about what it would have taken to fix Ross' hair. If you need a great hairdresser in the Carmel, Indiana area, check her out!

I'd also like to thank the random stranger who showed up in my LinkedIn feed one day, the very real Mr. Lasagna. Yes, y'all, it's an actual name. I got such a good chuckle out of it I knew I had to do something with it. My husband is descended from Italian immigrants, and I grew up with a second-generation Italian grandpa. So it warmed my heart to write Tino, who is a bit of an avatar for all the awesome Italian-American stallions I've had the privilege to know. I hope you enjoy him as much as I do!

And one last shout out is in order, for my fellow romance author, Sutton Bishop. If you enjoyed my preview of *Sirensong Falls*, you can thank her. She saved my butt on all the horse behavior details, thanks to her extensive experience showing horses. Love you Sutton! Check out her books on Amazon. They're awesome.

If you'd like to learn more about my inspirations and get great free bonus material, visit my website at www.lizajonathan.com, and sign up for my reader newsletter!

ABOUT THE AUTHOR

Liza Jonathan is a writer of hot, heartfelt contemporary romances with a magic mountain twist. A West Virginia native, she now lives in the flat, flat lands of Indiana. But as she's discovered, you can take the girl out of Appalachia, but you can't take the Appalachia out of the girl.

When she's not haunting the house at all hours working on her books, she has a job as a marketing writer for all things IT, and has had a long career in PR/communications that's taken her all over the Southeast. She lives in the Indianapolis area with her long-time husband, Paul, and their two nearly adult-aged sons, who are actively plotting their escape from the nest.

Wrecking Christmas, the first of the standalone Mountain Magic Christmas Romances, is the 2020 Winner of the HOLT Medallion for excellence in romance fiction. For more information about Liza, check out her website at www.lizajonathan.com!

CPSIA information can be obtained
at www.ICGtesting.com
Printed in the USA
LVHW031632181121
703740LV00001B/117